DEFY THE FAE

VICIOUS FAERIES
DARK FABLES WORLD

4

NATALIA JASTER

Books by Natalia Jaster

VICIOUS FAERIES SERIES

Kiss the Fae (Book 1)

Hunt the Fae (Book 2)

Curse the Fae (Book 3)

Defy the Fae (Book 4)

FOOLISH KINGDOMS SERIES

Trick (Book 1)

Ruin (Book 2)

Burn (Book 3)

Dare (Book 4)

Lie (Book 5)

Dream (Book 6)

SELFISH MYTHS SERIES

Touch (Book 1)

Torn (Book 2)

Tempt (Book 3)

Transcend (Book 4)

Cover design by Maria Spada
Map design by Noverantale
Typesetting by Roman Jaster
Body text set in Arno Pro by Robert Slimbach

For Cerulean, Puck, and Elixir—I will miss you

THE
SOLITARY WILD

THE FAERIE
TRIAD

EVERMORE
BLOSSOM

OAK

HAWTHORN   ASH

BATTLEGROUND

GLASSBLOWER'S
FORGE

REVERIE
HOLLOW

MARKET
SQUARE

CERULEAN & PUCK'S
CAGE

ELIXIR'S
WATER WELL

THE
SOLITARY
MOUNTAIN

THE
SOLITARY
FOREST

THE
SOLITARY
DEEP

N

W   E

S

FABLE DUSK
SANCTUARY

LARK, JUNIPER & COVE'S
CARAVAN

DARK FABLES WORLD

From the Book of Fables

Immortal wild. Immortal land.
Dwellers of the mountain, forest, and river.
You are born of eternal nature—
of the wind, earth, and water.
Yet that which is everlasting is not unbreakable.
And should you wither by the hands of others,
look not merely to sacrifice,
for another path to restoration lies in wait…

Prologue

Nine years ago, I met a lark. From between the bars of a cage, I caught her peeking through the shadows. Her gaze had shoved its way into my soul like a defiant gust of wind, a mutiny in the making.

She'd crept toward me on bare feet, with a bird mask strapped to her face. Through beams of iron, we watched each other. Then she opened her mouth—and a storm flew through me. Her feisty, reckless words tore me to shreds and strung me back together.

Oh, but what else can I say about her?

If you're brave enough to face this beautiful mortal, brace yourself. She will burst into your life like a gale, a force to be reckoned with. Her tongue will lash you as sharply as her whip.

But if you're skilled, you might draw a moan from her lips. If you're clever, you might earn her smirk.

If fate is on your side, she might kiss you. If you're lucky, you might find a way to deserve it.

If you're strong enough, you'll leap into the void with her.

And if you're very, very careful, you'll survive the fall.

~ Ruler of the Sky

Nine years ago, a huntress stalked my ass. My leg had been caught between the teeth of an iron trap when it happened. The son of a bitch munched on my calf like a chew toy, and I'd been bleeding all over the forest floor, when I caught sight of her antlers.

Fake antlers, which had pissed me off. Who the fuck wears a phony rack?

Her silhouette had been prowling through the woods. The antlers had been attached to a mask, the mask to a pinched face. Spruce green eyes sliced through the visor and targeted me.

Just like that, her candid gaze struck its mark and punctured my chest.

But it was the huntress's steady hands that did me in, the way they shoved apart the foliage like she owned the wild, then dismantled the trap's lock with quick motions, as if the contraption was made of paper, like it was a minor inconvenience.

And when she spoke in a smoky voice, my heart burned. So began my obsession with this mortal. Fuck, if she didn't turn my heart into a stalker.

Take this seriously: If you hunt her, she'll hunt you in return.

She won't back down, will never back down. Not my woman.

If you aim, she'll take you down first.

And if you're smart, you'll enjoy it.

~ Ruler of the Woodland

Nine years ago, a siren tried to drown me. Mortals had locked me inside a glass case filled with water. Yet through the darkness, her light appeared.

From outside the tank, gleaming irises swam through the murk, their radiance pouring into the container where I floated. Her stare anchored me in place—momentarily. For she was a human, and humans were toxic.

Fury had slithered up my fists. Hate had coursed through my blood. But when she rested her palms on the glass, I could not resist. I made my choice.

One breach. One touch.

She'd set her palm on the glass. Her warmth had seeped through and drawn my hand to hers, both of us pressing into the flat surface. Somehow, this fleeting contact caused my soul to rupture.

I wanted to punish her for this offense. I wanted to drag her under an abyss.

I wanted to keep her with me. I wanted to take her to the depths.

Perhaps I wanted to sink with her.

That is the power of this siren. If you make contact, she shall curse you. When she does, you will go deeper than you ever have.

While you descend, her light may lead the way.

And if it does, you'll go willingly.

~ Ruler of the River

PART 1

CERULEAN

1

She's naked and on her back again. Only this time, she's asleep.

Moonlight glosses my mate in a metallic sheen, stroking her skin like a lover. Even the sky yearns to touch her, to bask in her curves and the windswept cloud of her hair. The layers pour across the blanket—a mutinous tangle of tresses, as befitting her mutinous spirit.

The pile of unruly locks is evidence of the damage I'd done to her earlier, of the way I'd carved my fingers through that hair while pitching my body into hers, fucking her thoroughly until her moans launched to the roof.

The memory of Lark strapped around me and panting with ecstasy blazes hot in my mind, searing a path from my heart to my cock. Naturally, she owns both.

I crouch before my mate's sleeping form and gaze at those dormant features. Gentle puffs of air whisk from her parted lips, and strands of white slump across her cheeks.

The sight draws my fingers, the magnetic pull elemental, eternal, everlasting. I brush tendrils from her face, the better to admire. Oh, but there's my equal.

"Minn ó vjafnmadur," I whisper, then take her hand in mine and sweep a kiss across her knuckles.

Lark mumbles but continues to dream whatever feisty dreams inhabit her slumber. How I'd like to know what those visions are. But so long as they're peaceful, that's all that matters. If only one of us can rest calmly, let it be her.

Commonly, this mortal is an animated sleeper, twisting, turning, turbulent even while unconscious. On this eventide, she barely moves except to flop onto her stomach. The blanket drapes across her lower back, revealing the exquisite length of her spine, the swell of her hips, and the half-moon of a breast.

My tongue presses against my teeth. I glide my thumb across her cheekbone, then pull back before temptation gets the better of me. Waking her up after such a long and lustful session would be cruel—pleasurable, but cruel.

Funny that. Selflessness was immaterial to me until her.

My long coat buffets my limbs as I rise and stalk to the arched window, then flick aside the curtain. A thin line of indigo has sunk over the horizon, etching the range and outlining a dozen serrated peaks.

Shit. I'm late.

Dusk is approaching fast. My kin will stir soon, though two of them are already awake, providing they're more punctual than myself and assuming their own partners haven't distracted them. The latter is very possible.

My shoulder blades warm, then shudder like latches breaking open. Wings flare from my back, the panels slipping like air through my coat.

I toss my gaze over my shoulder. A smirk plies the crook of my lips as I pay Lark one more glance—always one more—then turn away and launch into the sky.

The wind greets me, the current flitting through my feathers and catching my flight. A particular cord of air rides beneath my arms, warning me of an incoming pocket that I pivot around. The atmosphere has a distinctly Faeish color at this hour, a gradient of slate blue indiscernible to the mortal eye, though I've attempted to show it to Lark.

The gust is also thicker at this speed, more so than in the human realm. The surge rustles my plumage, which sends a ripple up my vertebrae.

The Fauna Tower, the home I share with Lark, shrinks to a needle behind me. I face ahead, tuck in my arms, and spear above The Solitary Mountain's labyrinthine peaks.

The maze spreads itself wide and vast, a mural of stairways linking the zeniths together and step brackets carved into the facades. It wasn't so long ago that Lark defied the odds and conquered this land, crushing my efforts to sabotage her every move and obliterating my willpower in the process. She consumed me quickly, even while we crossed weapons and fired words at each other like grenades.

Torches writhe from the promontories, vines of foliage trickle down the bluffs, and the cliffs bite into the heights. I veer sideways and pass The Parliament of Owls, with its empty rotunda, its illustrious residents yet to awaken.

All except one. As a draft pats my back, my mouth slants. I sense his presence like that of my brothers and Lark—unmistakable and encompassing.

"Mmm," I ponder. "What have I forgotten this time?"

When I receive no reply, no message through the wind, I slow my pace and cast a sidelong glance to my right. The owl lands beside me and coasts, his horned ears spiked to the heavens, his profile austere but proud.

Tímien's head rotates my way, a single, aquamarine eye glittering. In his beak rests my javelin. He releases the weapon, lobbing it toward me. I catch the handle in one fist, spin it between my fingers, and jam it into the harness at my waist.

Chagrined, I incline my head as the raptor fixes me with a stern look. Indeed, he's right. I should have known. It's not the first trip in our lifetime together that I've neglected my weapon.

This is hardly an era of peace. Enemies masquerade as allies, and allies teeter on the brink of becoming enemies. I've lost my command over this mountain, and while Tímien still reigns supreme, every time I fly, I do so with a target on my back.

In short, I can fucking do better. That's what the owl's disapproving eye says.

I slow, as does he. Suspended above our world like weathervanes, we hover in place, our quills swatting the air.

"I know," I tell him. "I'm sorry."

Tímien beats his wings nearer. The reproach dulls from his pupils, replaced by a protective light that punctures my chest. I meet him halfway and rest my forehead against his.

"Father," I murmur.

He nudges me, a gesture that brands itself to the marrow of my bones. Lark owns my heart, and my brothers have chipped their way into it as well. But of all those I love, my father will always have been the first to introduce me to that emotion.

Blues and purples bleed over the pinnacles. A blast of air swirls around us, reminding me of the hour.

At Tímien's insistent hoot, I pull back with a mischievous grin. "Care to test your skills, old bird?"

My father's eye glints. We cannon apart.

I catapult toward the dark range, shooting forward at a velocity that would snap a mortal's neck but barely ruffles my wings. Tímien's evening call punches through the vista, rattles the slanted rowan branches, and shakes the stair rafters. We race at breakneck speed, swerving vertically around the plank extensions where Lark and I had traded blows—her whip against my javelin—before I sent a hive of hornets after her.

Shooting north, my father and I dive into a spiral around The Lost Bridges, the maze with its overlapping delirium of platforms, where Lark won her game and her freedom.

She won and left this place. Yet she came back to me.

She *came back.*

Tímien's cry yanks me back to the present, the shrill call aimed south of The Watch of Nightingales. The race ends abruptly. We stall as the jutting lip of a promontory beneath The Watch breaks into chunks and crumbles down the precipice. My pulse stutters, and my eyes jump from the destruction toward a queue of rams rushing across an underpass dozens of leagues below.

"Fuck," I hiss, then fling myself in that direction as a boulder drops toward the creatures who are trying to evade the onslaught.

I charge downward, my wings burning with exertion. The distance is too far. Blood rushes to my fingertips as I beseech the wind.

When it answers my call, I grab hold of a draft and crank my arm, hurling the gust in the animals' direction. The wind shoves the boulder away, chucking it into the abyss.

Another mammoth rock plunges. I reach it in time, ignoring Tímien's hoot and catching the slab several feet above the rams who gallop out of harm's way and disband into the neighboring rowan trees.

The weight of stone presses on my joints, the boulder's craggy exterior grating my palms. With a growl, I ram my fist into the rock. It cracks down the middle and splits as I fling the remains into the void.

My chest heaves, and my wings quake. That boulder could demolish a house. It could have smashed the fauna to dust.

Tímien rushes beside me. His thoughts travel through a funnel of air and match my own conclusion. This isn't the rams' territory. The animals must have been forced to migrate from their habitats.

That's been happening frequently in the past weeks, the landscape showing increasing signs of fading, losing grip on itself. With the fall of each terrain, the habitats are being disrupted, migration patterns shifting and causing territorial friction between the fauna as they seek places to dwell, to survive.

I cast my father a look. "I need to tell them."

No more gaming. No more racing.

We fly at a rapid speed while surveying the range. In the days since I last scouted the labyrinth, additional turfs have changed. One pinnacle has been shaved down to a stump, stair ramps have been severed like limbs, clefts have dented a handful of summits, a number of rowans have been torn from their roots, and The Mistral Ropes are fraying. Passages are getting blocked, routes altered, and natural resources diminished.

I clench my teeth and fly quicker. My coat flares open like a second pair of wings, the air bracing my naked chest.

My father soars above me, his wings spanning over my form like a canopy—or a shield.

Swiftly, we land on The Wild Peak. Originally, the highest zenith had stood at a lower elevation, but Lark winning her game had changed that. Her victory had forged this new apex, which now tops the range like a crown and has inherited the title.

The instant my boots slam onto the surface, my eyebrows stitch together, and my muscles click in awareness. I set one palm on Tímien's back, my other hand on the hilt of my javelin, and scan the vacant scenery.

An army of dwellers could populate this precipice. Instead, a single rowan tree dripping with glowing specks resides at the center. The crest is intact, secure for the time being.

Yet a mercenary chill winnows my plumes. The wind shifts, agitated by an unknown disturbance that has nothing to do with this meeting. It might be close or farther away. It might be retreating or approaching. That I can't decipher which is enough to set me on edge.

I keep my grasp locked around the javelin and glance at my father. A string of unspoken words project between us, the air carrying our thoughts to one another. Despite my verbal delivery earlier, we often communicate through the wind, preferring to keep our exchanges guarded, my words camouflaged by silence.

Tímien's assures me he will be close and then propels into the air, wings slicing through the fresh night. Above, he circles and keeps vigil. I watch him patrol as twilight descends, teal, white, and gold constellations nipping the sky's black canvas.

Another fluctuation in the current brings with it the scents of pine and spice.

I loosen my grip on the javelin, and my voice unravels like a bolt of silk. "Come now, don't be shy. That's hardly your style."

A roguish drawl greets me from behind. "You're late as fuck, luv."

"I'm fashionably late." I whip around and quirk an eyebrow. "What's your excuse, satyr?"

Puck reclines against the rowan's trunk. His bulky arms cross, a leather vest strains across his broad torso, and his shoulder-length red waves burn through the looming darkness. A pair of honed antlers sprout from his head like a deadly crown.

I might have just arrived, but he'd manifested from The Solitary Forest seconds later. That's clear. Even if I hadn't spotted him a moment ago, his scent hasn't had time to fully permeate the wind. Otherwise, the notes would be stronger.

While I haven't let go of the javelin, Puck's longbow and quiver recline against the tree like mere accessories. Evidently, my brother has more trust in our surroundings than I do. Ironic, considering I once ruled this mountain.

Notwithstanding, if Puck needs to arm himself, he can accomplish that in less time than it takes to blink.

The satyr's mouth slants into a devilish grin. He snatches an arrow from his cache and spins the projectile between the fingers of one hand. "What's my merry excuse?" he echoes, pretending to mull that over. "If you must know, she has green hair and wears the sexiest spectacles known to Faerie."

A puff of humor leaves my mouth. "Evidently, that obsession runs in our family."

"You going to let go of that weapon anytime soon? You're grabbing it harder than a cock."

"Did you see or hear anything when you arrived?"

The arrow stops spinning. Puck's mirth drops, and his brown orbs darken. "Do you see blood on this archery?"

So he hadn't been followed. Any Fae pursuing him wouldn't have lasted long. Though putting it mildly, that fact does little to alleviate the shitstorm churning inside me.

I retract my wings and examine the panorama. To the east rises The Congress of Ravens; I've promised to take Lark there, show her the landscape once I'm certain it's safe. Beyond that, an assembly of rocks forms a ramp, the extension suspended above a fermented bog that gurgles and reeks of brimstone.

Hoofbeats thud into the grass and stride across the vertex. The tinkling of Puck's earrings resounds as he halts beside me and matches my pose by the rampart. Our gazes fix ahead, but I feel his perception, his ability to read me as I can him, a connection long established over these past nine years.

I foresee his question before he voices it.

"What have you got?" Puck asks.

I continue scrutinizing the horizon. "There are many outlying regions of The Solitary Mountain I've yet to patrol. It's never-ending."

"Send someone else to pick up the slack, then. How about that spunky tumbleweed of a pixie?"

I swing my gaze toward him, my forelocks sloping like curtains across my face. "She hates it when you call her a pixie."

"She also hates it when Lark calls her a whippersnapper."

"Yet Moth is neither."

"Whatever." Puck shrugs. "I have a fetish for nicknames, I'm a pathological agitator, and I don't do things half-assed. Besides, why should your buxom mate get to have all the fun?"

My tone comes out part-droll, part-menacing. "Pay tribute to Lark's curves again, question what she does or doesn't do, and I'll rip out your silver tongue." Then I alter my voice to a nymphlike simper. "Dearest brother."

"My, my, my," Puck responds. "And here I was worried you'd go after my dick."

His impishness never ceases. He's been like this since we were striplings. "The Fauna Tower's animals already keep Moth busy, and she can only venture so far," I say. "Her compact wingspan lacks the stamina."

"Excuses, excuses. You're just a protective bastard."

Oh, fuck him. And so what if I am? This woodland satyr is no different, especially these days. Seducer he may be, but my brother would tear out his heart if it meant protecting the ones who matter.

My smirk wanes. "Either way, I haven't covered enough ground."

"Not sure if this helps, but it's a big fucking mountain," Puck drawls.

"And I have big fucking wings."

"Bragger."

"But even here, I can't help feeling an ominous presence."

Puck sweeps his hunter's gaze along the ground, his eyes shearing through the foundation, then he shakes his head. "No prints or breakage. Any chance you're overreacting?"

He's not serious, so I dismiss that with a flick of my fingers and return to assessing the wild. "Something's off."

"It's been off for a while," Puck answers with grim humor.

True. Our people are divided, which puts us on the minority side of this forsaken conflict. Watchful, vengeful, heedful eyes abound. Oh, that they do.

But this is something else, something more than spies or armed Faeries out for our blood, something that's only marginally traceable in the wind—a premonition that isn't what it seems.

How appropriate in Faerie.

A flurry disturbs the rowan branches. The leaves shake, the sound like a serpent's hiss.

My ears pick up on the noise, as do Puck's. In my periphery, his mouth twists.

"Oh, joy." Puck pitches his arrow into the grass, its tip puncturing the soil as he rotates toward the source and folds his arms. "Kept us waiting on tenterhooks, did you, luv?"

Elixir eats up the distance in a handful of steps. Long panels of black hair whisk around the harsh grooves of his face, and his open robe buffets his legging-clad limbs, all evidence that he'd manifested here in a rush.

Because he's not in his domain, located in the subterranean depths of this wild, Elixir has no familiar tunnel walls, babbling watercourses, or humid airways to guide him. I send out a thread of wind for his fingers to trace and follow. When he reaches us, Elixir's irises blaze gold, the rings skewering Puck. Amused, I watch the scene unravel.

"I keep no one waiting," is the extent of Elixir's reply.

Which isn't enough for Puck. "So you're not going to admit you were late for the same priceless reason?"

"No."

"No, you weren't late for the same reason? Or no, you won't answer?"

Elixir just stares at him through eyes that have incinerated far less antagonistic Faeries, and for fewer offenses. They wait to see who'll cave first. This should be easy for Elixir and impossible for Puck, who never shuts the fuck up.

The outcome would be predictable were it not for the subject matter and Elixir's newfound devotion.

He grumbles, "Unlike the pair of you, I can fuck my lady—"

Puck raises his eyebrows and mouths to me, *Fuck my lady.*

"—and still arrive when expected. That is not the reason for my delay."

"Oh, so you were brooding," Puck assumes. "My mistake."

"You insolent prick. I was brewing."

That clips the humor in two. The veneer drops from Puck's face. I straighten beside him while noting the bleak exhaustion dragging down Elixir's broad shoulders.

He's been working to replace the wealth of cures he lost during The Solitary Deep's flood. Unfortunately, ten weeks is barely sufficient time for him to redeem a fraction of his stockpile.

Without those stores, we stand a greater risk of losing this fight. Despite the remedies available in centaur territory, Elixir's hoard had been unique, to say the least. We need an assortment of cures, and we need mass quantities of them, should this clamor between the Solitaries amount to battle.

Considering we haven't made progress on the mysterious second path to restoring the fauna—the elusive answer to an enigmatic Fable of old—bloodshed is becoming likelier.

My brothers' features transform. The three of us exchange savage glances, plagued by the same fear.

Puck is built like a great stag, with his slab of muscles and earthen features. He can take down a redwood with a backhanded slap.

Elixir's aquatic body is built to withstand tsunamis. He has the reflexes of a cobra and the venomous inclinations of a viper.

Yet their expressions have never looked this brutal. If anything, these Fae have become more vicious, as have I.

Because now we each have something more precious to lose.

Lark's smile blows through my mind. I'm certain my brothers are doing this same, conjuring images of their mortal women.

We turn and align ourselves with the pinnacle's ledge. While Puck and I watch the eventide clouds, I imagine Elixir listening to them shift, seeing them in his mind's eye.

Shortly before meeting with our allies, we often convene here to share new information, which we pass on to Lark, Juniper, and Cove upon our returns. Meanwhile, the sisters tend to the fauna who have been misplaced or injured by the wild's demise. Those numbers are increasing, a fact that boils my blood.

Based on the lingering silence, none of us wants to start. That's because none of us have anything good to say.

Puck swears under his breath. "Fine. I'll go first. We're fucked."

"I applaud your optimism," I remark.

"Want to hold that against me?" he bites out. "Have it your way."

"The mountain is crumbling," I supply. "It's happening quicker than I foresaw. On my way here, I stopped a boulder from crushing a herd of rams."

"In addition to erratic drainage and overflows, the waterways in The Deep are becoming infested and undrinkable." The scales of Elixir's cheekbones flash. "There's no pattern to it. Cove and I have sought to find one, to no avail."

Puck knifes his fingers through his red waves. "The woodland's soil is showing signs of rot. In fact, it's so fucking rotten and so fucking random, I can't predict which patches will stay safe for grazing and which won't. Not to mention, I have spies on my ass, lurking just outside The Herd of Deer, and so help me, Cerulean, if you say—"

"I didn't say anything."

"Then I will," Elixir inserts. "You need to leave."

"Piss off and fuck off, luv. I don't need to be told the obvious."

"Then why do I hear that twinge in your voice?"

Puck falls quiet. It's true that Elixir isn't saying anything our brother doesn't already know and isn't already plotting. When it comes to Juniper's safety, Puck is always a hundred steps ahead.

Cypress has offered him and Juniper refuge in The Heart of Willows. Either Puck accepts that offer or finds sanctuary in the mountain or river.

None of these factors are problems. Something else is bothering our brother.

To our question, Puck emits a low sigh. "I hate doing this to her."

Elixir and I pause. Puck would never procrastinate getting Juniper out of harm's way. None of us would with our dearest ones.

His unease has nothing to do with indecision and everything to do with uprooting his woman after all she's been through. He's given Juniper a haven, only to make her abandon it again. Like us, Puck tore a foundling from the only home she'd ever known and tossed her into a deadly game. And now that she's survived, her reward is more upheaval, more of the unknown.

Speaking of the unknown, the wild has become foreign to its past and present rulers. That's yet another danger. And soon enough, the threats will inch nearer and eventually breach the boundaries we've kept secure. The walls we've erected will break down. Ultimately, no corner will be trustworthy or reliable.

Elixir hesitates. His mouth spasms with an unspoken thought, a truth that seems trapped in his mouth. Oftentimes, he's acted like this with Puck. Not that our serpentine shifter of a brother has ever been comfortable with verbal communication.

He clears his throat. "There is another reason you must act soon."

"Meaning?" Puck interrogates with a frown.

"You have an additional concern."

"*Meaning?*" Puck stresses, impatient.

Nighttime cloaks the sky in blacks and blues. Stars pinch the canopy with pulsating light. Elixir's irises are just as animated, the rings bright with indecision. He opens his mouth—

And the air changes course. The fluctuation raises the hairs on my nape and dashes the layers around my face.

It dawns on me that my father is nowhere in sight. Tímien must have stopped circling to check neighboring terrain. Either that, or something had distracted the owl, drawing him away.

Puck stiffens. Elixir's eyes tick toward the draft, hearing its progress and feeling its shape. Indeed, my siblings' sensory powers are fast. But when it comes to the sky, they'll never be as fast as its former sovereign.

My head snaps toward the current, toward the signs of approach, the traces of a predator. Time slows and accelerates. I feel it, then hear it, then see it—a sooty outline leaping from the rowan tree.

I lunge forward. My wings blast from my shoulder blades and flap wide, blocking Puck and Elixir from a set of talons.

2

Feathers spread like raised hackles, the panels flanking a large form glazed in starlight. Our attacker springs forth, talons slicing through the air.

My left wing takes the brunt a second before the honed tips would have severed Puck's head. Razor-sharp blades cleave across my plumes. Pain tracks from the barbs to my arms, and into my chest. I grunt but take the hit, my wing a shield between the enemy and my brothers.

Puck tumbles into a forward flip on his cloven hooves, snatches his longbow and quiver from under the tree, and pops upright with the weapon nocked.

From beneath his robe, Elixir whips out a pair of forked daggers. The prongs flash as fiercely as his pupils.

My brothers brandish their weapons but then spasm to a halt, momentary shock fastening their features in place. I don't have the luxury of pausing. I whirl my javelin, spin the weapon, and clash with the assailant's incoming blow.

Braced like this, with my weapon hinged against those talons, I take a second look and lose my grip. Yet rather than the sight, it's the great caw that chills my bones.

I'd thought the wings had been attached to a set of arms. I'd assumed the talons were affixed to a pair of lethal hands. I'd mistaken the predator for a Fae with avian features.

Fuck. This is no Fae.

The creature's piercing shriek tolls from the summit and slices across the vista. A pointed beak spears from its head, long talons protract from its feet, and its feral eyes target me. The figure spans the pinnacle—a majestic, obsidian vision.

It is a mountain dweller, a member of the fauna.

It's a raven.

The bird's form dwarfs mine, having shuddered to the size of a colossus. My dread renders me fair game. The raven sees as much and barrels headfirst into my torso.

I fly backward and hit the ground hard enough to leave a crater-deep imprint. The foundation quakes, sending ripples across the grass, thus yanking my brothers from their vertigo.

Puck aims and lets the arrow fly. The weapon rents the air and punctures the creature's limb.

The raven cries out, the sound cracking through me.

Elixir is more direct and less forgiving. With his features reinforced, he rotates his arms in a rapid-fire sequence. His pronged daggers chop through the air and catch the animal in its left wing.

The animal caws and veers. Its beak jabs, clanging with the daggers.

Although my brother senses its movements, can decipher them in his head, this isn't his domain, and he's lost that cord of wind I'd provided early. He's lost the path that helped direct him. His delayed reflexes illustrate as much.

Puck pounds across the crest. The raven detects his approach. It swerves and strikes out with its uninjured wing.

At the last moment, my brother springs into the air and leaps over the black panel of quills. Mid-air, he executes a full twist and looses another arrow, which sunders a talon.

The raven's pain peals through the night, penetrating my bones. Its rage is palpable as it whacks Puck off his hooves just as my brother lands. Then it swipes at Elixir, cuffing him in the ribs.

My brothers recover but not swiftly enough. The raven launches their way, hellbent on impaling them.

I vault into the air, circle the scene, and career in front of Puck and Elixir. On a roar, I reel back my arm and haul the javelin forward. The resistance of a helix blade meeting flesh robs me of breath. The weapon's spiraled tip hacks through feathers, the crunching of bone swarms my ears like a torrent, and the raven teeters backward.

Crimson sprays my hands. The beautiful corvid crashes on its side, its screech fading.

I hover in place, my wings flapping and then giving way.

As I land on uneven feet, my boots lose their balance. I let it happen, let gravity take me down beside the raven. My knees smack the grass, dropping me into a kneeling position, as if fate knew I'd seek immediate penance for this.

The sacred fauna or my brothers. I'd had no choice.

Grief clots my throat and steals the oxygen from my lungs. I bow over the creature and behold its eyes fluttering as they focus on me.

Puck and Elixir rush to my side and lower themselves. Our stunned pants flood the mountain peak. The reek of sweat and blood saturate atmosphere.

In Faeish, Elixir recites a lament. Puck brushes his fingers over the raven's wings. The creature lets out of feeble sound as he and I fixate on one another, as he struggles to stay alive.

Will he survive? Or have we forsaken him?

My hands shake, so I close them into fists. I was this dweller's peer once, his monarch and his servant.

How the devil did it come to this?

Puck whispers in a fractured tenor, "No fucking way, said the satyr."

It's rare to penetrate Elixir's facade, to break him down and expose his emotions. Only Cove is routinely capable of it. Yet Elixir's baritone sounds brittle, scraped raw. "I heard the wings beating."

That's how he'd known what we faced, long before the raven had cawed. He and Puck had identified the animal earlier than I had.

The choked words eject from my lips. "Have either of you encountered anything like this before?"

Elixir shakes his head. "I have not."

"Neither have I," Puck murmurs.

And of course, they haven't. If something this harrowing had transpired in the woodland or river, my brothers would have confided as much by now.

"Fables almighty," I rasp.

I lift my head to my brothers, our turmoil transcending into fury. Faeries have slain fauna out of self-defense, and we hunt them for food.

Likewise, animals have attacked us for the same reasons. In fact, during Cove's game, she had battled a bask of crocodiles with Elixir.

However, this is different. This hadn't been the product of hunger or territoriality. It had been premeditated, as if someone had enabled or somehow manipulated the corvid.

Never have our kin committed such a crime. Yet this had been a plot, a fucking war tactic.

Our Fae enemies are using the fauna as weapons.

3

I stagger into the wildlife park, pass through a slot between two coni-cal trees, and navigate dense thickets of foliage. Torches bloom from their posts, the flames contorting and throwing amber across the multilevel haven. Despite this, my vision falters, every shape tremulous and clouded.

Desperation gets the wiser of me. Instead of pacing myself and wait-ing for the haze to clear, I increase my pace. She hadn't been in the tower when I'd arrived; I hadn't sensed her, hadn't detected my mate's fragrance.

No, she's out here. She's roaming somewhere, presiding over this feral reserve like a feisty fauna goddess.

Loss and longing carry me across the lush paths and verdant lawns. Retracting my wings, I seek out her scent, my senses grappling the air, reaching for her aroma like it's an antidote.

In my haste, my long coat smacks against my calves. Sweat coats my bare chest. I'd flown here swiftly.

The slender horns of an antelope spear through the shrubs, the bo-vine's slow gait rustling the leaves. A cardinal spears across one of the up-per levels. A low roar scrapes through the park, a bush splits, and a pair of jeweled eyes shimmer at me like peridots.

The cougar hobbles my way, its body revolving sinuously despite the limp and severed rear paw. The sight stalls my progress, calms my need. There's always time for these dwellers, especially tonight.

I kneel before the creature and run my palm over her tawny back. The great feline purrs and burrows her muzzle into my side.

Through the wind, I communicate with the feline, assure her I'm well.

I scratch behind the creature's ears, then coax the female to leave me, watching as she saunters into the shadows, the rope of her tail swinging behind her.

The whiff of foggy mornings twines through the air. Although my wings have retracted and melted into my body, every plume quivers, ready to spring free. I resist the urge to soar. Instead, I lunge to my feet and trail after the incense wafting through the park like a mating call.

As the scent gets stronger, my legs pump faster, and her location becomes clearer. Sprays of vegetation and flora dripping from trellises get in the way. My left arm swats aside those obstructions. I reach the compact lawn where the gazebo sits at the edge of the world, the ornate pillars laced in moonflowers and lacquered in starlight.

And there she is.

A circular bath stands in the heart of the gazebo, the tub's lip curved outward for Lark to rest her head upon. It's more a pool than a tub, with its depth and width. My mate reclines in a film of steam. Her profile glistens with moisture, her face is angled toward the ceiling, and her eyes are closed. Those wicked, round, mortal ears peek beneath the froth of white hair piled atop her head.

Pixies must have set up the bath—the few servants who've remained—and added a water sample from The Mer Cascades, compliments of my brother. In Elixir's region, the mermaid pools flow with natural heat. A single drop will ignite the temperature of any water body.

The lapping of fluid douses my ears, momentarily setting my imagination ablaze. The bath is too high to see more than Lark's relaxed expression and the length of one arm draped over the side. Suds glide down her arm and fall from a single fingertip.

This view of her clears the fumes in my head. It washes away the tension, as light as summer rain. My shoulders ease, and the hectic yearning I'd felt earlier abates. The mere image of my mate is a breeze, a downy touch that coaxes me to relax.

Yet it's her voice that penetrates the most. "Sighhh," she moans, nestling deeper into the tub. "I could get used to this." But when I make no teasing reply, Lark fills the void and speaks to the gazebo's ceiling. "You left early. How'd it go?"

How did it go? How do I tell her?

My mouth opens, but nothing comes out. If I speak, I might choke on my words.

A sticky residue coats my fingers, only now registering in my consciousness. I drag my gaze from my mate to my hands, where crimson speckles my flesh.

Raven's blood.

My javelin is still caught in my grip. In all this time, I've haven't released it since the attack.

At last, the weapon drops. It plummets from my shaky fingers and hits the grass. The thud alerts Lark. Her eyelids bounce open, she rolls her head in my direction, and her eyes flare wide.

"Cerulean!" Water sloshes everywhere, and she's out of the tub before I draw another breath. Naked and drenched, Lark rushes to my side, her expression trenched with worry as she snatches my face in her palms. "For fuck's sake, Cerulean. What happened?"

Her gaze jumps from the red smears on my chest to the splotches on my hands. "Fables," she hisses, and her gray eyes swoop up to me.

I'm festering, falling, fuming with too many emotions to count.

I seize her cheeks, my head veers down, and my mouth fuses to her. A sound of surprise ejects from Lark's throat before she links her arms around my shoulders and digs her fingers into my mussed hair.

My nostrils flare as I pry her lips apart and flex my tongue into the wet depth of her mouth. Her own tongue latches to mine and curls into me. Yet instead of burning desire, my mate's taste racks me with anguish and terror.

Anguish for what I might lose next. Terror of what could happen to her.

Lark could have been there with me. She could have been exposed on that zenith.

I kiss her harder, rougher, faster. My tongue licks into her, the rhythm quick and famished, the way it is when I drive it between her legs, probing deeply into her slick walls. Lark meets my pace, as she always has. She catches my tongue and lances her own into me. Our mouths slant and thrust, sealed so tightly that breathing is hopeless.

I want to vanish into her, cloak her in my wings, so that no one can reach her, no one can touch her. None but me.

My fingers grip Lark's full, soaked ass and haul her against me. Her breasts mash into my torso, and those lovely, pink nipples toughen for more. The sweet thatch of her pussy bucks into my cock, and—

And then I remember the blood. Rather, we both remember the blood.

Our mouths split apart, and our foreheads pin together. We draw in harsh drafts of air, our exhalations colliding.

"Well, hell," she tries to joke. "You know I like a little domination now and again, so I'm not gonna complain." Then she whispers, "Talk to me, Cerulean. Tell me what happened."

"Something," I rasp. "Maybe everything."

"Is this more of your Fae speak? Because I'm not in the mood for riddles."

"Trust me. When I'm riddling, you'll know."

Lark peers at me, her brows knit with determination, and she strips the clothes from my body. Since I rarely don a shirt—why bother, when I can feel the wind rushing against my skin?—this takes little time. My winged ear caps go first, then the coat, which Lark shrugs from my shoulders.

As my eyes stray to her bent head, unconditional affection squats in my throat. She has only ever torn off my clothes in a frantic rush of heat and sex, all while muttering the filthiest, spiciest demands.

But this is infinitely different, the tenderness overwhelming. This is what it's like to be taken care of, to be part of an even exchange.

Her care for my care. Her mortal heart for my black one.

I toe off my boots while she unbuckles the waistband of my loose pants. I help her, kicking them from my sight. A breeze coasts across my thighs and cock, then descends to my unshod feet.

She guides me to the bath. We sink in, the water swirling around us and leaching the tension from my bones.

Lark maneuvers behind me and straps her arms around my chest, her limbs rise to flank my hips, and her ample breasts swell beneath my weight. The scars on her knees glisten, prompting me to run a thumb over the pulped skin.

Mist rises from the tub. With the back of my skull resting on the crook of her neck, I recount the details of the attack. Lark listens while washing the blood from my body. Crimson leaks into the tub and disappears, one of the many magnificent powers of water in Faerie—its ability to drain away filth and refresh itself.

My mate remains quiet, which is unlike her. Usually, she's vocal and visceral when reacting to news. Oftentimes, this involves a string of *fucks* and *fucking* and *fuckery*. Tonight, she's silent but for a sequence of gulps and a singular hitched breath.

Once I'm clean, we watch a vulture cut over the mountain range, the pinnacles encrusted with teetering trees and burning torchlights. From within the confines of this park, the cougar roars again, this time from further off.

Lark tightens her body around mine and buries her face in my nape. "Dammit, Cerulean. The raven could have disemboweled you. Don't you ever die on me, or I'll flay your pretty ass."

A tired chuckle pushes from my mouth. "I should be so lucky to suffer your retribution."

"Does this mean we're battling the fauna now?"

The dread in her voice is unmistakable. "We don't know anything yet."

"But the others need to know."

"Agreed. And soon."

We dredge up theories about the attack and who could have instigated it. How the fuck had this happened? What Fae would use the sacred fauna like this? Who would go to those lengths?

As we weigh the possibilities, the water never loses its heat. A pair of hawks shave through the air, emerald hummingbirds flit into the shrubs, and an owl hoots. The latter isn't my father. I'd know his call anywhere, would recognize the slant and slide of it from a thousand leagues.

Tímien had returned shortly after the chaos. A lane of snuffed torches on a nearby rampart had troubled him, as the flames never go out at night, so he'd swooped down to inspect the extinguished lights.

The simplest diversions are usually the strongest. Whoever set the raven on us had successfully distracted my father.

But upon seeing the raven, Tímien had gone into a frenzy, intent on dismembering the corvid with a thrust of his talons. Instead, I'd stopped him by communicating what had happened, that it hadn't been a scrimmage for territory or a hunting rampage.

This hadn't been the raven's fault. He'd been a pawn, an act of war. Some, like our enemies, might say the corvid was a casualty of war.

Bereavement claws at my chest. I would say the avian had been a tragedy.

Puck and Elixir had been shaken, but they're not of the mountain. This isn't their realm, and it wasn't one of the animals from their regions. Their fingers hadn't trembled this violently, as if gripped by a tempest.

My mate is the one who puts me back together, her embrace reinforcing the scaffolding once more. I take Lark's knuckles and race my lips over them. "Thank you."

She nips the tip of my ear. "Any time," she says, then waits a beat before asking, "Did the raven suffer?"

I swallow. "He was sedate. I tried communicating with him, but the animal was too weak to try." We sit with that for a considerable while until I'm able to continue. "I'll speak with The Parliament of Owls. There's no telling whether more corvids have been corrupted. Until we know for sure, The Congress of Ravens must be considered forbidden terrain for our allies. I know you were intrigued to see the place, but I won't risk it."

"Fine by me. I'm also eager not to be eaten."

"Except by me, I trust?"

"That a legit question?"

We do our best to laugh, but the mirth is stale. And Lark isn't finished.

"Will it live?" she asks.

"I don't know," I answer.

Elixir had evanesced while my father and I flew the raven to The Deep. My brother had been intent on transferring the corvid there, where he could bathe its wounds and see about mixing a cure for the creature's altered state. Though sorrowfully, Elixir hadn't succeeded with his limited ingredients, particularly without knowing what exactly had been done to the raptor.

For my part, I could hardly provide a solution. When Lark's game had ended, my magic had cleansed one of her wounds, preventing the possibility of an infection. For a while afterward, she had assumed that gift extended to any being who needed my help. But what I'd failed to clarify until recently is that my ability only works on her, because we're mated. Thus, I couldn't use it on the raven.

But wanting to be near the bird, to offer the animal whatever comfort I could, I'd remained by its side, then left with Tímien when the raven finally slept.

I tell Lark as much, though I harbor little hope. My javelin had skewered the avian deeply.

As a mortal who has spent her life rescuing animals, Lark's breathing catches. As a Fae who has spent his existence giving fauna victims of The Trapping a haven, a place to recover, I understand her reaction.

A peacock's remote call blows like a slender horn through the park, coupled with the echo of two rams galloping through the brush. Moonflowers droop from the gazebo's framework and perfume the air.

Our wet hands thread, in and out, over and under. I watch our fingers explore and feel Lark doing the same. Such a basic yet profound exchange, which I'd never known was possible until I fell eagerly under this mortal's spell, until a bond linked us eternally.

"I love you," I whisper. "To the ends of this earth, I love you."

Her voice thickens like syrup. "Back atcha."

Oh, but I know that sultry tone. I'm fully aware of the smutty intentions accompanying her intonation. Moreover, I hear Lark's blood flowing quicker now, as impulsive as a gust.

My mate wiggles out from under me, her movements tossing water over the tub's edge. She sits upright, twists to face me, and slings a glistening thigh across my lap to straddle me. Rivulets slide like fingers down her breasts, drip from the cherry tips of her nipples, and sink down her ample hips, where they vanish into that delectable patch of hair at the crux of her body.

She's a busty one indeed, full and shapely across the hips, providing so many places to sample. Fables help me. How I'd love to snatch those nipples in my mouth, then flick my tongue through those sprigs of hair and latch my lips around the stud hiding within.

I've done so countless times, physically and through the wind. Yet the craving never abates, and I'm certain it never will. Even now, amid grief and fury, I've found solace with her. And in that solace, the desire from earlier resurfaces, rising like the humidity encircling us.

Lark settles her weight onto my groin. "Get over here, you," she says, tugging me forward.

Ever at her mercy, I straighten into her waiting arms. They string around my shoulders while my own arms band around her middle, and we crush ourselves together. Our heads bow and burrow into one another.

A sharp sensation gathers at the corners of my eyes, moist and stinging like salt. This response is hardly Fae. Yet it feels natural while enmeshed with Lark, as all extraordinary sensations have felt with her.

Safety and strength. The antidotes to loss and longing.

That's what this hug offers. That's its power.

We stay like this, naked and soaking with each other, until my mate's impulsiveness resumes. Lark reels back and rolls her hips once against my cock, sending a bolt of lust straight to the head. As the water laps against us, the swollen flanks of her pussy abrade my crown and provoke the cruelest of teases.

I hiss and grip her waist. "You mutinous thing. Taking no prisoners, I see."

"You know it, baby," she pants while gyrating onto my cock. "You expected otherwise?"

The hiss morphs into a pained chuckle. "Dear me, never. In addition to your sassy mouth, defiance is among my favorite traits about you."

Her sneaky fingers wedge between us and strap around the stem of my cock, which hardens and throbs in her hand. "Then what are you waiting for?"

"Indeed," I husk, nudging my erection into her grip. "Does this mean you wish to be fucked by your wild Fae? By the one who was raised by animals? Do you long for his cock to fill you in this untamed park, where the fauna roam?"

"Yes," she urges. "Now."

A roar tears through the haven from one of the levels. Bushes shake in the vicinity, horns spearing through the vegetation as its owner passes by. And we are part of it, part of this environment in which creatures dwell freely.

Tonight, Lark needs to feel wild. I need that with her. To combat the rage and sorrow, we need the peace, the hunger. We need to feel all of it, to unleash all of it, to launch ourselves off the precipice.

With a groan, I lurch forward and yank my mate into me. Water thrashes around us, and the stars bite into the sky. My mouth catches hers, muffling her delectable moan and consuming the sound for myself, taking it like the selfish Fae I am.

My hips snap between her legs, our bodies rubbing, slick and sinuous. I roll my cock up the tight slit of her pussy, teasing out her whimpers. The crest of my erection is about to pitch high between her flushed walls, to fuck her beautifully, slowly, wetly.

A screech peals through the night, neither fauna nor Fae.

Lark goes still. I do not.

The noise snatches me by the gut. I shove Lark off my lap, whisk her behind my back, and thrust out my arm. The wind answers, blasting across the hollow and punching through the trees toward the source of clamor.

My other hand whips out. The javelin shoots into the air and lands in my waiting grip. It spins in my fingers and freezes, the helix tip angled toward the gazebo's threshold.

But no one's there. My ears pick up the commotion of fauna scattering to avoid the tumult, none harmed but all startled.

I listen as the gust I'd hurled across the park fades. In its path, I feel no disturbances in the atmosphere, no figures lurking nearby.

But something was there. Something was *there*.

Lark's voice slices through my head. "Cerulean, look at me!" She grapples my shoulders and wheels me toward her. "It was the gate," she says while framing my face. "It was only the gate."

I blink, stumped. My eyes stumble across the path leading to the park's main entrance, which always makes that infernal racket whenever a large enough bird lands on it. Any one of the resident avians could have been the cause.

"Fucking Fables," I mutter, chucking the weapon to the ground. "I thought…I thought it might be…"

"It's okay," Lark coaxes.

"I thought it was another raven…or a Fae who would…or anyone

32

that could…"

"There's no one else here. They can't get to us. Not you or me or the fauna. All right?"

It's not all right. I'd overreacted and mistaken the noise for the enemy, but I wouldn't have if that sound weren't a trigger in the first place. It's happened before, during Lark's first night in the tower, back when she had been playing my game, running the labyrinth. The sound had leaped out of nowhere and rattled me to the bone.

Since then, I've meant to fix the gate's hinges. So many times, I've meant to fix them, so they would never make that rusty fucking shriek ever again—so akin to a raptor in pain or a cage shutting its doors on a prisoner, a Fae stripling who can't escape.

A recollection sweeps through my head—young fingers clawing at iron bars and sizzling from the burns, mortal rods poking my forearms and scarring them.

My fingers. My arms.

My burns. My cage.

Under layers of flesh, my wings shudder. They want to burst free and carry me into the sky, where I can patrol the tower grounds.

I would have felt the enemy moments ago. I would have felt their proximity through the wind, through my senses.

Aside from that, I belatedly remember Tímien is perched on the tower's spire. Upon our return, my father had stationed himself there, set on monitoring the range and keeping vigil of the park. Not that he ever does otherwise, though this time he'd called for reinforcements, including the haven's resident hawks, a fleet of vultures, and members of The Parliament of Owls. They've been cruising overhead, guarding the refuge's borders all this time. If something had been wrong, the fauna would have known before I'd have.

Still, a raven had charged at us. One of my own had taken me off guard. The enemy has sent a message. They've made a move, and they'd done so with superb brutality.

It can happen again. It *will* happen again.

I tear out of the bath, my departure hauling a tidal wave with me. Water splatters the gazebo tiles and trails my footfalls as I stalk across the lawn and sweep my arm through the air.

At first, the wind doesn't answer. Yet it must sense my agony, because it takes pity and responds to my summons once more. Its power links with my own, enabling me to whisk up a gale.

Threads of blue and silver glaze the atmosphere. They inflate over the park like a half-formed crystal ball. The wind's shape and colors spiral, visible only to my eyes.

Mine and Lark's. I've been teaching her how to see the wind, and it's becoming easier for her to achieve now through the bond.

A set of hands materialize. They clamp onto my wrists as Lark wrenches me around. "What the fuck are you doing, Cerulean?" she trills. "What is this?"

But Lark knows, because she knows me, and she knows what I'm capable of. My mate knows because it's the same thing she would do for those dearest to her. Thus, I remain silent.

So she pushes me. I stumble, the movement clipping the wind's growth like a string before it can seal us in fully. The expansion pauses and whirls in place, covering only a portion of the grounds.

I snarl, "Dammit, Lark!"

"No," she snaps, wet strands clinging to her cheeks. "Don't do this. Do not fucking do this."

"I have to," I grind out. "The boundaries of Puck's cabin are no longer secure. Elixir's home may be next, or our home. If anyone—"

"They won't."

"They will."

"For shit's sake, Cerulean! You can't lock us in here! Listen to me, you overprotective fucker!"

I stride nearer, until Lark's naked body stands an inch from mine. "Do *not* fault me for keeping you safe. Do *not* underestimate how far I would go for you."

"You're panicking. You're overreacting."

"Blasted, brash, breathtaking woman!" I shout back as the tempest swarms around us. "You are not an overreaction! I would split the sky in half for you, I would demolish this mountain range, and I would massacre anyone who tried to stop me!"

"You think I wouldn't do that for you? Hell yes, I would. But this isn't the way."

"I won't let them touch you, I won't let them touch my father, I won't let them touch Moth, and I won't let them near these dwellers. I failed to protect my kin once, and I won't do that again!"

"What about my sisters? What about your brothers?"

My chest heaves—and caves in. I curl my free fingers into a fist and lower my arm. I hadn't intended to insulate us for long. Only until I could be sure, until my mate and I could figure out what to do.

I bow my head, brace my hands on my hips, and fight to suck in oxygen. "A member of the fauna was turned into a weapon tonight," I murmur to the ground. "If that happens to more of them, we won't stand a chance. The Fae can't defeat their sacred dwellers any more than they can fell a hurricane. It's impossible."

Lark goes silent for a moment before taking my hand. "But the haven is neutral. And going the extra mile with a forcefield—no matter how impressive that stunt was—won't solve anything," she says softly. "It'll only do the opposite. It'll disarm us by keeping out the ones who mean everything to us."

The park is where we've been meeting at large with my brothers, her sisters, and our allies from all three regions. I trust their instincts. They're intelligent, they have their own powers, and they would know how to guard themselves until we reunited.

Be that as it may, Lark's right. I could regularly disable the wind for them to pass through, but still. I can't put up a shield, not against our family and allies, not for a second.

"I'm sorry," I whisper. "The bond is...very strong."

Lark expels air. "It sure as hell is."

"I don't...know how to..." My cursed throat bobs. "I don't know how to protect you without losing control."

"Sounds savage."

Her flirty tone draws a rueful chuckle from me. I glance up to find her batting her lashes with exaggeration, and we laugh.

Yet almost instantly, we fall silent and stare at one another. That all-consuming pull urges us closer.

The bond is eternal and more potent than anything I've ever felt. Being a Fae of the wild, having been raised by animals, and considering the gruesome things I've done in the past, my protective instincts are on the primitive side.

My fingers steal out to cup Lark's face, my thumbs tracing her rounded ear. My mate's arms strap around my waist, and she palms the base of my spine. On reflex, my forehead presses to hers.

Constellations tap a rhythm into the sky. Their brightness illuminates the pearlescent streaks in Lark's hair. My fingers can't resist sinking into the damp strands.

She shivers. "You fucking villain."

My lips quirk. "I think you've forgiven me."

"Depends on how you plan on apologizing."

"And now you've intrigued me."

Her fingers descend to my ass. "Would you say being mated has perks? Don't ruin this with riddles. Just answer me, pretty Fae."

I spear my hands through her roots and murmur, "Oh, but I'll do more than answer. I'll finish what we started."

Indeed. I always do.

A kiss for a kiss.

A fuck for a fuck.

With that in mind, I palm Lark's scalp and haul her mouth to mine.

4

Three minutes later, we blast into the tower with our mouths locked in a battle for dominance. Our arrival jostles the curtains of the open windows, the panels flapping from the disturbance. Darkness cloaks the entrance, studded by moonlight and torchlight as we stumble hectically across the foyer and into the great room.

Flames emboss my mate's flesh in orange. If we weren't already naked, we would be shredding one another's clothing by now. Pity we've forsaken that opportunity. It's sublime whenever Lark's greedy fingers strip me bare, though it's even more enjoyable leaving her slinky dresses in tatters, ribbons of fabric discarded in our wake.

Lark claws through my hair, fuses my lips with hers, and splits herself wide under me. Our tongues wrestle, slick and hot. I angle my head and sink my lips deeper into hers, licking and savoring the heat of her moans.

As the noises clutter Lark's throat, I feel every shape of her breath, every texture of her need. Damnation, each time I take her is riveting. I can never make her come deeply enough, long enough, loudly enough.

Never. Fucking. Enough.

Though, I'll die trying.

Lark nips the tip of my tongue enthusiastically, and I grunt as the briny tang of blood leaks into my mouth. She must taste it as well, because she makes a feline noise and licks the residue of blood.

Fuck. Passion and pleasure coalesce, rushing to the head of my cock and hardening its length to the point of anguish. The shaft thickens, pushes high, and bloats the veins across my skin.

On a groan, I nudge my teeth into her plush lower lip, relishing how she trembles and flings herself into me. I crush her against my chest, my hands disappearing someplace down her back.

Our mouths slant, layer, and rock. Her tongue flexes beneath mine, sketching and probing. It's delirium, yet it just won't do.

My mate agrees, because we drag ourselves apart. We stare, sucking in tornadoes of oxygen.

"Fuck the bedroom," we say in unison.

It's magnetic, intrinsic, how we move together. We spin one another around, and I stalk her backward, while she clings to my hips and tugs me forward. Feverish exhalations pump out of us. Her breasts hang heavy and erect at their centers, but more importantly, her pussy glistens in the dark, the lips slick for me. The exquisite sight bolts a direct path to my crown.

From the moment I first saw her, how many times have I craved this mortal? How many times did I want to feast on that feisty, fiery, fierce mouth? How many times did I want to kiss her, fuck her, love her?

I'm still counting.

When Lark's spine hits the nearest wall, there's no pause, no delay. I grip the plump crescents of her ass and hoist her off the stone floor.

Lark has the same idea. She jumps off the ground, hopping onto me, into my arms. Her legs string around my waist, and her clit grinds into the ledge of my cock.

Stuttered noises rush from us, a joint sound that breaks through the great room. Oh, we know what we're doing in broad twilight, in the middle of the tower's most frequented space, where the servants might overhear or see what we're doing.

Public displays have become a delightful habit from the moment I first touched Lark. Therefore, the exposure stops neither of us.

How utterly Fae of my mate. And how like her reckless, rebellious self.

My sac aches, my erection rises between my hipbones, and a bead of liquid pools from the slit. Lark sighs with relish. She wedges her hand down to reap that droplet, swiping her thumb across the line of my crown, which darkens from her touch.

Bringing that thumb to her mouth, she flicks her tongue and tastes me. I shudder, my eyelids drooping as I watch. She shall pay for this anguish.

With a hum, I etch my tongue across the seam of her lips, demanding they open for me. Lark emits a half-chuckle, half-whimper and complies. Our mouths tilt and clutch, the depth urgent, the pressure increasing.

My lips find her tongue and suck with force. Like this, just like this, I draw on her until she's coiling into the plate of my torso, and her nipples grow taut, the peaks cementing into pebbles.

Perfect. So very perfect.

I wring myself away, releasing her mouth only to swoop down and snatch the first nipple between my lips. Lark gives a cry and arches into the wall. Her head thuds against the surface while her fingers scrape through my hair, pinning me to her breast. I indulge her need, following the sounds of her pleasure and circling that raw nipple with the point of my tongue. She tastes marvelous, like sin and sweetness itself.

Her moans scatter, the rapturous echoes spurring me on. My mouth pulls on the nipple in slow, leisurely tugs, then inches away to brush the tight flesh with my lips. The touch is feather-light now, roaming over the swell of her breast, the pit of her nipple.

I continue the torture and lay siege to the other breast. My tongue swabs the underside, rides up her skin, and my mouth engulfs the crest whole.

"Oh, shit," Lark chants. "Cerulean."

A growl rolls up my throat. I consume the name, consume all of her.

She mewls and yanks me closer, urges my lips wider around her. I nudge my waist further into the vent of Lark's limbs, and her thighs spread, knees steepling high and heels linking beneath my ass, which begins to roll.

The stem of my cock slides along the crease of her pussy, the swollen walls drenching me in her arousal. Slowly, fiendishly, I repeat this maneuver. Then again…and again…and again.

All the while, I suck her into a stupor.

Blood gushes to my erection, rosy splotches color her stomach, and perspiration gathers across my tailbone and her collarbone. We sweat through it, work ourselves into it.

Still, it's not nearly sufficient. I bracket my palms on either side of her, lift my mussed head and watch her face as the engorged crown of my cock glides through her folds. My entrance spreads her open a scant inch, just an inch to start.

I rock my hips attentively. Lark's walls flood my hard flesh with heat. She feels tight, soaked, glorious.

"Oh, Fables," Lark utters. "Yeah."

"How deep am I?" I rasp. "Indulge me. Tell me, pet."

"You're…" She flicks her waist forward, lurching it against mine, so that we reel as one. "You're inside me only a little. The top of your dick is probing me like a cruel son of a bitch."

Wicked humor rumbles from my chest. My body enters hers another forsaken inch, then another, then another, which pulls afflicted moans from her.

"And now?" I murmur while nudging her with long, shallow pumps until she's sopping wet, and I'm as stiff as metal.

"You're a bit deeper now," she keens. "Barely halfway. I feel…I feel your cock's tip inside me…but not the base, and it's so good, but fucking hell, if you don't fill me to the brim, I'm gonna scream."

"I'd like to hear you scream," I whisper, my muscles clenching, burning from holding back. "I'd like to tear the climax from your throat. You know I can do it. You know how long a Fae can last—"

With the snarl of a sexual deity, Lark grabs my face and wrenches my gaze to her ravenous one. Those mercury eyes flash as she makes her command. "We're of the mountain, hon. I don't want you to go deeper. I want you to go higher," she mutters. "Now fuck me. And do it with your wings out."

My lips slant in what I suspect is a devilish grin. "Your wish is my will."

The plumes bust from my shoulder blades. Two vast panels of blue and black snap outward, the lashing sound reminiscent of her whip—another toy that we've used during our erotic escapades.

My feathers bristle from the mounting tension, their velocity smacking across the room. The impact throws a flurry through the space. Vines of foliage, which spill from hanging pots, swing above us like pendulums and clack into one another.

The moment my wings have overwhelmed the room to capacity, I clamp onto Lark's ass and launch my cock into her. Her spine curves, and her cry shoots to the rafters. Fables eternal, her folds seal around my erection, seizing me from the apex to the hilt.

My head falls to her neck, where I groan, breath hot against her skin. "Unearthly fuck."

Her nails scratch my back, thread through my wings, and drag over the vanes. "Do it," she pleads. "Now."

Such delicious torment racks my joints. Indeed, with what I'm about to do to this precious female, anyone will hear. They won't be able to tune it out.

Without further preamble, I cover Lark's mouth gently with my palm and whisk into her with measured thrusts. My backside pitches forward, my cock swinging up into Lark, hitting that cinched spot that makes her shout. In a vigorous tempo, I contort my hips and pull those moans from my mate, the need a carnal thing, an unrelenting thing.

Her moans slam into my hand, muffled but still audible to the servants' ears. I don't want her silenced, quietly taking my cock. No, I want her rapture blasting to the heavens. I want to hear her dominate this tower. But while I cherish our notorious penchant for fucking in open spaces, another part of me wants to keep this between us, however futile at this point.

I undulate my hips, my erection slippery with her arousal as it pumps in and out of her. The feel of her slickness covering my skin drives me to madness. My length broadens, the pommel of my cock so inflated it hurts in the most decadent way.

My free hand clamps onto Lark's wrists and jerks them overhead, fastening her to the wall as I piston my waist, lashing every inch into her. Firelight dances across her pleated face. She bows into me, mouth open and raging with noise beneath my palm.

Each moan grates from her chest, in tandem to my thrusts. Her pussy tightens, spasms with every fluid entry and withdrawal.

My own mouth falls open, groans shaking from my throat. I put my entire frame into the effort, the elation traveling to the edges of my wings.

Lark's teeth nip my flesh. She's had enough restraint, and I can't refuse her, won't ever refuse her. With a hiss, I jerk my hand away, releasing the noises she makes, which run rampant through the great room.

On impulse, I reach for the wind. Once it answers, I snap my fingers.

A breeze strikes like a match against the logs in the central pit surrounded by sumptuous chairs. Timber explodes into flames. They scald the tower with additional light, more ways to see Lark, to watch her face while I make her convulse.

But not yet. Oh, not yet.

When I reminded her how long a Fae can last, I wasn't being casual. My body keeps going, keeps pumping. This isn't over until her throat is raw from crying out, until the orgasm is ready to shove her off a precipice.

With my other hand still claiming her wrists, I thrust into Lark with precision, increasing my pace and going higher, higher still. I won't stop, not even if the momentum threatens to crack my spine in half, not even if the pain threatens to suffocate me. And when she's falling, I'll gladly plunge with her.

My mate twists her hips with mine, unable to keep still. I growl, clamp onto her thigh, and hook it over my waist, adjusting the angle of my cock. Then I pick up speed and hurl into her. Her exquisite pussy wraps around my length, saturates it to the base, and catches each deep pivot. Disjointed whines fall from her lips and collide with my own guttural moans.

She's so open, so wet, so mine.

I'm so buried, so hard, so hers.

Together, we shout. Yet still, we deny ourselves.

And do it with your wings out.

Always be very careful what you ask of a Fae. Fail to do so, and I'll show you what my wings can do.

My shoulder blades flex. The wings start to beat, their magnitude hauling me into Lark, the plumes' intensifying the force of my cock inside her wet folds. I use the leverage to our advantage, the feathers' velocity and mass strengthening every lurch of my waist, my wings helping me to fuck her more, and more, and more. It sends the roof of my cock striking into Lark's folds, pushing us to the brink.

Lark shrieks with pleasure. "Holy...fucking...shit!"

"You wanted it," I murmur roughly. "Now ride it."

We unleash. I let go of her thigh, then brace her even higher against the wall. My beautiful mate nods, spreads her legs wide, and plants her soles on the walls. With her knees flanking my lunging ass, she takes every flap of my wings, her pussy grabbing my cock as it surges higher, higher, higher.

Shredded groans pull from my mouth. Sobs roll off her tongue.

My hand loosens from her wrists and tangles our fingers together. Our hands ball into a single fist above us, while my other arm flattens beside her head.

My abs crunch, perspiration building over the ridges as I work my cock, plying her swollen walls. Wafts of sweat and moonflowers throttle my senses. The scents throw me into a tailspin, into a place where madness, mayhem, and mutiny coexist.

And I love it, I love this bond, I love her.

Secured in my arms, Lark presses her bare feet firmer against the wall. She uses it for support and jolts on my cock. Her divine tits pucker, the nipples sliding across my pectorals.

Our hips smash into one another, tireless, hopeless, ruthless. My waist thrashes with hers, the motions sinuous and frantic.

And while I'm capable of drawing this out until our bones fracture, I'm the one who loses the battle. "Lark," I grate. "Please."

She grabs my jaw and mouths against my lips. "Who's got your trapped?"

"You do," I pant.

"Who's riding your cock?"

"You are."

She nods again. "And who's going to make you come?"

I felt my retinas burn into hers. "You will."

And we launch at each other. The wet clamp of Lark's pussy sucks me deeper, harder, longer. The bud of her clit abrades my erection, and when it does, we're lost.

My heart disintegrates, my head dissolves, and my cock throbs for mercy. The impact of my thrusts splays her wider, makes her wetter. I pound into her with ardor, and she takes me into her with abandon.

I holler. At this rate, she'll make me shout until I'm hoarse, but not before I make her scream first.

My wings whip the air, casting me into her. The quills tremble, and the vanes sizzle, the heat traveling from the plumes, to my heart, to my crown. It's so critical, I can't tell which will expire first.

At last and too soon, her cries multiply and begin to fray. Her quavering thighs give in and twine around me once again, as if needing me to hold them up.

"That's it, Lark," I encourage. "Take it there. Take it right there."

"Don't stop," she implores. "Keep fucking me, Cerulean."

"Eternally."

Our moans turn ragged, strung out. Lark's breasts pit into my damp chest and jostle with our movements. I wedge my thumb between us and pat the kernel between her legs, stroking that sweet little clit jutting from her center.

Her desire pours down my length. Her walls contort, and her eyes tense, almost there, nearly there.

Another roar builds in my lungs. I pitch into her quicker, quicker still. Her dripping slit parts so easily for my erection, her body catching the brunt of my hips.

Her pussy flutters around me. She's about to come so beautifully.

For a moment, I can't remember where my free hand is. Then I recall one is strapped to hers overhead on the wall. We're holding so tightly, my circulation prickles, but I don't let go, will never let go of this—of her.

On the verge of losing my voice, I crash my mouth to hers. Lark moans and kisses me back, our tongues fighting.

My cock whips through her folds, splitting them with swift, shallow thrusts. My fingers tease her clit until her cries taper, and her pussy tenses.

We go still for an instant. And in that instant, our open mouths press together.

Then we shatter.

Moans vault from our lungs. Heat and blood collide where my body throttles into hers. It hurls us over the edge, pleasure spasming from my crown and quaking with her own climax.

Lark comes with a splintered cry, a violent tremor rushing through her body. At the sound, I shout against Lark, my cock spilling into her warmth.

Our hips ride the climax, rolling lazily, then ceasing. We collapse against one another and go limp. My face rests against hers, our bodies heaving for air, and her fingers drape through my layers.

A breeze rustles the curtains. I thumb her cheeks, overwhelmed.

Outside these walls, the mountainous panorama surrounds us. Yet here, with my mate, I'm more home than I've ever been.

Her body wraps around me, my cock still lodged inside her. Tangled and naked, we pull back and stare at one another. Remembering where we are and how many residents must have heard us, we break into exhausted laughter.

"Whew," Lark compliments. "Your stamina is one sexy turn-on. I'm impressed."

"I wouldn't compliment me so soon, my only one." I quirk a devious eyebrow. "If I recall, you told me not to stop."

Lark yelps when I fly us to a window ledge, prop myself onto the sill, and set her ass on my lap. My torso aligns with her back, so that my chin settles on her shoulder, and she faces the mountain panorama. While cupping her breasts, I roll my hips, entering her slick pussy from behind.

Her head flings back. Another moan surges from her as she grabs the overhead arch, enabling her body to take my thrusts. Our waists grind in sync while facing the open range, swatches of wind chasing through Lark's hair.

When I tilt my hips in a new angle, Lark cries out with enthusiasm. Her walls spread for me once more. She moves in cadence to my hips, her buttocks swaying on me, her lovely spine revolving.

She's enjoying the view and the sinuous pump of my cock under her. Oh, but when my mate requests that I keep pleasing her, I always honor my promises. She loves the heights, and I'm going to make her come at the top of the world, where she belongs.

5

The door slams shut. My heart clatters as the bars shudder around me, the cage trapping me in its maw. Hinges screech on impact, the sound cutting into my ears like an owl crying in pain.

The human hands that bolt the trap vanish, its male owner dashing into the woods while carrying a metallic net. Nearby shouts collide—the lilting calls of my kin and earthen hollers of the enemy. The clang of steel pierces the night. So many shrieks and bellows overlap, because they've attacked my home, and they've taken our animals.

They have taken my family. The humans have taken them all.

Father? Where are you?

My small fingers lurch out to clutch the grille. Yet the instant my skin makes contact with the rods, the reek of charred flesh invades my nostrils. Smoke curls, the tendrils singed at the edges. I see it, see how the air burns.

I yank my fingers back in shock. A guttural noise shreds from my mouth, but I clamp my lips shut to conceal the scream from being audible, airborne, apparent. If the mortals hear me utter a sound, they'll slice off my tongue, for fear of trickery. They know better with Faeries.

My digits tremble. The pads blister as if I've dipped them into a cauldron.

Iron. They've thrown me into an iron cage.

Please come! Please help me!

A merciful breeze filters through. I grasp it desperately and try to communicate with someone, anyone of my world. I don't know where I am, but my rescuers can follow the wind if I deliver it to them carefully, like a trail of breadcrumbs.

Éck er jérna!

I'm here!

Except no one answers. They're too busy defending themselves or being slaughtered. Even if they weren't, I remember too late. I can't communicate through the elements in the mortal realm.

Éck er jroddur.

I'm scared.

Avians caw, and a wolverine howls. The shapes of their calls are clear; they're looking for me, scrambling for me although the humans have them trapped, too. My eyes jump across a human field of high grass, yet I don't see them, can't get to them, can't save them.

I recognize the echoes of my wild family, their agony scraping my organs like razors. I whimper and squeeze my eyes shut, but I still hear them searching for me, fighting to get to me.

Ok éck er mede jvjartade.

And I'm heartbroken.

I curl into a ball on the floor. The owl mask strapped around my heads conceals half of my face, and the midnight-dyed plumes catch a single tear. Moth made me this mask.

Have I lost her, too? Have I lost all of them?

Another avian wail dashes through the branches. I know the texture of that frantic sound. Panic shackles my lungs, so that I can't speak, can only listen as Tímien fails to reach me in time.

They've got him now. They've got me, too.

They've separated us.

My body hunches over, and my face burrows into my upturned knees, and I sink my teeth into my lower lips until I taste blood, until it trickles down my chin. Rage and fury and terror bend my knuckles inward. Inside, I screech until I've lost my voice, until only a scant breath remains.

"Father," I whisper so low only the wind can hear.

After that, all goes deathly silent—and so do I.

Then suddenly, the human returns. He crouches down, peers at me through angry eyes, and says, "You made us do it. It's all your fault."

I growl and launch upright to charge at the man, then I halt in place.

My clouded gaze staggers across the bedroom. Midday leaks into the space, screens of golden light pouring across the carpet. All is still and quiet but for a draft that teases the curtains, the hanging planters, and the ivy dripping from the turret ceiling.

Panels of linen canopy the bed. The sheets pool around my waist, and a layer of sweat coats my naked torso. My fingers choke the blanket's edge, but I loosen my death grip as awareness consumes me.

Nonetheless, I overturn my palms to examine the fingertips and the length of my arms, merely to check, to be certain. The digits are smooth, not a blister in sight. Scars pockmark my arms, however they're old, not fresh.

My breath rushes out. I bow forward and cleave my fingers through my hair, which only makes a greater mess of it.

Lark had done the rest, numerous times last night while I made love to her.

Across the room, a mounted feather adorns the opposite wall. The quill is stripped in buff and tan, its overall shape slightly warped.

The joints of my back unwind as I stare at the relic of Lark's childhood mask. I remember her gray eyes watching me from behind the visor. It was the first good thing I'd seen since the mortals caught me.

Beside me, feminine curves weigh down the mattress, the sight drawing my gaze. I roll toward my sleeping mate. Lark's cheek sinks into the pillow, and her breathing rustles the fabric while she curls a fist beneath her chin.

A grin splits my mouth. I lean over and drop a featherweight kiss to her temple, then scoot to the edge and rise from our bed. Lack of sleep pulls on my muscles, but respite is unthinkable now.

A pair of silken trousers drape over the chair by the fireplace. A tired, gravely sound rumbles from my chest as I saunter toward the pants. While stepping into them, I regard the central fire basin, which is filled with trumpet flowers. They glow in the dark like a miniature, phosphorescent garden, the puckered white petals releasing a peaceful, verbena scent.

The pit in the great room is fine since we don't sleep near it. But we never use this fire basin because the threat of ashes building in the grate reminds Lark too much of her youth. And while I'd intended to have the basin ripped out, she hadn't wanted that.

"I'll never get over my fear that way," Lark had said.

Instead, I'd filled the space with these trumpet flowers from The Watch of Nightingales. My mate had been pleased. Often, she likes to curl up beside them as they glimmer.

Beyond the arched windows, the sun hovers like a coin in the sky. Filaments of wind twine around the mountain peaks and slip between labyrinthine bridges.

Careful not to rouse Lark, I grab my javelin from its stand, pluck the case holding my flute, and harness both. With the flute strapped to my back and javelin affixed to my hip, I exit the bedroom. After padding down the stairwell to the tower's first level, I stride through the great room and into daylight.

An endless dome of blue and yellow greets me, along with the stuttering chirps of birds from the wildlife park. My father is no longer perched on his spire, so he must have migrated to the west end overlooking the park.

Instead of heading in that direction, I stalk east to the promontory fronting my home, where the lip of this zenith juts into the void. The wind is more active in this spot today, its thrust battering my hair.

Tufts of green fill the valley, the treetops concealing The Solitary Forest. Far below that, deep under the crusts of this earth, flows The Solitary Deep.

The question remains, have other animals of our world been manipulated? And by what fresh devilry can that have been achieved?

Even Elixir had been unable to shed light on the mystery, at a loss to recall a single brew capable of turning the fauna.

I brace my foot on a boulder, reach backward over my shoulder, withdraw my flute, and spin the instrument in my hands. My fingers poise over the keys, my lips purse against the plate, and a melody flutters out. A current catches the music, cascading it across the lawn as gently as a zephyr.

Until recently, the notes I used to play had been artful, spiteful, or sensual—or all three. This had been true particularly while luring a mortal to their doom, glamouring them across the threshold between their realm and ours. Even then, there had been an elegance to those knavish compositions.

Today, the tune is out of my previous character, yet I take to the notes like my wings take to the heavens, swiftly and naturally. The music encompasses memories of one face, one silver lining in my past.

I remember the last game played on this mountain, how I had tried to sabotage Lark's efforts in the labyrinth. Instead, I'd come to her aid several times, mere seconds after hurling danger in her path.

Constantly, I made excuses. I'd dressed her wounds in Moth's cabin, telling myself the mortal needed to be mended for practical reasons, for her to keep playing the game.

I had convinced myself that breaking Lark's fall from The Mistral Ropes had been a debt owed, because she'd guessed my true name. With that moniker in her grip, she could have wielded power over me, but all she'd wanted was to be called by her own name, a request that stunned the shit out of me.

Names aren't to be trifled with in Faerie. They're sacred. And for Lark, her name had been more valuable than magic.

In that moment, I felt inadequate, humbled, and enthralled by this woman, more so than I'd already been.

Technically, I did owe her for that. Veritably, Lark's actions had entitled her to my help at The Mistral Ropes.

But that's not why I'd caught her when she plummeted.

All the times I dueled with myself. All the times I attempted to thwart Lark. All the times I undid my heinous efforts moments later.

All the times I wanted to massacre any mountain Faeries who came near her. All the times I sent a tempest toward those who had come close to harming Lark.

Gales had shoved Fae skulls into cliffs. Squalls had wrapped around throats. I had wanted to do worse, just as I had wanted to slay the poachers who chased Lark into Faerie in the first place.

From the minute this mutinous creature entered my world, I had been torn in half, unable to stop myself, unable to stomach Lark's hurt, unable to let my actions stay their course. She'd penetrated my head, disarmed my soul, and gripped my heart.

I hadn't understood why. Not until the masquerade.

Still, Lark had claimed me even before that. Slowly, and then suddenly, it happened.

I fell in love.

Then Lark won her game by nearly dropping to her death in The Lost Bridges. She had released my hand after I fought to hold onto her, while she dangled over the valley. And although I'd thrown myself after her, mindless to break her fall with my tattered wingspan—desperate to at least try—Lark had already saved herself.

She'd chosen to surrender her life, to spare mine so that I wouldn't plunge with her. She did that for love.

That had been the ultimate sacrifice. That is why the cliff we landed on had grown. That is why she won.

Lark went home afterward. Then she came back to me. I didn't deserve it, but she came back.

My fingers dance over the flute, the melody skipping across the lawn. Whatever it takes, I won't let Lark's choice be in vain, won't let her suffer, won't let anyone rob my mate of this life, of her happiness. I shall hold up this mountain with my bare hands before I let it crumble, if it means keeping her safely on top of it.

The air sways, bringing with it traces of her. My lips quirk as I blow. Perhaps I show off a little.

Lark's shadow drapes across the grass. "Catchy tune."

I play through the end, then I lift my mouth from the instrument. "I was going for elusive and too rare to last. I'd hardly call that a tune you can catch."

"Tell that to my whip."

With a chuckle, I slide my gaze over my shoulder. "Is that a fact?"

One of my linen shirts hangs off Lark's body and buffets her upper thighs. That ravishing little gold cuff encircles her thigh like bait, and the shirt's neckline plunges low, offering a tempting half-moon view of her breasts. With her white hair avalanching down her curves and her toes exposed under the oversized garment, she's equally adorable and provocative.

"Dear me," I murmur while flipping the flute between my fingers. "You're quite the delectable sight."

She plucks the sides of the shirt. "What? This ol' thing?"

I swing fully toward her. "I could rip it and make the infernal thing look older."

"I'm sore as fuck, but I'll take you up on that later." Lark cocks her head. "Another nightmare?"

Visions of the cage assault my mind. We've described our recurring nightmares of The Trapping in gruesome detail before, though I'm in no mood to rehash.

I jam the instrument into the harness across my back. "The fresh air and music help to settle the images."

"Tell me about the music, then," she suggests. "Never heard that one before. What inspired it?"

"You," I say. "Us."

The way her complexion flushes is out of character, as is the shy dip of her head. She tucks a lock behind her ear, then glances at me. "You composed a tune for us?"

I soften my voice. "If I say yes, what then?"

My mate's eyes glisten. Her awed features kindle my soul with tenderness and rancor. I know why she's looking at me like this, long before she says it. "No man has ever...done something that like for me."

I'm going to dismember every male who ever touched her, bedded her, fucked her, used her, and then left her.

"I'm no man," I say. "But I'm yours."

Lark smiles. "The music is pretty painful, but it's also beautiful."

"That, it is."

The wind whisks against us, resounding with a low whistle. I suspect we're not moving closer to each other because if we do, that shirt won't stay on longer than a second. After our antics, we really need to come up for air.

We admire one another, her small grin doubtless a mirror image of mine. It's enough to wipe out the residue of my nightmare.

Then I feel it—the change in air pressure.

Then Lark sees it—a presence at my back.

Fury and fear expand her pupils. Those emotions do the same to my reflexes.

She and I exchange a single look, then we move.

In unison, Lark unspools the whip I hadn't noticed in her hand until now, and I whirl the javelin. I cross the lawn in seconds, surge in front of her, and pivot. My weapon blocks the soaring dagger mid-flight, knocking it off its trajectory toward Lark's skull.

Steel glints and topples to the ground. In sync with my motions, Lark's lashes out her whip, which strikes past me and hooks the weapon's owner by his ankle. With a deft jerk, she yanks on the slack and sends the Fae to the grass.

The instant he smacks against the promontory's rim, my mate executes a second lash that nooses the figure by the throat.

Then we're on him. Lark and I blast ahead and slam to our knees above the Fae, who's flaming hair and sweltering yellow eyes match the shade of his skin and smoking wings.

Anxiety cramps Lark's face. She recognizes the firebird Fae, a member of the trio who'd attacked her during her game. At The Lost Bridges, one of them had tried to throw her off a platform, but I'd skewered him with my javelin. Nevertheless, he and his flock have been prominent figures in her nightmares.

A snarl grates from my mouth. It takes a mammoth amount of willpower to refrain from bulldozing my fist through the crate of his chest.

Lark regroups. Her teeth flash as she wraps the end of the whip around her fist and uses the leverage to make him gag. She plants her foot on his clavicles and leans in. "Touch me again, dickhead, and I'll fuck up your world."

The firebird glares and speaks through a roasted voice. "More than you already have?"

With deadly eloquence, I rest the helix tip of my javelin over his heart. "Who sent you?"

"I came on my own."

Lark tightens the whip, dislodging another gargle from him. "Try again, hon."

"I will," he swears. "Trust me. And next time, I'll aim for your—"

My fist rams into his face, bone cracking and blood spurting from his loose teeth. Violence sizzles my knuckles. Another threat to my mate, and the next blow will separate his head from his neck.

"I'd rather not ask again," I murmur. "Who. Sent. You?"

The firebird just cackles and sputters through rivulets of crimson. "You won't see us coming. You won't see his next move until it's too late, just like last night," he foams. "Just like now."

From his boot, the Fae pulls another blade, which spears toward Lark. Again, we move as one. She jolts on the whip and stalls him in place while I block the knife's flight with the hilt of my javelin.

On a hiss, I twist and use my weapon to shove the knife back the way it came, straight into his torso. The blade shears through flesh like a stake and punctures his lungs. Then I spin the javelin in the opposite direction, the tip ripping open his left wing.

The Fae's eyes pop in surprise, then gleam like a zealot's. He goes limp and puddles to the grass. Life slowly leaks out of him, the blisters of his pupils on the verge of dulling.

It's one thing to rupture a mountain Fae's organ. But to mutilate their wings is an act of barbarism. However, I'm not done yet.

Kneeling, I thrust out my palm. The wind shoves the Fae across the precipice and sweeps him over the cliff's ledge.

He's too weak to fly, but he's still alive enough to shriek on the way down, not only from the fall but from the speed. At this elevation, it is never a quick descent. Yet I'm hardly satisfied until the wind hears my appeal.

Air pressure condenses further, fabricating a descent that lasts much longer. The Fae shall suffer on the way down. He'll be conscious of every league closer to the ground, with nothing but anticipation to keep him company.

His screeches whittle to a puff, but I still hear him. Shortly before he lands, the wind breaks like a chain, and gravity rushes through like water from a ruptured dam. The buildup of his fall compiles, which makes the crash harsher, wilder, and messier.

A gust blusters in his wake. Then all that remains of him is a smoking puddle on the forest floor.

I rise slowly and turn to Lark, who slumps to the ground and gawks at me. Several dots of red have spritzed across her cheek.

We lock gazes, then drop our weapons and grab for each other. I crush her to me and press my lips to the crown of her head, and she flings her shaking arms around my waist. Together, we stare at the promontory's rim, over the side where the Fae had plummeted.

You won't see his next move until it's too late.

His next move. So they've established a leader.

Someone who would defy natural law by turning the fauna into weapons.

Someone who would deliver an assassin into a neutral wildlife haven, where survivors of The Trapping roam.

Someone more extremist than my brothers and I have ever been.

6

However, if this leader fancies himself more vicious, they're wrong. Push us, and we'll drive our fists through our adversary's heart.

He wants to start a game? Oh, we're good at that.

Hours later, on the brink of eventide, the moon is but a rendering of itself, a sketch of white in the inked sky. Cobalt brushes the vertexes in drowsy strokes, which will soon dissolve into nefarious shades of black and blue—a hybrid color I'm well associated with, from my hair, to my wings, to my lips. Once nighttime cloaks this region, the midnight shade will deepen, and thick piles of clouds will hover above us.

It's going to be one of those overcast evenings. I consider it a perk.

Lark and I wait at The Lost Bridges. She sits on the planks of an upper suspension, with her legs filed between the rungs and her feet dangling over the valley. She's watching a butterfly bounce across the sky, its wings flashing like foil.

I crouch on the woven rim of a parallel rope bridge, grasp one of the railings, and lean over the void. My eyes scan every garland of wind, every swaying overpass and creaking extension.

Spanning multiple levels over The Solitary Forest, these bridges have no structure to their arrangement and no concrete direction, though it may seem otherwise. Traverse any set of planks, yet travelers will never reach the opposite side. Rather, they'll only end up on a different gangplank, at a different elevation. That's the artifice of this individual maze.

Few souls know how to master it, apart from myself, Lark, and the fauna. Otherwise, most mountain Faeries can't make sense of it, to say nothing of the ones in the woodland and river.

That explains the scowl Elixir wears when he manifests several paces from me, swaths of onyx hair whirling around his scowl. "Curse you," he mutters through gritted teeth.

I can't help my smirk, so I don't bother trying.

Instead of pushing me off the edge—we leave those manic antics to Puck, who's done it to me in the past when I wasn't looking, just to see how long it took for my wings to sprout—Elixir continues to fester in silence. Unlike our impish brother, relying on gravity wouldn't satisfy the river ruler. When ticked off, he would rather use his bare hands to crush someone's skeleton than let a measly tumble off a precipice do all the work.

Hopping off the rope ledge, I retract my winds and lean against the frame while crossing my arms. A shag of hair flops over my brows as I regard my surly sibling. Mer scales glitter from the ramps of his burnished cheeks, a long robe hangs like smoke off his shoulders, and dark leggings adhere to his limbs.

I imagine this is the highest he's ever stood and the driest environment his legs have ever endured. I wonder if his shifter instincts get antsy this far from the water, as my aerial nature does when confined so far underground in his realm.

"I did send you instructions," I defend. "How difficult could they have been?"

My brother's growl only intensifies, but the sound of Lark chirping her delight cuts us off. We swerve toward the commotion. Elixir listens, and I watch, as my mate leaps to her feet, then dashes across the bridge toward her sisters.

Cove and Juniper rush in her direction. The wind blends locks of teal, green, and white together as they smash into a hug. It doesn't matter that they saw one another less than two days ago. The trio routinely greets one another this way, as if they've been parted for months.

It could be the residual effect of what my brothers and I did to them, back when they were our pawns and playthings. Now guilt pricks me, as it always does when these females occupy the same space.

Cove's teal eyes sparkle as she brushes her fingers through Lark's windswept tresses, a gesture so very human, so otherworldly to a Fae. And although Juniper's green eyes brim with affection, her fondness is of the attentive and diligent sort. She steps back to take Lark's measure, checking whether Lark's appropriately dressed for the elements and sufficiently armed with her whip.

A spear is anchored at Cove's hip, the weapon's sharpness a dire contrast to her flowing, shell-white dress. Juniper wears an ankle-length vest over a shirt and pants that cinch just above her knee boots. Her ponytail swats about as she hitches her crossbow over one shoulder.

Lark bumps the pair with her ample hips. "About time, missies."

"It's breathtaking up here," Cove says.

"Literally," Juniper adds while surveying the horizon of rowan trees and torchlit summits.

As Lark starts pointing out vistas to her mesmerized sisters, Elixir's profile softens, and I feel a grin tugging the corner of my lips. That is, until he remembers he's pissed and rounds on me.

"Explain yourself," he demands.

To the point, indeed. However, one other brother is less subtle.

"What the fuck are we doing up here?" Puck interrupts while moseying across the planks toward us, his red hair blazing like one of the bluff torches.

Halting a foot away, he slouches one shoulder against the railing, his chin cutting a path from Elixir to me. They stare my way as if I'm the epitome of a prick for summoning them to these heights.

For all intents and purposes, Lark and I chose a location remote from The Fauna Tower. It had to be a safe distance from our most vulnerable animals, should we be followed, as well as someplace few Faeries would know how to ascend.

The bridge maze had been Lark's excellent suggestion. None would be able to solve its layout, which made it ideal for concealment plus evasion.

I'd sent detailed instructions on how to manifest here, though it had required a cache of energy. Based on Elixir and Puck's labored outtakes, they've used up precious reserves of magic.

By contrast, Cove and Juniper had had it easier coasting on Tímien's back. My father must have parceled them off and vanished quickly, intent on watching the sky with his brethren.

My mouth twitches. "Too much of a draft for your antlers to handle?"

Puck's eyes narrow. "Leave my rack out of this, asshole."

"The location was necessary," I tell them, then turn and guide my brothers across the network of bridges until we reunite with our partners, where Lark and I explain the reasoning behind meeting here instead of our usual outlet in the wildlife park.

Daunted silence trails in the wake of our story about the firebird Fae. Several hardwood bridges croak beneath sloping tails of air, and other crossways fashioned from intricately braided cords swing. Clouds pack around numerous extensions, blotting out half of the maze.

A flock of avians spear through the powdery haze. My ears locate the rhythmic flap of my father's wings, not thirty leagues above.

Puck mutters under his breath. He tightens his arm around Juniper's waist from behind, and she leans into him while frowning in thought.

Elixir hisses while looming beside Cove. I sense my brother's instincts—the desire to injure, to strike fast. That he has nowhere, and no one, to take his venom out on is a challenge for him. By now, he would have sent someone crashing to the ground.

Puck notices this, too. "For fuck's sake. Cerulean, give this anaconda something to break. Preferably nothing connected to the bridge we're standing on."

However, Elixir's lady is the first to make an actual move. "Fables help us." Cove swerves toward Lark and cups a hand to her sister's cheek. "Did he hurt you?"

"Hush," Lark says while removing Cove's hand and kissing the knuckles. "That bloke hurt me? Who do you think you're talking to? Besides, I had backup."

I move closer to my mate. "He wouldn't have split a hair," I vow, hearing the deadly edge in my own voice, like silk gliding over the curve of a dagger.

"What did he want?" Juniper asks.

"My severed tits for his collection box?" Lark guesses, referring the human bone charm that had ornamented the Fae's forehead. "That, and my mortal heart on a platter, along with Cerulean's."

"Tell me you lopped off his cock as payment," Puck requests.

"Guess we missed that opportunity," Lark says. "We were too busy throwing that piece of shit off the mountain."

"That was going to be my second suggestion."

Lark's mouth slants. She might have snorted if the matter were funny.

Juniper analyzes. "Your frazzled state must have given the enemy an incentive to trespass. They assumed you would be off your guard, not expecting a second attack in the span of a few hours."

It makes sense.

"The more pertinent question is what do about it," I prompt. "How do we respond?"

"By killing their leader," Elixir says.

"By hijacking the pissant," Puck amends. "Then killing them."

"By spying on the wanker first," Lark counters. "Then hijacking, then killing."

"By talking," I answer in unison with Cove and Juniper.

The three of us glance at one another before all hell breaks loose from the other half of our band.

"Wait." Lark rounds on me. "We're going to do *what*?"

I clarify, "We'll call a meeting with our enemies."

"Are you fucking kidding me?" Puck ejects, the black streaks beneath his lower eyelashes creasing. "We're going to *talk to them*? After what these fuckers did, that's our plan?

"Cerulean, those meddlesome shitheads corrupted one of the fauna, then their leader sent a lackey to trespass on the wildlife park—fucking sacred ground—and finish the job. After all this time gathering allies, training with them, and preparing for a battle, you want to sit down and have a chat instead? That's not your sport, luv."

"It is when we don't know what we're up against," I bite out. "If you think we won't be in combat during our conference, you're gravely mistaken. And by the fucking way? It wasn't one of woodland fauna that was compromised. I'm not taking this lightly, so don't test me on this, Puck."

"It's a sound plot," Juniper agrees. "Weapons will be fired, only of the verbal sort." She nudges Puck. "Since when have you ever underestimated the power of words?"

The satyr falls quiet, his face strung tight but his closed mouth proving he sees where this is going. Faeries would expect physical backlash. They won't expect diplomacy, especially not after what happened.

The steps to being vicious are to observe, then to listen, then to manipulate. That's how you get your targets to spill information they don't want to confide. Always, that's the trickster's way.

"There's time," Juniper insists. "We still have time to break through the Fable's hidden message and find the second way. Jumping into warfare will make that impossible. No matter how far they push us, we might only have one chance. And when you're hunting with only one shot—"

"Better make sure it's clean," Puck finishes while gazing down at her. "Bloody true."

Elixir's still fuming about our plans. Pacing himself is hardly his nature. I can't begin to count how often Puck and I had to stop him from going on a murder spree against the mortals who took part in The Trapping. Even though restoring the fauna requires sacrificing humans through games, it had sometimes taken half a dozen forest roots and just as many slaps of wind to hold Elixir back.

It's understandable. He lost his parents the night we escaped.

Nevertheless, Cove whispers into Elixir's ear, which causes the vengeance to dim from his eyes. His jaw hardens, but he gives a clipped nod. "So be it."

We agree, and I send an invitation through the wind. There are no roots, nor waterways in this location, so Puck and Elixir lack the means to dispatch their own missives. My element is the one outlet available from this bridge, and although we don't know where the enemy resides, the wind will find them.

It will know where to look.

Similarly, it will know how to travel and make itself accessible. Communication in Faerie is simple yet complex. If need to be, the wind can meld with the roots, and from there with the water. The essence of my dispatch can morph itself from one element to the next, enabling it to migrate between regions.

No matter where the recipient dwells, the invitation will be comprehensible. And receiving a response shouldn't take long. Faeries are often too curious, too intrigued by surprises.

In the meantime, another concern has been plaguing my mind. Wordlessly, I seek out Elixir's attention and wait for him to seize on it. His features smooth out once he hears the delay in my respiration, his gaze fastens to a spot just below my eyes, and his baritone loses its serrated edge. "The raven lives."

My joints buckle, and a huff of relief flees my lungs. The group lets out a collective exhale, though it's swiftly replaced by apprehension.

"But will the raven try again?" I speculate.

"Doubtful," Elixir says. "Whatever they did to him was temporary."

Fury stirs up like debris within me. Be that as it may, I set my palm on his shoulder. "Well done."

My brother wavers. "It was not only me. I had help after you left."

He must mean Cove, who kept us company at the raven's side before I departed from The Deep and flew home with my father. I glance Cove's way, but the woman shakes her head, and her eyes stray to a point behind us.

Whatever she sees, it triggers a pleased light in Puck's eyes. Likewise, Juniper beams at the approaching sight.

At the sound of hooves, I turn as a towering centaur breaks through the mist. Beneath a horned helmet, his dark visage is as timeless as the earth itself. His olive irises match his mane, tail, and coat, and the orbs shine with friendship when fixing on Juniper.

"Always an honor, moppet," Cypress greets.

"The honor's mine, friend," she replies.

He grins, then his irises spark like embers when they land on Puck. "Satyr."

"Centaur," Puck quips.

A faithful sort of kinship brims between them, one that's distinct from my camaraderie with Moth, heightened in some enigmatic way. It takes a moment for the equine to look away and turn his attention on me. "When a call comes from the infamous Three, it must be answered."

I incline my head. "Cypress."

"Cerulean," he replies.

"According to my brother, you helped him tend to the raven after I was gone. I should be the one who bows to you."

"Nonsense. A ruler does not bow."

"Haven't you heard? I forfeited that title."

"Also, nonsense. Once a ruler, always a ruler."

"All the same, name your favor."

The equine grumbles with dignity. "We centaurs are healers, but we do not pawn off our assistance on a whim, much less for deals. Our gifts are offered freely. That is our way." He glances at the heavens, then says, "Long have I wished to view the stars from this point. If you insist, that and the animal's recovery are reward enough."

Only Cypress and I can see through the dense canopy to the celestials. Centaurs are intimately acquainted with them, though on a different level from mountain Fae. It's more spiritual than physical, more divine than fundamental.

The giant Fae shifts his hooves on the planks. "Now tell me why I am standing thousands of feet above my home."

"Come now," I say. "Are you implying the view isn't worth it?"

"Ask someone who's seen it before," a feminine voice grunts.

My mouth turns up as I regard the runty figure who flutters into the scene, her paper-thin wings vibrating with umbrage. Moth shoves through the clouds in a maelstrom of resentment. Her gauzy dress cocoons her diminutive shape and makes her look at least five hundred years younger than she is.

My sister-in-arms perches two fists on her hips while glowering at Lark and me. "You left a mess."

Lark clears her throat. "Right. Sorry about that."

"No, you're not. One day, you human nuisance, I'm going to pick off your eyelashes one by one while you sleep. And I will enjoy it."

Because Moth's not serious, I atone with a repentant tilt of my lips. "Our apologies, Moth."

"I'm not your housekeeper, you insatiable juveniles. If you're going to fuck like rabbits on my turf, at least gather your clothes afterward."

Fuchsia erupts across Cove's cheeks, whereas Elixir's impatient expression doesn't alter.

Cypress isn't listening. He's too busy consulting the stars.

Juniper merely rolls her eyes.

And Puck...well, Puck is Puck. The satyr gives us both a thoroughly impressed look. "My, my, my," he gushes. "Getting frisky on sanctified grounds? You've gone pagan."

To be clear, Lark and I had satisfied our cravings inside the tower. That aside, we did neglect to retrieve our clothing from the gazebo.

I open my mouth, but Elixir interjects. "At last," he mutters.

A voluptuous female with silver blue hair saunters from the opposite end of the bridge. Her eyes are as prismatic as crystals, which match the scales capping her dark-skinned shoulders. Sheer, flowing pants buffet her thighs and cinch at her ankles, and a harpoon-shaped lance rests across her back.

After taking stock of the elevation, Coral raises one fluid eyebrow. "This is quite high," the water Fae announces in a syrupy tone, as if confiding a scandal. "And a positively excessive journey for a summons. But of course—" she bows to a beaming Cove and a restless Elixir, "—my liege's wish is my command."

"My wish," he grouses, "is to stop wasting time and proceed."

"Mind telling us why you've chosen the most elusive region in this mountain for a meeting?" Moth proposes, her rump now perched on Cypress's back.

All heads swoop toward Lark and me. After a silent exchange with Puck and Juniper, Cypress deduces, "Because this is not a meeting."

"Hardly." My mouth crooks with fiendish intent. "It's a game."

7

Rather, it's a game of wills and willpowers. It's a power play, with moves and countermoves.

My mate and I bring Cypress, Moth, and Coral up to speed on the details, from the raven's attack to the firebird's foiled attempt in the wildlife park. Dismay contorts Cypress's face, and Coral's eyes thin to slits. Moth is less restrained, but once she has ceased cursing and kicking the poor air, we move on to the impending meeting with the enemy.

Negotiation is unlikely, since we tried that after everyone recovered from the flood that ravaged Elixir's domain. Compromise and reason have gotten us nowhere. Indeed, under normal circumstances another conference would send the wrong message—that we're either naive or bluffing. Yet after recent events, it will present our side as controlled, durable, and resilient.

Rage weakens a fighter. Weakness makes a warrior careless. Whoever is leading our enemies, they need to see that we're anything but.

It's time to issue a harsher threat, all the while slipping between the cracks and gathering every bit of information we can. That includes why and how our opponents compelled the raven, and what sort of leader can influence his followers to breach the tower's sacred haven.

As for the type of meeting, Puck suggests a roundtable involving alcohol. "Booze tends to loosen tongues and fuck with inhibitions," he says. "Especially if the bottles are curated and spiced by me."

"Except we host it here," I specify. "In The Night Aviary."

Everyone gawks, as if I've gone mad.

A rather predictable response follows. "You're shitting me, right?" Puck points across the range to the glass dome, home to hundreds of birds and the Middle Moon Masquerade. "Bringing them to the aviary is like dropping a fox into a chicken coop."

"Very much so," I agree. "We're the foxes."

"You sure about that? Because from where I'm standing—"

"If I were you," I murmur slowly, "I would stop right there, dear brother."

Question my motives when it comes to the mountain fauna, and no sibling shall be safe from me. I have my stealthy reasons, and since when has this lot ever doubted that?

Realization alights Lark's gaze. "You're gonna place a shield on 'em."

"On all of us," I say. "The wind won't let our visitors get near the avians or anyone who matters to me. But we need to see if our enemies are tempted to turn the animals on us, or at least to parse through any hints about how they do it, should they fail to tell us outright."

Puck's stance relaxes, and his lips tilt with mischief. "Clever, brother."

Juniper nods. "It's a good strategy, with a contingency plan."

"Won't they guess what you're doing?" Cove wonders. "If they know your powers?"

"They will not," Elixir assures her. "No Fae reveals the extents and drawbacks of their abilities."

"Not willingly," Coral expands. "That would cut out the element of surprise."

"Plus, the opportunity to commit deceit," Puck adds. "Where's the fun in that?"

"Be that as it may, you will not need to tempt them," Cypress predicts. "They will tell you how they influenced the raven."

"You'll provoke it out of them," Moth says with a grin. "You always do."

My mouth quirks. "Only if the rest of you provoke them with me."

We expect Moth, Cypress, and Coral to be there. However, they insist that will dilute the impact my brothers and I have as leaders. Lesser numbers will appear more confident. Everyone agrees to that.

We'll pick through the enemy's weaknesses and pick apart their strengths. We'll seek to find the chink in their armor.

Whatever threats our band sets on the table will come from us alone, not from our allies. We can't speak for them until they've learned the details, but we can't involve them until we have clearer information.

My father will attend the meeting along with The Parliament. Tímien is certain none of the owls have been influenced like the raven. As a former sovereign of the wild and a dweller of the sky, I can detect this as well.

As for the multitude of other fauna across this region—birds, bats, rams, cougars, antelopes, and mountain goats, among others—it's anyone's guess. The notion ghosts up my spine.

Moth, Cypress, and Coral disband. The rest of us stay behind and line up along the bridge, where we face a labyrinthine mosaic of suspensions, planks, and ropes, all capped in shawls of dense fog. This far up, the only sources of color are Puck's inferno of red waves, Juniper's green tresses, and Cove's watery locks. Elixir is a cloaked python dominating the shadows, whereas my mate and I blend in with the firmament.

A draft whistles through the maze and disturbs one of the lower-level bridges. A caw shears through the night, and the subtle twitch of a torch glints from The Watch of Nightingales.

None of us second-guesses our decision. What we speak, we cannot unspeak.

"Well," Juniper states, twisting toward everyone. "Now that we have a plan, we can move on to a recurring problem. What about the Fable?"

"You tell us, missy," Lark says.

"I haven't unearthed anything new." Juniper rolls her shoulders, as if to release a kink. "But I'd like to test a theory."

With that, she glances at Elixir. Everyone follows her gaze and settles on him. My brother hears our heads veering his way, but when his attention ticks over to Juniper, his irises flare, briefly but safely. Then he looks away.

How intriguing. My brother often responds like this with her.

It's not lost on Cove, who watches him carefully. Nor does the reaction sneak past Puck, whose brows stitch together. But ironically—seeing as it has to do with his woman—he doesn't comment for once in his outspoken life.

Likely, he doesn't want to interrupt Juniper. She resents being cut off. All of us have learned the unfavorable consequences of that.

Lark's sister trots away, retrieves a pack slumped nearby, and returns while plucking the Book of Fables and her spectacle case from its contents. Feathers, branches, and droplets emboss the tome's spine. The hinges have dulled over the centuries, and animals including lions, bears, wolves, hares, and ravens embellish the cover.

Puck takes the bag from Juniper, and after she perches the glasses on her nose, she thumbs through the pages until reaching the most crucial one: the Fable created with its mysterious passage about the second way to the preserve our world.

"I'm still hunting through this," Juniper prefaces. "One, other potentially coded messages stored inside the book. Two, any historical clues that predate common knowledge. Three, additional changes in font that I might have missed during my last reread. Four, feasible patterns in the Fables' titles. Five—"

"*Five?*" Lark exaggerates.

"Five," Juniper snaps, a scowl leaping off her face before she returns to the book. "Five...and this is important...any changes in texture."

Elixir hears something preemptive in her voice because his features purse. "Texture," he repeats.

"Creases in the pages that form shapes or words, thickness that emphasizes passages the way an underline mark would, or areas where the parchment is smooth or coarse," she explains. "Or perhaps the textures of the letters and sentences themselves. What if there's something there? Any of us could feel that." Juniper swipes off her glasses and meets Elixir's remote stare. "Unless we aren't meant to. Unless the signs are hidden."

Perceptive, indeed.

Our earlier hope that Elixir might have access to the second way, given his power to see what others can't, had waned after The Deep's flood.

Prior to that event, Elixir had insisted he knew nothing, despite the role his Unseelie ancestor and her Seelie nemesis played in the Book of Fables. Since then, Juniper has narrated the tales to him, but it hasn't unveiled a forsaken thing. He seems to know as little as the rest of us.

Yet this idea has merit. What if Elixir feels his way through the Fable, touches and follows it as he does the humid mist or the tunnel walls of his domain? What if he uses texture to guide him?

Puck gives Juniper a proud wink. They must have talked about this at length.

Elixir hesitates until Cove presses into his side. "I will try," he grunts. "But I promise nothing."

Juniper's shoulders rise with confidence, and she extends the book to him, the pages spread open. I restrain the urge to move in closer. Elixir isn't a creature to be smothered.

Those gilded orbs cascade shut. Our group waits as he rests his fingers on the title, then glides them like water over the parchment, from the illuminated artwork—raptors, stags, and serpents—to the paragraphs. His digits sink down the page, gliding from left to right like a wave, his arms moving as though he's playing the harp.

Then his hands seize up, halting on the last word. His eyes flip open, and he growls in frustration before yanking his fingers back.

Fucking Fables. I lean against the railing in defeat and tuck Lark into me, trading sad grins with her.

Puck's chest falls. Juniper's face sags as she draws the book to her small frame. Regardless, the speed at which she progresses from disappointed to pragmatic is a testament to her nature. Puck once likened her to a steadfast tree, and I can see why.

Come to think of it, with her eyes unfettered, the irises transcend from the green of a woodland to something infinitely more vivid, almost Faelike. I would spend more time on that oddity if my mind weren't toying with me, and if the probability weren't beyond farfetched.

"Well." Juniper pats the book's binding. "It was worth a try."

"Or two," Puck advocates. "Or three."

"He's right," Lark says. "Could take more than one attempt."

Ferocity and something akin to shame dig trenches into Elixir's face. Long strands of black hair tumble over his profile as he stalks to the opposite side of the bridge, where he grips the railing. The scales of his wrists glint like shards of glass.

Cove hastens to his side, rubs his bicep, and murmurs, "You tried."

While they whisper in private, Lark makes the best of it. "What's next on your list?"

"Ten other possibilities," Juniper says lamely, her sullen expression suggesting it's not an impressive number.

"Aww, is that all?" Lark endeavors to tease. "You'd better work on your quota. Need some help? I'll be really quiet in that fancy library of yours. I promise." Then she turns to Puck. "You're spoiling her good, by the way."

"Is there any other way?" he asks with a roguish grin.

My brother had added a new level to his cabin and built a library for Juniper, which contains mortal and Fae books, illuminated manuscripts, scrolls, and lexicons. It's another reason he doesn't want to pry her from their home, even though he will.

Juniper harrumphs and shoves the Book of Fables into her pack, along with her spectacles. "Leave it to me to read the correct texts. Unlike you, I've studied all of them."

"Gee, I'd forgotten that fact," Lark singsongs. "Thanks for the thousandth reminder."

That bumps a smile out of Juniper, and we all chuckle. Though, I stop when the air shifts. I spin as the draft rushes against my coat, drapes itself across my shoulders, and funnels a message to me. I heed its contents and flick my fingers, done with listening.

My gaze sweeps over Lark's face, then every member of our band. "We've received our answer." And my lips curl. "He's coming."

He'd left his signature on the wind—an echo of his voice, a thrash of sound reminiscent of simmering liquid about to reach its boiling point. The noise is less akin to the brush of wind and more like a surge of water.

Subtle hints exist within a Fae's inflection—rhythms, patterns, depth— which indicate their origins. Now I have an inkling of which sort of Fae we're dealing with. But for confirmation, I glance toward my brothers and describe the voice.

"He isn't of the mountain," I say.

As I'd suspected, Puck shows no sign of recognition. "Don't look at me. From what you describe, it's not the burr of a leprechaun or the tenor of a faun, to say nothing of a forest nymph's lilt or a brownie's incessant squeaking. I don't know that voice."

But Elixir's pupils ferment with hatred. A lashing growl rips from his mouth. "I do."

8

The following eventide, we're ready for him. Across the range, I fly beside my father, and Lark sits astride the nightingale with whom she's developed an affinity. The bird has shifted its size to accommodate her, and the air lifts Lark's hair, tossing it around like a white sail.

She's wearing a silver dress. The succulent design was fabricated by Moth, with delicate chain links for straps and a skirt that flashes like lightning when Lark moves. Additional intricate chains thread through her hair, gathering it into various layers while letting the ends tumble down her back.

She's breathtaking. She's dazzling. She's enticing and—

I slam into an air pocket. The downdraft yanks me under so fast my wings invert.

"Shit," I grunt, beating my plumes until I'm level again.

Lark's knowing chuckle skips across the sky. It's my fault I can't stop staring at her long enough to concentrate. Regardless, I toss her a fiendish look. The more she laughs, the longer I'll fuck her tonight.

When we land at The Night Aviary, Tímien and the nightingale shrink and dart inside. Torches light the gravel walkway, molten orange shadows licking the curves of my mate, and her dress remains an obstacle I'd very much like to tear from her body.

It's the neckline. I blame the forsaken neckline. The infernal thing plunges between her breasts, revealing crescents and an intolerable strip of skin.

Actually, no. I blame every stitch of the garment, every place it touches her, every thread that's driving my cock up against my pants.

"You're a cruel being," I warn her. "I see you mean to torture me for eternity."

"Payback." Lark drapes her arm through mine and drizzles her gaze down my gem encrusted black coat, which falls open to reveal my torso. "Hot damn. Guess I could accuse you of the same thing. I miss the sexy wings, though."

"Consider it a tease for a tease."

"Impeccably disheveled prick." She sidles closer and flirts, "Remember the last time we were here?"

I lean into Lark's precious ear and let my whisper glide over her like silk, "I remember every taste, pet."

I recall the vision of Lark sneaking into the masquerade, pretending like she owned the place, ours faces covered in masks, the sly game of hide-and-seek as she tried to find me, and the frequent glimpses I stole through the crush of rutting figures, the dance in which her body grated against mine, and the retreat into a dark room, where my mouth feasted on hers. I remember the savory taste of Lark's moan on my tongue and the realization that she was the mortal who had stolen my heart nine years ago.

The mammoth vultures guarding the entrance from an overhead mantel regard us placidly as we pass through. Inside, the corridor broadens into a domed structure capped in thousands of panes of glass. Foliage crochets through multiple levels where broad hammocks hang. Raptors either walk on gangly limbs across the walkways or flit through the vegetation, the avians' flights rustling the greenery.

At the nexus, a towering hawthorn tree rises into the heights, its branches canopying the rafters. Starlight dapples the levels, and flocks of cyan and copper wings flutter in and out of view, the whooshing flap of their plumage audible.

On the ground level, where the masquerade's dance floor had once been congested with grinding couples, a long table outlined in high-backed chairs stretches beneath the hawthorn.

Everyone is here. Cove wears an ivory gown, and she's inhaling the blossoms of a honeysuckle bush. Elixir bends his head and murmurs to her. His gold-cuffed robe is more lavish than usual, as are the boots encasing his feet and the loose shirt and leggings.

Puck swaggers our way in buckled leather and without a shred of formality. His rumpled waves look as though Juniper spent half the night yanking on them. In comparison, Lark's bookish sister is a vision in a velvet gown so scarlet it rivals her lover's hair.

Lark whistles. "Hubba hubba."

"Why, thank you," Puck croons.

"Not you, asshole," my mate jokes, then admires Juniper. "You're looking mighty fine, hon. But I thought you said only hussies wore red."

Juniper shrugs. "I changed my mind."

"Which is why we have one less set of drinking glasses in our kitchen," Puck remarks. "I was clearing the dishes and might have broken them when I saw her."

"How many were you holding when they slipped from your fingers?" Lark wonders.

"One," he says with a wolfish grin. "The first was an accident. The rest just got in the way. We needed countertop space."

"Nice work," my saucy mate compliments her crimson-faced sister. "Glad to see you've accessorized, too. The dress goes well with the crossbow."

Weapons flash from each of our garments. It had been a trial locating the ones that got swept away in The Deep's flood, but we'd managed to restore them.

Chalices and trays run down the table's length. The latter bears flagons of blackthorn wine, spirited nectar, and effervescent water flavored with woodland spices. As everyone finds their seats, Juniper takes stock of the banquet. Her mouth scrunches into a grimace, and her intakes falter, trying not to inhale the mixture of scents.

Across from her, a frown yanks Puck's features downward. "My, my, my. I thought you loved cranberry nectar."

"It's not the drinks," she excuses. "I'm just tired."

Puck doesn't look convinced. Elixir listens to them with a perturbed expression. I'm not sure I believe Juniper, either.

Tímien and the nightingale are perched on the hawthorn's shallowest branch, which extends over the table. Our band watches a troop of owls cruise inside, sling-shotting through the air on ebony and flaxen wings, each quill shining at the tips.

Lark's sisters go slack-jawed at the congregation. In synchronized form, the raptors split and take up residence on the lower boughs, every member claiming a different spot. Their arrangement is carefully considered, offering views of each chair as well as the entirety of the aviary.

We sink to the floor, bowing to the fauna and then rising. They peer down at us through irises glossed in aquamarine and citrine, the wide eyes so piercing they could be medallions.

Despite signs of the wild fading, the river and forest fauna are more remote—and thus, more removed—from this conflict. However, the animals of the mountain are increasingly aware of the tensions. They sense the impending scrimmage between Faeries of the Solitary wild.

We genuflect to the raptors. Straightening, I twirl a finger, and the wind answers my call. My digit whisks up a thin film of air, invisible to everyone but me, the owls, and Lark, who notices fragments.

The wind agitates into a sphere that bloats around the hawthorn, where the aviary birds roam. A smaller globe forms over our band, which adapts to us as we move.

Afterward, Tímien communicates on behalf of The Parliament. It's time to prepare ourselves.

I heed the message and nod to everyone. "He's near."

"I'd say I'm a little closer than that," a male voice drones.

We turn—all except Elixir, who's already facing the arched entrance. He must have detected the Fae's arrival moments earlier, because a hiss is skittering across his tongue. Each of us seizes our weapons, holding fast to our bows, spear, daggers, whip, and javelin.

Elixir plants himself in front of Cove, whose delicate features are taut, equal parts stricken and livid. We'd known who was coming. Yet knowing and seeing are two different experiences.

The water Fae fills the doorway, a single thumb hooked into the pocket of his pants and a dark shirt clinging to his frame. Markings peek from the neckline, hinting at the tar-black whorls inking the rest of his torso. Beneath a stream of murky green hair reminiscent of a marshland, black smudges leak from beneath his lower eyelashes, as if he's weeping oil.

Several scales glitter at the temples, but for a merman shifter, Scorpio doesn't have as many incrustations as Elixir.

Scorpio raises his brow at our display, as if we've overestimated and overreacted. On that note, he stands without an entourage. The only thing he's brought is the trident buckled to his back.

The prick lifts his arms, palms up. "If I'm not mistaken, you were expecting me, right? Your love letter said this was a meeting, not an execution. What did you think I would do?" A spiteful grin reveals a row of whittled teeth. "Take you by surprise?"

My fingers itch to throw a few cyclones in his direction, tie those windstorms around all four limbs, and use the air pressure to draw and quarter him. To be sure, we'd have one less nuisance to deal with. That is, if we discount the Faeries who follow him and outnumber us.

Elixir stalks forward, his fingers choking the forked daggers. Protectiveness isn't the only thing that propels my brother forward. It's the fact that Scorpio's lucid eyes are focused on him. Somehow, my brother can sense this.

Elixir's glare ignites. "I blinded you."

"You did, didn't you?" Scorpio pretends to mull that over, then hitches a shoulder. "So…I guess you missed?"

"That's impossible," Cove utters.

"Not really," the merman dismisses.

Elixir and Cove had told us what happened during the flood, how Elixir had blinded Scorpio while underwater. That, plus everything else that transpired during Cove's game had been enough to fuel Scorpio. It had motivated him to lead our kin against us.

Yet my brother's powers are supposed to be irreversible.

So how the Fables is this bastard able to see us?

Scorpio has the nerve to genuflect to the owls. "Esteemed ones."

The raptors dissect him with their medallion eyes. My father bristles right up to the horned tufts.

An order from the owls sails to me through a current. I disarm at their behest, and the rest of our band takes the hint, lowering their defenses.

Rather, everyone does but my dear brother, whose capacity for venom exceeds Scorpio's by a thousandfold.

"Elixir," I say. "The Parliament has spoken."

I'm the only one who'd been able to hear the command, but the impetus behind my actions had been obvious. Reluctantly, Elixir complies. While jamming the daggers into the baldric beneath his robe, his pupils blaze with rancor.

With all the vicious elegance I can muster, I gesture toward the table. "After you."

And with all the malicious entitlement Scorpio fails to contain, he strides into the aviary while barely paying the resident birds notice.

Ah. So he doesn't expect any of these avians to take his side, nor is he interested in trying for them.

I parcel this observation to my father, who agrees. His counsel flocks to my ears, cautioning me to take heed.

Scorpio's intentions are selective rather than random. To that end, I reserve this fact for later but keep the shield in place.

In any case, Scorpio has less interest in the fauna and more interest in Puck. They've never officially met, and while my brother's sinful, seductive, shameless reputation precedes him, it's hardly a shock when the cobbled muscles and stag antlers draw Scorpio's appreciative eye. Most Faeries can't resist the lustful magnetism of a satyr, especially if that satyr is Puck.

As Scorpio passes my brother, the merman's uncensored gaze wanders south. No stranger to physical temptations herself, Lark catches the exchange and snorts, "Get in line, bloke."

Puck isn't clueless. He knows the effect he has on others. "There is no line," he corrects, then aims his gaze at Juniper. "Not anymore."

Juniper pelts Scorpio with a possessive glare. But the sight of them together only causes the merman's mouth to twist in distaste, as if he's lost his appetite.

With a flourish, I offer Lark my arm and guide her to the table.

The players take their seats. The Parliament won't intervene, preferring to observe unless it's imperative. Tímien will communicate on their behalf, but only if necessary. Owls take care with what they say, every utterance between them and Faeries is heavily measured, and the raptors prefer to suspend judgement until the end.

Puck slouches in his chair, props his hooves atop the table, and crosses them. He picks up a stirring spoon meant for the nectar and twirls it between his fingers. "Well, fuck me. I was hoping we'd start guzzling without you. Rude, I know, but the nectar was getting warm. Nobody likes it room temperature."

Scorpio unhitches the trident and sets it beside him as he fills his seat. "You were also hoping for a larger head count."

"About that. Where are your minions? I went to all this trouble, setting the table. What happened? Only you could find time in your schedule? Or did the prospect of Elixir scare everyone away?"

"I don't know what you're talking about." Scorpio fetches his chalice, pours wine, and lifts the vessel in a mock toast. "I'm just here for the drinks."

"I wager it was my charisma that kept everyone away, then. It tends to intimidate others."

"Why bother with a coterie? It takes only one Fae to state terms, and one to reject or accept them."

"In other words, you're a control freak."

"Probably. Anyway, I'm done talking to you."

"You're done when I say you're done, luv."

"You should be blind," Elixir demands.

"Yet I'm not," Scorpio gloats. "Apologies for disappointing you again, Sire."

Although he occupies the furthest seat from his ruler, the distance between them is moot, powerless to stifle the tension.

"Elaborate," Elixir clips. "Either do so, or choke on your wine. Make your choice."

Scorpio's features click into place. He knows what that means, knows what Elixir can do from this distance. Wisely, the merman sets down his goblet. "Elaborate?" He taps his chin. "That sounds like it'll take work."

"True work is for the strong-willed," Juniper recites.

Puck smirks at her. "Book of Fables?"

"Journal of Juniper."

"Even better. Honestly, I was wondering how long it would take you."

Scorpio grunts. "Too bad I'm not interested in secondhand teachings from a human."

"Watch yourself," the satyr warns, swinging his head toward the merman. "That human is my woman. Make a mockery of her, and she'll make an ignoramus of you. And when she's done, I'll say I told you so."

The Fae scoffs, then regards Elixir with a blithe expression that neglects to conceal his smugness. "The flood weakened you, and the saltwater weakened you further. Need I say more?"

No, he needn't. Elixir's countenance shifts in comprehension. The flood and salt had expended his energy, thus decreasing the strength to wield his power. Because of that, the magic hadn't cemented to the point of irreversibility. As a result, blinding the merman had been temporary.

Cove peers at Scorpio and shakes her head. "The vial that salted the water. You took it from Elixir's den, didn't you?"

Scorpio refuses to acknowledge her but just stares at Elixir. While struggling with him underwater, Cove had noticed a vial hanging from around Scorpio's throat. She'd torn it from him and hurled the contents at his face, which had brined the water.

What she hadn't intended was for the water to nearly drown my brother—but it must have been on Scorpio's agenda.

And Coral, Elixir's first-in-command, had reported seeing Scorpio loitering in the den shortly before the flood began.

The merman tilts his head. "I must admit. I expected a less civil response than that, Sire. You must be getting soft…slowing down."

Elixir's visage tightens. "Are you familiar with the pyre viper?"

Scorpio twitches. His index finger ceases tapping against his chin.

Amusement travels across The Parliament. I can tell by the shift in the air.

For my part, a grin slants across my mouth. The pyre viper is an extinct reptile of Faerie, a dweller that once existed during the age of the kelpies. According to lore, the viper had been the slowest of serpents, yet it had delivered the harshest venom, which melted its victim from the inside out.

Just because a creature moves slowly, that doesn't mean it's not the most brutal of killers. My brother may have given his heart to a mortal, but he's never lost his capacity for ruthlessness. One would think Elixir has provided Scorpio with plenty of opportunities to learn this.

At this point, the only reason Scorpio still possesses the husk of skin encasing his body is because of our location. We'd cited this meeting as neutral. Faeries are duplicitous, but they always keep their word once a bargain is made.

That isn't to say Elixir won't make good on his threat once we leave here.

The merman regroups. Suspicion cramps his face as he takes The Parliaments' measure, then considers the setting with renewed scrutiny. "This location seems a reckless choice for a meeting." He glances my way. "Or a shrewd one."

Good. He's remembering not to underestimate me.

That will make Scorpio overextend himself and sift through every word I speak, searching for a riddle. And when my targets try that hard, they stop paying attention to their own secrets, stop monitoring their own demons.

I won't need to toy with my words. None of us will.

We just need to rile him up enough, so that he fucks up without realizing it.

"What's the point of this meeting, I wonder?" Scorpio prompts. "To threaten, bargain, or declare war?"

"We're here to get answers," Juniper lists. "Then to make demands."

"Then to threaten your ass, if you refuse," Lark says.

"And then get you drunk," Puck adds. "That'll be my job."

"After that, we'll talk about bargains," I finish.

"And besides that, what's my incentive for being here?" Scorpio questions.

"To leave with your cock still attached to your body," Elixir says through gritted teeth.

"You'll answer us," I say. "Then you'll agree or disagree, and then you'll make your own shoddy demands, then you'll receive our rebuttal, and then you'll leave."

"I didn't hear you acknowledge the 'declare war' part. Where's that on the schedule?"

"Meh." Puck shrugs. "We don't need to serve you expensive wine to do that."

At the mention of alcohol, Juniper looks queasy. She ignores the nectar Puck had claimed she loves so much, opts for a flagon of herbal water instead, pours a generous helping, and tips back the contents.

I recline in my seat and circle my finger around the chalice in front of me. "You declared war two nights ago when you compelled a member of the fauna."

"Good point," Scorpio concedes. "Though usually once war is declared, meetings are forfeit."

"Forfeit-schmorfeit," Puck says. "Isn't it funny how Faeries like to break their own rules?"

Which brings me back to my original statement. "How did you do it?"

As if flummoxed, Scorpio bunches his mouth and lifts his arms. "Magic?"

The Parliament bristles. A smile cuts through my face. "I won't ask twice."

"And I won't answer at all."

"We can do this the easy way or the Cerulean way."

Juniper stamps her chalice onto the table. "This doesn't make sense. Steering the fauna into combat is the same as sacrificing them. It goes against your nature, not to mention it does the opposite of preserving the lifecycle. It's no better than what humans did in The Trapping."

The merman's features contort, turning the black smears under his eyelids into slashes. "Those animals were murdered by inferior lowlifes of a different race." His elbow hits the table as he points at her. "By enemies outside of their world."

"We are not an inferior race."

"The fauna of The Trapping were caged and maimed with human iron. They weren't killed by natural causes, nor in their own realm. That's why your uprising has endangered our world—because your desecration went against the cycle."

He directs his attention to The Parliament, though he avoids Tímien's gaze. "The raven, on the other hand, was different. It was acting within in its territory and with Faeries. That's a natural combination for this world. Besides, it was running on its base instincts. I merely enhanced them."

The Parliament lances him with formidable stares.

"What about the assassin?" Lark interrogates. "You know, the wanker we sent packing off the side of a cliff."

"I can't take credit for that imbecile," Scorpio discards, returning to the members of the table. "Apparently, you failing to get yourself pecked to death disappointed the miserable sod, and he got ambitious on his own. Faeries are impulsive when scorned, especially if their *sovereigns*—" he glares at Elixir, then Puck, then me, "—betray them."

"The firebird Fae attacked us in your name."

"Well, I'm not going to complain about that. It's flattering."

"I did not betray anyone," I draw out. "None of us did. We're trying to save our world."

"By siding with—and fucking—the humans we're supposed to sacrifice," the merman sneers. "You're mated. Repugnant, but I sort of get it. Destiny is hard to flip off." He jerks his chin toward Puck and Elixir. "What are your excuses, alphas?"

Puck tsks. "My, my, my. Now who said anything about our choices needing excuses?"

"There's another way," Juniper petitions.

"Lies," the merman spews. "Lies you're telling the pitiful number of followers you've converted."

"As much as we like playing mind games, doing so to accumulate allies isn't one of those times," I contradict. "Can you say the same? Because from what I'm hearing, enhancing the raven sounds like a fancy way of saying you manipulated the creature."

"We're the ones liberating the fauna," Scorpio blusters. "You're the ones putting them in danger by siding with the enemy and causing this internal battle."

"Is that what you're telling the Solitaries? Is that how you're indoctrinating them?"

"They don't need to be swayed. They'd already been mobilized to the right side by being who they've always been. You three were the ones who pissed on our culture, mocked our history, and broke our trust—all for the sake of mortal pussy." His lip curls. "In that respect, I'm surprised these females are still in one piece. Brittle as paper, they are. Who knew humans could handle being fucked by Faeries?"

"Who knew Faeries couldn't handle losing to those same humans in a game?" Lark parries with a honeyed grin.

Scorpio glowers at her, then regards me. "Mentally feisty but physically feeble. Do you have to be careful not to shatter a bone while driving your cock into her? Is that part of the kink?"

Fury sets my tongue on edge. "Be. Very. Careful."

Although the wind shield is still up, Tímien shifts on the branch, putting Scorpio into his line of flight. It's a reflex more than anything. He knows not to fight my battles, nor Lark's.

The merman, on the other hand, doesn't have a fucking clue what's good for him. Without thinking, he snatches his chalice, takes a deep swig, and sets the vessel down. "Spoken like a Fae who's buried himself so waist-deep in his whore, he's lost track of his balls."

And that's when he begins to sizzle. Red floods his complexion, and the veins sliding up his throat glow orange like flowing lava.

True, I could have shoved a tempest into his chest and blown him out of the aviary. Or perhaps I could have conjured a batch of sharp quills and hurled them like darts at the merman's vital organs. The options are numerous.

But I'm not the one doing the damage.

Elixir fills his chair to capacity. His features have tapered in concentration, the wrathful expression fixed in place like a chess piece. A curtain of onyx hair falls around his face as he glowers in the Fae's direction.

I hear the rush of liquid surging back up the merman's esophagus, the wine he'd just swallowed backtracking to his trachea, and bubbling to a melting point. The merman rumbles, as though the alcohol is boiling him.

Water in The Deep isn't the only body of liquid my brother can wield. Moreover, possessing the traits of a serpent has also graced the river ruler with similar abilities.

Truly, Scorpio should have taken Elixir's reference to the pyre viper more seriously.

Elixir growls, "Apologize."

"'The sake of mortal pussy' and 'waist-deep in his whore,'" Lark quotes. "So original. I hope you weren't thinking I'd be insulted, because I'll tell you what. My pussy's as gorgeous as my whip and as well-preserved as my backbone."

When I had told him to be careful, that is precisely what I'd meant. Lark has a tongue that doesn't require backup. And while I'll never denigrate her by assuming she needs a shield, neither will I sit back and let her take the brunt alone. Always, we defend each other.

Under the coat, my wings ripple, the plumage ready to spring. I'm about to add my own brand of threat when Elixir repeats, "Apologize to my brother and his mate."

But when Cove touches his arm and gently squeezes it, a reluctant muscle ticks in Elixir's jaw. Instantly, Scorpio slumps in his chair. The red hue drains from his skin, the simmering veins traveling up his throat snuff out, and scalded gasps pour from his lungs.

It could have been worse. If Elixir had delayed any longer, the effects would have reached Scorpio's tongue, permanently scorching it. As it is, I'm sure the blisters hurt.

The minute he recovers, the Fae grunts through the pain and slams his hand on the table. The goblets and flagons dance, clacking like bones. "See what they've done?" he splutters to Elixir. "They've turned you against us!"

"Says the one who sent a raven to kill me and my brothers."

"I did what I had to for the sake of our land. But they—" he gestures at Lark, Juniper, and Cove, "—they've trapped you with their own form of glamour! Humans lie, and they use those lies to distort what happened during The Trapping. They would make you believe they had no choice, that they were forced to massacre our kin and the fauna, when really, they're using our vulnerabilities against us. All the while, they're plotting to do it again!"

"That is propaganda against humans," Juniper rebukes.

"The chosen Fable you so confidently speak of is propaganda. Its hidden message wasn't penned by the Folk but by mortal scribes with an agenda."

The huntress scowls, as if he's committed blasphemy. "The agenda was to inform people."

"This alleged second way you advocate for doesn't exist. It's a myth. It's a mirage. Matter of fact, maybe this has nothing to do with the scribes. Who's to say you didn't invent this scam? Who's to say you aren't misinterpreting the Fable on purpose and mangling the truth?"

Incredulous, Juniper stabs her finger onto the tabletop. "The text is there. You can see the font discrepancies that reveal the hidden message. It's in print, accessible to anyone who isn't too lazy to pick up a book."

"Oh, I'm sorry," Scorpio rasps with feigned humility while clutching his chest. "I suppose if it's on paper, that makes it true—that the fate of our world rests on the whims of a few humans who've been dead for centuries."

"You want to get slapped with another valid example? Fine. Not only did ancient Faeries contribute to the scribes' tales, but the Fables were endorsed by the Seelie witch who established one half of this land.

"What's more, she embedded a spell in one of the Fables. She did that to counteract a curse, which her Unseelie nemesis placed on a water well in Reverie Hollow. Cove enacted that curse and then broke it, by way of the Seelie witch's spell. *That* is the truth."

"And how I'd love to be educated on the nature of truth by a culture with the ability to lie."

"The broken curse is *proof*," Juniper disputes, exasperated. "It confirms that what's archived in the Fables is legitimate. Or are you saying the stories got it wrong? That you don't use glamour, you're not immortal, and your fauna don't have the ability to shift sizes? Have you even thumbed through the contents?"

"Next you're going to claim that salt and hawthorn berries ward off enchantment."

"I've learned my lesson about those fallacies, but most of the tales are correct."

"The basics maybe, but what you're talking about is a cipher, a message that has somehow escaped our notice for eons, but which you seem to have uncovered after less than thirteen days of being here." Scorpio's eyes slit. "How convenient."

Juniper raises an impervious eyebrow. "It's called making an effort. Perhaps you should try it sometime."

Puck presses a fist to his mouth, concealing a grin. Lark outright snorts.

The scales laminating Scorpio's temples glint. "I've heard about you. The bookish bragger who's a walking encyclopedia for the Fables. It's impressive that such intelligence can fit inside such a compact body." Like a glutton for punishment, he glances at Puck. "How does she manage to wrap her legs around you?"

The stirring spoon in Puck's hand bends a fraction, too imperceptible for anyone sitting on the opposite side of the table to notice. The rest of us see the motion, and Elixir hears it, his head jerking toward the noise.

Nevertheless, Puck smiles. "Guess I'll have to repeat myself and add a bonus warning. Insult my woman again, and when she's done verbally scrubbing the floor with your ass, I'll finish where Elixir started. That's how you'll find out what it's like to have my hands wrapped around your jugular. And I have very big satyr hands."

"If we're taking turns on him, I'm next in the queue," Lark volunteers. "I own a whip."

Scorpio ignores her and slurs to Puck, "Well, I got my answer. She wraps them pretty tightly. Like a leash."

The utensil in Puck's grip snaps.

In one unified move, the sisters rise from their chairs like a pack of tigresses.

Scorpio looks impressed. "Human solidarity. How cute."

"You jealous there's no one standing up for you?" Lark asks.

The merman's features spasm, as if pricked by needles. An instant later, his expression blankets, concealing whatever emotion had just squeezed through. "To envy a human," he belittles. "What do you have that we don't?"

Lark crosses her arms, white hair cascading down her frame. "You try living through plague, and then we can talk about strength. You try raising an orphan who needs a family, and then we can talk about magic. You try living fearlessly within a short lifespan, and then we can talk about power." She unwinds her arms, flattens her palms on the table, and leans forward. "You try facing an impenetrable enemy with nothing but your bare hands, and then we can talk about courage."

"We all want the same thing, just by different means," Juniper campaigns.

"And that's where the argument ends," Scorpio fumes, his throat inflamed and voice raw. "This is our fight, not yours. We will never side with humans. They're weak, they weren't ordained with magic, and they abuse their fauna. They have no respect for their natural world, which is why they defend themselves like savages by attacking ours. The only advantages your ilk have are iron and lies; one of those, you used to dismantle our realm, the other to steal our rulers. We'll save our world without you, and then we'll deal with your race later."

Cove has said very little until now. But when she gazes at him, her eyes reflect some type of awareness.

In a soft tone, she asks, "Who broke you?"

Scorpio's murky head snaps toward her. For the first time, confusion stumbles across his countenance, followed by astonishment. His eyes waver on her, as though struggling to escape from a snare.

At length, he tears himself away. The male's temper radiates off him in waves as he vacates his seat, intending to level himself with the sisters.

Chair legs scratch the floor. Elixir, Puck, and I wrench from our own seats—and our fingers jolt toward our weapons—before the Fae straightens fully.

But instead of reaching for the trident beside him, Scorpio grips the back of his chair and snarls at my brothers and me. "Reject your mortals, send them back to their world, and rejoin our original efforts to restore the land."

"You'll forgive us if we tell you to go fuck yourself," Puck answers.

Scorpio tilts his head at The Parliament, then us. "Then you'll forgive me if I keep doing what I'm doing. The raven was one of many candidates. For the greater good, perhaps I'll be forced to try for something closer to home next time. The Pit of Vipers, for instance."

Elixir's baritone cuts across the room. "The fauna are sacred."

The merman's pupils flare at him. "Then stop me."

My father seethes with his avian kin, their thoughts mirroring mine. This is why Scorpio's here. This is why he accepted the invitation.

Since he couldn't assassinate us with the raven, he's trying to use the attack as an incentive: rejoin their side or things will get messier. If we pursue our own path, he'll target more fauna.

Dying of natural causes doesn't harm the lifecycle. Whatever method he used to enhance the raven must have been organic, otherwise it would have endangered this land just as The Trapping had with its human iron.

Scorpio swipes the trident, attaches it to his back, and stalks from the table—then changes his mind once he's at the exit. Pausing on the threshold, he pats the jamb in thought, then swerves to face us.

Or rather, he fixates on Elixir. "You know, when you blinded me, I was upset—enraged, even. But during that spell, something interesting happened. My senses changed, became more acute than they already were. It gave me an idea of what it must be like to be you, and that gave me rather tangible understanding of how to decipher what's inside a brew—what it contains, merely from its scent and the sounds it makes when everything's stirred together.

"By the time I got my eyesight back, those senses dwindled, but I haven't forgotten what they taught me. And that got me to thinking about a particular ingredient, one you possessed before the flood washed it away. And that got me to thinking about all the ways that ingredient could be used. I guess you could say that blinding me led to inspiration." He ducks his head in mock subservience. "Thank you for that."

Before leaving, he finally pays Tímien a single, fleeting glance. Then he bows like a hypocrite to the rest of The Parliament and quits the room.

My eyebrows knit. I send a message through the wind, asking the vultures to confirm whether he's left the mountain.

Their reply comes swiftly. He has evanesced.

My shoulders unwind. The wind shield drops, the film evaporating.

Knowing Scorpio's truly gone means I won't be forced to launch after him, make sure he doesn't seek out additional mountain animals to exploit. Yet while he'd threatened as much in front of The Parliament, he had also genuflected before leaving. That means Scorpio really thinks he's being pressured to take this action, that we're forcing his hand.

Which also means he doesn't have limits.

Avians flit through the hawthorn branches. Light from the celestials pours through the glass dome. At first, no one speaks.

Then from his end of the table, Elixir grunts. "I know how he did it." My brother's eyes fizzle like liquid. "The Evermore Blossom."

The Parliament shuffles, Tímien narrows his lone eye, and Puck groans.

My mate and her sisters frown in puzzlement—especially Juniper, who's clearly aggravated she's never heard of this flower.

I release a gust of breath, round my seat, and clench the back. "The

Evermore Blossom is a singular flower, only one of its kind in existence, and potent enough to amplify the natural instincts of any creature. That's what Scorpio had meant about 'enhancing' the raven. It wasn't hunting or defending its territory, but it was demonstrating feral dominance. A mere snippet from the petal had been enough to stoke that impulse. To say nothing of what the entire flower could do to a legion of fauna."

Cove asks, "Is there an antidote?"

"In Faerie, antidotes are for poisons," Elixir replies. "Intrinsically, this plant is a strengthening agent, a boost that cures what is lacking. You cannot create an antidote for something that already functions as a remedy."

"Technically, it's a loophole," Puck translates. "The cocksucker is basically abusing the flower's original purpose and calling it enhancement instead of manipulation. On the surface, he can't be accused by the Solitaries of violating the sacredness of the fauna." He whistles without humor. "Very cunning."

"Very Fae," I remark.

"Then let's destroy the flower before he harvests more," Juniper resolves.

"It's called the Evermore Blossom for a reason," Elixir revokes. "It cannot be destroyed."

"Neither burned, nor contaminated, nor diced into pieces," I say. "It can't be replicated or pulled from its roots."

"Oh, come on," Lark protests. "Nothing's wholly eternal. Not even the three of you."

"You're right. But the only way to destroy the Evermore Blossom is for the wild to fade, which isn't exactly ideal. And even if we could destroy it, the flower is located on enemy turf."

"Marvelous," Puck vents. "An indestructible weapon confined to fatal terrain. So he has access to the plant whenever he wants."

"Scorpio knows we can't get to the flower without risking our lives," I say. "And there's nothing to be done against the blossom even if we reach it. Regardless, he withheld this information until the last minute, when his willpower faltered." My eyes swing toward Cove. "I suspect you hit a nerve. It provoked him to supply us with a stronger exit speech."

Cove winces, eyes solemn. "Actually, his exit speech was meant for Elixir."

My brother's jaw softens as he threads their hands together. "You underestimate your effect on even the fiercest of Faeries."

"Maybe, but that's because there's only one fierce Fae whose reaction matters to me."

To that, Elixir's mouth slants into a furtive grin.

Juniper goes rigid and addresses The Parliament. "If he wants to use more of this Evermore Blossom on the fauna, he could breed an army of animals."

"Potentially," I concur on behalf of the owls once Tímien has projected their reply.

"The Solitaries won't go for it," Puck contests with a shake of his head, his earrings tinkling. "Sure, enhancement through a natural source gives them an outlet, but everything has its limits. One raven, yes. A handful of dwellers, probably. A stampede of sacred fauna at their behest, no."

"Oh, brother," I reply. "Never underestimate the double-standards of a Fae who's operating on an anger streak. We can't lie verbally, but we can lie to ourselves."

"Denial is an intoxicant," Elixir says. "For they shall convince themselves what they're doing is just."

"Either that, or he'll find a way to blame us for 'being forced' to expand to large quantities of other fauna."

Juniper squares her shoulders. "So, we stop him by—"

"By removing his heart from his body," Puck votes.

"By winning this battle," Lark proposes.

"By stopping the battle before it begins," Cove counters.

"I was going to say, by solving the Fable," Juniper rebuts. "That will spare the fauna and prevent war in the first place."

By all means, The Parliament concurs with her on this.

I deliver their concession aloud and summarize, "Essentially, we stop him by doing what we've been doing."

"With an extra perk," Lark hints and glances at Cove with a twinkle in her eye. "Seems we didn't need Fae maneuvers to pry open Scorpio's mouth."

"That, we didn't," I agree.

While my brothers and I excel at riddles, mischief, and mind games, we hadn't needed to flaunt those skills tonight. To be certain, Scorpio's fuse had been as short as his cock and required little effort to penetrate. But when it came to uprooting his secret weapon, not to mention his vulnerability, my brothers and I can't be credited.

Fae trickery hadn't made the enemy's tongue rattle. Human empathy had.

9

My javelin arches and collides with Moth's forearm, which surges upward to thwart the blow. The impact would have splintered a human's bones, but with her, it's a mere snippet of sound. Standing in the wildlife park lawn, we face each other over the rim of my weapon.

Vines swing in the breeze, conical trees surround us, and a hawk loops by. This upper level offers a vast prospect of the labyrinth's southeastern range, which leads to The Night Aviary.

I push back to threaten one of Moth's greatest assets—balance—then quirk an eyebrow. "Your concentration is wavering."

"Rubbish," she argues, pressing her twig-sized arm into the javelin's handle. And because the female can't let a criticism go unpunished, she turns it around. "Your aim is shitty."

My smile broadens. "Shall we see about that?"

Defiant glee brightens her topaz irises. "Try me."

She shoves me backward, and we charge it into. I spiral my weapons and execute several rounds of strikes, which Moth counters with her fists and limbs. She pops into the air and zips around me, and I swerve to match her speed, though I keep my plumes retracted. Although we're nearly the same age, our appearances hardly suggest as much. The span and force of my wings would blast her runty frame into the ether.

She compensates with agility, velocity, and pure grit. Her papery wings vibrate faster than a hummingbird's, and her punches block my attacks. I spin my weapon overhead and windmill around her, and she vaults over the shaft as it sweeps beneath her bare toes. Mid-jump, I seize the advantage and thrust my palm toward her, tossing a pocket of wind her way.

The flurry knocks Moth toward the ground. Her growl shaves through the park, but she recovers and dodges the next squall, then elbows the javelin from my grasp.

The weapon pitches upward, then shoots downward like a beak. Smoothly, the helix blade lands, the tip puncturing the grass.

Heaving, Moth and I wheel toward one another. She pants but grins, her complexion flushed. "Ha!" she boasts, pride and nostalgia consuming her voice.

The sight digs a trench into my chest. It's a rare thing to see her joyous, a departure from her surly glowers and disgruntled huffs. With members of our band swapping opponents during practice, she and I haven't trained with one another often enough.

This feels like old times, back when we were younger, in our early hundreds, and hadn't known the realities of war. During those fledgling years, I'd often held back, as had she. It had been innocent child's play, of course, sometimes with my wild family joining in.

Tonight, neither of us had disrespected one another by restraining ourselves. It had been a fair fight.

We share a look of remembrance. Sadness and fondness flows through the silence.

"How are you?" I ask. "Truly?"

Inevitably, Moth's wings bristle. She crosses her arms. "Why wouldn't I be fine?"

"I didn't say you weren't. I asked how you were."

She shrugs and glances toward the feral roars scrolling in the distance. The bridge of her nose scrunches.

I know that look. After losing her parents in The Trapping, these animals became her kindred. She adores the park's dwellers, despite how many times she pouts about mucking up cougar shit. In a heartbeat, Moth would take a knife to the stomach for any of these creatures.

"They'll survive," I vow, stepping closer. "We'll make sure of it."

Moth's wings lower, the filmy panels curling inward. "What about you?"

That trench burrows deeper. I've never known either of us to be vulnerable with each other, the candidness of it foreign. Admiration and devotion aren't unusual, but it's not in a Fae's nature to be sentimental.

She hedges before peeking at me with incandescent orbs. Those eyes have seen her parents die. Over the years, they have kept me aloft when I thought I might plummet, and they've clung to me for the same reasons.

"I've missed this," she admits.

"Me, too," I intone.

"I miss when it was just for fun, when it was safe."

"But was it? Was it ever, really?"

"Yes and no." She gulps. "I just can't…I don't know what I'd do if…"

My breath caves in. The sight of her draws me near, my palm buttressing her cheek. "I'm not going anywhere. Neither are you."

Comfort flashes across her face. Naturally, it lasts only until the incoming fragrance of a storm fills the lawn. At which point, cantankerous lines bunch along Moth's forehead, and her spine snaps to attention.

"Melodrama," she gripes, though with less bite to her words than there used to be. "The humans must be corrupting us."

A chuckle skates from my lips. "Oh, but what a divine corruption it is."

"If you say so, but I'm leaving. Fauna duties call, and I smell a pest approaching." Moth knocks her shoulder against mine. "And don't you trash my park this time. Take your clothes with you, or there'll be hell to pay. Oh, and widen your stance, or you'll never beat me. Remember: Cerulean of the sky doesn't miss."

I smirk. "Remember: Moth of the mountain doesn't yield."

She leaps into the air and flaps off toward the lowermost level where the cougar roams. After she's gone, I saunter toward the javelin and strap my fingers around the shaft, then pause. Starlight and torchlight converge where I stand, and my lips quirk in awareness. Another string of familiar scents twines around my senses, coupled with the audible unspooling of a rope.

Mischief deepens my grin and tightens my fingers around the handle. I tear the javelin from the soil and whirl. The weapon catches Lark's whip mid-flick, the smack and clang lacerating the air.

The perpetrator tosses me a saucy grin. In silence, we appraise one another.

Moth was right in predicting the outcome of this scene. That pewter dress hugging Lark's waist and flaring wide at the hips will need mending in several minutes, for I intend to shred the garment to the point of uselessness.

In the meantime, her weapon has coiled around the shaft. Notwithstanding, I'm not that easily beaten.

We launch into our own round, the moves and countermoves like a provocative dance—intrinsic and primal. Our pants grow heavy, hectic, heady. With every pass of our defenses, we prowl around one another, propelling ourselves closer, as if in ritual to a mating call.

My grin broadens. Her cheeky tongue sticks out at me, yet I scent the desire heating her blood and dampening between her thighs.

Lark's whip cuffs my weapon. The javelin slices around her next lash.

As the cord flays in my direction once more, I rotate and block the attempt over my shoulder. Craning my profile her way, I taunt my mate with a wicked grin. She hadn't seen the move coming.

So she tricks me back. It a feisty move she's never shown me, the whip bounces off my javelin and winds around my chest, snaring me in place and spinning me in front of her. With my torso trapped, the savvy mortal yanks me forward like a prize. We crash together, our bodies beating hard for oxygen.

"Well, I'll be damned," Lark purrs. "I've caught me a wild one."

"Mmm. You've been keeping that nifty little move a secret," I compliment.

"What do you mean?" she teases, her breath stalking across my lips. "I just learned that one. I'm a woman who improvises."

"Is that a fact? Because I should warn you, it's unwise to speak untruths to Faeries. In our world, there's a price for mortal fibbing."

Lark drags a single finger from the pulse at my throat, down the plunging V of my shirt before pausing at my bared navel. "Is the penalty a stiff one?"

Her innuendo dabs another grin into my face. "Painfully." I push in closer and husk, "Severely."

"And if I continue to defy you? Just what are you gonna do about it?" Lark's tongue darts out and licks the upper bow of my lips. "Take me prisoner?"

Mutinous creature. She laughs as I shove the whip to the grass, hurl my javelin beside it, snatch her hand, and stalk through the wildlife park. My arm thrusts outward to shove aside vegetation. Yet no matter how many leagues we cross, the tower rises too fucking far away.

My wings itch to sprout, to carry us to our destination swifter. But what can I say? Prolonging the bliss has its own tantalizing virtues.

I compose myself while guiding Lark across the lawn. In the tower, the servants are nowhere in sight. Though based on a distant tinkling snigger, I wouldn't put it past them to spy on our progress. Pixies are about as discreet as forest nymphs.

They'll know not to disturb us once we reach the bedroom. And at this point, I don't give a shit who hears us. Neither does Lark. We'd already crossed that threshold the other night in the great room.

My mate and I speed through the first level and up the winding staircase, our haste increasing. At the top floor, we charge down the vestibule toward the framed curtains that function as a common door would, blocking out sight and sound. As my palm shoves forward, a burst of wind blows back the panels.

The instant we storm through, we're on each other.

At the same time Lark tugs me against her, I growl and snatch her mouth with mine. While the curtains fall shut, I wrench her lips apart, spreading them like limbs and fitting myself to her. My tongue pitches between the damp seam of Lark's mouth and flexes against her in a steady cadence.

A lovely moan skitters from her throat, the sound like embers igniting me into a frenzy.

My palms span the humps of her ass and heave her against me. While my tongue rakes through her lips, I walk her backward. We stumble across the rug, passing the fire basin packed with glowing flowers and its surrounding chairs, where I once bent Lark over and took her steadily for an hour until she had wailed herself hoarse.

Now she throws her arms around me, her fingers launch into my hair, and she fastens onto the back of my head. This urges us nearer, harder. Her swollen breasts lunge into my chest, the nipples solid, and need seeps from between her legs, the musky aroma like a marvelous drug.

Despite their loose fit, my clothes chafe. The harder my cock gets, the more it wedges itself against the trousers.

Lark must feel the same inconvenience, because she squirms. We peel ourselves apart only long enough to fumble with my shirt. Her fingers grip the material and give it a feral pull, wrenching the offensive piece from my torso. A distinct tear pierces the room.

While making unsteady progress to the bed, I crush her dress in my fists and cram it down her curves, taking the skimpy, platinum-laced undergarments with them. The fabric shudders down her hourglass frame, inches of soft flesh baring itself.

Her breasts inflate with each breath, and her nipples darken, the disks erect. That swatch of hair at the nexus of her body conceals the tight line of her pussy. My mouth all but waters to taste her pleasure.

That will be my first agenda.

Except Lark's mouth fuses with mine once more, then she swings us around at the last moment. My knees hit the mattress. The instant they do, she pushes me down, so that I land upright on the bed.

Like a feline, Lark slinks onto my lap. Her thighs split around my waist, straddling me.

Not one to be outdone, I pry my mouth from hers and nibble on her bottom lip, tugging on it until she keens, the sound gritty. My teeth graze the arched outlines of her flesh, teasing and taunting, then descend along her neck, where her pulse thumps.

I band my arms around her and continue my onslaught, my incisors sliding along her clavicles and down to those lovely mounds of flesh. Her stunning tits prickle as I scoop one in my palm, lower my head, and take it in my mouth. Lark whines, and her ass gyrates on my pelvis, smearing wetness on my trousers, which we've yet to remove.

I groan into her breast and suck her in, then lash my tongue over the nipple, circling the ruched skin and patting the tip. Lark mumbles something incomprehensible and arches into me, urging her breast into my mouth while her digits claw through my scalp.

How she loves to draw on the roots. How I relish the pain of it.

My tongue swabs at her, and my mouth draws on that breast before switching to the other one. Another hard cry vaults from her mouth, which morphs into an ambitious grunt.

That means she wants her turn.

Thus, she takes it.

My mate does her worst, her fingers scaling my ears and flicking off the bronze caps. Her fingers trace the edges, ascend to the peaks, and thumb the tips.

The ministration shoves a hot bolt of lust up my cock, which jumps to attention. A low growl of warning creeps up my throat. If she continues to torment me, this will be over far too soon, whereas I have many devious tasks yet to accomplish where her pussy is concerned.

Nonetheless, she persists, her fingers brushing my earlobe and skimming over the points. On a hiss, I veer back and seize her cheeks. We stare at one another, panting with exertion and a restraint I scarcely feel, nor mean to tolerate.

Yet in this stare, everything slows. The stress of wanting, of coveting, of dominating subsides. This profound thing between us calms our exhalations.

Poised over me, Lark's heavy-lidded eyes rove over my face before sinking to my abdomen. Her swollen mouth parts, so that puffs of air fall from her lungs. Her hands have vanished once more into my hair, as if she needs it for balance, lest she fall.

Except I'll leap into the abyss and catch her if she ever does. Always, I'll catch this vixen.

Again, she lifts her head to scan my face. As though reading my thoughts, her lips break into a tiny grin, so very fragile, so very rare for this spitfire. Some form of crafty intent banks in her eyes.

She cranes her head to pass her tongue across my lips, licking the thin pleat from one end to the other. My wings flare, thrashing outward from my back. I'm about to flip this mortal onto her back when she claims me first.

Her fingers sink between us and cup the length of my erection. A disorderly hiss blasts from my mouth. As the heat of her palm melts through the textile, my cock expands from stem to crown.

Patiently, Lark rubs the flat of her hand up and down. The abrasion thickens me even more. Just like that, she's takes me captive.

Lark pants, "I have three rules. One—" her fist inches upward until I gasp, "—don't move. Two, hold your tongue. And three—" she halts her movements, "you're forbidden from coming until I say so. Understand?"

A great shiver rattles my quills. "You shall pay for—"

However, every potential bargain, riddle, tease, appeal, promise, and threat crumbles on my tongue like dust. I choke on the words as those wily digits vanish into the waistband of my trousers. Heat envelops me as Lark straps her fingers around my rigid cock, her grip fixed at the base.

To further her point, her other hand glides beneath my sac and balances its weight, her digits massaging. Air drains from my lungs. My fingers grasp her buttocks, clasping her to me, clinging to her for mercy's sake.

A sigh of approval flutters into my ear, along with the turbulent shiver of my wings. I have the presence of mind not to clench my teeth so hard they crack.

We glance down, watching as Lark nudges the trousers just enough to free my aching cock. The head springs between us, its girth enlarged, the veins dilated, and the tip flushed.

My length flexes and spans higher. Lark hums with delight.

With unhurried precision, she swipes her thumb over the head and gathers the bead of liquid that has leaked from the slit. After another droplet rolls into her hand, she coats it over my foreskin, then cups her pussy and withdraws with her fingers glazed. She runs her arousal down my shaft, braces me in her grip, and oh, hell on earth…

Lark…

Her wet fingers encase my erection. And they begin to pump.

My hands clench her ass. "Fuck," I mutter.

She tsks. "I'll forgive you for that one."

A pained chuckle flees my mouth. Vicious woman and her rules.

With her digits encapsulating me, my mate siphons up and down. With every rhythmic tug, she tempts the groans from my throat, which never escape my lips. I withhold them, all but the short and swift puffs of oxygen.

With our foreheads pressed and sweating, we stare at her hand fastened around me, pumping me to the brink. Each draw on my cock inflates its size, until I'm as firm as a lever.

As Lark reaches the crown, her thumb traces the incision at the apex, then again, and again. All the while, my mate caresses the sensitive pouch with her other hand. My eyes veer to the back of my head, which lolls backward and hangs heavy.

The ends of my hair skate over my wings. The friction ripples from my cock to the length of every rachis, to the marrow of my immortal bones. It's gradual at first, but the tempest builds.

Eventually, I can't stand it, because fuck, she does this so well, and it feels too heavenly, and to hell with the consequences.

Rules are meant to be broken. Such is the nature of a Fae.

I break the first one as my hips move, jutting up into her hand. And perhaps Lark has forgotten too, because she moans with me and drives her grip down, while I buck my cock higher. I chase the motions of her hand, offering myself to it, my abdomen contouring with the movements.

I commit the second infraction. Groans topple from me, along with her name.

As for the third rule, I do my utmost to obey until my bellows take on a desperate note, begging for more. The sounds grow louder, resound for longer.

I suffer through it until Lark leans and whispers, "Now, baby."

Like a wild thing springing from its cage, I veer my cock into her hand several more times, then my wings tense. My joints spasm and release, molten heat gushing through my cock. I come with a hard, grating shout and spill into Lark's hand, my body jerking into it.

White sparks of light inundate my vision, and the wind tosses my hair in my face, as if I've stirred up a tornado. While bracketed on my elbows, my head falls forward. Lark catches my lips and swallows the sounds of my rapture, all the while fisting my cock, drawing out my climax to the last drop.

The instant I slump, the wind funnel ceases. Shit. Indeed, I'd incited a miniature cyclone.

Pillows litter the floor, the overhead linens canopying the bed are tangled, and the torch sconces have been snuffed. Starlight enamels every furnishing in the room. The hinges that usually display our weapons are empty, because earlier in the park, we'd flung the javelin and whip to the ground.

Disoriented but still conscious of my release coating her hand, I sweep my fingers through the air, and the breeze wipes her skin clean. This convenience had entertained my mate to no end when I'd first done it.

Her digits comb through my hair, then balance my jaw and raise my face to hers. "Your eyes are so damn blue when you come," she gloats, utterly thrilled with herself.

The vision kindles a new determination. I feel my eyes slitting, my stamina resurfacing.

Lark yelps as I seize her hips and fling her onto the bed. Her back hits the mattress, the expanse jolting beneath us. Her legs split as I land between them, my hips tucking into that vent, which radiates heat and slickness.

"My turn," I growl against her mouth.

"Then make it count," Lark says just before our lips clamp.

She kisses me with a craving that rouses my cock anew. She kisses me as though she's already fucking me, mindlessly yet deliberately. She kisses me with a desperation that squeezes around my sinful heart like a fist, as though this won't last because the world is falling apart. She kisses me with an emotion so profound it rarely fails to stagger me.

I kiss her back like a glutton, as though I've endured nine years of famine. I kiss her back as if I'm fucking her in kind, deeply and tirelessly. I kiss her back with a voracity that promises I'll never let her go, never let this fade, because if the world falls apart, I'll fly us into the firmament where nothing and no one can touch her. I kiss her back with an emotion so unconditional it rattles me to the edges of my being.

Our mouths clutch. My tongue licks against hers, but it's not enough.

I want her moans in every possible octave, from sighs and shouts. I want her cries at every possible speed, from slow to fast.

I want those beautiful noises shredding into the fucking air. I want her so depleted that she's never been happier.

My lips wrest from hers. "Grab the headboard, pet," I whisper. "You'll need it."

An eager light glazes her pupils. She nods and gropes the notches affixed behind her.

Unlike my mutinous one, I assign no rules to this. My mate would only shatter them faster than I had.

I coast down her body while planting open-mouthed kisses over Lark's skin, from her flushed throat, between her quivering tits, and over her twitching stomach. Her knees steeple around my head of their own volition. Though, she'll have to do better than that.

Settling at the hot nexus of her legs, I glance up and toss her a nefarious look. My arms hook around Lark's knees and splay them wide, opening the gap of her body.

Between two strips of hair, her walls flutter apart. Slickness runs between them, her flesh pinkens under my gaze, and that sweet kernel projects like a button. Fables almighty.

I remember one of the first things I'd said to her when she answered my summons and arrived in this world looking fierce and fuckable. Even then, her proximity had sparked through my veins like an electric current, jolting me in a resentful yet remarkable way. It's a wonder I hadn't fallen off my throne in The Parliament's rotunda.

Her name had intrigued me.

The rare bird that sings while flying.

Indeed. And tonight, my mate shall do just that.

Pinning her to bed, I sink in and drag my tongue up her slot. Lark's back snaps off the mattress, and a hard cry pops from her mouth.

My mouth burrows in. I trace up and down the seam, lapping up every flow of moisture. Each pass of my tongue swabs her opening yet drenches it all over again. Dampness seeps down my palate as I lick her folds, my tongue spreading her intimate lips apart.

And then I slide into that beautiful pussy. My tongue thrusts, pitching into the hot cavern at a steady tempo.

My wings brush her scarred knees. Every piston of my tongue pushes a groan from Lark's helpless mouth.

She releases the headboard, grabs the roots of my hair, and rolls her hips. Fuck, she rides my tongue like it's my cock, like she's pleasuring herself. And I adore it what it does to her shouts, how it chips them apart.

The taste of ginger and vanilla drips onto my tongue. Yet I need her wetter, so much wetter. I want her pussy aching and her clitoris throbbing like a drum for me. I want to engulf her fully, then make her soar.

First, I twirl my finger, summoning a slender rope of wind. It tapers and braces against her entrance. Then my digits grip her tighter, split her folds wider. After that, my tongue glides up her core to the small root of flesh distending from the hair.

While I do this, the wind grows dense like an appendage and eases into her opening.

Like this, we claim her from both points of pleasure. And at the same time, the wind and I feed on her.

I strap my lips around her clitoris and suck. And as my mouth encases that perfect little peg, the wind begins to coast in and out of her.

The next whimper frays into an amplified moan. The headboard rams into the wall.

Lark's face thrashes from side to side. "Oh, fuck!" she sobs. "Cerulean."

I release her momentarily. "Do you feel that, pet? Do you feel my tongue and the wind? Do you feel us fucking you?"

"Yeah…"

Very good. My mouth refastens around her clit and tugs gently, steadily until she's inconsolable. My tongue flicks against the nub, licking it rhythmically. I sketch the peak, dabbing at it, patting it.

In unison to that, the tail of air plows inside her. Each entry reaches those hidden places I can't physically go.

But I feel them. Oh, how I feel them.

Lark keens, weeping with a mixture of frustration and euphoria. Her hips grind into me, spurring me on while parting her legs more for the air to probe her.

I bob my head, my lips affixing to her, pulling on my mate as the wind enters her. I lick her steadily, and the rope of air plies her repeatedly, following every helpless sound. It's endless, vigorous, lasting for so long that I forget everything but her moans.

Yet again, it's not enough.

My mouth releases Lark. The draft slides out of her and disappears.

She whines in need as I ascend her body and set a finger to her lips. "Shh," I whisper.

I have additional plans. And let no one say I've lost my penchant for scheming.

As my cock braces against her soaked pussy, she understands. In unison, my hands and her heels shove the trousers down my limbs, freeing me completely.

Panting, we waste little time. Lark slings one leg around my waist, and I hitch the other high, bending it and flattening the front of her calf against my chest.

With a firm swing of my hips, I pitch my cock into her.

Lark cries out. My mouth falls open as her walls seal around my length, clutching me to the hilt.

Once I'm rooted, we move. With measured control, I rotate my hips into her, plying her with the full length of my cock. The hot, wet clamp of her body expands, taking my weight and width. Pain and pleasure infuse my veins and flow through the rachises of my feathers.

I glide in and out of Lark, withdrawing to the head, then sweeping back in. The pace is moderate but feverish. My waist slings into her, my tip works into her. Our gazes lock as our hips beat tougher, perspiration building at the base of my spine and between her breasts.

I fuck her affectionally, passionately, endlessly. She fucks me back, her waist jutting into mine as her face contorts with something akin to loss and longing.

That, and love.

We labor for this, drive ourselves into a trance, our moans colliding. With a vicious growl, I go deeper, harder—but not faster.

I want this earned. I want this to leave an imprint inside her.

Mine. She's mine.

And I'm hers.

"My equal," I rasp. "I love you, Lark. I have always loved you."

"I love you, too," she cries. "Oh, gods. Cerulean...don't stop."

"Never," I swear. "When I make you come, I'll start over again. I'm never stopping."

There are no gods on this continent. Nature is our divinity, and if deities exist, it is outside our hemisphere of knowledge. Yet with her in my arms, I'm making love to a goddess.

Lark seizes my ass, which flexes with each plunge into the warm cleft of her body. Her folds squeeze my lunging cock, and her grasp urges me to give more, to push her farther.

I lift my torso off the bed and staple my hands on either side of Lark's head, the better to see her, to watch what my cock does to her. Her stomach bunches with mine, her legs link around my snapping waist, and she rises her hips to meet my thrusts.

I hiss and increase the momentum, surging into her with short, bucking thrusts. My thick crown strikes in...out...in...out. Her lips part, moans leaping off her tongue and joining my growls. The creases around her eyes clench, and the damp walls of her pussy clench, and everything in me clenches.

The orgasm tosses her into the void. Lark comes, her pussy gripping my cock, her walls pulsating and then unraveling around me. I maintain a steady pump as Lark's broken cries launch to the ceiling, the sight of consuming my vision.

Yes, my precious Lark.

Fly. Sing.

Once I'm certain she's reached those heights, I throw my head back, throw my hips into her, and holler. My cock strains and then releases, the climax extending to the fringes of my wings. I shout, coming for so long that my vision blackens, my body convulsing.

Heaving, I collapse into her spent arms. We sag against one another while striving for breath. My face burrows into Lark's neck, and her mouth presses into the point of my ear.

The constellations douse the room. My wings slip into my back, her limbs flank my waist, and our stomachs rest together. Most glorious of all, I'm still inside her, unwilling to leave her body.

As the time passes, we remain that way, tangled and listening to the calls of wild animals from the park.

Eventually, Lark utters, "You spoil me rotten."

Amused, I lift my head. Propping my temple on my upraised fist, I glance down at my mate's face, her cheeks brimming with sated color. "You flatter me, mortal."

"And you love me, Fae."

I feel my eyes kindle. "That, I do."

Lowering my head, I take her lips. Lark sighs into my mouth and kisses me back, her tongue moving languidly with mine. The moment our mouths break apart, fitful noises slide from our tongues, both of us riled up to fuck again, to savor this one emotion worth fighting a war for.

My hips nudge, my firm cock rolling leisurely and deeply inside Lark's heat. She moans, linking her ankles over my ass and angling our hips together.

Yet before I can fulfill my desire to make love to her for a second time, a whistling sound reaches my ears. I go still, then register the familiar noise. Lark does as well, seconds before the crossbow bolt whizzes through the draperies and stabs the wall opposite our bed.

There's no note attached to the projectile, but there doesn't need to be. We know who it's from. This greeting is the equivalent of someone throwing pebbles at a window frame.

We glance at the bolt, then untangle ourselves. My cock slips from Lark's body, and we sweep aside the blankets. She throws on my shirt, which hangs halfway down her thighs, and I step into the loose trousers before we charge to the window.

My mate halts before the arched view. I tower behind her, brace both forearms on the frame, and glance over her shoulder in wary amusement.

Below, Juniper stands on the lawn. Her head cranes up at us, green eyes punching through the darkness.

As I'd suspected from the lack of blood clotting the air, she's in one piece and not sporting a gaping wound, which extinguishes the first immediate concern.

To the contrary, spectacles perch atop Juniper's nose. Through the lenses, her pupils reflect the urgency of a human who hasn't had much sleep, of someone who's been in the throes of distraction and obsession, and who's been captivated by an undeniable temptation.

Which leads to the second conclusion: She's been reading.

She's been reading and has something vital to share.

It's not the first time this has happened to us, though Lark and I were in a more…complicated position…the last time Juniper interrupted. Wisely, she has learned her lesson and elected to summon us from outside.

"For fuck's sake, hon," Lark gripes, crossing her arms so that my shirt sleeves drape over her knuckles. "Can't you let your sister orgasm in peace?"

"Get dressed," Juniper orders in a hushed tone.

"Why the fuck are you whispering? You worried one of the resident llamas are gonna overhear you?"

"And get down here this instant. Both of you."

"Before I get my second wind with Cerulean?" My sullen mate peeks at my amused face. "Pun intended."

I suppress my chuckle. "I'm sure she has a good reason."

"I do." Juniper looks elated with herself. "I know who can tell us the second way."

10

We stride across the lawn and meet the others at the promontory's ledge. White, gold, and teal celestials nip the sky. It's a clear and windless night as two raptors soar in the distance, over the jagged teeth of the mountain.

I would call out to Moth, if she weren't in severe need of rest. Whatever we're about to learn, I'll share later.

Puck, Juniper, Cove, and Elixir wait at the lip of the overhang. They turn and register my state of undress, along with Lark's. Neither of us had bothered to heed Juniper's order and cover ourselves further, apart from Lark slipping into a pair of skimpy undershorts beneath the oversized shirt.

Not to mention, my mate's hair looks like it's been through a monsoon, and I doubt my hair is any tamer.

Elixir listens to the minimal rustles of my pants and her shirt, draws his conclusion, and rolls his eyes. As if he's any less chaste. The man can barely keep his temperature down, much less his feral appetites in check around Cove.

Speaking of the lady in question, she flushes a rosy tint but smiles at Lark, glad to witness her sister's happiness.

Puck absorbs the sight of us with relish. "Look at you two, fresh from another merry round of perversion."

"Fuck you," I say with a grin.

"Tsk, tsk. Seems to me like your mate already took care of that."

"Actually, we weren't done," Lark informs him.

Juniper plunks her crossbow on the grass. "Well, would you care to put your sex drives on hold for a rare second?"

"You're one to talk," her sister replies. "You're the one humping a satyr."

Junipers opens her mouth but gasps in surprise as her fingers shoot to her stomach. Her complexion blanches, the pasty hue clashing with the new brightness of her eyes.

Cove moves to brush back Juniper's hair, but Puck gets there first and frames her shoulders. "You all right, luv?"

"It's nothing."

"It's been nothing for months."

"You don't need to fuss. I'm fine."

She doesn't look fine. Lark and Cove want to question it as well but think better of the impulse. My mate once said her sister loathes people doting on her.

Elixir glances away, as if he can see rather than hear the exchange.

Briefly, Juniper leans into Puck's touch. After that, she straightens, granting none of us the chance to gainsay her. The female shoulders the bag she'd brought and pushes forth with a stubborn but admirable tenacity.

"When was the Book of Fables written?" she begins, the question directed at all of us.

Lark sighs. "Tell me you didn't assemble us here for another quiz."

"Oh, honestly," Juniper berates when no one else responds. "Doesn't anybody but me pay attention to the book's front matter?"

"Frankly, we wouldn't dream of outdoing you, hon."

Juniper addresses our group, the pace of her voice accelerating. "Don't you see? We've never investigated what year it was created, when it's such a simple task." She rifles through her bag and pulls out the Book of Fables, then whips it open to an early page and stabs a finger into the parchment. "Look at the date."

With the book spread before us and leveled in her palms, we crowd around the text. Elixir reaches out, sets his fingers atop the page, and traces the content, awareness flashing in his pupils.

I see the reason, as does Puck. It's era of the ancients, including the Seelie and Unseelie witches of old.

Granted, this information is commonplace, seeing as the witches were the first Faeries to call the Solitary wild home. Also, they played vital roles in Elixir and Cove's story, from curses to counter spells.

Yet Juniper watches us, as if this long-known fact is a revelation...or perhaps a glaring reminder. Oftentimes, the obvious gets neglected in favor of novelties and enigmas. One lives with certain fundamental truths for so long, they become obsolete. They fade into the background like wallpaper, present but no longer remarkable.

Cove turns to Elixir. "You've never told me what happened to your ancestor in her later life."

"The Unseelie witch lived long enough to sire a child, which led to my mother Lorelei's line," he answers. "Then she perished alongside her Seelie nemesis during the scrimmage between the Pegasi and the dragons."

Puck grunts. "Not to detour, but if there's any behemoth more antiquated than a witch—or Pegasi, or Faeries—it's a fucking dragon. They're as old as nature itself, which makes them the strongest race."

"We know a thing or two about that event," Lark contributes. "The Pegasi lost that battle. That's how they became extinct in your world, apparently along with the last remaining Fae witches. Seems the latter tidbit didn't make it into the Book of Fables, though."

"Actually." Juniper flips the pages. "It did."

She halts on a Fable that uses fauna as a metaphor. Yet as she interprets the paragraphs aloud, the meaning becomes so clear it's an embarrassment that we Faeries hadn't made the connection.

Puck, Elixir, and I have the decency to look contrite. Our kin have spent eons calling ourselves the superior race, believing ourselves so impervious we never gave credence to the Fables. We never took it seriously enough to delve in, other than perhaps Puck, and even he hadn't uprooted this information.

The Fable is a retelling of the witches' demise.

As for the human editions, Juniper reasons the story fell into obscurity when copies were created and distributed to mortals over generations. Seeing as this is the first true edition, with tales that aren't in the later volumes of my mate's world, it makes sense that humans wouldn't have known about this, either.

Juniper claps the book shut, her wan complexion competing with those vivid green orbs, which sparkle with bookish intoxication.

"You look like you just read the longest smut scene in your life," Lark says.

Juniper ignores her. She tucks the book under her arm and counts off her fingers. "One: The witches played a major role in the scribes writing the Book of Fables. Two: The witches allied with the Pegasi against the dragons. So three: The Pegasi were around during the scribes' era as well. And four: The Pegasi told Cerulean the first way."

Hence, they might know something else. After they died, those winged horses had transformed into a landmark of nature, and that's where their apparitions exist to this day.

"The Horizon that Never Lies," I say.

"Correct." Juniper glances at everyone. "I mean, it's mortifying that we didn't draw this conclusion right away. The Horizon told Cerulean the first way. Why wouldn't they know the second?"

My hopes crash to the ground. I sigh, not eager to inform Juniper she's grasping at straws. "I hate to be the bearer of unfavorable news, but I've already asked the Horizon about this. After you revealed a second way existed, Lark and I went to them."

Elixir frowns. "You did not tell us."

"We were gonna," Lark defends. "Everyone was busy doing their parts. We went to the Pegasi a few days before the raven attack, but we were out of luck. Cerulean and I didn't know how to tell everyone without mucking up our sense of hope. And then everything else happened..."

Thus, there was never a good moment to rub salt into the wound.

I glance at Juniper, rueful. "Although we thought Elixir would be able to bring the second way to the surface, I wanted to exhaust the possibilities. Sadly, my attempt didn't work. The Horizon had no answer."

To that, Juniper whisks off her glasses. "But what did you offer?"

The prompt gives me pause. The Pegasi won't provide answers unless the asker makes an offering.

To further complicate matters, the question may only pertain to the offering itself. It can't be random or unrelated.

"We offered the only thing we could—a piece of the mountain, a stone from the range's highest peak where Lark won her game," I tell them. "Our question was about saving this land, so offering a segment of it seemed the most promising option. Needless to say, it hadn't sufficed."

An alternative crosses Juniper's face. While there's triumph in her expression, there's also sacrifice.

More than anything, Puck sees this and more. "What have you got?"

"Something the Horizon will accept." Juniper's eyes glisten with resignation as she holds up the book. "We have this."

11

Wildflowers carpet the ancient summit. The flora sways as we stand in a row across the rampart.

Our gazes aim toward the sun crawling up the sky. Elixir's acute senses pick up the warmth of its rays and hear the changes in scenery, the environment shifting from eventide to daybreak. The rest of us study the tapestry of zeniths, ochre and rose hues marbling over the range.

The Horizon that Never Lies.

Tímien circles above us with several accompanying Parliament owls. Although this is an ideal time to visit The Horizon without being monitored, no chances are being taken. The flock is keeping surveillance for us.

Elixir shakes his head. "We would be surrendering the source material on a gamble."

Juniper clutches the book to her chest. "It's the only way. And it's only one page."

"It's never just one page to you," Lark empathizes, her voice softening in a way that's foreign to my kin but remains a strength in her people—a fact I hadn't appreciated until her.

"Well," Juniper says. "I've got the Fable memorized."

"Cypress truly agreed to this?" Cove asks, unable to believe it.

"Wonders never cease with him," Puck replies with fondness. "Even if it took a level of convincing only Juniper could achieve."

"It wasn't just me," Juniper argues. "He did it for you, too."

"Usually, I fancy taking the credit as much as you do, but this was all your doing."

"You underestimate your influence on him."

There's an earnestness to Juniper's reply that grabs Puck's attention. The satyr wheels toward her, his earrings tinkling with the movement. "Meaning?"

Juniper wavers, as if she's said too much. "Just that he was your friend before he was mine, and he's loyal to you. And to this cause."

This isn't a lie, nor is it the whole story. Although the Folk are unable to speak untruths—and we compensate by being masters of evasive word manipulation—our inability nevertheless attunes us better to mortal lies. Because we spend our lives dancing around dishonesty, we detect it easily in humans.

Juniper knows this. What's more, she's no stranger to Puck's shrewdness. His knack for cunning and perception are the stuff of lore.

Either she's too anxious to remember these facts or she's concealing something. The statement could have been innocent, but it hadn't sounded that way.

My dubious brother continues to stare at Juniper. Meanwhile, the remainder of our band considers the landscape, with its infinite vista of cliffs and the fringed woodland below.

Long ago, Cypress and the centaurs of The Solitary Forest had made an eternal oath to the last surviving scribe who'd penned the Book of Fables. The centaurs had vowed to keep the tome safe, to be its keepers. According to Juniper and Puck, it hadn't been easy for Cypress to approve of this venture.

However, for the sake of our realm and its fauna, the centaur and his kin had concurred. Juniper's logic, combined with Puck's sovereignty and devotion, had persuaded them.

While discussing this at The Fauna Tower, Juniper had stressed we wouldn't offer the entire book. We need only to offer the page containing the Fable itself. That will be sufficient.

Except one vital concern remains. It may only be a single page, and Juniper may be able to recite the text by heart, but that doesn't atone for the loss. She has proven there are other ways to find hints within the parchment—texture and lettering style, for instance. We'll be forfeiting our access to that.

An offering for an offering. It's a cruel bargain and indisputably Fae. But for survival and to avoid war, loses are inevitable.

To that end, Cove and Elixir had endeavored to find clues by visiting The Grotto That Whispers. Located in his domain, the age-old pool chronicles the history of this wild. Yet nothing new had come of it. Our band has been searching for answers and reaping none.

And at the rate Scorpio and our enemies are going, we must move swifter if we wish to avoid carnage.

This is our last resort.

I stride forward and offer Juniper my arm. She inspects the crooked elbow with uncertainty, then glances at Puck, who nods with encouragement. It rinses away the apprehension and replaces it with conviction. She places her crossbow on the grass, tucks the book to her side, and loops her free arm through mine.

I guide her to the rim, bend toward her ear, and whisper, "Call them."

Before I can elaborate, she asks, "How?"

"With your voice or your mind. Either will do. Trust me, they'll answer."

Her profile creases. It's the not concrete sort of instruction she prefers. Nonetheless, she straightens her clothing, tamping down the wrinkles. "Er...Horizon, we'd like a word. Show yourself."

At first, the air goes still, the quiet so expansive I barely hear the flapping of my father's wings in the welkin. Then the atmosphere oscillates. It funnels in several places, as if stirred by spoons, before slowing.

The blurred embodiments of winged horses float before us like phantoms—faintly distinct, reduced to shapes as diaphanous as fog. This is but a hint of what the Pegasi once looked like before they fell.

Cove gasps in wonder. Juniper must have temporarily forgotten her agenda, because she gawks with the fascination of a scholar.

Her mouth opens, but I place a finger atop her lips. "Let them speak first."

The Pegasi hover in swirls of prismatic color, their hazy wings outstretched and their filmy manes flying like pennants. "Juniper of Reverie Hollow," they greet as one, their voices overlapping. "And Cerulean of the sky. We see you've brought a party."

My mouth curls into a smirk. "I expect introductions aren't necessary."

"We know each of you. Lark and Cove, also of the mortal world, Puck of the woodland, and Elixir of the river. To what do we owe this pleasure? A deal, perhaps?"

"Is there ever another reason?"

"One at a time, then. Or choose your ambassador."

Juniper steps forward while holding up the Book of Fables. "We have a question for you—about a Fable in this book."

A lengthy pause follows. "We haven't beheld that anthology in ages. How good of you to share it."

From behind, I imagine Puck restraining a derisive sneer and Elixir slitting his eyes. Fake politeness is the first stage of making a bargain. We respect the Horizon, but that doesn't mean the Pegasi are above calculations and negotiations.

They were once flesh and blood, after all. Half-fauna, half-Fae. The latter part still knows how to get what it wants.

To the contrary, their response causes Juniper's features to lift. "Our question has to do with a page that says—"

"Juniper," I interject in a low tone. "Be very careful."

"So true," the Horizon responds. "You must pace yourself, dear mortal."

"Stop talking down to her," Puck warns, his threshold for reverence thinning, while Juniper's sisters audibly bristle, and Elixir continues to glower.

I give each of them a cautionary look and mutter to Juniper, "The offering must be explicitly revealed before you ask the question."

With no guarantees, it's a risk. That is the nature of trading in Faerie, a fact that has my brothers and me on edge.

Juniper gazes at the book with resolute sadness, then rifles through her skirt pocket for the spectacles. After dropping them on her nose and flipping through the pages, she folds the crease and gently tears the Fable from its spine.

The sound rips through the summit. She cringes, then lifts her arm to show the parchment. "This Fable says there's a second way to restore the fauna."

"Yes," the Horizon echoes. "Cerulean and Lark have recently beseeched us about this."

"But you didn't give them an answer."

"The offering was inappropriate. That forbids us from answering or providing any knowledge of the subject."

"Fine, but this offering is entirely adequate." Juniper recaps the details about the hidden message. "Are you familiar with this Fable? Did you know about its secret passage? Do you know the second way?"

"Those are three questions and only one offering."

I resist the urge to roll my eyes, whereas Lark mutters, "For fuck's sake."

Juniper frowns, then amends, "Will you tell us the second way?"

"Do you mean, *will* we?" the Horizon wonders. "Or do you mean, *can* we?"

Shit. My eyes clench shut.

"Will you?" Juniper insists, her green eyes intent behind the lenses.

"You have elected to speak with confidence, then." From there, the Horizon muses, "A second way. If such a thing exists, it is a marvel and could be a triumph. But we cannot tell you the way. That is our answer."

Several variations of "What the fuck?" project from two visceral voices behind me. A softer voice unfurls a dismayed breath. And the last voice seethes.

Juniper's profile collapses. "But...that can't be."

"You told me the first way," I grate. "How can you not know the second?"

"Because both ways have originated from different sources, Cerulean. Just because we speak truths about our world does not mean we have all the answers."

"Bullshit," Puck gripes, aligning himself behind Juniper. "You know something else. Say it."

The Pegasi flutter their wings and remain quiet for a moment. "You've always been a canny one, Puck of the woodland. It's rather annoying but attractive. How do you accomplish that?"

"I'm a satyr. Need I say more? Now give my woman the leftover detail you're withholding."

A collective sigh filters through the wind. "We do not know the second way, but you do—no, not just him," they scold when everyone turns to a flummoxed Puck. "All of you know. Or rather, you will know once you tap into the capacity."

"Oh goody," Lark says. "More riddles."

Juniper's gaze becomes remote, as if she's in shock for being wrong.

"Forgive me, but this makes no sense." Cove approaches, the scalloped straps of her dress swimming in the breeze. "If you can't tell us the answer, how can you assume that we know?"

"Because each of you radiates with the knowledge. That much is clear."

"Please. At least tell us how the scribes knew about this second way but not you? How did mortals know something so archaic?"

"Because they got their information from an age-old source," answers a raspy baritone. "One older than the Horizon."

We turn to Elixir, who stands apart from everyone. In the wake of his response, his gaze travels across the ground in thought.

"Correct," the Horizon vouches. "We don't know the second way, nor who supplied this information to the scribes, because the solution predates our existence. The second way is something far older than us. It is something that has existed since before our time, as has its source. That is the only possibility, and this is our answer. Do what you must with it."

The wind snatches the parchment from Juniper's fingers and carries it toward the Pegasi. When the leaflet reaches them, it vanishes, as though consumed in their grasps.

After that, their forms bleed into the firmament, their wings and manes beating until those disappear as well. A draft of wind passes through us, billowing our clothes and the surrounding wildflowers. All is quiet on the crest apart from my father's quills cutting through the air with The Parliament.

Instead of yielding an answer, more questions have arisen. And we've lost the page.

In silence, we process this. Anger spreads over the vanes of my wings. Elixir scrapes through his hair, tousling the black cascade. Cove and Lark slide worried glances toward Juniper, who teeters on her feet, as though the conversation has yanked the ground from under her.

Once more, she doesn't look well. Her complexion has lost its luster entirely, dulling it to a chalky pallor. The only facets that retain their brightness are her irises.

Not that she's been looking sprightly lately, but it has worsened since the Horizon spoke. It's hard to tell whether something else is wrong with her, or if the news has made her ill, or if she's reeling from having surrendered the Fable.

In an instant, Puck is at her side, his face cinching. "Luv?" But when she makes no reply, his jaw hardens. "Fuck this. We're leaving. Now."

But we don't return to the tower. Instead, we travel to The Solitary Forest. I fly while Tímien, members of The Parliament, and Lark's nightingale arrive to ferry everyone there.

The aromas of woodsmoke and fur permeate the environment as our fleet lands. Oaks canopy the wilderness, their muscled trunks capped in awnings of green that splay over the ground. Acorns litter the floor like small, brown studs.

Lark jumps from the nightingale's back. My boots hit the ground beside her, and my plumes condense against my back. The woodland is a compression of thickets and gnarled trees, with many areas less accommodating to my wingspan. Though to say the least, it's nowhere near as claustrophobic as Elixir's domain.

The moment I take a step, my heel releases a chunk of dirt, which crumbles into powder. I furrow my brows. The soil flakes beneath my soles, dehydrated as though it hasn't drunk from a downpour in ages.

"Shit," I mutter to the ground.

"Son of a bitch," Lark whispers, following my gaze.

In a mortal weald, this might be nothing. However, this environment has always been ripe, rich, robust. Now the earth's dark, umber color and moisture has reduced to a parched tan, which extends beyond to who-knows-where.

Lark scans the undergrowth and casts me a grave look. My sharp gaze must validate her thoughts.

Despite these grim hints, candles flicker from the branches, in the guise of chandeliers. Gilded light sketches the cluster of trees and the lone raccoon with blazing lime eyes that skitters past us. In the distance, a fawn springs over a stump, though the creature appears ganglier than it should.

It had been clear without Puck saying as much that Juniper was due for a much-needed breath in the place she now calls home. Based on the scenery, we've arrived in a copse near the boundaries of their cabin.

My brother had said the enemy's been closing in on his turf, though they've yet to breach it. The Herd of Deer will be secure for only so long, and Puck has been preparing to leave with Lark's sister.

I've no doubt they'll end up in The Heart of Willows, with Cypress eager to host them. His domain is neutral territory, exempt from bloodshed. Though, that might count for little these days, considering Scorpio's actions.

Puck dismounts one of the great owls and helps Juniper down, then he braces her shoulder and bolsters her chin with a single crooked finger. "We're here, luv. Come back to us."

"Sacrifice," she mumbles at last, setting her palm atop his. "That was the first way."

My eyes scan the forest floor in contemplation. "So the second way is older than sacrifice."

"But what method could possibly be older than sacrifice?" Lark asks. "And what source is older than the Pegasi?"

After a moment silence, Cove's voice shines through. "Unity."

There's a collective pause as we regard her.

Of course. After the battle at The Gang of Elks, when Juniper's game ended, we'd theorized about the second way being the opposite of sacrifice. We had talked about unity and revisited this in The Deep when Cove and Elixir joined our group, right before the flood. And we've been debating on this since.

Unity is the reverse of sacrifice. Also, it's indeed an older act.

"The Horizon didn't give us the second way," I say. "But it did just confirm we're on the right path."

"Okay, so if the second way is about unity after all, then we're still missing the actual method of unity," Lark summarizes.

I nod, grinning at her. "We'll get there."

Lark takes my hand and links our fingers together, seeking reassurance. I squeeze back, savoring her touch, the firmness of her grip.

For a moment, time ceases as we stare at one another. My gaze clings to hers, and the grooves around her eyes soften.

We'll get through this. Somehow, we'll find the answers, and I'll do everything in my power to keep everyone in this copse safe, so help me.

She's mine. I'm hers.

No other truth exists.

The mating bond courses through my veins, along with so much love that I know she sees it. I know because the same emotion is reflected at me.

A sickly noise breaks our trance. We split apart and veer toward Juniper right before she flattens her palm on the nearest tree trunk, keels over, and vomits.

Puck makes a shocked noise, then snatches Juniper's green hair, holding it back while the contents of her stomach splatter the ground.

Lark and Cove rush toward her, leaves crunching beneath their boots. However, Puck's already there. He rifles through Juniper's pack, withdraws a waterskin, and pours liquid down her throat, then snatches a leaf from a bush and urges her to chew on it.

I recognize the plant. It will refresh her mouth, wash away the residual taste of her sick.

When she's done, Puck balances Juniper in his arms and wipes her brow while she sags against him.

It's a rare sight to see my brother alarmed. "Juniper," he utters. "Fables almighty, luv."

"It'll pass," she persists.

"It won't fucking pass. Tell me what's wrong."

She wheels toward him and clutches his arms. "I don't know." She shakes her head. "I don't know."

"Do you have a fever?" Cove tries to soothe. "Aches or pains?"

"No, but something's...not right."

"That's it. I'm calling for Cypress," Puck says, then punches his arm toward Elixir. "Are you going to just stand there?"

But he knows Elixir isn't a doctor. He can brew curatives like a chemist or a potioneer, but he can't analyze ailments apart from venom or poison-induced ones. Few Faeries can since illness isn't a regular concern. The centaurs are the ones remotely capable of identifying maladies to the most accurate degree.

I approach the huddle. "Faeries can be cursed, poisoned, wounded, or incapacitated through bargains. But they don't get sick. Not in the way humans do. And there are no other mortals presently dwelling in this realm."

"There's no way you could have been exposed to a contagion," Puck agrees, stroking Juniper's cheek. "So what's causing this?"

After a pause in which Juniper's baffled countenance transfers to her sisters, some sort of realization flashes in Cove's teal eyes, which bloat to the size of saucers. "Oh, Fables," she gasps.

Lark is right behind her. "Holy shit," leaps off my mate's tongue.

I'm at a loss, so I merely shrug when Puck and Juniper swing their heads toward me for clarification.

"Okay, that doesn't help," Puck snaps to the females, his glare jumping from them to the water Fae who's busy compressing his mouth. "How about you, chatterbox? You want to fill us in on why my woman just lost her breakfast?"

At last, Elixir sighs and rubs the bridge between his eyebrows. "Because she's pregnant."

PART 2

Puck

12

Don't get me wrong. I fancy a good jest, especially if I'm the one responsible, and especially if it's graphic. Except nobody in this band is laughing.

I stare at Elixir, waiting for him to deliver the shitty punchline. But it doesn't come. Not that I'd expected it to from my broodingly-monosyllabic-prick of a brother, who wouldn't know a wisecrack from the hole in his sculpted ass.

Mischief is the guilty pleasure of randy woodland Faeries, not his lot in The Deep. All the same, I couldn't have heard him right. This has to be some tacky attempt at a prank.

Either that, or it's a truly fucked-up version of sarcasm, seeing as his announcement is the kind of news I've only ever imagined hearing. It's the kind of reality that isn't possible. Not for me and Juniper.

But again, humor and banter are hardly Elixir's expertise. Even if it were otherwise, he wouldn't stoop so low to make a mockery of something like this.

Apart from a doe traipsing through the forest about fifty feet away—probably Sylvan, from the sound of it—silence crams the forest. In my periphery, everyone gawks at Elixir, who finally turns to face me. His eyes are the sort of gold that glows in the dark, but it's his pupils I'm more interested in. Frankly, they're what keep me from balling my fist and ramming it into his face. Those orbs are the lethal black of a basilisk's skin, and they're as sober as any Fae who can't lie. Because like an idiot, that fact had escaped me for all of three seconds.

He's incapable of bullshitting. He's serious.

Because she's pregnant.

No. Not a chance.

For obvious reasons, my brother's got to be wrong. For all his acute senses and mastery of perception, he's made a mistake.

Juniper can't be pregnant. I would've known. After living with this woman for well over two months, I would have sensed it. I would've seen it on her face, scented it in her blood, and heard it in her voice.

Right? Wouldn't I have?

Or not. Only fated mates can read each other that way.

Because she's pregnant.

The words ring in my ears like alarm bells, the sound of them about as foreign as Elixir giggling or Cerulean slurring. I feel my eyes blinking, then I veer my head to Juniper, who's still clutching my biceps for balance. Any moment now, she's going to shed light on this mystery, interpret where Elixir's brain cells have gone wrong.

Problem is, Juniper's features have slackened. Her wide eyes fixate on Elixir, as if he's just narrated a Fable she's never read.

And now I'm damn sure she's as confused as I am, because it's taking her longer than me to process his statement.

Candle flames twitch from the oak branches. The earth crumbles beneath my hooves, the soil about as dry and useless as my tongue. My leather vest cinches in my ribcage, suddenly tighter than it's ever been.

Juniper and I move in unison, pivoting toward Elixir. Forget the visceral-but-ordinary, *What did you just say?* Neither of us are the types to ask someone to repeat themselves. It's boring, not to mention a waste of energy. We heard him just fine.

"That's impossible," Juniper and I say at the same time.

Elixir's eyes flash. "No. It is not."

"In that case, I overestimated you," I tell him. "Or does everybody else here need to spell it out?"

"He's a Fae," Juniper rehashes, her voice rising to a hysterical octave. "I'm a human."

"It is rare for Faeries to conceive," Elixir acknowledges. "Rarer still for woodland Solitaries."

"And rarest of all for satyrs," I finish, the fact tasting bitter in my mouth. "Where are you going with this?"

"It is rare," Elixir repeats placidly, then strikes quickly. "But it's not rare for mortals."

Juniper and I fall silent. His point hits truer than a honed arrow. It echoes through the great oaks and burrows as deeply as the exposed roots weaving in and out of the soil.

My brother's right. Juniper being mortal isn't a barrier—it's a breakthrough. It's a defiance against every natural law in my world. That's why it's never been considered, never fathomed by my kin or her people.

Nothing like this has happened before. Not in our recorded history.

Yeah, satyrs are the one type of creature in this wild who have a sexual appetite for humans, particularly if those humans are virgins. We're the only Faeries who fuck them. I've pounded enough mortals to outperform a brothel, mostly with males.

As for the female humans our kin have seduced and bedded, none have ever carried a Fae inside them.

Then again, none of those satyrs have ever fallen in love with their conquests. That emotion is also a rarity in this world. Faeries are intrinsically less capable of it, and most of all satyrs, who are the least likely to lose their hearts to anyone, much less a human.

My woman and I not only broke the mold. We shattered it to fucking pieces.

Maybe that's why I hadn't known. Everything I've felt for Juniper, everything I've done with her, is so wildly new and unfamiliar, that it's kept me from recognizing the signs fated mates would have detected immediately.

The possibility...the actual possibility that this is happening...drains me of words. I can't speak. I can't think. I can't feel the weight of my fucking antlers. My tongue lolls around in my mouth like a sloth, and the fringes of surrounding greenery blur.

Wings flap. Shadows launch off the ground.

The Parliament members quit the scene. Tímien and Lark's nightingale flee the premises too, likely to keep vigil while the drama unfolds.

Several nearby figures slip through the cracks of my consciousness, reminding me of everyone else's presence. Our clan has kept their mouths shut this whole time, probably pacing themselves and giving us our due moment. But now the voices burst like a dam from the sidelines, overlapping and getting as tangled as a thorn bush.

Female voices try to get Juniper's attention, to ask if she's all right, but she doesn't answer. Meanwhile, a male's whisper seeks me out, murmuring in Faeish, but I ignore the hell out of it.

Cove gives up on Juniper and glares at Elixir with an intimate sort of fury. And good. He deserves to be in deep shit with his lady.

Instead of her customarily benevolent tone, her voice cuts through, as sharp as her spear. "How long have you known about this?"

Elixir is not one to hedge. "You know the answer to that."

"You should have said something," she charges. "I've asked you more than once why you kept looking at Juniper like you knew something important. I asked why your eyes flashed when you shook her hand right before the flood. I *asked* you, and you said it was nothing to worry about. You lied."

"I omitted," he corrects, rueful. "Cove—"

"Don't *Cove* me. Never mind that you kept this to yourself." She flings her arm toward me and Juniper. "You should have told *them*."

"Hon, it wasn't his news to tell," Lark broaches. "It wasn't his news to even find out about."

"Brother, are you certain?" comes Cerulean's annoyingly eloquent murmur. "You mean to say, you sensed Juniper's pregnancy shortly before the flood?"

There's a pause. "I heard the child."

Clarity returns. The words grip my lungs, my stomach, my fucking heart.

As my head whips toward Elixir, I catch Juniper doing the same. This feels all sorts of wrong, finding this out in public and by accident, instead of us alone together, naked in bed, in the dark.

And why the fuck hasn't she looked at me, even once? Whereas I've been casting her glances constantly.

Elixir speaks to Juniper. "When I shook your hand, I sensed movement inside you. I heard blood flowing around some type of form, outlining its shape. It was like…like an embryo floating."

Because her sister doesn't respond, Lark asks, "How could you hear that?"

"The water Fae have acute senses to fluid, but it's more than that," Cerulean explains. "Fae children are so entrenched in the womb, they're beyond audible detection in the beginning. However, Elixir is a brewer who learned to inspect what's occurring in any form of liquid. And while his senses were already powerful, they were honed further when he lost his sight."

Elixir nods. "The embryo is too deep for other Faeries to locate. But not for me."

"I've been feeling jolts in my stomach," Juniper says.

"Of course, you have. The embryo is in flux, and you're the mother. It is normal."

That's when it hits me with the force of a felled evergreen. It's true. Juniper's pregnant. She has a mini Juniper-and-Puck growing in her.

My woman's pregnant. And it's mine.

It's ours.

There's a seed inside her, made from one of the countless days and nights we've gone wild together, fucking like there was no tomorrow. We'd planted that seed during a moment when I'd been rooted inside her body.

My throat bobs as I swallow hard. I imagine that tiny nugget floating in Juniper's womb, brimming with the soul of the woodland, with her intelligence and my…my what?

What the fuck do I have to offer a sapling?

Too many emotions surge together and swarm my head. From the cold blast of shock, to the worst case of scared-shitless I've ever known, to a nauseating bout of inadequacy, to something warmer, brighter, and more intoxicating than sex. I know what it is, but it's never been this potent, not even when making Juniper come for minutes on end.

Happiness. That's what this heady feeling is.

I'm happy.

Fables al-fucking-mighty. I'm going to be someone's father. By some crazy miracle, I'm having a kid with the sexiest, smartest, strongest female to walk this forsaken earth.

I wheel toward Juniper. But her profile remains latched to Elixir, riveted on the facts he's just laid out. With each passing second, her features crinkle, from the small patch of skin between her straight eyebrows to that stubborn chin. If there was ever proof of reality sinking in, it's that expression.

That expression, which is on the brink of a scowl.

That scowl, which climbs up her face the moment she vaults my way.

Dammit. That's the Mayhem Face. This isn't the reaction I was hoping for.

"Juniper," I begin but don't get a chance to finish.

Her glower deepens, those green eyes vibrant with accusation and warning me to back off. They conceal what's beneath the surface. Those depths reflect everything she won't let the others witness, everything she can't hide from me.

I see it and feel this truth right before Juniper turns on her heel and marches out of the copse. Bushes shudder as she charges away, tracking in the direction of our cabin. Her crossbow and pack with the book stay behind.

Awkwardness settles over the forest. Cerulean and Elixir hesitate to show pity, knowing how I'll take it. Cove moves to go after her sister, but Lark snatches the female's arm to stop her, then Lark shakes her head wordlessly.

It's the right move, because this is my battle. Mine and Juniper's.

Also, my woman should know by now that I don't go down easily. And I don't give up easily.

This isn't over yet. It'll never be over with us.

"Fuck," I mutter, then drive my fingers through my hair and stalk after her.

13

Candlelight spills across the wild as I stride through condensed shrubbery. This route is more cramped, but it's quicker. She moves fast when she wants to, although she's never been one to retreat. No, she's always been the type to either stand her guard or step into the fire with her chin nocked high.

This is different. This is so fucking different, I barely register the tempo of Juniper's movements or her lingering scent—the hefty aroma of a campfire. Those familiar signs usually lead me to her. This time, my senses are too jumbled by a bunch of shit at once—elation, fear, more elation, more fear—it's hard to focus.

Only two reinforcements point me in the right direction. One, experience. I know where Juniper goes whenever she's upset, which isn't far from our cabin. And two, her boot prints. They stomp through the soil, marking the way for anyone who has a knack for hunting.

I scan the environment, but there's nothing to worry about. The enemy might be lurking on the borders of The Herd of Deer, but the fuckheads haven't crossed that line, haven't reached this turf yet. Otherwise, Juniper wouldn't have ventured this way weaponless. Not to mention I'd sure as shit be manifesting in her wake, flopping her cute ass over my shoulder, and returning her to safety.

I pace myself, giving her time. Nonetheless, I smack a wooly creeper out of the way, and the miserable thing snaps in half. A pinecone crunches beneath my weight, likely brought here by a woodland critter from some farther area of the forest.

By now, I know why she's pissed. Juniper hates when guarantees fail to stay guarantees. She despises being proven wrong.

My ribcage clenches, as if it might crack open. It's a brittle feeling, like my bones have been worn down. And it takes me a moment to recognize the emotion. To say the least, it's not a feeling my woodland kin deal with often. We're too busy having fun, having revenge, or having orgasms to experience anguish.

So this is what it's like to be hurt. This is what it's like to be wounded by someone who means everything to me.

Even shittier? It's a lot harder than being furious.

My brothers and Cypress have never had this effect. Fae bed partners haven't, either. I guess it comes with the territory of loving someone. It gives them the power to smash your heart to a pulp.

She's not doing it on purpose. I understand why she took off, but that doesn't get rid of the ache.

I just...wish she was as fucking ecstatic as I am.

My limbs pick up speed, cutting through bushes and patches of foliage. The momentum keeps my fist from denting the nearest trunk. Putting it mildly, the trees would take offense.

At last, I break through the crush of greenery and step into a glade. One of the oldest trees in the forest towers overhead, its wizened branches splaying wide like an umbrella. Spastic candle flames line its boughs and throw orange light onto the acorn-scattered grass.

When I first introduced Juniper to this landmark, her quizzical eyes had glowed with enthusiasm, for obvious Juniper reasons. Outside the cabin's library, it's become her favorite place to read and study the Fables.

Tonight, she idles beneath the proud tree and contemplates the grass with her back facing me. Her suede skirt is the color of currants, a fetching shade that always brings out her blushes.

Sylvan is with her. Candles sketch the deer's majestic form, her antler crown strewn with shamrocks.

My companion bumps her muzzle against Juniper's shoulder, and my woman responds by stroking the creature's russet fur. She twists enough to lower her forehead against Sylvan's, and the picture is so poignant, it stalls my tongue.

That's my family. Soon, a new member will be added to it.

Now that her profile's more visible, my gaze skims Juniper's face and then staggers across her stomach. Her free palm rests there, either shielding it or bracing what's inside. I have a strong feeling she's been doing that since before I'd barged in here.

Just like that, my breath is gone. My fucking heart isn't far behind, that volatile organ having a tantrum inside my chest. She's never looked more stunning—or more livid.

Her spine goes rigid, and her jaw sets, those huntress instincts kicking in. She knows she and her companion aren't alone.

Sylvan's head swings my way. As recognition floods the animal's orbs, she pulls away from Juniper and trots on spindle limbs toward me. My palm glides across the deer's back in greeting, the fur under my skin cropped but soft.

"Skijari," I joke quietly. "Traitor."

Although my companion and I can communicate through the roots, Sylvan offers no signals. She just leans into my touch, then backs up and clomps past me, exiting the glade as though aware of the conflict. Animals can sense tension between fauna mates, so maybe she's getting the same vibes.

The moment Sylvan's gone, I cross the grass. Except I only make it halfway before Juniper cuts me off, her voice fired up like kindling. "How did this happen?"

My hooves stop ten paces from her. I scratch the back of my head. "Well, luv. When a satyr and a huntress love each other very much—"

She whips around. "This isn't funny."

"Am I laughing?" I deadpan.

Those spruce eyes are forests, prickly and capable of burning. Her index finger stabs in my direction while her free palm remains on her stomach. "You said this wouldn't happen. When we first had sex, you told me it wasn't possible. You said we were safe."

"Because I fucking thought we were!" I grind out, wounded pride now whittling to something more familiar, more wieldable.

And shit. Unlike Juniper, I hate when I'm right. This is for sure why she's pissed.

I speak slowly to calm myself, to keep myself from grabbing and kissing her, to keep the mishmash of emotions in check. "You heard Elixir. Compared to Faeries, it isn't rare for humans to hatch a few eggs in their short lifetime. Your people have that privilege, not us."

"Not every human does," Juniper concedes. "Some try forever, but it doesn't work for them."

"My point is your humanity made the probability higher."

Her mouth trembles. I take another step forward and then—fuck it—consume every bit of space separating us. My body halts inches from hers, our shadows merging across the grass.

I duck my head, fasten my gaze to hers, and refuse to muffle the awe in my voice. "This is real."

Juniper stares at me, my words slipping through the cracks. After that, it happens in one fell swoop. Her features crumble, and she turns away while cupping a hand over her mouth.

Gone is that habitual composure. Gone is that indomitable resilience.

I don't know another being who's withstood what she has. This woman thought she lost her sisters forever, only to be glamoured, humiliated, and thrown into a cage in The Redwoods of Exile, then trussed up like a hunk of game, all by my orders.

She was hunted at night, tracked through this wilderness like prey by a legion of howling Faeries.

She sat through a feast where my kin secretly tried to drug her with food and drink.

She bargained with us, braved the forest Faeries' scrutiny.

She got glamoured again, then was trapped with me in a Fae ring, then traded blows with a bitchy nymph who tried to suffocate my woman into the dirt.

She battled my kin in The Gang of Elks, saved Sylvan from death, and won her game.

She survived a near-drowning at Elixir's hands, back when he didn't know who she was.

In the end, Juniper found it in herself not only to forgive me, but to love me—from my troublemaker smirk, to my non-existent morals, to my black-sheep soul.

Through all that, this huntress never wavered. But she does now.

Everything compiles on her face. The carefully erected scaffolding tips like an uprooted tree. I feel it like I feel the overdue sensation of my ribs cracking.

If she suffers, I suffer. That's how it is.

Juniper's gutted over losing that crucial page from the Book of Fables. She's fuming that we'd both neglected the obvious about breeding.

But mostly she's mad at herself for not having anticipated this, for not connecting the dots between Fae infertility and human conception, for not drawing the logical conclusion after how awful she's been feeling. Even now, stress churns under the surface of her flesh, the sound audible to my ears.

But none of these problems are what's really breaking her. None of them explain why her eyes glisten with unshed tears.

No, something else is tormenting her. For the immortal life of me, I can't tell anymore if she's clutching her womb purely because she's ill or shocked—or if it's because she's plagued.

I clamp onto her shoulders. "Juniper. For fuck's sake. Say something, anything. Or at least, tell me if you're all right."

"I'm all right." Her voice splinters. "The nausea passed."

"What about everything else? What are you feeling? What are you thinking? Talk to me."

"I don't...I don't know."

Okay. If that's her answer, this is really fucking bad. "Why won't you look at me? Why haven't you been able to face me since we found out?"

"That's not true. I've been looking at you this whole time."

Except it's been taking a shitload of effort. Whatever else is shredding her, she won't let it out. Some confession is pushing itself up her throat, but she's refusing to let loose.

"What is it?" I press. "I'm here with you. Tell me."

Juniper shakes her head. "I can't...I don't know if..."

Another thought jumps into my brain. My hands fall to my sides, my hooves thud backward, and the question lurches off my tongue before I can muzzle the fucker. "Is it me?"

Her head snaps in my direction. "What?"

"Have I ruined this for you?"

"Puck." The confusion fades as Juniper translates the rest, which must be smeared all over my face, which causes her eyes to widen. "Puck, no."

"You could've had a human. Not a satyr with a history of being a malicious asshole, a morally grey whore, and a marginally redeemed villain. You could've had someone better to be the father." My throat bobs, a growth inflating there, making it tough to speak around it. "Are you afraid the babe will turn out like me? Is that why you're unhappy?"

A strained moment passes. Juniper's expression crinkles, then she narrows her eyes like I'm the dumbest dumbfuck in this forest.

At which point, she breaks from her stance and shoves my chest. "Fables, Puck! I'm not unhappy. Yes, I'm furious but not wallowing. And I'm not angry because it's yours. That's the good part, not the bad one." With a grunt, she clamps a single palm on my cheek to bring me closer, then whispers, "Look. Closer."

I do what she wants. My gaze probes every inch of her features, from the tilt of her brows to the facets of her eyes. Oh, I'd noticed the change in her irises a while back. From one day to the next, they'd turned from a coniferous spruce to a deeper hue, their clarity amplified like stained glass.

Juniper had also noticed it. And honestly? We'd assumed it was the result her extended life. She'd taken half my immortality. Why wouldn't that show some physical signs?

We couldn't have been more wrong. Now we know the real reason her eyes have brightened.

As for the random moments when she didn't seem well, it had worried me. Mostly, she'd hid a lot of it. But when she hadn't, she kept making excuses for why she wouldn't approach Cypress for a remedy. Up until tonight, I'd been ready to drag her to The Heart of Willows.

Now we know the reason for that, too. And she's scared of it.

That's what I see while looking closer. Anxious lines stack under her lower lashes. Her chin is crinkling. And her right foot is doing that thing where the heel swings from side to side, her toes rubbing an impression into the dirt.

That's what happens when she's nervous and doesn't want to show it. I'd missed that very telling sign.

My woman is afraid. Her left hand isn't arrested on her stomach like she's going to be sick again, or like she wants the contents of her womb to vanish. She's cupping it like she wants to maintain a hold on what's there.

My head whisks up to meet her frail expression, as naked and vulnerable as it's ever been. This is what she's been fighting to hide. She hates looking weak rather than indestructible.

The discovery loosens the knots in me, even while it punctures holes in my chest. "Juniper." I take her hand from my face, thread our fingers together, and press my mouth to the fist we make. "Don't you know by now? Don't you know you can show me everything? Don't you know how I'll always see you, no matter what?"

Candlelight brushes streaks of gold through her hair. Her lips wobble, then split open and spill. "What if something happens to them, Puck? What if we can't protect them in this war? What if I make a mistake, raising them? What if I don't know how to do this right? What if I can't teach them things? What if something goes wrong?"

I wait a beat. "Are you done, luv?"

"At present."

My forehead lands against her. "And what if you stop what-iffing?"

"You know, you're thinking the same thing."

"I am. And eventually, I'll panic like you're doing now. But I'd much rather spend this little one's first hour with us by being happy. This is their first introduction to you and me."

Juniper startles, her features shifting in comprehension. "I hadn't thought of that."

As I pull back and stroke her cheeks with my thumbs, I hear my own gritty timbre, heavy with hope. "Are you saying, you want this?"

"Fables, I'm so young," she rattles off. "And you're my age multiplied by a factor of ten. We haven't been together long. We've barely lived in the same home long enough to establish who gets which side of the bed."

"That's my fault. I keep rolling you across the mattress."

"Neither of us knows the first thing about being parents."

"We can learn," I murmur. "I think we're mighty good at that."

"This is the worst timing. We're not prepared."

"We weren't prepared for lots of things, but we kicked fate's ass anyway.

And you know how I feel about needing to know everything in the first place. It's overrated. I can remember several episodes during the game when we locked horns about this. The eagerness to be right all the time gets in the way of discovery."

"I know, but we can't be clueless, either. This is something I just…don't know how to do in the slightest."

I lean in and swipe my lips over hers. "Like you said, neither do I."

Her breath hitches, then releases. "Not yet."

"So again: You want this? Because if not, there are ways to undo it, herbs that Cypress has mentioned working on the mountain and river Faeries, on the occasions over the centuries when they didn't want offspring."

"But you've been wishing for this your whole life."

"I got what I've always wanted, luv. I got you." When her eyes mist, I husk against her mouth. "I want you happy. That's my wish. So if you're not ready, or you don't want to, just say the word—"

"I do." She nods. "I want this."

My words falter. "With…me?"

"Yes." Juniper inches away, her pupils glimmering with fascination, like she's uncovered a new Fable. "Puck. Right after I came here, I felt another jolt. And I've been feeling more of them ever since."

I launch back. "This whole fucking time?"

"On and off. Nine times. I counted."

Naturally. But whatever quip I'd been about to make leaks from my tongue her hands claim mine and draw my palms down. Juniper settles them on her stomach, my broad digits spanning her form.

Nothing happens. Yet I swear to Fables, I might pass out from waiting.

Then after a minute, a tiny sort of pressure bumps against my flesh, like a seed while it's growing. I've known plenty of trees before they sprouted roots and rose into their prime. But it's nothing compared to this.

That bump is us. That's the sound of us.

I glance at Juniper. My eyes must be wide as hell, because a laugh pops out of her mouth.

"It was like the moment I realized I love you," she reminisces. "In the rain, caring for you that much, wanting you forever, all came unexpectedly.

And when I fled to this spot, I felt something shift inside me, and again, the feelings just happened." Another chuckle leaves her mouth, this one strong and solid as she twines her arms around my neck. "I'm scared, but I want this. I want us."

Several pleasurable things follow. My heart explodes, my mouth lifts into a roguish smile, and I exhale. "Well, I'll be fucked," I say, then grab her face and crash my lips to hers.

14

Juniper moans, the flex of my mouth pulling that savory noise from deep in her throat. The sound is made of smoke, the noise shooting to my ears like a rush of adrenaline, penetrating and addictive. Even better, the texture of that moan oozes down my tongue, her pleasure melting into me.

My throat unleashes its own rugged sound, sharp and guttural enough to chop down a fucking redwood. I groan, steel my arms around her middle, and snatch her ass in my palms. Hoisting her off the ground, I stroke my tongue between the wet crease of her lips, pushing them wider.

Damp heat swirls around my tongue as it flexes against hers. Juniper's fingers shave through the hair at my nape, her grip urging my mouth harder into hers. Prickles dance up my scalp and scatter across my antlers.

Fuck. That's an aphrodisiac more erotic than if she'd fondled the tips of my ears.

My cock jumps. I hiss into her mouth and work my jaw with hers. Another moan cracks from her lungs, and I swallow the living shit out of it like a famished beast. Her taste plunges straight to my balls, which tighten under the breeches.

Everything about this woman drives my senses wild. Juniper's pert tits rub against my pecs, and her warmth seeps through my vest, nipples so hard I feel them poking through our clothes. More than that, just thinking about the small form tucked inside her brings savage cravings to the forefront.

I'd made her come hard. And she made me come long. That's how we'd made something even better.

My nostrils flare, scenting the musk of her desire. Wetness is dripping between her sweet cunt with each pass of my tongue. How I'd love to drop to my knees, yank up her skirt, and feast on that banquet until she dissolves.

But when she skates one hand to my cheek, clutching the side of my face like something rare, something worth holding onto, my head explodes.

With a snarl, I grasp her ass and lunge her against me. I haul my mouth into hers, tongue lashing between her lips.

The kiss detonates. On a stunned cry, Juniper surges her body into mine, her mouth falling open wider, welcoming the steady thrust of my tongue, the tempo like a pulse.

Palpitations beat the hell out of my chest. My dick stretches beneath the leather pants, so fucking hard I'm going to combust any second.

Satyrs don't lose control of themselves. Ever.

That's another rule she's dismantled. And I have zero complaints. This mortal can ruin my self-control to smithereens whenever she wants. It's all kinds of fun.

Never talking my mouth off hers, I back Juniper up against the ancient oak. Leaves and acorns rain from the branches. Her spine hits the trunk, and I brace one hand behind her head to keep the bark from scraping her, while my other arm links under her thigh and yanks her limb off the ground.

Hitching her leg over my waist, I nudge my hips between the V of her thighs and continue to kiss the shit out of her.

My lips smash into Juniper's, licking into her, lapping each of her moans. Maybe this kiss should have been sweet, tender. Instead, she's an overachiever, and I'm a satyr with a huntress fetish. We attack each other with obsessive swats of our tongues, as if snatching this moment for all it's worth, because we only get one shot to savor it.

Bloody true, because this moment only happens once, just like our first kiss. There's no repeat, we get no do-overs, and we've never taken less than everything. Any other way is impossible.

Juniper's mouth fuses to mine, both of us slanting and jutting as if we're fucking with our lips. I growl, snagging her tongue and sucking hard. She whimpers, melting under the rocking pressure of my mouth.

Her skirt flutters around my waist, my cock sliding along her crease, that gorgeous pussy throbbing, hot and soaked. I feel it, smell it. And soon, I'm going to do a lot more about it.

I want her naked and panting, with strands of green hair stuck to her cheeks. I want her legs cinched around my snapping waist. I want her delectable cunt parting for my cock, and I want her shouting.

Soon. Not yet. Prolonging the inevitable is part of the charm.

With that in mind, I slow the motions of my lips, lolling them against hers. Juniper sinks into the ancient oak, her mouth yielding under me. Our tongues sweep together once, twice more, before I pry my mouth from hers.

On a stuttered gasp, she peers at me as my forehead sags against hers. I slump into her, my arm tacked above our heads. Our thick breathing chips apart. It could be from finding out we're no longer two people but three, or it could be the havoc our mouths just wrecked, but I like to think it's both. It ups the ante.

Juniper's fingers trail over the sides of my face. I latch my gaze to hers, and the crook of my mouth tips upward.

Dammit. More than ever, I love the fuck out of this woman.

After dragging ourselves apart, we return to the others with our hands laced tightly. Only one force breaks us apart. Lark and Cove squeal the second we get to the copse, make a mad sprint to their sister, and I get out of the way fast as the females crush Juniper in a hug, with my woman wedged between them like a sibling sandwich.

Cove holds her sister's face and whispers, "Congratulations."

Lark echoes the sentiment, hooting, "And here I just thought your eyes had gotten greener from fucking a satyr." I take that as a compliment as Lark plants a wet kiss on Juniper's cheek. "I'll wager that beautiful runt will inherit your brain."

Cove gets teary, Lark beams, and Juniper's face softens. In a way, I get this picture. I know these looks from the stories she's told me, plus what my brothers and I went through. It's the look of those who've lost their parents or never had any to begin with, but now have a chance to do better for their own kin.

While Lark and Cove gush over her, Juniper glances my way. Her eyes gleam, and I fixate on them until a hand rests on my shoulder. My head swerves to meet Cerulean's blue gaze.

"Well done," he says with a grin. "To the both of you."

I can't help the smug smile that wraps around my face. "Guess this'll make you an uncle." My eyes travel over to the quiet, broody one several paces away. By way of forgiveness for him not telling us, I jut my chin at Elixir. "You, too, blabbermouth."

Relief passes through Elixir's eyes. He absorbs the words like water— swift and transparent—before inclining his head.

Everyone switches. Cerulean and Elixir approach Juniper to offer their best wishes, while the giddy committee of humans jumps all over me. Lark elbows me and makes a raunchy joke, and Cove pats my jaw, and both order me to spoil my family.

That new feeling of euphoria intensifies. From these players to Sylvan, I have a family now. Hell, if I won't tear the world from its roots for them.

It's midmorning, and everyone's tired. My brothers and their women head back to their own turfs. I take Juniper home to the cabin, where we crash onto the bed, and I keep kissing her until those bright eyes close.

Way too many hours pass until I wake up, my eyes crusty with sleep. I groan, flop over, and reach for her, my hands as eager as they ever were.

Except my fingers feel nothing but air. All I find are rumpled blankets.

Nightfall filters through the window, illuminating the log walls and burning candles. Dusk must have come and gone a while ago.

She always does this. She's always the early riser, I think with a sloppy grin.

I hustle out of bed, opt for a pair of loose pants instead of leather breeches, and ignore the long, bronze leaf earrings on the nightstand. If I put them on, she'll hear me coming. It'll be enough of a challenge to keep the huntress from detecting the thud of my hooves.

But we balance each other that way. She knows what sounds to pay attention to, and I know how to mask those sounds. Makes for a merry game.

It's not as if we haven't used this to our advantage in the past. I've introduced Juniper to roleplay—prey and predator, the hunter versus the hunted—and it's a kink she's fond of.

Except I'm less interested in that right now. Instead, I'm more interested in relishing this all-consuming, weightless feeling that makes me feel as if I'm fucking levitating.

It's fun, being happy. It's rare these days, feeling nothing but that.

I want to gloat. I want revel in this moment. I want to pack it in before the shitshow continues.

I amble down the stairs, expecting to find Juniper either baking in the kitchen, reorganizing the cupboards, or curled up with the Book of Fables on the couch. But when I round the corner from the foyer into the living room, I halt. And so does my breath.

In the room's center, the trunk around which this cabin is built rises like a spine into the beamed ceiling. A small inferno blazes inside the fireplace carving through the trunk. The windows overlook the woods, where a cluster of oaks are veiled in mist and shafts of starlight.

Otherwise, it's dark enough to see one's reflection in the panes. That's why my woman is standing in front of them.

With her back facing me, she studies herself in the glass while wearing nothing but a tunic that barely covers her ass. Her small fists rest on her hips, her green head tilts, and her eyes squint through the lenses of her spectacles. She uses them purely for reading, but she's got them on now, as if she's parsing through a line of text instead of her likeness.

Firelight skims her thighs and toes. With those tresses whisked into a messy updo—huh, not like her—and those spectacles perched on her nose, she looks every bit the sexy scholar. One who's currently appraising her form.

My brain calls it quits the instant Juniper settles a palm on her stomach, draws a deep inhalation, and purposefully bloats out her womb. Like that, she turns to inspect the way it makes her belly expand.

Uncertainty shadows her face, right before something much better animates it. Those irises brighten, and her lips part in a slow, proud smile.

I damn near lose my mind. Watching my woman like this, seeing a preview of how she'll look, I can't think straight. The only thing making sense inside me right now is this blissful, drunken sensation.

Lust shoots like an arrow from my hooves to the tips of my antlers. In seconds, it has my blood in a tailspin and my dick standing up.

Juniper goes still, a bashful pink climbing up her throat. Her eyes shift to my reflection behind her. "Spying, satyr?"

I slouch against the corner of the wall. "What can I say? I have a crush on you. And you're looking mighty spyable."

"And…" She changes her pose to something simpler, her back straightening and palms spanning that pretty stomach. "And, um, what do you think?"

My mouth and cock have the same answer. "I think it's a good look on you."

"Really?"

"Really." I hoist myself off the wall, swagger across the living room, stall inches behind Juniper, and speak to her reflection. "I have a confession to make."

With dry humor, Juniper adjusts her spectacles. "This should be epic."

I band my arms around her middle and thread my digits with hers, so that both our hands cover her womb. Leaning down, I murmur in her rounded ear, "You're giving me impure thoughts."

The molten words have the best effect, causing a ripple down her nape. Juniper curls into me, her head lolling as my lips trace the shell of her ear. Then something snaps her out of it, and she whips her head upright. "Antlers."

It takes me a bit to catch up. "Come again?"

"Will the baby have antlers?" A drop of panic leaks into her face. "What if I can't carry—"

"Shhh, luv," I assure Juniper with a kiss to her temple. "Satyrs and fauns grow them after being born. And it takes a while."

"How do you know for sure? You came from a seed, not a womb."

"Because all Faeries with horns grow them after they're born." I tighten my hold on her. "Go on. What's next?"

"What on earth do you mean?"

"Tell me what else is on the list of questions and to-do's you wrote after leaving our bed cold."

Juniper bunches her lips to hide a grin, but she doesn't deny it. Her toes rub against my cloven hooves, as if seeking warmth. "For a start, we still haven't determined when it happened."

"But you have a theory," I deduct. "Me, too."

We gaze at each other through the glass, gauging one another's thoughts and whether our hunch is the same. Outside, fog glazes the oaks. Leaves drip from the branches, moss embroiders the trunks, and somewhere nearby the Herd are grazing with Sylvan.

Juniper exhales. "The Seeds that Give."

I nod. "Pretty much."

That's when it must have happened. That's where woodland Faeries are born, so it stands to reason that's also where they have the slightest chance of conceiving. Of course, that's assuming one's partner is a human who can undo that impossibility.

It had only taken one time. During the Middle Moon Feast, I hadn't been able to stand it anymore, wanting this mortal and not being able to have her. Until that night, my cock had been nearing critical mass, my balls suffering from a drastic case of sexual purgatory. But once the bonfire really got started, both of us had shred ourselves bare and gone rogue.

The next query takes shape across Juniper's pinched face. "I'm still bleeding. Not now, but I have been. How's that possible? More than anything, that would have made my condition obvious earlier."

"Ah, that." I shrug. "Faeries being immortal means things take longer. With the rare Solitary who carries an infant, the signs don't show up that quickly, apart from queasiness. Since you have half of my immortality, and the baby's half-Fae..." I drift off, letting the rest speak for itself. "Don't expect your monthlies to end for a while, much less for the baby to grow as fast as it does for humans."

"Sooooo," Juniper draws out, "how long does a Fae pregnancy last?"

"Years."

"What?!"

"Technically three." When her eyes bulge, I bark out a laugh and crush her to me. "Don't worry. You won't show until it's closer to the end. With Faeries, everything happens at a slow pace, then all at once."

"But if you're saying queasiness is the exception, does that mean I'll be nauseous the whole time?"

"Nah. Just in the beginning, during the first few months. Since it's been about that much time already, it should pass soon. After that, you won't feel anything but a jolt here and there from our kid. And you know what all of this means? We'll still have the next few years to ourselves, plenty of mornings, afternoons, and nights to fuck like maniacs and soak up our alone time. Sounds like a plan, don't you think?"

"How do you know all this?" she asks, nonplussed.

I rub her arms up and down. "Don't be pretentious. I grew up in the sex capital of the Solitary wild, I was its most popular resident, and in a thousand-plus years of banging more Faeries than I can count, I *have* learned a thing or two about the outcome of coitus. Even if it's impossible for woodland Faeries, it still happens for mountain and river ones."

"Fables, I'm sorry." Juniper's brows tip inward. "That was unfair of me."

"And don't apologize."

"I don't want to argue."

"Now who said anything about arguing? Tell me you won't allow sex toys in our house, and then we'll have a problem."

"There's enough going on. When it comes to this—" she glances at her stomach, "—I don't want an ounce of distance between us. No discord. No awkwardness. No disputes. I don't want to fight."

I lean in and ghost my lips against her ear. "Then let's fuck."

Juniper's breath catches. I hear it like a root stretching through the soil, deep and subtle. Peach creeps across her cheeks, the color so pronounced it reflects against the window as much as my red hair and her irises.

I crave seeing those treats and much more. I may be a taken satyr, but I'm still a satyr. And when it comes to temptation, I'm one evil son of a bitch.

Like a hunter, my gaze captures Juniper's. I hold fast until she can't look away, even if she wanted to. Every shred of playfulness drains from my face, my features dark and intent on her. Still, she hasn't released that breath.

Good. Very good girl.

With our gazes pinned together, I grip her waist and tug her into me. This way, she feels the heat radiating from my chest and my cock stretching between us, hard as steel and erect against her compact little ass.

Juniper's mouth parts, and her eyelids flutter, yet not a single puff leaves her throat. At the sight, need flows freely through my veins, the onslaught surging to my dick. It hasn't let up since this conversation began, though it's behaved itself so far.

I lean my chin over Juniper's shoulder. "You remember that night?" Then I twist my head and graze my lips over her cheek. "The night I made you come for the first time?"

Juniper gulps. "Yes."

I descend to her jaw, letting my voice trail over her flesh, down the side of her throat. "I still remember the clamp of your sweet, virgin pussy around my cock," I murmur, barely audible. "I remember hitting a tight spot that made you whine."

Her head lolls onto my shoulder as I slowly pop open the closures of her tunic, one by one. When her eyes threaten to fall shut, my fingers waver. "Don't," I tell her. "Don't look away, or I'll stop."

Juniper blinks. Her head doesn't rise, but she refocuses through her lenses.

Much better. My mouth sketches her pulse point, that small button starting to pound like I'm sure it's pounding between her legs.

"I remember you strapped around me," I say, nudging open the flaps of her shirt once they've come undone. "I remember your breasts pouring from the neckline of your bodice—like this," I enunciate as her sweet tits fall into view, the skin of her nipples roughening into pink studs.

Juniper's chest rises and falls, inflating her breasts with every pant. She stares as I reach up and swab my thumbs over the disks, tracing their circular shapes. They stiffen further, the teasing brush pushing the oxygen from her lungs in one long blast.

"Oh…," she gasps, arching into me. "Oh, Puck."

Hell. Yeah.

"I remember the noises you made." My fingers abandon her nipples and finish off the last of the shirt's clasps. "So supple and strong, even while my cock broke through you, over and over. Your cunt took it so wetly, so warmly."

She licks her lips, reaches behind to claw through my hair, and wraps her hand around the base of an antler. I hiss in satisfaction. It's the same as pulling on my roots or the troublemaker under my pants, only a thousand times better.

My digits grip the tunic and split it open, baring her naked body to the night outside the window. Her flushed tits sit heavily on her chest, her flat stomach trembles, and the sprigs of hair between her thighs glisten. A tiny nub rises from her cunt, the sight parching my throat.

Fables have mercy. My cock twitches, thick and throbbing.

On a hum, I lap at the pulse of her neck, then ride my lips along her shoulder and back to that sensitive crook. "I remember you wanting my cock to go faster." I plant a teasing, open-mouthed a kiss on her flesh. "I remember doing as you wished, fucking you so thoroughly until you shuddered around me."

"Puck…," Juniper heaves, grinding her rump into my dick. "Do you want that memory again?"

"No," I husk. "What I want is to watch you like this." My voice is so low now, it's nothing but a pinch of air. "I want you to know I'm watching. And I want you to see it, too."

"You want us to see each other while climaxing?"

On a groan, I lift my head and snarl into her ear. "I want that."

"And do you promise to fuck me good?" she asks, making it sound like an innocent plea. "Will you fuck me so very good that I can't keep my eyes off us? Will you fuck me like a satyr? Will you do that for me?"

Growling, I seize her jaw and swivel her face up to mine. "Fuck, yes," I rasp, then seal my mouth with hers.

Our lips slant and clutch, firm and deep and everything at once. I pry her open and stroke my tongue inside, the flat sweeping into her. My lips ride hers, grinding us together.

Juniper moans, both of her hands now clinging to the nape of my neck. She takes my kiss the way she takes my body—wholly, hotly. Always a slow buildup before we hit the ground running. After that, no limits.

Like soulmates if not fated mates.

Like wild things and deliberate creatures.

Like a human and Fae. Like hunters.

I lick past the seam of Juniper's mouth, her lips yielding under mine.

My tongue skims hers, every flick urging another moan from her lungs. Our bodies fit and rock, the curves of her ass gyrating with my dick.

A feral sound rumbles from my chest. I tear my mouth from hers, and it takes Juniper's eyes a moment to flutter open.

Once they do, I bite her lower lip, then brush them with my own. "Watch," I mutter.

Her head swings toward the glass, where our reflections stand. Our chests siphon for breath, and a layer of sweat shimmers down her body. Her shirt hangs open, but I don't take it off.

Instead, she holds onto my nape. We stare as my knuckles track down over one lush breast, across her pert nipple, then down to her navel. Her thighs spread on reflex as my fingers sink between them and comb through the hair covering her pussy.

A whimper breaks from her mouth, but she keeps looking, keeps watching with me. My own mouth unhinges as I brace my palm over the crease of her body. Instantly, heat and arousal drips from the cleft, damn near scrambling my brain.

"Shit, Juniper," I mumble.

She makes another pained noise. "Puck. Right there."

"Where, luv?" My wrist presses into her clit. "There?"

"Yes. More. I need—"

"Shhh," I coax.

But she does the opposite, crying out as my palm cups her cunt and begins to rub. I contract my hand, curling my fingers and stroking her, petting her while she rolls her hips. I massage her folds while our gazes stay linked, our mouths hanging open and throwing loud noises into the room.

My thumb finds that kernel of nerves and begins a steady caress over the distended flesh. I etch that peak, tracing around its swollen shape, then patting it until she's sobbing with need and soaking my fingers.

I seethe with approval. All the while, we stare, our pupils blazing on each other.

The space between her brows crimps, the spectacles shifting with the movement. A muscle rams into my jaw. My thumb presses harder into her clit, rolling that sensitive little peg with my digit.

She goes with it, moaning out loud with me. And when that's too much and too little, I swirl her wetness around the oval opening, spreading it. Then I slip my hand forward and sink two fingers into her pussy.

My growl hits the ceiling, and Juniper cries out. Her walls cinch around me, sucking me in. It scorches as I probe my digits higher, thrusting nice and slow and long.

Juniper keens, jutting her waist on top of my hand.

"That's right," I encourage her. "Ride them."

She nods, straddles my fingers, and whisks her hips, meeting the steady pitch of my wrist. My free thumb flits against her clit, everything moving in sync.

But there's more. I see it in Juniper's likeness while she chases the pleasure, the hunger so potent, it makes the head of my cock bulge.

Somehow, I manage to utter her name. And she knows to let go of my nape, reach behind, and shove down the front of my pants. I manage the rest, stomping them to the ground.

I see Juniper's eyes rove over my naked abdomen and glimpse the thick, ruddy crown of my cock. We move quickly. She returns her gaze to me in the window, and I grasp one hip, fixing her in place.

But instead of gliding my fingers out of her and entering from behind, I pivot my hips, thrusting my cock against the folds of her ass. The impact shoves my fingers deeper into her.

A startled moan cracks from Juniper's mouth at the sensation.

A smirk coils across my face. This is yet another new one for us.

I do it again, rocking my hips forward, the motion propelling my fingers higher, deeper still. Like this, I maintain a sinuous pace. I pump my cock from behind, which pumps my hand up Juniper's cunt from the front, which draws gravelly noises from her lungs.

"Ah," Juniper gasps. "That's...oh, Fables."

"Open your thighs more, luv," I instruct. "And brace the window."

She flattens her palms against the glass and broadens her stance, thighs splayed wide. I put my whole body into it. My hips siphon, working my cock against her, the force throwing my fingers in and out of her.

My chin lands on her shoulder, and her temple sweats against my jaw, and we watch, and watch, and watch. My hips unleash, charging forth. The brunt of my dick causes my fingers to strike through her slick grip.

The pace is relentless. Juniper snaps her hips into my hand, her wetness leaking all over me. With each piston, the friction builds from my balls to the base of my cock, and straight up to the head.

I fuck her like this, my waist hauling forward, the momentum driving my fingers higher, deeper, harder. Fractured moans peal from my woman's lips. Flames from the fireplace hurl light through the space, but the whole place could burn to the fucking ground, and I don't think we'd stop, can't stop, won't ever stop.

Juniper's soaked walls tense. A plaintive noise spills from her tongue, and I want my cock in her so badly, I might scream.

But not yet, because I'm going to make her come about six or seven times tonight. This is only the first.

I reel my hips, breaking into quick, shallow thrusts. My fingers are dripping from her pleasure. They ply her with every pass, curling into her slot, drenching her.

She shouts, whisks her body into me, knowing I need it, too. I'll always need it from her.

We ride each other. She launches backward and I cast forward, our bodies colliding, slamming together from both ends. Juniper's hands fly from the window and rip through my hair while she slings her cunt atop my fingers and punches her ass into my dick.

"Puck," she begs. "Come for me, Puck."

Oh, fucking hell. She didn't.

"Come on," she entreats, swiping her tongue under my jaw. "Please. For me."

But yes, she did.

Stamina renewed, I growl and swing my hips against her. The force plows my fingers into her so deeply that she moans, and moans, and fucking moans.

The tension ratchets up, then springs apart. It hits us at the same time. Juniper gives a hard, prolonged cry, the walls of her pussy quaking around my knuckles.

I bellow my pleasure, the release spasming through my cock. Warm fluid surges from the slit. Swearing to Fables, I try to cup my hands over it—something a satyr usually wouldn't do—but Juniper shakes her head and presses herself in, letting my fluid permeate the tail of her shirt.

We roll together, riding out the aftershocks. My chest pounds for air, my breathing torn like a sheet. Juniper sighs, her fingers doing that thing they do after sex, brushing through my scalp.

And when it's over, we sure as hell don't slump.

Not us. Not this time.

We move in unison. Only then do our eyes quit the window.

My fingers slip out of Juniper, and she whirls just as I hoist her against me. My mouth crushes with hers. Our tongues writhe as I push the gaping tunic off her shoulders, promising myself to wash it later.

The fabric puddles on the floor. I palm Juniper's thighs and heft my woman off the ground. Kissing her senseless, I carry her across the living room and mount the stairs.

She laughs into my mouth. I let out a half-snarl, half-chuckle.

The library I'd built for her is on a new level above our bedroom loft, an addition I'd erected around the oak's central trunk. I take the steps three at a time, stride into her sanctuary with its desk, bookshelves, and oversized reading chairs. I'd once found Juniper asleep in one of the seats and watched her for an hour before scooping her up and taking her to bed.

Neat stacks of notebooks and quills cover the desk. I wouldn't dare mess with her arrangement without permission, so I pause beside the furnishing and lift my brows. "May I?"

Juniper nods vehemently, excitement inflating her pupils. "Yes."

And with a single swipe, I launch my arm across the tabletop. The writing instruments and notebooks clatter to the floor.

Depositing her on the desk, I unfurl my woman across the surface and spread her limbs. Leaning over her, I bracket my palms on either side of her waist. "Be a good pupil and stay down for me."

"Give me a reason to," she taunts.

My mouth twitches. Now we're talking.

Never underestimate the kinks of a satyr. Without looking away, I curl my fingers into my palm, beckoning the earth. The central oak trunk vibrates, a lone branch cracking from the column and stretching like an arm, which splits into four.

Juniper gasps as the boughs catch her wrists and ankles, spooling around them and pinning her. The wonderful thing about Faeries is, we excel at interpreting meanings in rather creative ways. So if she wanted a reason to stay put, I've just given her one.

With her naked and splayed in the middle of her domain, where books loom around us and her stationary materials litter the floor, it's a fetching sight. Her tidy, orderly world has been upended, disrupted by yours truly.

Yet those pupils expand, a thrill flashing through them. With me, she doesn't mind the clutter. I'm allowed to make a mess of her, a privilege I take seriously.

Her neck bobs, heart thumping there. As for her smart little pussy, its flushed and slick from the last orgasm.

Juniper's pleasure is my command. The branches are only secure enough to position her, without being too constrictive. Moreover, she knows that she needs only to speak the words, and I'll release her.

Instead, nothing but trust and rapture stare back at me.

I kiss her lips once, but a whine peels from her mouth as I pull away and straighten. Standing before the desk, I grab her hips and draw Juniper to the edge, pitching her knees high. The branches encircling her wrists stretch like elastic, and her arms lengthen overhead.

Molten heat pools in her cunt. My cock jumps, the engorged head darkening, and my balls hang heavy with need.

I poise the crown at her slit, palm her waist, and slip inside her with excruciating slowness. Juniper's breath hitches again, like it did when we started this beautiful shit. Love and desire wrap around her features, just the way I like it.

Her fingers bend inward, hands fisting the branches. I can't tell if she's suspending herself for something harder and deeper, or if she's clinging to the boughs for composure.

Either way, we'll find out.

I withdraw my hips in one prolonged movement, patiently exiting her to the roof of my dick, then sinking in once more. Juniper's mouth hangs ajar, and her toes curl. With a wily grin, I tug my cock from her again before gliding in between her drenched folds.

Not in a hurry, I roll my hips, her pussy catching every leisurely thrust. The moment she whimpers, my lips part on a silent groan. Fables, when she makes that sound.

Her knees quiver, and her heels press into the desk. She groans and wiggles her hips, lifting them to meet me halfway. It's all she can do while strung up.

We pant into it, our hips bumping lightly. Her cunt seals around my cock, wetting it to the base, and dammit, it's the stuff of fantasies.

I ease in and out of her at a gradual pace, making it last and last and last. Juniper's moans narrow to cries. I'm right there with her, growling low in my throat.

The friction and momentum are a torment. Even so, I keep it up, keep going like this. And it's like making love and fucking all at once.

Anguished pants fill the library. The desk rocks under us.

I bow over Juniper and clasp her fingers while probing my cock into her. My ass contracts between her bare thighs. I groan in tempo to our waists, and she cries out, our breaths colliding.

My pecs brush her tits, rubbing gently. The head of my cock glides between her walls while she soaks me in her arousal. Sex with Juniper has always been elemental, heightening every sensation beyond what I'd thought possible.

I can last for as long as we want. If she asked, I would do this forever.

Tonight, I'll pretend it's an option. I'll make her feel like nothing else exists, that we have all the time in the world.

That's why I go even deeper. Juniper bows off the desk, her eyes squinting shut and her cunt flexing around me. I slant my cock against a spot that makes her eyelids flutter and then do it again, and again, and again. With every steady beat, I ply that knot of pleasure, the crown hitting it carefully, deliberately.

Juniper's moans escalate. Her fingers squeeze mine, so I brush my mouth against the knuckles to relax them.

When her grip unravels, I hoist myself up and return to standing. I sling my hips back and forth, riding her moans, claiming each of them.

Her knees clamp my sides. Her nipples point to the ceiling, breasts jolting softly. She rounds her waist with mine, taking me in.

My ragged growls scrape through the room. I cup her ass and pump us to the brink, until warmth climbs up my shaft, and my bones tense. I may have the branches fastening her to the desk, but she has me just as pinned to her.

Juniper yanks on the boughs. Then her eyes blast open, her pussy convulses and melts onto me, and she comes with a long cry.

While it happens, Juniper watches me unleash with her. I pitch my cock with short jabs of my waist, then pause and hurl my head back as liquid heat gushes from my crown. A roar vaults up my throat and grinds from my mouth.

As it does, the branches unfurl from Juniper. They shrink and vanish back into the oak tree, leaving not so much as a crevice in its wake.

With a satisfied sigh, Juniper rises to catch my mouth with hers, swallowing the sounds rushing from my lungs. I smirk against her lips, then inch back to plant kisses up and down her throat, snarling and nipping her every so often until she chuckles.

After that, we progress to the nearest reading chair.

15

While prowling through The Gang of Elks, I take stock of the forest's state. Fir needles poke the night air, though a bunch of leaves and pine-cones have fallen, crunching into flakes under my hooves. It happens for several months every year, but not this early, and not this amount.

I squat on my haunches, pluck one of the stalks off the ground, and twirl it between my fingers. In other areas, broken branches lack green rings inside the bark's flesh, the contrary brownness a sign the trees are dying.

At this rate, it feels as though the woodland is being held up by sticks.

"Fuck," I mutter, chucking the needle leaf. Worse, the soil is infertile in this area, like it was near our cabin when our band had returned from The Horizon.

Tinder's reports have been yielding shitty news. He's been scouting The Wicked Pines and The Swarm of Rats, both of which remain under my rule.

Cypress says neutral ground in The Heart of Willows is faring well. But as for the rest of this wilderness, who the hell knows? Most of the woodland has been claimed by our enemies—from The Roots That Take and extending all the way to The Skulk of Foxes and down to The Bonfire Glade and The Seeds that Give, plus everything south of where I'm stand-ing. That arrangement has chopped our fellowship's turf into two pieces, blocking off our travel routes and forcing us to manifest, thus draining allied stamina on a regular basis.

As a ruler, I should have access to every corner of this land.

As a traitor, that's not the case anymore.

Still, there are obvious signs. Bears and badgers are roaming through this area. Residents of The Skulk of Foxes are migrating to Cypress's home, searching for new dens because the old ones are caving in on themselves, for no elemental reason. That's according to the foxes who've been willing to communicate as much to the centaurs.

My fingers spear through my hair. I set my free hand on the trunk of the evergreen beside me and close my eyes. "Talk to me," I whisper.

The trunk's coarse hide vibrates with life from within, humming like the inside of my cello. But the sound is feeble, its bark parched. I can't hear a damn thing. Not a single crumb of information broadcasts from the tree, which would take energy it doesn't have.

It's preserving itself.

A grisly pang squeezes my chest. The trees in this wild are my teachers, my superiors, and my friends. And they're fading.

My eyes clench tightly, then flip open with a vengeance. Everything went slowly those first years, but now it's speeding up.

What will be left by the thirteenth year? Or will this just be a desolate wasteland, the last green stem straining for candlelight and starlight that aren't there, that burned off before then?

Juniper. Our kid.

Sylvan. My brothers. Their women.

This land. The fauna.

Everything.

"Fuck that," I hiss.

I clutch the fir tree, infusing whatever strength I can, then rise. Minutes later, I manifest back to The Herd of Deer and head straight for the glade with its ancient oak.

The sound of her voice dissolves the dread gnawing through my bones. Pushing through the thicket, I lean against an oak, the corner of my mouth ticking up.

Juniper sits on a stump with a notebook open on her lap and those sexy lenses topping her nose. Combine that with the studious blouse, cinched vest, ankle-length skirt, and a tendency to fire a weapon, and I've found me an academic who's as intelligent as she is deadly.

A gaggle of Fae striplings squat on the grass, encircling her as she reads a story about a water dragon who swims through raging oceans. Pint-sized nymphs, dryads, and leprechauns listen avidly, their legs crossed and their eyes wide. Several brownies observe from their perch in the branches. And to my surprise, a runty centaur sits among the group, the equine's short limbs curled to the side.

It's a filly with a chartreuse tail. I recognize this one, having played with her once during Juniper's game.

Although these are the striplings of allied Faeries, does Cypress know one of his own is here? His kin are usually more sequestered than this.

"And the dragon said—" Juniper pauses for effect, *"'—I shall protect what I don't yet know, for therein lives my strongest magic.' With that, she dove into the depths and saved the drowning mortal."*

The little Faeries gasp. They explode with questions as Juniper closes the notebook.

She places a finger to her lips, silencing them. "Remember what I said the last time?"

"Wait for your turn, and the answer will be greater," a lanky faun with horn stumps recites.

I raise my eyebrows. Impressive, considering Faeries aren't the disciplined types.

My eyes click to the silhouettes skulking between the trees, the figures auditing Juniper's performance without showing themselves. They always do this. It had taken Juniper's tenacity and my roguish, ruling grin to sway our allies into letting her read to their wards.

Although woodland Faeries don't have their own offspring, elders volunteer to guide the runts until they come of age, the way guardians of nature would. And while these subjects may still follow me, they don't entirely trust Juniper or her sisters. It's not a transformation that'll happen overnight. Which is why they stay on the sidelines, making sure the striplings aren't being brainwashed.

Reclusive behavior is in a Solitary's blood, apart from the sacrificial games and training for this battle. But I've also got a feeling Juniper's scheduled readings have the elders hooked. Why else would they be still as stones whenever she narrates from the pages? My ears and eyes sure as shit can tell the difference between restlessness and idleness.

Pride loosens the kinks in my muscles.

Juniper's attention roams, then lands on me. Behind the spectacles, her eyes spark like embers. It's a cheerful look that jumpstarts a fresh bout of lust.

When she gains her feet, the runts scatter to their reclusive guardians, though not before casting me awed glances. I screw up my eyes and features, making them guffaw as they leave.

Juniper busies herself, removing her spectacles and polishing them, then packing them into a hardwood case. The young centaur is the last to quit the area. She rises to her hooves and lingers, gazing at Juniper with fascinated curiosity before noticing me.

The filly's eyes widen with guilt. She sighs and canters in my direction.

"My, my, my," I remark while crossing my arms.

"Don't tell," she begs, her head cranking up to mine.

"I take it Cypress didn't give permission?"

"He likes your mate as much as he likes you, but he doesn't want me traveling here alone. I was supposed to ask first and secure an escort." The filly turns up her chin, just like someone else I know. "But I don't need a fucking filly-sitter."

"The mouth on you," I mock-lecture.

"I'm eight-hundred," she defends, her rear hooves kicking up dirt and her tailing swatting about. "I can manifest this far on my own, and I met your mate long before these other saplings did, back when she was hiding in The Heart of Willows. She was nice and interesting and mortal, and I just...now I want to know more.

"She tells stories about Faeries and humans, and I like them. I want to learn about her people. Are you going to tell?"

"Meh." I shrug. "Cypress is my friend, not my conscience." I bend forward and tap her nose. "It's our secret, but next time? Ask. Make him feel important. He likes that."

Her posture straightens, confidence bolstered. "It's a deal, sire."

"Ah, ah, ah. A vow, not a deal."

She grins cheekily and springs into a gallop. Her small form vanishes before she reaches the trees.

"You were good with her," that smoky voice observes.

I twist my head and find those scholastic eyes staring back, brightening the forest from two feet away. Juniper's got the notebook under her arm, and she's flushed from reading.

I slouch like a delinquent. Basically, like a satyr. "I've had practice with Tinder."

"He looks up to you, too."

"Something like that. You seemed mighty rested." I take the notebook and wag it like a tail. "It looks as if you actually slept."

Juniper's cheeks mottle, despite the censorious glare she darts at me. She's private, her audience has barely left the premises, and I'd fucked her multiple times yesterday. After driving my fingers into her, then giving her that shattering climax on the desk, I carried Juniper to one of the reading chairs, knelt at her feet and sank my tongue between her legs. Even an insatiable faun wouldn't be walking upright after all the things I'd done to corrupt this human.

Juniper grabs the notebook, but the flirt in me doesn't let go. We fall into a gentle tug-of-war until her lips fold to keep from chuckling.

I finally let go and strap my arms around her. "Get over here," I groan.

She melts into my kiss, the force of it prying her lips open. My tongue strokes deeply, coaxing a moan from her throat.

Sadly, Juniper pulls away too fast and fondles my vest collar. "Papa should know. I want to tell him."

I stiffen. Her father is one of the main reasons she reads to the Faeries in the first place. She has memories of him doing the same thing with her, Lark, and Cove.

My woman had wanted to pass that on, to give the striplings an escape, something to enjoy despite everything that's happening around us. Once a week, they gather to hear the stories Juniper's begun scribbling in her notebook. She'd started right after our first night in the cabin.

Of course, she wants to see her father more than ever, to tell him in person about the wee sapling. Except there's a problem, which I don't need to rehash.

"I'm sorry, luv," I murmur.

Juniper nods, ever the pragmatic of her sisters. They had been planning to see their father, to sneak into their world and reunite with him in secret. She'd also wanted me to meet the man who raised her.

Instead, all kinds of shit has gone down since then, from The Deep's flood to the raven attack, to the point where it's become too dangerous to leave Faerie. With the Solitaries on our asses, we can't afford to gallivant into yet another enemy territory. That'll just compile our problems—and our opponents.

And now that Juniper's pregnant, any risk has become a dealbreaker.

Lastly, traveling to Juniper's father could mark him as another vulnerability, as a target or bait to be used against us.

"You can send him a letter," I suggest.

Juniper's head flips up, longing etched in her voice. "I was thinking the same thing."

"Then do it. Write one with your sisters."

"But we have to be cautious about delivering it. After Lark won her game and returned to Papa, her stay didn't last. She was there and gone again. Nothing could be gained from lying outright about her reasons for leaving home willingly, since the townsfolk would only see through that. Having Papa tell them she'd left to be close to me and Cove made sense at the time."

I know all this. It was a motivation the family believed everyone would understand. It was also the truth, aside from Lark's desire to be with Cerulean.

"What are you getting at?" I ask.

Juniper frowns, the cogs and wheels turning. "But what if knowing she'd gone back to be near her sisters eventually inflamed the villagers? What if our captivity here triggered their anger, not only on our behalf but humanity's? What if it created another incentive to rage about your kind? And what if that drove them to watch the house?"

My eyebrows knit. "You think spies are keeping tabs on your father."

"I think nosy people are keeping him in their sights. By now, why wouldn't they? If that's true, how do we send a message and guarantee it won't be witnessed or intercepted? If they're not embittered about us being taken by the Fae, it's still plausible they'll be sniffing around to see if we turn up at the house again.

"If they see Papa receive tidings in any form deemed strange, or if they manage to steal the letter without him knowing, they could find out what's happening here. They won't believe we're still on their side. They'll conclude we've turned on our people, been seduced by Faeries. And that could endanger Papa." She rocks on her heels. "You think I'm overanalyzing things."

"I think you're worried," I tell her. "Though yes, you tend to overcomplicate, for good reasons and with good instincts. Except you once told me how you and your sisters were outcasts there. That alone provokes me to do serious damage to your neighbors."

"It doesn't matter if we were outcasts. The people of Reverie Hollow don't need to fret about our wellbeing, as if we're family. They only need an excuse to riot."

I cup her face. "Remember being called to Faerie in the first place?"

Juniper gives a start. Her forehead wrinkles with the realization that she hadn't examined this obstacle from all angles. "I'd forgotten."

Sylvan had been glamoured while delivering Juniper the summons from me. No one in her world would have seen the deer as anything other than a mortal animal. In which case, sending one of the fauna to transport this message won't be a problem.

"The logistics seem obvious now," Juniper sighs. "I should have made that connection."

"We've had more than usual on our minds. But we'll make sure the letter gets to your father," I say. "Tímien is the quickest traveler and the hardest to spot. He can carry the message undetected."

Relief smooths out the trenches across Juniper's forehead, but her nod is cut off by a gasp. She jerks forward, her hand falling to her stomach. "Oh!"

I encase her in my arms, keeping her balanced. "Another jolt?"

"It was just stronger than expected. It's never been that intense before."

"Guess our wee sapling is becoming as restless as you."

She forces out a chuckle. "Probably."

I'll see if Cypress can give her something for that, so she's comfortable. Which reminds me, we need to tell him soon. That centaur's an unflappable fucker, but it'll wound him if he finds out secondhand.

Then something else drops into my head like a rock, knocking the oblivious right out of me. "Oh, shit." I glance at Juniper. "You think this is the answer?"

Juniper blinks, taking a second to understand. "To the Fable's hidden message?"

"We talked about the second way being something older than sacrifice, something that's also the opposite of taking life. We talked about unity ticking both boxes. Combine a human and Fae with the rarity of a kid, and there's our method of unity."

"Giving life instead of taking it."

"Hell, yes."

"But this land would be restored by now. I've been pregnant long enough for that to happen. Instead—" she gestures to the sagging oak branches, dry earth, and waning glow of the overhead candles, "the environment keeps wilting."

"Not unless our kid actually has to be born," I point out.

We stare at one another, optimistic. I can taste the flavor of hope so potently, it almost makes me tipsy.

But once I'm nearly there, doubts crawl in. Then Juniper's face cinches, and she shakes her head.

"Too simple," we say at the same time.

Not easy to conceive, but too simple when we consider the Fable's lines.

Therefore, follow your Fables, heed your neighbors, and look closer.

"Heed your neighbors," Juniper contemplates. "And look closer."

"Doesn't fit," I conclude.

"I just don't see the connection between heeding our neighbors, looking closer, and a making a child. It doesn't align in a logical way. No, the second way is something else, some other form of unity."

Fuck. She's making the Scholar Face. Sexy as it is, my woman's also unfortunately correct.

She rubs one of my earrings between her fingers. "We should discuss it with the others, get everyone's opinion, just in case."

"Go through the motions," I agree. "Sounds right."

I drag my arms from around her and stride to one of the oaks. A message to our clan should go through the roots without a hitch. These trees are still hearty enough for that.

My palm clamps onto the trunk, and my back faces Juniper while I speak. "I've got to hand it to those old scribes," I say. "If they wrote a Fable none of us can decode, they were pretty skilled at—"

But I smell it before I hear her cry out. The briny reek of blood clots the air, thick and free-flowing to my ears.

I whip around just as my woman collapses to her knees, red pooling like a river between her legs and a scream ripping from her lungs.

16

I see her, blood pouring from her body. I see my woman, clutching her womb and howling on the ground. I see my unfated mate, my steadfast equal, my willful love in agony.

Her name tears from my lungs as I pound across the dirt. My hooves slam against the earth. I crash to the forest floor beside her, my knees stamping into the grass and cracking open an acorn shell.

"Puck," she shrieks, reaching for me. "Puck, I can't...I can't...make it stop!"

"Luv," I rasp. "Hold on. I've got you."

Another bellow rips from her mouth as I scoop Juniper into my arms, lurch upright, and haul ass through the woodland. I smash through bristling thickets and bushels of moss, and jet around the oaks. Dried chips of mulch crack under my weight. My arm whips out to smack a low branch out of the way, the limb snapping in half and splitting from the tree trunk.

Juniper's blood seeps into my vest and races down my arms. Her cries thin out and then fade altogether as her head slumps against my chest.

"Juniper," I heave, alternating between peering at her and checking my route. "Juniper, no no no no no. Stay with me, luv. Stay awake."

She mumbles, "Hurts," before her eyes flutter shut.

Terror ices my veins, propelling me faster, though it's not fast enough. It'll never be fast enough. I can't fucking manifest with her. And I can't stop to send a message, but even with my speed, I won't make it quickly.

My hooves skitter beside a trunk, which I grasp, my fingers digging into the bark. I'm shaking so badly, my grip is seconds away from bending the tree.

I close my eyes and shove a message down through the roots, fear tracking through my spine. Releasing the tree, I keep running. Greens, browns, and golds blur past my vision, and Juniper's featherweight breath skates across my collarbones.

Moments later, the call is answered. A russet figure gallops into my path and stops, shamrocks trembling from its antlers. Clouds of air puff from the deer's snout as her black eyes train on me, then seize on Juniper. Alarm flashes through my companion's pupils as I heft off the ground and land on her back.

She's spearing through the wilderness before I'm fully settled. Sylvan bounds over a ravine and shoots forward. The instant we clear denser terrain and emerge into open forest, her form shifts and expands to double her size.

Faeries have the power of speed, unmatched only by certain fauna. My friend is one of them. Even without having to shift sizes, Sylvan usually outpaces me.

With her limbs extended, she vaults across The Herd of Deer and heads northwest, knowing where we need to go.

The cabin would be swifter, likely safer. The problem is, it's even likelier that whatever Juniper needs, we won't have it stored at home. My woman had made sure we had a cache of basic remedies for battle wounds and mortal diseases, but I'm not about to risk going there and realizing nothing at the cabin will work for her.

And I have no fucking clue what's wrong with her! Only two other beings might know how to help Juniper, and one of them is closer than the other.

Sylvan sprints across the wild, crossing through territories that whirl past us. Time lags and accelerates in tandem, but Sylvan is wise enough to avoid turfs now polluted by our enemies. That makes detours essential, yet she reaches the place we need to go in half the time it would have taken me.

We dart through a filmy, shimmering wall and pass into a valley clustered with titanic, leaf-woven pavilions and yurts. Emerald willow trees shudder in the breeze. Overhead, a few constellations are mobile, zipping through the sky.

Centaurs emerge from different corners, murmuring to one another when they see us. The small filly from yesterday trots into the scene, her gaze worried as she takes in the grisly sight.

The deer and I cut across the candlelit stone paths to a yurt the size of a villa. As Sylvan halts in front of the entrance, Cypress bursts through the willow vine flaps. His hooves stomp the grass, his horse tail swats the air, and his long hair falls from the tether at his nape.

My friend's eyes narrow on me with surprise, then expand on Juniper, limp and soaked in red. Horror warps his dark features. "Bring her inside," he hastens, whisking the foliage panels open.

I jump off Sylvan's back and bolt through the entrance. The deer's form shrinks before skittering inside after me.

The walls are made of additional threaded vines, floor pillows occupy Cypress's tent, and a fire burns in the center. The kindling spits embers like flecks of lava. Sylvan paces left and right as I kneel and settle Juniper onto the cushions. My palms clamp over her face, but that smears blood on her cheeks.

With quaking fingers, I yank on her vest and blouse, shredding the garments open. An embroidered band harnesses her breasts, and I don't see any gashes below her navel. But as expected, when I ruck up her skirt, it's a different story. Blood stains the matching drawers that cling to her hips and waist.

My hiss fractures in half. "Juniper…"

"What happened?" Cypress asks while tossing me a cloth.

I catch it in one hand, then rattle off the details while peeling Juniper's clothes from her body. Cypress traces her flushed skin while I clean the blood and swaddle her in a blanket.

The centaur works rapidly, pouring something from a miniature carafe down Juniper's throat, which we get her to swallow while she's half-conscious. Silvery fluid dribbles from the remains down her chin, and I swipe it with a fresh cloth. The dose seems to work against the pain, because her breathing evens out, and the bleeding stops. But her flesh is hot, and her lips are ashen.

Sylvan lowers herself next to Juniper. The doe curls close enough for my woman to nestle in.

As Juniper rests, Cypress pulls back, gazing at her in confusion. "The sedative will make her comfortable for the time being. For a mortal, it will suffice temporarily, but it is no better than a tonic to a Fae, and it is no solution." He shakes his head. "I know little of human ailments, so I cannot fathom this one, nor decipher how to remedy it. Though, it seems to be rooted in her womb, which does not make se—"

"She's pregnant," I tell him, bunching Juniper's hands in mine.

Cypress's head swings my way, his features arrested in shock. Briefly, something else crosses my friend's face—something as fragile as glass, but it's gone too quickly to consider it more than a figment of my frenzied mind.

"How is that possible?" he questions.

"The Seeds that Give," I say. "It happened there, on the night of Middle Moon." I latch onto his gaze, the dregs of panic filling my mouth. "I can't lose them, Cypress. I can't do it."

He opens his mouth to speak when a faint voice gusts between us. "Puck."

My attention snaps to Juniper, those green eyes dull and hooded as they glimpse me. Relief floods my stomach. I hunch over, kiss the space between her brows, and stroke her hair.

"Hey there," I whisper.

Her gaze clings to mine, then travels across the tent to find the centaur and deer hunkered around us. Her words are sluggish, as if she's speaking around a mouthful of gauze. "Cypress…Sylvan…where…"

"The Heart of Willows," I answer. "You scared the shit out of us."

"Why? What did I do?"

"Later. You need rest and—"

"My spectacles. My journal."

The lenses and notebook had slipped from her grasp when she collapsed, and I'd left them in the forest. I'm about to promise I'll get them for her when my brothers and Juniper's sisters race into the tent. I can only guess Tímien and the nightingale flew them here. Cove has Juniper's notebook clutched to her chest, and Lark's got the spectacles.

"Juniper," Lark screeches.

"Dear Fables," Cove exhales as she and Lark huddle around her.

Cerulean and Elixir idle in the periphery, with Cypress clomping backward to join them. My winged sibling retracts his plumes and nods at me. "My father was circling the valley and heard her scream. By the time we reached the glade and saw the blood, you were gone. We checked the cabin first, but it was clear where you had gone."

Cerulean casts Juniper a concerned look. Elixir furrows his black brows as he listens to the commotion and inhales the residue of blood.

Only his presence would get me to budge from my woman's side. If Cypress can't say what's wrong, Elixir's the only other option.

I squeeze Juniper's hands, then release her and launch off the ground. Stalking his way, I mutter under my breath, "Cure her."

Elixir's gaze strays toward me, a mind-blowing gleam of empathy reflected there, which has less to do with visceral reflexes and everything to do with the human he loves, how she's influenced him. "If I can, I shall. But my brews are not fully restored."

"Your mixtures only poison or cure, right? Then cure her. Whatever it takes." My words grow hoarse. "Please."

"You do not need to ask."

Elixir places a hand on my shoulder, then his attention seeks out Cove. He follows the sound of her intakes, snaking past me and lowering himself on his haunches before the small group. My brother's black mane falls over his shoulders, and his scales ripple with light as he inclines his head to Juniper. "May I?"

Lucidity clears the fog from Juniper's features—all but her irises, which have lost their luster. She's fully conscious now, though wan and beading with sweat. She leans up on her elbows, her voice threadbare. "What's wrong? What is it?"

"We don't know yet," I say, striding to her and sinking to the ground.

"I need room," Elixir instructs.

Cove ushers Lark from their sister, but I'm not moving. Neither does Elixir ask me to as he braces his hands on Juniper's stomach, feeling her contours through the blanket. The bronze caps on his fingers twitch, and he closes his eyes.

Juniper's hand steals out for mine, her fingers clammy and digging into my palm. Our pulses smash together. I know her fear like she knows my own, because it's the same one.

Everyone in the room goes still, apart from Sylvan bristling her tail in agitation. Elixir's eyelids wince, then flare open. Gold floods the room, but the sheen isn't blinding. It's aware—and disturbed.

If my brother's one thing, it's direct. "Your child," he says to Juniper, and it's the first time I've ever heard him sound this ominous. "It's depleting your strength."

"What does that mean?" Cove asks, her lisp thickening.

"How the hell can that be happening?" Lark demands.

Juniper's face pinches with dread. "It means the child is too powerful for me."

"Because she's human," I grate out.

Elixir nods. "The embryo is likely divided, equally mortal and immortal. But its form is robust, as powerful as any Fae. So when I listen to your body, the flow of your blood and the tempo of your heart, I hear them faltering. This wasn't the case when I first detected your condition. The change must be new."

"Meaning?" Cerulean insists from beside Lark.

Juniper glances at me. "Meaning I'm not...I won't be able to..."

She won't be able to carry the kid. Not through to the end. They're linked, so it's not a question of one or the other.

If she dies, they both die.

Every ounce of blood inside me drops to my limbs. Just last night, she'd been petrified of not being able to protect our kid from this world. Not once had we considered we'd have to protect them from Juniper as well, from her inability to bear their power.

Timbers crackle, sparks dashing from the fire. Outside, the willows shiver throughout The Heart of Willows. The ambience should be a comfort in neutral territory, but right now, it reminds me of a reptilian shudder, like a snake hissing.

"Elixir." My head clicks over to him. "Tell me you have something for this."

But he makes no reply. Instead, his metallic orbs dim.

"Cypress?" I press, swerving to my friend.

The centaur's face twists in misery. "Such a restorative is unheard of..."
But then his expression transforms, the pleats flattening. "Wait. Elixir, if
there were indeed an ingredient that could aid Juniper, would you be able
to distill its properties?"

Elixir considers the question. "My reserves are limited. Chances are
high, it would need to be the sole ingredient necessary."

"It would be."

"In that case, yes."

"Then there might be a way."

Everyone veers toward Cypress as he explains, "There is a plant that
may help Juniper. Its extract could provide her with the fortitude to bear
the infant safely. Moreover, it would create a protective coating around
the womb, like a wall of muscle. If anything happened to Juniper from
then on, this would barricade the embryo from harm and enable us to
extract it, then plant it in The Seeds that Give. No matter what, that would
ensure its survival."

"Like a backup," Juniper interprets.

"You won't need a backup because I'll kill anyone who tries to get
near you," I tell her.

Cypress flattens his palm in a mollifying gesture. "In any case, this
plant will help, Fables willing." But he wavers and glances at Elixir. "It is
a botanical magnifier."

My brother's face ticks, as if debating Cypress's meaning. But a second later, Elixir's eyes radiate in understanding. "Magnifier," he repeats,
the word heavy on his tongue.

My best friend nods. "The very one."

Cerulean frowns. "Might you two be forthright to the rest of us?"

"I second that," Lark says. "For the record, I'm no fan of cryptic information. We've been getting enough of that from these Fables."

"Out with it," I say.

A muscle leaps in Elixir's temple, his scales glinting. "I am familiar
with the ingredient. It once graced the tables in my brewing den before
the flood."

Cypress rubs the bridge between his eyebrows. "It is the Evermore
Blossom."

This news cleaves through the room like an arrow.

I bow my head, a slew of curses stacking on my lips. Unfortunately, neither my best friend, nor my brother are fucking with us. They'd be the last ones in this wild to try.

The Evermore Blossom.

The flower Scorpio used on the raven. The flower that can't be destroyed for shit, can't be replanted anywhere else, and can only be found in one place.

By magnifier, Cypress and Elixir had meant enhancement. The extract would intensify Juniper's strength, reinforce her while carrying our kid.

It would save hers and our kid's lives.

Problem is, there's only one Evermore Blossom in existence. And it's located just south of The Seeds that Give, right in the crotch of enemy terrain.

My gaze stalls on Juniper, whose grave expression rearranges itself, resolve folding across her features like a shield. "I'll go."

"Not a chance," I snap.

"I'm a huntress. I'm smarter than you."

"I can't agree more, but while you'd make the most formidable companion under any other circumstances, you can't take that gamble."

I wait, knowing she's already aware of this. It's a dangerous journey, and Juniper's too feeble. Her chest sinks, hating the notion that she can't be of use, can't contribute to her own safety.

But finally, she grabs her spectacles. "Well. If can't exercise my hunting skills, I can still exercise my mind."

Except when my woman shifts, she notices her bare shoulders and legs sticking out of the blanket. In an extremely delayed reaction, her eyes bloat. "Where are my clothes?"

I manifest to the cabin, where I collect enough fresh clothes and research materials for her, including the original Book of Fables and plenty of parchment. Since the group had already brought Juniper's notebook, she'll have enough to keep her occupied.

By the time I return to The Heart of Willows, Sylvan has retreated outdoors to find a stream. Our band convenes in the tent to make plans.

Juniper and I tell everyone about the fleeting speculation that her pregnancy could be the answer—the key to restoring our fauna, our world, and our existence. It's a legit theory. But like we'd already realized, it doesn't match the Fable's content, doesn't work with the tips we've been given. After deliberating, everyone agrees.

Although Juniper grunts about not wanting people to fuss, Elixir and Cove will stay with her, for curing and nurturing reasons. We need the one who's able to brew the remedy to stick close. And we need the one who's capable of keeping her sister calm to camp here as well.

As an extra precaution, the community of centaurs will minister to Juniper, if any extra healing arts become essential. Cloistered in this neutral landscape, everyone will be safe.

Cypress volunteers to go with me. Lark and Cerulean are right behind him, one eager to act for her sister, the other unwilling to let his mate go anywhere without him.

Hours pass quickly. Dawn bleeds through the tent and gilds the space.

When we're done harnessing our weapons, I say, "Better to travel when the Fae are sleeping."

"I have several routes mapped out," Cypress supplies. "The alternate paths are meticulous, but they will help us evade detection."

"I'll scout the area from above," Cerulean offers.

"I reckon myself pretty good at solving mazes," Lark says while harnessing her whip.

Elixir is busy running his fingers over a stash of bottles Cypress had brought in for Juniper, from oils that will relax her muscles to a fizzing drink that will cool her temperature.

Juniper sits upright in a hammock the centaurs have erected for her. She's pouring through the Book of Fables while chewing on the temple tip of her spectacles. She's not reading but worrying, and she's trying not to show it.

I open my mouth to say something, anything that will get her to smile.

"Excuse me," a soft voice interjects.

All heads swing toward Cove, who's perched in a chair with a stack of Juniper's notes in her lap. She sets one of the leaflets down, struck by a thought. "The Deep's flood happened because the wild is fading, which had already been changing some of underground's geography. Doesn't it stand to reason parts of the woodland might have changed, too? Perhaps not yet in massive ways, but even the smallest shift in terrain can alter a traveler's route, throw them off course."

Fuck it all. She's right.

Warmth sweeps across Elixir's face. As for the rest of us who hadn't considered this logic, we continue to stare at Cove until it makes her uncomfortable.

She scoots in her chair. "I mean, it's possible. Elixir and I saw lots of subtle changes throughout the river, which amounted to a big change in the end. Not that you'll experience a flood in the forest—they don't have massive waterways like that, right? Anyway, my sister and I have rescued animals often enough to know that the path isn't always straight, and we're not even talking about the mysteries of Faerie.

"Nature has a mind of its own, and with the wild decaying, the environment could shift at any moment. You might run into barriers and need to detour or find another way to the Evermore Blossom. And if that happens, that will make it difficult to get where you want to go without being noticed."

A grin spreads across Juniper's face. "Wisely done."

Pink stains Cove's cheeks. "I learned from the best."

"It is a valid prediction," Cypress concedes. "The best we can do is be mindful."

"And have another set of eyes," a feminine voice announces from the tent's entrance.

The centaur goes rigid as a lithe figure steps through the yurt's threshold. Her footfalls are tentative, hardly the usual sashay she once mastered among her woodland kin. Yellow petals crowd the nymph's dark hair, a floral dress drizzles down her body, and stacks of color dust her upper eyelids, ranging from yellow to green.

Lark and even compassionate Cove look ready to tear the female's hair from her scalp. Cerulean's blue eyes narrow to slits. Elixir merely stares in the female's direction, impassive and the only soul here who can relate to her despicable actions.

Fury blazes from my hooves to my antlers. "What. The. Fuck?"

"I asked for her," Juniper says, prompting me to swing her way. "Cove beseeched a centaur to call on Foxglove—on my behalf. My sister wasn't too happy to heed the request, but in any event, she's more than correct about the wilderness. If there's a remote possibility the landscape is going to give you problems, you need others who know the forest."

"Cypress knows the forest," I grit out. "Sylvan knows the forest."

"But you have to plan for all contingencies. Foxglove's the chief nymph. She has her own knowledge of this land."

"The chief nymph," Foxglove muses from the entrance. "I like that."

I pivot toward her and snarl, "Not happening."

The female crosses her arms, the movement displaying the same dagger she'd used during the battle at The Gang of Elks, when she tried to save Sylvan. "I'm here because of your mortal. Not you, handsome."

"Her name is Juniper. If memory serves correctly, you strangled her and buried an arrow in my best friend."

Foxglove cranes her head high but avoids Cypress's withering stare. "I attempted to fix that blunder."

"You failed. Sylvan lives only because of Juniper."

"Okay, I'm not here to nitpick. I came to repay a debt."

"My, my, my. Now who said anything wanting your cheap-ass redemption?"

"You could have come after me for what I did. I heard through gossip that Juniper stopped you, and that's why I was allowed to stay on allied turf." Foxglove glances at Juniper. "I owe you for that. Besides, in The Gang of Elks, I saw what you and Sylvan meant to each other. The respect and kinship between a Fae fauna and a mortal…it made me think differently."

She exhales and redirects her attention to me. "Fine, everything that happened made me think differently. If Juniper wants me to join you, then I'm joining you."

"You forget I'm still the ruler around here," I growl.

"Going against your darling's wishes? Good luck with that." Foxglove flips a lock of hair over her shoulder and wheels toward the exit. On her way out, the nymph pauses in the shadow of Cypress's glare, embarrassment staining her complexion. "Sorry about the arrow."

The centaur grunts. "You are fortunate I am ancient. I have lived long enough to learn the virtue of picking my battles. But if you ever betray Puck's trust or harm his mate again, I will decapitate you myself."

Her profile crinkles with regret, then evens out. She sidles away while saying, "I'll be outside."

The willow vines flap closed behind her.

Lark whistles. "If I didn't want to murder that hussy, I'd be impressed with her sass."

Sure. I'll give that bitch credit for having the nerve to show her face here. That's about all I'm capable of.

I whirl to Cypress. "You're okay with this?"

"I understand this," he defends. "As will you, once you calm down. Juniper's intentions have merit. I believe Foxglove means to atone, however much we both should like to wring her neck."

"Motherfuck," I say, ingesting lungfuls of oxygen and then laughing without humor. "There you and my woman go again, ganging up on me." I cast my head to Juniper. "I make no guarantees about trusting her."

Juniper grins sadly. "I wouldn't be loved if you did."

Cove rises and loops her arm through Elixir's. "Let's give them a moment."

I stride over to the hammock, then think better of placing my weight there. My ass drops onto the chair beside her, and our hands clasp. I'm tired and terrified and pissed off and too madly in love for my own good.

Now that everyone's gone, Juniper's voice crumbles. "Puck—"

"No," I say, my gaze whipping up to hers. "No fucking way."

"But—"

"I'm not losing either of you." I snatch her face in my hands. "You're not going anywhere. Understand?"

After a moment, her chin steadies. "I would argue if I had the energy."

"Save it for later. You'll be here for half an eternity—both of you. That's plenty of time to fuck with my sanity and win every debate."

She rests her forehead against mine, her outtakes stirring with my intakes. "I love you, too."

Bloody Fables. "You have no idea, luv," I murmur before my mouth seizes hers, my tongue swiping in to taste every bold thing about her.

Minutes later, I drag my lips from Juniper's. Her voice cracks as she traces my profile and makes me promise to live, to come back to her, and for Fable's sake, don't do anything I'd normally do.

I grin against Juniper's mouth and kiss her once more, and again, and again. I duck my head and stroke my thumb over her stomach. Then I pull myself away and stalk outside before I can change my mind and go back to her.

Every step is a thousand. Every second is a brick on my shoulders.

My brothers and Juniper's sisters idle beneath a willow, while Cypress and Foxglove exchange words off to the side.

On my way to them, a runty voice begs, "Let me go with you."

I halt and glimpse a centaur stripling with a chartreuse tail and mane. It's the lively rulebreaker who'd attended Juniper's reading without Cypress's permission.

The filly's eyes glitter with bravery. "I can help, too. And in a battle, I can fight."

I hedge, then squat in front of the centaur and fold my hands between my knees. "You're quite the fan of my woman."

"I told you...I think I could like humans," the filly says. "I want to help yours. Let me, please?"

"You can help Juniper by staying with her. She needs others around, Faeries who'll keep listening to her stories. Do that for me, and I'll consider it a favor."

"I'm not gullible."

"And I'm not lying."

She bursts into mollified chuckles, the humor rinsing away her disappointment. "That's because Faeries can't lie," she scolds.

"Oh? And here, I'd forgotten."

"Very well. I suppose I can be Juniper's soldier then. I'll guard the tent and maybe hear a tale or two."

I bump her chin with my knuckles. "Brilliant idea, luv."

As I stride away, my hooves accelerate. My longbow and quiver shudder against my back, the archery a familiar ally in a world where everything has turned upside down.

Funny. Once in this dark forest, I challenged a mortal to win an impossible hunt.

Now I'm the one playing a game. Now I'm the one who has to face the wild and hunt something that just might be unhuntable.

17

Sylvan's hooves pound into the earth beneath us, debris snapping under her weight. The woodland spirals past in a montage, patchworks of color prickling the edges of my vision.

Several dozen paces to my left, Cypress gallops. My ears pick up on the tempo of his limbs, which carries additional weight.

Slinging my head in his direction, I discern a sheet of dark hair threaded with yellow petals whipping through the creepers. My least favorite nymph sits astride the centaur, an arrangement neither of them had been thrilled about. Still, it was better than expanding this gang to include an animal for Foxglove to ride. And if need be, say if they reach their breaking points and can't stand one another anymore, she's skilled at moving swiftly on foot.

Each of us knows how to cover ground while avoiding exposure, our combined pace light and agile. Regardless, a team clustered together could make too much noise, cause more commotion, and attract unwanted attention. Keeping a set amount of distance is essential with Solitaries, who are used to watching from the outskirts. If any Fae makes a perfect spy, it's one that has spent their immortal life cloistered.

We ride straight, then splinter farther apart milliseconds before breaching enemy lines.

Red foxes blink from the crevices. Trees with barbed trunks and spiked leaves flicker by, and a passel of boars sprints from our path. With every league we consume, disturbing new signs turn up, from the rotted wood of a fallen trunk to the dulling green of the canopies.

We avoid the Fae homes and shops nesting in the recesses. I lean forward as Sylvan lances through the area. The weald is quieter here. It's as though the environment has lost its ability to exhale.

It's also murkier despite the midmorning hour. Half the candles are nothing but fizzles, either snuffed by residents or extinguished by natural causes. It's hard to guess which.

A shadow passes overhead, a silhouette of wings flaring across the ground. My mouth slants at my brother's ability to flit through the wild without clipping so much as a single leaf. And all while securing Lark in his arms.

Cerulean's father seems to have vanished, probably on his own unexpected mission. He hadn't responded to Cerulean's last call before we rode out. His silence is unusual, but then, nothing has been normal lately. In war times, everything gets skewed.

Anyway, I doubt the owl would be thrilled to know what his son's about to do without him there, protective avian that he is. Must be nice to have a parent who reacts that way.

South of The Passel of Boars, a small avenue exists wedged between The Bonfire Glade and The Seeds that Give. That's the crack we need to slip through.

While nearing our first destination, my eyes scan the route ahead and catch on a thread flashing like tinsel between the trunks. I pull back, using my limbs to alert Sylvan. She skids to a standstill as I lift my arm in a halting motion, knowing everyone can see it.

The barest sliver appears, a single filament as thin as a fiber and invisible to the most perceptive of woodland dwellers. But it's not invisible to a hunter. The wiry strand extends inches from the deer's hooves and knits through the mesh of undergrowth.

Evidently, our foes have taken precautions against an invasion. Crafty, but my traitorous kin should know better. Spending part of one's youth with their calf punctured by the iron teeth of a human trap will make a Fae more sensitive to spotting bait.

A mirthless snigger puffs from my lips. Me, trespassing in my own realm. Sure enough, it's come to that.

Ground beetles hobble across the grass. The loom of a spider's web stretches like elastic across a branch. A ringed tail slips between the vegetation.

The weave is too complex for Sylvan to shrink and slip beneath, especially with her antlers. The fauna can grow small, but not to the size of a thimble. Everything, from nature to magic, has its cutoff point.

I jump off Sylvan's back and guide her through, my hooves stepping over each thread. From the sideline, I catch Cypress and Foxglove doing the same, the nymph having dismounted. Though, I'm not sure how my brother's reacting, but I can only guess he and his mate are circuiting, scouting the perimeter for watchers or signs of an impending attack.

Sweat coats my nape. One thing I can't disguise is my hair, the red visible from a good distance and impossible to shield with a hood, on account of the rack sitting on my head. Better not dwell on that.

The filaments have been harvested from a nasty plant that grows close to The Deep's entrance. Scorpio and his cult are quite the industrious fuckers.

It takes forever and a fucking day to wind through the lattice of wires, expertly camouflaged like a Fae ring. I step and twist. At one point, I duck while ushering the deer beneath a strand affixed high off the ground.

One touch, and the fibers will slice deep enough to cleave through bone.

One stumble, and I can say goodbye to my cock. It's that kind of trap.

My eyes narrow, scrolling across the dense environment as we keep moving. Countless threads later, we trail over the last one—and I whip out the longbow.

Leaping in front of Sylvan, I nock it, swerve, and let my arrow fly. It punctures the dryad charging my way. A scream peals from his mouth, the staff dropping from his hand and blood spraying from his chest.

The rest of them leap from the shadows. More dryads and fauns and leprechauns, armed with bows, staffs, hammers, axes, saw blades, and throwing stars. I can't help the disappointed sigh—"Ah, fuck," I mutter—before I shove the deer out of harm's way and throw myself into it.

Sylvan totters backward. The Solitaries won't hurt her, but they might snare my friend as leverage.

I dodge and spin while firing another round. I tumble forward, pop up, and two arrows through a pair of throats, crimson splattering the wilderness.

An axe flares in my direction, but it falls from the leprechaun's fingers as a dagger hacks through his wrist. Foxglove straightens from her throwing stance and races into the scene.

An arrow with illuminated fletching spears through and puts a crater into a faun aiming at the nymph's back. The earth shakes as Cypress smashes through the foliage, his weapon braced and the splayed horns of his helmet dotted in red specks.

Sensing a figure behind him, he rears and stamps his hooves into a dryad, launching the Fae into the sky.

I pivot while entreating the roots of a tree, which break from the ground. Muscled cords of bark throw clumps of soil across the forest. Completing a full turn, I ram my free palm in front of me, launching the roots toward an incoming body like a battering arm. The second the Fae lands, the bark clamps around their form and crushes what's left, bones audibly crunching.

Another figure jets my way. I flick out my hand, lobbing a single root that belts around the leprechaun's throat. As my splayed fingers curl into a fist, the root squeezes. And when I jolt my arm backward, the bark twists the assailant's neck.

I've asked enough of this tree, so I relax my arm. The root drops along with its brethren, and the cords stitch themselves back under the earth.

My bow does the rest. I sweep under a flying axe, then flip an arrow between my fingers and jolt the tip over my shoulder, the arrow piercing through another Fae's larynx.

A javelin spirals through the air and pins a faun to the nearest trunk. The outline of wings shears across the woods, the quills sharp and seizing the enemy's attention. Cerulean swoops down. Lark jumps from his arms, her boots hitting the grass as my brother snatches his weapon and soars toward another faun.

Lark hooks a female dryad and brings her down. In a fluid series of moves, my brother's mate reels in her whip and lashes backward through the gap in her legs, striking a charging leprechaun heading her way.

"Fables almighty," one of the fauns gasps, the fear bright and authentic in his eyes as he perceives my brother and his mate.

Then the Fae glimpses me, as if the reality of this surge—against the ones who've reigned over this land for the last nine years—is only now striking him.

I want to explain. I want him to understand, to see it all differently, to realize it doesn't need to go down like this, to know I'm still here, fighting for this world, if only from another angle.

The faun wavers. He whirls and dashes into the trees.

Shit. If he reaches his clan, if he reaches Scorpio, more will come, more will intercept. If I let that happen, we'll risk getting to the Evermore Blossom.

My arrow is up and firing before my head catches up. The arrow lodges into the faun's spine, launching him into a hedge.

By the time he lands with a thud and a final screech, it's over. Fatal silence sweeps through the forest, punctured only by the harsh pants coming from each of us. Blood clots the foliage, the stench thick in my nostrils. We stand, heaving among the slaughter.

Humility bites into Foxglove's face. She nods to Cypress for saving her, and he bows his head. I manage the same to the nymph, seeing as the female had shielded me from a leprechaun's axe. Besides, I'm too shredded to hold a grudge right now.

I glance at the faun lying still in the bushes. I targeted him while he'd been fleeing. I'd done that to an unarmed Fae, who'd once been my kin.

The longbow drops from my hands. "Fuck," I grit out while dicing through my hair.

"Brother," Cerulean murmurs.

"Puck," Cypress says.

I hold up my hand, shutting them the hell up. I need this. I have to feel this, to know what it's worth for my kid, for Juniper, for this forest, for all of them. I need to face it and remember.

They wait as the aftereffects unspool through me. At one point, a snout nudges my arm. Sylvan must have shifted to a smaller size and stashed herself in the recesses until the fighting had ended. But now, she appears in her normal height and nuzzles me until I run my palm over her fur.

After that, we collect the fallen and set them to rest beneath the awning of a tree, where they fade into nothing. Then I swing myself onto Sylvan's back and say in a voice chafed by sandpaper, "Let's go."

Cove had been right, and so had my woman. The wild's topography has morphed in places, turning a gully into a chasm too wide to spring over, plus the western fringes of The Bonfire Glade have filled with an impassable overgrowth of stinging nettles.

We reach the margins of The Seeds that Give by late afternoon. The passage is barely recognizable with thorn vines roping through the place, so coiled and stocky none of us would be able to strap our arms around the stems fully. Our only choice is to split into pairs, to find a way around the brambles and signal one another once we've located an outlet.

Cerulean and Lark take to the sky, blending in with the clouds. Cypress and Foxglove go west, and I ride east with Sylvan.

Two hours later, the deer and I take a break. While she grazes, I round a corner and halt in the gap of a fern thicket. My brows furrow at the sight of Cypress and Foxglove bickering inside a glen laced in fronds.

"I'm telling you, we're going in circles," Foxglove gripes under her breath.

"And I am telling you, that is the point," Cypress argues, staring down his nose at the female. "There is a pattern in the thorns, which I suspect is obscuring a channel that we can pass through. The more we retrace our steps, the more the pattern makes itself clear."

"Hogwash, centaur. I enjoy illusions as much as the next Fae, but there's no way a path is hidden in those brambles. They're as thick as your eyebrows."

"Leave my eyebrows out of this debate, tiny nymph."

"Whoooo are you calling tiny?"

I fold in my lips, muffling a chuckle. I've got to hand it to Foxglove. As much as I hate her, the female's got a whipcord tongue like Lark. Plus, it's funny watching someone other than myself exasperating the centaur.

Foxglove folds her arms over her breasts. "I'm curvy and tall for a nymph."

He mirrors her pose. "But not for a centaur."

"Whatever. It still doesn't make me tiny. I'm not Juniper."

"No one is Juniper."

"Such fondness for the mortal," Foxglove marvels. "Though, I guess I'd be more surprised if I were talking to a covetous faun, not a dignified equine. You don't sound remotely jealous. How do you manage that?"

I feel my eyes slit. What the fuck does that mean?

Cypress steels himself, yet apprehension twitches through his features. "I cannot fathom what you're implying."

"How nimble you are," Foxglove praises. "You can't fathom because, technically, I haven't voiced anything specific yet. Nice way to lie without lying, but I think you understand me clearly. Your satyr might be ignorant, but I'm a nymph, and I've seen you two together plenty of times, as if friendship is still enough for you."

Despite whatever she's referring to, Foxglove's compunction finally gets the better of her. "Anyway, we're wasting time."

But when she turns to leave, Cypress's words stop her. "How would you recognize such ties, when you have never earned a true friend in your immortal life?"

Foxglove's bare feet pause. Hurt creases her profile as she rounds on him. "Maybe not. But as the nymph who witnessed you barrel into The Herd of Deer when I had Puck trapped with Juniper in a Fae ring, it became pretty clear. I saw your face—that ferocious expression because your satyr was in trouble. That wasn't the look of a friend protecting a friend."

Cypress bares his teeth. "He is not *my* satyr."

"No, he isn't. Puck is Juniper's. So I repeat: You hide the effects of that fact remarkably well, considering."

"Considering what?"

"Considering you're in love with him...what?" Foxglove squints at Cypress in confusion, then follows the sudden direction of his gaze, which has landed on me.

18

I stand on the fringes, watching them. Foxglove's words take a minute to penetrate my skull and root themselves into my brain. Even then, it's as though they're speaking in a language I've never heard.

Considering you're in love with him.

You're in love with him.

With him.

With me.

Cypress's dark features practically blanch. Stricken, his eyes widen to the size of dinner plates—guilt, vulnerability, and something else flaring in his pupils. It's a combination that looks wrong on him, out of proportion to his personality.

Or maybe I've just never stared hard enough.

The foreignness of it strikes me dumb. My tongue seizes, unable to budge for about ten seconds.

Once it loosens, I step into the glen. The first thing that comes out is a question I've never bothered to ask in my depraved existence. "Am I interrupting something?"

Foxglove's steep cheekbones blaze with mortification. Call me a hypocrite, but it's either that or some phenomenon resembling a conscience.

Her gaze swerves toward Cypress, but when he makes no reply, she swivels back to me. "Kind of," she squeaks.

Kind of. Sort of.

But I couldn't have heard the female right. She must have misinterpreted something in the past, because there's no way my best friend is carrying a torch for me. Cypress doesn't pine. He never has over anyone.

The look he's giving me must be the result of bafflement and denial. He's as stumped as I am that Foxglove, interloper extraordinaire, has gotten it all wrong.

This is a joke. It's not real.

Relief eases my shoulders. "Come on," I say to the nymph with a dry, incredulous laugh. "What cliquey, gossipy woodland Fae spoon-fed you that rubbish?"

The nymph balks. She casts Cypress another uncertain glance, but he just idles, his expression wrung out like a towel. The silence goes on for so long, it starts getting awkward.

Foreboding climbs up my sternum. I feel my smirk loosening like a cord, like an object slowly unraveling. "Cypress?"

"I'm, uh…" Foxglove breaks from her stance and gestures clumsily to the nearest gap in the trees. "I'm just going to…" She trails off and makes a break for it, escaping between the fronds.

By the time she's fled, the mirth has disintegrated from my face. I don't need a mirror to know this. Every muscle above my neck feels unhinged, just like the rest of my insides.

This isn't a joke. It's real.

Cypress mutters in Faeish, ducking his head with shame. His jaw ticks like he's trying to reinforce himself, but then those sage eyes rise and settle on me once more.

And there it is. Fables, if I don't see the truth sitting plain on his face.

Foxglove had been right. For once in her life, she'd been so bloody right.

My best friend is in love with me.

The shock hits me like a pail of ice water. My hooves carry me back a step, compromising my balance. Yet as I steady myself, Cypress has a split-second reaction, his massive frame spasming toward me, as if worried I'll fall.

It's the same type of reflex that blows through me every time Juniper loses her footing or shows any sign of being hurt. It's protectiveness. It's an impulse stemming from a deeply rooted place.

Memories crack open and spill out like yolk.

When Juniper's game first began, Cypress, Tinder, and I had crossed paths while hunting for her. The centaur had muttered something back then.

Some attachments do not wane.

During the Middle Moon Feast, Cypress had watched us both with a strange kind of conflicted loss I hadn't been able to understand.

That time I challenged Juniper and Cypress to an archery contest, he'd averted his gaze while she and I shared a heated look.

And when Juniper and I got trapped in the Fae ring, Cypress had ridden in with deadly fury strung across his face, not only because Juniper was in danger, but because he'd caught our kin beating me.

Every time Cypress had gazed my way. Every time we laughed together. I should have seen it. But being a satyr and a fucking idiot, I hadn't.

My friend's expression crinkles, as if pained. He turns away, the scrolled longbow and quiver of glowing arrows trembling with his movements. He takes a moment, then his baritone comes out as firm as stones. "You were not supposed to find out."

It's a moot point that I'd normally tease him for. That is, if we were talking about anything else.

My chest caves. I murmur, "How long?"

I hear him swallow, the confession leaking out as slowly as sap. "The year we met."

"Fables." I thrust a hand through my hair. "Cypress, I…"

"You were no different than every woodland Solitary," he reminisces, a sad grin shaping his words. "Except in one capacity: You had an earnest heart. You told me of your wishes to be part of a family, to raise one of your own, so very unlike the casual whims of a satyr. Yet you hid this yearning well. I admired your ability to soak up the pleasures of life, despite what it denied you.

"Then one day, you boosted the confidence of a young Fae named Tinder, a runt who idolized you but failed to defend himself when a crew of leprechauns mocked him."

"I remember that day," I say. "You were there when I pulled Tinder aside."

"I was," he replies. "And I have never forgotten how you knelt and tousled his hair, how your words stoked light back into his eyes." Cypress huffs. "I cannot stand that nuisance of a Fae, but I could not look away as you encouraged him. You were not merely a debauched satyr but a leader with the instincts of a father. Under that coltish smirk, you were selfless and honorable.

"It was not the thought of your touch that stole my heart. It was how you touched someone else, made them feel valid and valuable. In that moment, I treasured you. The passion was unlike anything I had known before, and I would have done anything to stay by your side."

My throat contorts. "And you did."

After a pause, his voice frays. "I did."

All this time, he's been there.

All this time, he either listened to stories about me sticking my cock into countless other Faeries or literally stood guard during the orgies.

All this time, he watched me with Juniper, watched me fall hard for her.

All this time, he wanted me. All this time, he stayed quiet.

All this time, he never left.

I think about the canvas he'd painted of the place we met, which hangs in the cabin.

I think about that night at home, when Juniper had baked Cypress a pie and explained it was "comfort food."

She knows. At some point, Juniper had found out.

I'd had a feeling they were keeping a secret, but I trusted that whatever it was, it was between them. Plus, I had wanted them to like each other because Cypress is my family, too.

I shake my head. The motion emits a tinkling sound from my earrings, which shivers across the glen. Hearing it, Cypress's shoulder blades pinch inward, as though the noise stings.

Has it always been this obvious? Was I always that fucking blind?

The sight of him crushes my chest. I'm an asshole for tearing my friend apart.

But I won't insult or break Cypress by saying I'm sorry. Outside of my brothers, he's the last Fae I'd want to hurt.

"I don't know what to say," I admit. "I'm...I don't know what to say."

Cypress snorts. "That is out of character. You always have something to say. It is annoying."

The chuckle jumps out of me, mimicking the sudden exhale of humor coming from Cypress. Finally, he clomps around, his tail swishing. Tenderness relaxes the plains of his face. "Are you happy?"

"You know I am," I answer. "She's everything to me."

"Juniper is a good mortal. She deserves you."

"I'm the one who's a lucky prick."

"Nonetheless, your happiness is what I wish for. More than your love."

"What about you?" I broach. "You happy?"

"You are here. Our home still exists. My kin live yet." Cypress gazes upward and speaks to the layers of leaves. "I shall never know your touch, but I know what it is to love you, even if on my own. That feeling belongs to me and cannot be taken away." His face lowers to mine. "So yes, I am happy. And I see that look, Puck. Never fear. Long has my desire been cultivated, but I shall always be your friend."

The relief is immediate. I don't want to lose him, but I would have understood if he decided to separate himself after this battle. "We're good, then?"

He harrumphs. "What do you take me for? A disloyal centaur who cannot function beyond the call of his loins?"

Now the laugh busts out of me. "A merry point, for sure."

"You should know me better."

"I should." I give him a deliberate look. "But I do now."

Cypress's mouth slants fondly. "It is nice to be known, at last in every way. And I congratulate you both. For each of you are precious to me."

"The feeling's mutual." Warmth and humility tighten my throat. "I know it's not a Fae thing to say thank you. But...thank you, friend."

We trade grins, but then Cypress's eyes grow distant, some knowledge hitting him. "The gap in the thorn path," he muses. "I know the way."

Thank fuck. I call the others through the roots before we rush out of there, collect Sylvan from her grazing spot, and meet them by the brambles.

Cerulean, Lark, and Foxglove are contemplating the wall of spikes twisting through the channel, but they whirl at the sound of us, their weapons anchored. Seeing me and Cypress with the deer, they relax the javelin, whip, and dagger.

I snort while jogging up to them. "Some of you are losing your sensory prowess if you couldn't recognize the sound of our hooves."

Cerulean's blue mouth slants. "Consider it paranoia after being ambushed."

"Fair enough."

"Speaking of which, those earrings might as well be wind chimes in enemy territory."

"I take mine off, you take yours off. That's how we deviants do things in the woods."

"There's a distinct difference between my ear caps and your dangly trinkets."

"Too bad. I'm not removing them, so get used to it. We didn't get attacked because I made too much noise, or you're underestimating every Fae in this wasteland. I can move with stealth while wearing earrings, bangles, and bells—all while plucking a cello, swaggering on cloven hooves, and wielding a longbow. Not to mention the multitasking I can achieve while fucking. Try me, I dare you."

"That was a really long answer," Lark wisecracks.

"I dabble in really long answers," I snark back.

Cypress alternates between inspecting the welkin and assessing the serrated hedges. "We have a source to guide us."

Realization lifts Foxglove's face. "The stars."

He scans the firmament for the celestials only centaurs and Cerulean can see during the day. "They are difficult to track through the canopy, but several of the fern trees we'd passed while 'going in circles'—" he gives Foxglove a reproachful look, "—had lost their leaves. The skeletal view enabled me to study their pattern beyond the blue, though it came to me rather delayed. They will make it easier to discern the way, rather than circuiting until the outlet becomes clear."

He catches my brother's eye. "Cerulean."

My brother nods. He gives Lark a swift kiss before a set of midnight plumes snap from the back of his long coat. He takes to the sky, his shape as thin as a knife as he cuts above us, vanishes for a handful of minutes, and then swoops back. Hovering over the thorns, Cerulean points along the route in confirmation, then vaults ahead to keep watch from above.

Sylvan shrinks just enough to maneuver through the web. Because I don't have the same advantage, Cypress sways forward while advising over his shoulder, "Puck, mind your antlers."

I groan under my breath. "I swear, you and my woman are two of a kind."

"I consider that a compliment."

"You should because it was."

"I'm wondering less about Puck's hard rack and more about your colossal size," Lark comments to the centaur. "Here I was, thinking the satyr was bulky."

"The centaurs of old know how to navigate the confines of this wild," Cypress intones. "It is inherent in us, more than any woodland Fae. I will manage."

Bloody true. He'd done fine while slipping through that webbed trap earlier, as I knew he would.

While stalking behind him with Lark, I glimpse Foxglove beside Cypress. Contrition lines her profile as she peeks at him and mouths, *Sorry.*

He merely shakes his head, indicating she shouldn't blame herself for what I assume was that outburst earlier, when she'd publicized his feelings in front of me.

We filter under a threaded arch, the brambles as honed as tusks and whittled enough to pierce the bones of an elk. Knowing the thorns of this forest, if the tips don't kill their quarry, the poisonous sap contained inside them will.

Any fauna with an established habitat in this area might attempt to pilot through, despite the confusion. Not only is the land fading, but certain parts of its nature are doing so in a mighty fucked-up way. The thought churns my gut.

It's a tight squeeze at first. But sure enough, a channel materializes in the clutter of shoots, the path disguised like a riddle.

Lark grouses, "Son of a bitch."

Foxglove hisses as she jerks to avoid a bramble.

Sylvan has no trouble, whereas I duck my head more often that I'd like to admit, my antlers in danger of getting hooked in the mess, which would probably ensnare me for a while. These thorns aren't easy to saw through.

At the possibility, a vignette flips like pages through my mind. The black teeth of a trap sinking into my calf. A human forest shivering around me. My blood dribbling onto the leaves. The acidic stench of iron burning into my flesh. The distant sound of fauna and Fae cries, and the cold slam of cage doors.

I blink, tearing myself out of the heinous memories. As my eyes readjust, I glance around in surprise.

We're through.

The timberland spreads outs, emitting the succulent whiff of fruit trees. The Seeds that Give materializes. Golden orbs shaped like strawberries droop from the branches, their aroma heady. If I had the time to feel nostalgic, I'd take advantage.

Except I can't. We're through. And we're close.

I hustle past the group, my limbs plowing into the dell and its orchard. Everyone brings up the rear. Sylvan gallops, her muzzle pumping in tandem. Cerulean's wings crimp and vanish into his body as he lands and races across the ground, Cypress's hooves kick across the earth, Lark's boots crunch twigs, and Foxglove's bare feet slap the underbrush.

Right outside the dell's southern border, a cul-de-sac ends in a vertical rock facade. We skate to a halt.

I pivot in a full circle while muttering "What the fuck?"

"It should be here," Cerulean says, his wings already retracted.

"The flower?" Lark asks. "Where?"

Finally, I see the next obstacle. I seethe and point upward, along the slab of rock crowned in heaps of foliage. "There."

The Evermore Blossom grows at the top of the woodland's only cliff. It's a modest elevation compared to the mountain range in Cerulean's home. Common knowledge speaks of an incline leading to it, enabling Faeries to pay the flower worship or—on rare occasions when a Fae is feeling desperate, planning to turn a raven against its kin, or trying to save his pregnant lover—clip a piece of its eternal petals, which grow back.

But the upward slope isn't there. At some point, it must have collapsed. Chunks of it are piled at the summit's base.

Cypress reads my mind and spells out the problem. Yet again, Cove and Juniper's theory about shifting terrain is correct.

Cerulean saunters backward. "I can fly there."

"No, you can't," I hate to say. "The fern trees are spread wider than a faun's legs, and the canopies shield the flower so thickly, it's impossible for even a dragon to breach them. Risk penetrating one, and you'll bust a wing, Cerulean."

"Can't any of you just manifest?" Lark insists.

My brother shakes his head. "We need to know exactly where we're going when we manifest."

"To the fucking *top*."

"In Faerie, it's more complicated than that," Foxglove sighs.

"When you manifest, either you or someone who's directing you needs to know the destination precisely," Cerulean clarifies. "It's a force that guides, and it's tedious, but magic is hardly straightforward."

"None of us in this band have ever visited the flower," I finish. "We've never had a specific reason to pay it homage. In general, most Solitaries haven't made the trek here."

"Not even to bloat your magic muscles?" Lark balks.

"Not even then," I say. "However arrogant and vain Faeries are, to enhance yourself with the Blossom would topple a Fae's pride. Most of us have only ever been aware of the Evermore Blossom from history."

"I know few centaurs who have made the journey, purely to offer tribute to its existence," Cypress divulges. "Regretfully, I am not one of them."

"Then how the hell did Scorpio manage to get up there?" Lark broods.

I grunt. "A woodland Fae could have played gopher for him, or Scorpio mounted the zenith himself. Though I doubt a merman shifter with sea legs is capable of it. Water Faeries aren't the best climbers, unless the incline was stable when he was here. Who the fuck knows or cares?"

We trade bleak looks. Seems there's only way to reach it.

Cerulean is a no. Likewise, Cypress and Sylvan are out of the question. Not that I'm eager to stand around mulling this over.

I stalk forward, but a hand shoots out and snags my elbow. "You won't make it," Lark protests, her mortal accent as twangy as her sisters'. "You've got too much weight and width on you, handsome. Even if you didn't, those hooves wouldn't grip a damn step, much less a nodule. Without knowing how the pinnacle is shaped higher up, there's no guarantee you'd find the right brackets or recesses to brace yourself."

"Ask me if I give a fuck," I growl. "Juniper is my woman."

"And she's my sister. This job is mine."

"No," Cerulean snaps, his pupils dilating with fear. "Not you."

"You see the vegetation packed up there? I'm the only one besides Foxglove who can fit through. But unlike her, I know my way around a bluff."

The nymph raises her palms in surrender. "Not arguing with that."

"Do I really need to point out how I scaled your labyrinth and won?" Lark reminds my brother. "I'm going."

His face cinches, torn between protecting her and backing off. "Lark…"

Seeing my brother's compressed features, she cups his cheek and murmurs, "Try and stop me, pretty Fae."

But he won't. Cerulean has never told Lark what to do, she would never listen anyway, and I can't argue any more than he can. She has as much right to save Juniper as I do.

Cerulean's mouth tightens, then tilts in amusement. "Mutinous thing, indeed."

She plants a quick kiss on his lips, then surveys the cliff before locating two rifts. Tightening the whip to her hip, Lark clamps on and hoists herself up, then glances over her shoulder at us. "Anyhow, I can climb better and faster than you magic fuckers."

Cerulean grins. I can't help my snigger.

We crane our necks as she scales the rock slab like a critter, her feet and hands catching on places I'd failed to notice. Clouds of white hair tumble down her back. Her dress flaps around her limbs. The skirt's multiple splits allow her to move spryly and flashes a cuff around her upper thigh.

Foxglove looks impressed. "Limber and looking good while doing it, and in a skirt no less. How is she accomplishing that?"

"Watch and learn," Cerulean gloats.

His mate's body shrinks the higher she gets. Periodically, she uses her whip to hook onto exposed joints. At last, the vegetation shivers and consumes her form, and her boots slip into the foliage.

We wait. And wait. And wait.

My ears pick up her footfalls and leaves that shake in the breeze but nothing else. The time lapse chews on Cerulean's certainty, his smirk twisting into a grimace.

Inevitably, my brother starts pacing. His statuesque limbs threaten to dig trenches into the soil as he strides back and forth like a panther, all while scowling at the bluff. He's so wound up, those wings are going to burst from his back at any minute.

Cypress ushers forward, his eyes trained on something falling. The whip plummets from above and smacks the grass, with a gilded petal secured to the end. The object shimmers like a kaleidoscope. It swirls from copper to bronze, then gold to silver, with the tip undulating as though it's floating in water.

We gawk at it, then jump in place as Lark's feet hit the ground. A smarmy look of glee stretches across her features as she wipes her palms together. "Ha!"

Cerulean expels a typhoon's worth of air, takes Lark's face in his hands, and husks, "You drove me mad."

"Won't be the last time," she jokes softly.

"What did the flower look like?" Foxglove marvels.

Lark pulls away from Cerulean and thinks about it. "Like a miniature starburst layered over endless other starbursts. The petals are every metallic shade I've ever seen, and they're in constant motion, like they're swaying to music." She smiles to herself. "Cove would love it."

"Gutsy woman," I say, by way of gratitude.

The whole petal is more than we need, but I like how this mortal thinks. Too much is favorable to too little.

I bend to pluck the petal off the ground, but it disappears before I touch it. A small figure snatches the petal in its mouth like a toy, then scrambles backward to regard us.

The moment my eyes land on the creature, the irony is comical. I recognize the snout, the coarse fuzz streaked in brown and black, and the beady, peridot eyes. The little boar blinks at us, its tail swatting about.

Juniper and I have crossed paths with this meddler before. Everyone tenses, then relaxes with easy chuckles when they register our visitor.

Either history has a repetitive sense of humor, the boar passels are migrating south, or this wee thing has an adventurous streak. Either way, the shoat is further from its farrow than it should be.

I'm about to hunker down and ease the petal from the animal when it notices Sylvan. Enthusiasm brightens the shoat's eyes. It's the sort of gleam that promises mischief, and I'm not only one realizing this. We all sense it at the same time, each of us pausing to frown.

I go still. "You've got to be fucking kidding me," I mumble, then leap forward.

The boar squeals—everyone shouts, "No!"—and scurries into the forest. Our band charges after it, racing through the wild at a breakneck pace because the shoat is fast for its size. It slips in and out of crawlspaces, forcing us to veer and swerve and jump over obstructions.

It goes on, too far and too long. I lose track of the terrain, sweat beading down my spine as the environment changes. It grows broader, smeared in the undercooked colors of an early sunset.

Something about this area jogs my consciousness like an alarm. Cerulean hollers, shouts at me to stop, to turn back.

Sure. That's what a smart person would do, except I'm running on instinct and can't stop.

Lark can get us another petal. But it's more than that, because the second I vault through a line of trunks, something's not right about this landscape.

The grass is thinner and grows taller. A charred scent scorches the air.

The boar stops, grasping the same thing. It trots this way and that, gauging its new surroundings. That's when it strikes me dumb. I skitter in place, my eyes wide on the snare inches from the boar's hooves.

The creature moves to flee, its weight triggering the click of hinges. I lunge, shoving the animal out of the way and rolling across the ground. A set of fangs bites into my shoulder, pinning me to the stalks. My flesh sizzles, the pain searing into me, the pungency of burned skin inflaming my nostrils.

I land on my back, unable to rise, as if the trap's teeth are leaching the energy from me. Only one substance has this effect. I remember the feeling like it was yesterday, like it hasn't been nine years

Iron.

Which means this isn't the snare of a Fae hunter. And I'm not in Faerie.

That's when a figure materializes above me with wide eyes and a shocked expression that instantly erodes into hatred.

It's not a Fae. It's a human.

19

No, it's not just one human. It's a pack of them. Three males, in fact.

They're staring down at me, their figures blocking the mortal sun, which is sinking below a mortal landscape. A plain of high grass shivers, the fields stretching into the distance, heading toward the pitched ceilings of a small town.

Reverie Hollow.

Images of shackles and cages flash through my mind. I shake off the haze and try calling through the roots to my kin, but it's useless outside The Faerie Triad. I must have run fast and far past the border without realizing it, too frantic to pay attention to how much distance my Fae legs had consumed in seconds, too desperate to catch the boar and retrieve the petal.

The animal is nowhere in sight, but I hear it squealing from a remote spot, its noises audible only to my senses. The smart little thing had retreated quickly once I'd pushed it from the trap.

I focus on the men, whose eyes have slitted in triumph as their gazes slide from my cloven hooves, to my antlers, to my pointed ears.

Encounter a healthy Fae while you're alone and unarmed, and you'll turn and run.

Catch an injured Fae who's impaled by iron, and you'll become a lot more confident.

One of the men has shaggy hair as dark as spilled oil. As he plants his hands on his thighs and leans down, his face seems familiar. "Well, if this isn't the best catch in The Dark Fables," the cocksucker gloats. "I don't know whether to skin your hide or saw off those antlers for my mantle first."

"How about you swallow my fist instead?" I snarl through my teeth.

The man glowers and spits on me, which is quite the lazy response. He's bare-chested, his torso carved with scars made by claws, talons, and canines.

What kind of human gets munched on by that many fauna?

The trio watches me spasm in pain, their iron trap chomping on my flesh. Heat sizzles through my veins, and the world blots at margins, coupled with the minced sounds of voices screaming.

Everything happens too fast and too slow. The commotion snags their attention. All three heads whip up, their profiles going slack at whatever they see, right before the men lunge toward a pile of crossbows and let the bolts fly.

Using what strength I have left, I haul myself onto my elbows. Ahead, two of the men charge and fire at my brother, whose midnight blue wings scissor into view. Lark vaults across the grass while looping her whip overhead, Foxglove throws her dagger, and Cypress roars while loosing an arrow.

My eyes jump across the scene, my mind sluggish despite what I'm seeing. The presence of iron is weakening Cerulean, his javelin failing to strike true. It also penetrates Cypress and Foxglove, their senses diminishing so that both miss a set of easy targets.

Only Lark is unaffected. Except something else stops the female in her tracks. As she gazes across the fields at the dark-haired man, a stricken look distorts her face. Her gray eyes are haunted, flashing with recognition.

He's familiar to her, too. The man squints back, then sneers with malice.

They know each other.

This being Lark's village, it's no surprise but…

"It's the whore!" he yells. "She's on their side!"

His minions aim at her, then shriek as Cerulean's left wing prunes one of them across the throat. The quills shave through his flesh so fast and sharp that blood sprays from his neck.

Lark recovers from her paralysis and hooks her whip into the second man, the honed lash resounding through the field.

My brother veers into the sky and cannons down again. His eyes slit with fury, and not just because the men went after his mate. No, his rage is older than that.

During the next lap, their leader dodges my brother, only because the iron is slowing Cerulean down. That's when my gaze stumbles across the X of crossbow bolts inked into the base of the human's spine.

Wrath fires up my muscles. That's why his face struck my memory, as much as Lark's.

He's a trade poacher.

This litter of shitheads are the ones who chased Lark into Faerie, dead set on raping and slicing her to pieces. They're the ones my brothers and I had fun with right after that episode. They're also the same breed of fuckers who kidnapped and forced my woman to do their dirty work when she was a foundling. They might not be the very ones, but close enough for me.

All hell breaks loose in my soul. I'm seething and launching off the ground before reality catches up with me.

The trap still has its jowls sabered into my flesh. Heat leaks down my arm, which burns like a pyre. Spots burst, making me dizzy. A guttural bellow launches up my throat, though I fight to keep it in as I sink back down, my knees cracking into the grass.

The chaos intensifies, with my kin and the mortals wielding their weapons. Red sprays the earth. Howls fill the air. One of the mortals shoots a flaming bolt heavenward. Several minutes later, a bell tolls from the village like a bad omen, and voices multiply, accompanied by a stampede of hooves.

The bolt was a signal. The town knows we're here.

The land of Faerie and the mortal realm seem to close in like walls. Enemies exist on both sides, fencing in on our small band, which teeters in the middle.

On the fringes, Sylvan rears in hysteria, her pupils trained on me.

The dark-haired human notices her and yells, "Get the deer!"

No!

My fingers reach for a yew-wood longbow that isn't there because it had tumbled when I'd fallen into the trap. Not that I can wield it with one arm. Tendrils of smoke curl from my shoulder. I grip the trap, keyed up to tear the fucking thing from my body, but the contact scorches my palm.

Cypress hits his mark at least, skewering one of the injured poachers through his chest before the man can target Sylvan. But if there's one thing the mortals know about Faeries, it's that the fauna are sacred to us. They know she's precious to my race.

She's precious to me. And more humans are coming, about to outnumber us.

The caustic stink of iron roils my senses. I growl as the dark-haired poacher snatches the back of my leather vest and hoists me upright. He grunts in shock and stumbles forward while struggling to maintain a hold.

"Heavy fucker," he mutters while dragging me off the ground.

As he does, something nips at my temple—something that feels like the tip of a crossbow bolt.

Lark stalls, her whip slumping as her eyes hook onto the sight. The poacher has a bolt aimed at my head. The rest are brawling, so it takes them a moment to register this, in addition to the scent of iron, the pounding of horse hooves, and dozens of shouts. A mob of humans gallop our way, armed with iron daggers, maces, swords, arrows, and—for shit's sake—pitchforks.

A single object is potent, but countless ones? My head swims from the noxious stink saturating the air. I wrestle against the mortal, who would normally be ripped in half by now, but my joints are too leaden.

My gaze strays to Sylvan. There, hiding behind the deer is the boar with the Evermore Blossom petal tucked in its teeth.

Once in the mortal realm, a Stag protected a Boar...

It's not an existing Fable, but Juniper would appreciate that line. She could write something about it in her journal.

A bolt spears into the air and hacks through Cerulean's left wing. He hisses, buckles from the sky, and crashes to the ground, some of the quills charred as he rolls. In seconds, the other surviving poacher lodges another bolt in my brother's right wing, pinning him to the grass like a butterfly.

A howl breaks from my brother's lips, while another one tears from Lark's mouth. "Cerulean!" she screams, vaulting toward him, only to be yanked backward by Foxglove, who slings an arm around Lark's middle.

My brother's mate screeches and kicks the air. "Get the fuck off me, you bitch! Cerulean!"

But my brother just puffs through the pain and gives them both a vehement look, one the nymph had seen but his mate hadn't. It's a silent demand to stay back. And it's the same warning I'm already giving Cypress, my head whipping from side to side, because if he tries to save me, I'll murder his equine ass.

Terror seizes Cypress's face as his head clicks between the incoming throng and the mortal trapping me. But I nudge my head, indicating the shoat, and my mouth forms one word.

Juniper.

My woman and our kid need that flower to survive. But if the rest of our band get caught, that won't happen.

At least two of them have to retreat, to provide backup along the way. But neither does it make sense for one figure to stay behind, to try rescuing me and Cerulean on their own. None of them can handle these many humans at once, and this amount of iron will suck Foxglove and Cypress dry before either Fae lifts their weapons for another round.

Cypress's features tighten with barely contained restraint. Time lags, and I see them in slow motion, moving as if through sludge. The centaur whirls and speeds toward the boar, whom he scoops off the ground.

Lark is next. Foxglove shoves her toward Cypress, who plucks the thrashing human and dumps her onto his back while she wails my brother's name.

Sylvan allows the nymph to leap astride her, then casts me one more tormented glance before leaping into motion.

Crossbow bolts arch but never hit their mark as my kin rides hard, shrinking to nothing as they disappear into the borders of our home.

Everything blurs after that. The two surviving poachers throw hissy fits, not bothering to mourn their dead ally. Instead, they console themselves with my brother and me. Hands push me forward. As the trap's iron teeth sink further with every motion, my stomach heaves from nausea.

The bolts are removed from my brother's wings. Hands wrench Cerulean off the ground, his limp plumes dragging across the grass. His head lolls, barely conscious.

And then they're on us. A clan of mortal faces charge into the scene on piebald and chestnut steeds. I count at least two dozen figures.

Could be more. Probably is.

They chant in victory as the poachers present us to them like game mounted on a plaque. They know who we are from the tales, from the stories about the Infamous Three and their unmistakable traits. I mean, we even sent some of those tales their way.

The humans form a circle, eyes wide or narrowed, faces contorted or stunned.

One of them yells about the time we drove nails into a glamoured mortal—actually, that had been Elixir.

Another spews about a time her son came back from Faerie so lovesick he slit his own wrists—and okay, that had been me.

Another rallies how his mother had gone mad, fearing every sweep of the wind after it shoved her to the ledge of a balcony and suspended her there for hours—and yeah, that had been the pretty Fae beside me.

And another time, and another time, and another time...

The grievances accumulate. To them, we're the vicious ones, and they're right.

But I also remember the fauna crying out. And I remember Faeries trying to save us and getting slaughtered. And I remember Elixir's mothers dying in front of him. And I remember them caging Fae children—us.

Who's right and wrong? In this continent, who's innocent and who's evil?

What would my woman say?

A scene like this is never complete without a little punishment. The dark-haired poacher sneers. "All alone, eh? Seems your so-called friends left you."

Those words pollute the air. It takes a dozen pairs of callused hands and a dozen attempts to dump us over the horses, which ends up requiring reinforcements and a wagon, chiefly because of Cerulean's sagging wingspan.

I float in and out of awareness until the pitched buildings and crammed shops of Reverie Hollow come into view. Tents and stalls are scattered through the market square, a breeding ground for mischief and a venue my kin have stalked many times while glamoured.

Faces materialize from doors, windows, and alleys. Additional shouting and noises follow. So much human noise.

Cerulean is hunched but more lucid than before.

The iron teeth vanish from my shoulder, which is likely a hunk of meat by now. I feel the magic leaching from my fingertips, the iron slurping up every drop of it.

After I'm done blinking, my gaze lands on the rod. It's a hard motherfucker carved of iron and looks like it's been whetted, the way it points at me like an angry thing. It's thin and long, which means it'll give a fair beating to the body, the kind Fae skin won't forget.

One rod turns into a pair of rods.

Chains bind my wrists, then Cerulean's. They're not made of iron, but they're strong, and they do what they're supposed to.

A pole appears out of nowhere, erect in the square's center. They press me on one side, my brother on the other, our backs aligning.

That's when my tongue strikes a bargain. "No," I mutter. "Turn us the fuck around."

All right, that isn't exactly a bargain. But this isn't how I want to learn my lesson, if there is a lesson to be learned, which I don't think there is except that life isn't fair, and things are about to get even shittier.

But I feel Cerulean's pulse ramming against mine. I'm not about to let him take this alone, with nothing good to fix his eyes on.

The mortals actually oblige me, maybe because it's the first time I've spoken. Or maybe it's because, as Faeries, Cerulean and I still have some clout.

They spin us around to face each other, with only the tall pole separating us. Our gazes cling as they hook the chains shackling my brother's wrists with mine overhead, then slice the clothes from our backs. Two humans stand behind each of us, the rods primed in their hands.

My brother's blue eyes glitter, not with fear but relief. Lark is safe. That's why.

I know that feeling well. Juniper will get her cure. She'll live, and so will that little sapling inside her. That's all I give a shit about.

If I never see her again…touch her again…

Cerulean stares at me with a somber grin, one loaded with trust. Like a brother. Like family.

My throat swells as I bunch our fingers into a fist, lean sideways past the pole, and press my forehead to his.

The first combined iron lash jolts us toward one another, but we keep staring, keep watching each other.

The second lash sends fire across my back. My teeth grind, and my flesh singes, and my fingers strain with Cerulean's as we hold on.

The third lash cleaves through, shredding my skin. Cerulean bites his blue lip until it bleeds. I imagine our bodies torn to ribbons, because this is The Dark Fables, and it's a vicious world. Things rip easily here. And some of those things can't be mended.

The tenth lash makes it impossible to hold back. Skin and sinew go up in flames. I can't tell if Cerulean screams first, or if it's me.

Then I think about a face I've never seen, a small figure I've never met.

Juniper's green hair and my brown eyes. Juniper's intelligence and my smirk. Juniper's voice and my antlers.

And by the thirteenth lash, I know. It will be a girl.

20

My eyes crack open, crud sticking to the grooves. A cold, hard surface is mashed against my face. Rancidness gushes into my nostrils, the odor of barbecued skin so potent it slaps me awake.

I'm slumped on my side, lying in a heap on a steel floor. Reflexively, I flop onto my back.

The second I do, fire scalds my flesh, incinerating me from the outside in. My back screeches as though it's been used as a whetstone for blades. Agony sucks the oxygen from my lungs one second before I'm seething and cursing the universe.

I roll to my side again, dry heaving onto the floor. Every movement scalds like fuck. Every inhale tugs on that pain. My skin feels as if it's been poached like an egg, and my shoulder throbs as though it's been mauled by a grizzly mama bear, clawed and gnawed to a bloody pulp.

Between the snare and the whipping, the humans had done an expert job on the husk I'd once called a body. Lucky for me, I hadn't rotated onto the wrong side and killed my bad shoulder. Red craters pit into that area, the sight resurrecting the memory of that trap I'd fallen into.

For a while, I stay put. The lash marks blister, and the iron teeth marks throb. Then like a miracle, a chilled breeze sweeps across my skin, icing what's left of my carcass and dulling the burn. The wind's presence reminds me I wasn't alone in that market square.

Groaning, I haul my upper body off the ground. My gaze stumbles across the tattered blue wings splayed a few feet away, the plumes sagging over a crumpled form. A tapered ear peeks from Cerulean's midnight hair, he's as bare-chested as I am, and his face is twisted in the opposite direction.

Panic hits me until I see his chest rising and falling. He's alive.

On the flip side, we might as well be sealed in a catacomb. Darkness pours around us, the ebony sky spanning my vision and shrouding chunks of the scenery.

The faint slopes of a vale rise on either side, with briers coiling up the inclines and a small creek trickling nearby. From what I can make out, I've never seen this part of Reverie Hollow. Not that I've spent a lot of time here since The Trapping. Over the years, I've usually lured humans by playing my cello from inside The Solitary Forest.

If I had to guess, this is an unfamiliar section of the woods where I'd gotten snared as a stripling. That's about all I can tell. Where we are in relation to the place I'd met Juniper, the market square where I'd lost half my hide, and the fields stretching between our world and the mortal realm is unclear.

How long have we been here?

My eyes stray over the rail of bars enclosing us, each one giving off the corrosive smell of iron. Four walls. Bolted door. Seems history is repeating itself, though nine years ago, it had been a set of jowls for me.

My brother was the one they'd locked up. He's been terrified of cages ever since.

Wincing, I sit up and glance his way. The quarter moon hovering beyond the cage illuminates one high cheekbone. For a minute, I'd thought the cool wind blowing onto my skin had been my brother's doing, but I'm wrong.

Even my voice sounds mangled, shredded to bits as I croak, "Cerulean."

"Won't work," a male voice mutters. "He's out cold."

My head snaps toward the figure squatting outside the cage. I expect to see one of the humans, maybe the dark-haired poacher whose gullet I'd like to squash in my fist.

Only it's not the poacher. It's not even a mortal.

Scorpio hunches a short distance from the bars, too far for me to punch my knuckles through his heart. The grille slices his face into halves, and smudges pour from under his lower eyelashes. One would think he's been crying black tears.

Dark green leggings and a long, sleeveless shirt cling to his frame. And like Elixir and Foxglove, he gets around barefooted. Of all the mermen capable of shifting between land and water like my serpentine sibling, it has to be this dickhead.

Inwardly, I have a million and one homicidal thoughts. Each involves his dismembered body, starting with his itty-bitty cock.

Outwardly, I settle into a lazy pose, despite the mayhem this does to the trenches marring my back. "If you're here for a conjugal visit, I'm taken."

The Fae's smirk is vacant, unable to reach his eyes. He notches his chin toward Cerulean. "They cut his feathers."

Rage surges through my blood. "You'll have to be more specific."

"If you want names, there's a steep price for that information."

"There's also a steep price for baiting me. Go ahead and try it."

"Knowing which humans pillaged your darling brother would allow you to avenge him properly. You're not willing to bargain for that?"

"You must have me mistaken for a desperate sod who doesn't know the difference between a deal and a trick. I invented that kind of mischief. If you're looking for an easy target, you've picked the wrong cage."

"Mostly, it was merchants who looted from Cerulean's wings. The trade poachers took a few feathers, too," Scorpio volunteers in a low tone. "Trophies like that fetch a hefty mortal price, more than the tusks, fangs, and fauna heads they like to display."

That bit of knowledge brings a snarl to my mouth. "Why the change of heart?"

The Fae shrugs, the moon's reflection coasting across his shoulders. "A bargain would have been nice, but my offer was just a warm-up. I have other goals."

Goals being a euphemism for an ultimatum. I'm not about to fall for his bullshit, so I wait him out, which does exactly what silence will do to a visceral Fae like this one. It provokes him.

His pupils detonate as he clips his head toward the cage. "Look what they've done to you," he instigates. "Look at how they've taken revenge." While I just stare, his fanatical speech quickens. "They've mutilated you.

They've stripped you of magic. They've caged you as if The Trapping never ended. It's only a matter of time before Elixir is next."

"Ah yes," I muse. "I'm sure Elixir's welfare is at the top of your list."

Aggravation thrashes across his features. That, and spite.

Honestly, he left himself open for it. Elixir has dealt this pissant several blows—from minor, to mortifying, to massive. Scorpio's interest in Elixir begins and ends there, and I don't have the patience to pretend he isn't using my brother as an agenda. Not while my shoulder has about twelve holes in it, and my back is cooking like it's mounted on a fucking rotisserie.

Scorpio leans closer, setting a palm on the ground for balance. The posture reminds me of a reptile about to spring. "Your torture won't satisfy them indefinitely. It'll only stoke their confidence and boost their ambition. Imagine what these mortals will do to more Faeries if they ever catch them again.

"You think the humans will stay docile forever? We've been striking back for The Trapping, but that'll last only so long before they stop cowering and start realizing battles can be fought twice. The only way to snuff out the problem is by sacrificing them, as we always have. It's what they deserve. This—" he gestures to the cage, "—proves it."

"Get to the punchline," I tell him. "As it is, you've interrupted my nap."

"I'm here to offer you both a truce. All you have to do is join us, side with us again, lead us as you once did."

Well, I've got to hand it to him. At least he's not power hungry. His passion isn't to overthrow us, it's to exact retribution by any means necessary, and to act on impulse. Such is the visceral nature of a water Fae, to say nothing of how malevolent Elixir used to be.

But when the merman's rant fails to lift my eyebrows, Scorpio grimaces, as if betrayed all over again. "Juniper has a father, yes?"

I go still, and he uses that reaction to drive the knife in. "Where was he during your whipping? Why didn't he show up to stop them?" Scorpio tilts his head, swamp-colored hair slanting over his face. "Perhaps the man wanted you and your brother to die for taking his daughters in the first place. Perhaps he was there and let it happen. Or perhaps he wasn't in the crowd and felt elated to hear later what happened."

It's a direct shot to the gut. But from what Juniper's told me about the man who raised her, he wouldn't do what Scorpio's saying.

Or maybe…he would.

I know what it's like to love her. I'd never crush Juniper, let someone she loves die, no matter how much I detested him.

But now…now I also know what it's like to be a father. My kid isn't born yet, but already the vision of someone doing to them what I once did to Juniper brings savage thoughts into my head. The sort of thoughts that involve putting a hundred arrows into my victim, after I've cheese-grated the flesh from their body. Without a second thought, I'd do it.

Why wouldn't Juniper's father have the same reflex? Why wouldn't he want me, Cerulean, and Elixir dead?

My jaw locks, suppressing any outward reaction. "How much did you see?"

"All of it," Scorpio gripes. "Your adversary woodland kin sent word to The Deep. First, there'd been a raid in the wilderness between Fae opponents. One side lost, according to the faded souls whose essences still lurked in that spot after they fell. Solitaries patrolling that region caught wind of it before those essences had time to vanish completely. Your work, I assume?"

"They pounced. We reacted."

"It happens, especially if you cross into enemy turf. Must have been important, whatever you were doing."

I don't answer that because this bloodhound isn't stupid. Both attacks in and out of Faerie had taken place in range of the Evermore Blossom. But since we've got no plan of using the petals on our fauna like he's done, Scorpio's fishing for a motivation. He can't guess why we'd go there otherwise, and he doesn't know about Juniper.

Scorpio sighs. "That's right. I can't be trusted."

"What can I say?" I hitch my good shoulder. "I'm picky about the mermen I share secrets with."

"Are you considering sharing secrets?"

"Depends on how much my back keeps hurting."

My reply comes out like a purr. His eyes alight. Satyrs have a particular knack for seduction of all forms. I've laid it on thick enough to entice him, to make him think he might have a chance of parting my ass later and pounding into me.

Ultimately, my brother and I can't stay locked up. That we're still alive means the mortals aren't done with us yet, and they've got lots of iron in their toy collection. If fooling Scorpio will get us out of this cage, I'll do what I have to, including flirt my balls off with this motherfucker.

Like well-behaved prey, the water Fae creeps nearer. "As for the whipping, a brownie traversing along the borderline witnessed an outbreak between your band and three mortals, which escalated into more. Those tidings came to me a lot quicker than the first, so I manifested into town."

"Oh, the benefits of glamour. Between all that spent magic, you must be exhausted."

"I'll live. But will you?" A rabid hiss slides from his lips, the sound evoking his river origins. "Join us, and I'll set you free."

"Two problems. How? And what about my brother? He's not awake to make the decision for himself."

"To the first, it's called a mortal key. From what I hear, the blacksmith keeps a duplicate in his forge."

"Being mortal doesn't make them idiots," I drawl. "That key would be forged from iron."

"I'll find a way around that, like I found a way around you three. To the second, convince Cerulean later. Satyrs are legendary tempters, are they not? Recruit him or speak for yourself, and he can rot into a corpse here."

The blithe suggestion raises the hairs along my arms. "Your devotion is touching."

I'm clever as fuck, but sometimes my mouth gets in the way of my brain and ends up going in the opposite direction. I might have sounded a little too insulted, a little too dedicated to a Fae who's not actually related to me by blood. Basically, I'd sounded a little too much like a human, or a brother, or both.

Scorpio's brows furrow. "My devotion is to my world. Yours is the one in question. We all saw them butcher our kin. I'm fighting for the wild because that's the vow I gave, and nothing will sever that."

And my mouth keeps talking. "Come to think of it, you never answered Cove's question."

He twitches, his scales throwing embers of light across the grass. At our meeting, Cove had asked the merman who broke him. I'm starting to think she was onto something.

Scorpio's gaze trips toward the illuminated flecks that splatter the ground. "No one broke me," he says. "I broke them."

Huh. I wasn't expecting him to answer.

Then again: water Fae.

His attention stays tacked to the ground. "I had a grandfather. Centuries of fatal bargains and pointless combats between Solitaries who held a variety of grudges narrowed my family down to the two of us. I worshipped him." Scorpio's mouth twists. "During The Trapping, the humans caught my grandfather while he was trying to save someone."

To say the least, I was hoping Scorpio's story would be flat, hollow enough to disregard. Moth had lost her parents to The Trapping. Cerulean had lost the fauna family who raised him—all but Tímien. Elixir had lost his mothers, and I almost lost Sylvan.

Countless Faeries were deprived because of the uprising. I can't argue with Scorpio there. Only months ago, I was delighted to drop my human sacrifices into a hunting game. The ones who refused got shackled in The Redwoods of Exile, where they either keeled over from thirst or were eaten alive by predators.

I'd watched both happen and hadn't flinched.

But didn't Scorpio just say he'd done the breaking, not the other way around? How does that fit in? And who was the grandfather trying to save?

I'd ask, but it's pointless. Only a smidgen of me cares about the answers. My woman and our kid might still be languishing on the brink of death if the petal doesn't work, my brother has been tortured to within an inch of his life, and my back feels like it's been deep-fried for brunch.

My shit-list keeps getting longer. I've got plenty to keep the dregs of my sanity occupied.

In any case, Scorpio's blinks, and his features wad into a grimace. He's reached his threshold, as far as emotional bonding goes.

He considers the iron bars. "You could always stay here. I could let the humans do my job for me. Eventually, Elixir will come sniffing for your whereabouts, and they'll lump him with both of you. Without the ruling Three, the Fae on your side will have no leaders, thus no one cementing them together."

I shrug. "You're underestimating the ones fighting with us."

"You mean those paltry mortals who spread their legs for you?" While my knuckles curl, he contemplates the question. "They may have won their games, but in a war against the whole of our Solitary wild, I'm not worried. It could be amusing, watching them struggle without you. It might be even more fun if I capture one of them, see what it's like to hold them prisoner."

He licks his lips. "Perhaps I'll leave you here and make good on that idea. Perhaps I'll find out all the different ways your whore can scream—"

My hand cannonballs through the grille, clamps onto his nape, and hauls him forward. Scorpio's forehead hammers into the bars, his scales roasting on impact just as badly as my arm. I don't give a toasted fuck, don't mind the burn because trapping him like this feels too good.

The merman growls, jerking backward in vain as I fasten him against the rail and lean so close my lips almost touch the bars. "Big mistake, luv." I jolt him backward, only to slam him again into the grille, the force making the cage shudder. "And now who said anything about you leaving?"

I've got him where I want him. I can stay like this for an eternity, or at least until two of two things happen—first, this moron reaches medium-well temperature and, second, the humans come back and find him with us.

In any case, if it's between sharing a cage with this fucker and letting him go free, the choice is easy.

Except I'd forgotten a minor detail. No Fae travels without a weapon.

The flashing tip of a knife lurches through the bars. A hand intercepts, catching Scorpio's wrist inches from the side of my throat and shackling the merman in a steady grip.

"Careful now," Cerulean whispers from beside me, his voice fatally calm. "Be very careful about playing with sharp objects, or you might drop one."

Whatever residual strength my brother has salvaged goes into that grip, clenching so hard Scorpio's fingers snap open.

Cerulean swipes the hilt with his free hand, but the sautéed merman manages to break from our combined grips and lunge backward.

Griddle tracks cinder his forehead. His scales radiate, throwing light across the vale. I should have suspected that just because his trident had been absent, that hadn't meant he was brainless.

The merman touches his charred flesh and seethes at us. "Suit yourselves. Let the mortals have you." With that, he fumbles through the pocket of his shirt and tosses a small pouch into the cage. "Brought you a care package."

Cerulean casts the gift a dubious glance, but I was done pacing myself a while ago. I snatch up the parcel, rip the thing open, and watch a single petal flutter to the floor. It's shaped like the point of a starburst. Shades of copper, bronze, gold, and silver fluctuate like a prism, each color melting into the next.

The Evermore Blossom shimmers between us like a sucker punch.

"By any chance, did you need that for something?" Scorpio brags, then rises and walks backward. "Two down. One more to go."

He strides from the cage and slips into the briers as if they're made of water.

"Now you see him," I mutter to myself. "Now you don't." Afterward, I slump on my ass, my earrings tinkling as I drive a hand through my hair.

Cerulean picks the Evermore Blossom from the ground and reclines sideways as if he's lounging on a throne. He winces with the movement yet still manages to look graceful, even while in pain.

His dark blue hair slides across his cheek as he studies the petal, which sways hypnotically in his hand. "He was bluffing, Puck."

"I know," I growl.

"This petal isn't the same size."

"I said, I know."

It had taken me a second too long to register that. The sample Lark collected had been smaller, likely from the flower's center. Scorpio's decoy is bigger, potentially from the outer edges of the blossom.

He must have amassed extra petals in advance while picking from the Evermore Bloom. His petty threat about enhancing more fauna proves he'd anticipated needing more. In that case, he had been fucking with us. He'd guessed we were in enemy territory for a piece of the flower, even if he hadn't known what for. And upon hearing the mortals had caught us, Scorpio had assumed we'd be ripe for coercion.

So he'd brought one of the petals on the way to Reverie Hollow, just in case he needed to either barter or rile us up, make us believe he'd intercepted our band after they had escaped.

Seeing as I'd pissed him off, the scorned merman chose to spite us rather than use the petal as a final bargaining chip. He might be formidable, but like Elixir had once advised us, Scorpio's also just that transparent.

I nudge my chin toward Cerulean's sagging wings. "I heard you're missing a few. How are the rest?"

He grimaces. "They've certainly felt better."

"Can you fly?"

"Not with this much iron in my system. It appears Scorpio possesses quite some reserves if he withstood the element long enough to sustain a conversation with you, of all Faeries."

"Wise ass. Just how long were you awake before coming to my rescue?"

"Long enough to be quiet about it."

And that's why he's the refined trickster of us three.

"Anyway," I continue, "I've learned multiple times from my woman how far persistence can take anybody. Scorpio was maniacal enough to deal with the iron, the same way an Unseelie Fae will carve an extremist mantra into their flesh."

On that note, I slide the knife over to Cerulean. "Better keep that hidden. Got any clue how long we've been out here?"

Cerulean glances at the inclines and briers flanking us. "A few hours or a few days. It could be either. Though, I'd say the former based on Scorpio's timing and the state of your back."

"Ugh." I rub my shoulder. "Did you have to remind me?"

Tired chuckles pull from our mouths. However, they peter out once Cerulean's breaths turn shallow. Short puffs scrape from his mouth, and his complexion bleaches as he casts about the cage, trauma resurrecting itself like a phantom.

Shit. The location is hitting him.

"Hey." I nudge his calf with my hoof. "Let's play a game."

"For once, I'm not in a gaming mood."

"Aww, don't be bashful. Tell me something, luv. Just concentrate and switch one memory for another. Could be anything, see? So long as it takes me off guard. That's the objective: Try and rattle me. I dare you."

Cerulean's eyes slide over to the creek. "Do you remember the time Elixir made a test brew that dyed your antlers purple?"

I cough. "Fables and fuck, you're good at this."

"It was a lavender color, if I'm not mistaken."

"Oh, now you're laying it on thick."

"I still remember the flummoxed look on his face and the appalled expression on yours."

I groan. "Serves me right for volunteering to be his guinea pig."

Cerulean's mouth ticks. "To be fair, he'd claimed it was supposed to mend a crack in your crown."

"How much do you want to bet he wasn't as regretful as he looked?"

"Apologies, satyr. I already lost that bet to Moth when it happened."

I huff with laughter. "We'd just become rulers."

He nods. "Brothers."

The three of us had decided that day to bond ourselves, pledge ourselves to each other. If we had to lead the wild, we'd do it as one.

Reminiscing slows Cerulean's outtakes and soothes his pallor, at least so he doesn't resemble a ghost of himself. Good, because to get out of this, we might need to rely solely on one another. Who knows what state our band is in, or where the fuck Tímien has vanished? There's no telling what could be keeping any of them from reaching us.

Least of all, if I let myself stew on what's happening with Juniper, I'll self-destruct and puke my intestines out.

Since picking a lock with a petal or a knife won't get us anywhere, Cerulean stores both under his wings. Beyond that, our choices are severely limited. The Evermore Blossom is an amplifier for endurance, vitality, and natural instincts. It has the power to enhance strength but not against the effects of iron, so the petal can't help us there. It won't leach the iron from our blood or stitch up our wounds.

As for magic, that's reduced outside of Faerie.

Glamour? Yes.

Manifesting? Yes.

Beseeching nature's help? Yes.

Doing any of those things after being flogged by iron rods? No.

Calling through the roots or wind? Also, no.

Apart from some cute parlor tricks, iron wipes Faeries of most abilities. Lastly, without the longbow and javelin—who knows where those are?—an escape is going to take creativity, plus a lot more rest.

Already, Cerulean's sinking to the floor. My head drops onto the flat of steel, my eyelids falling shut.

After that, consciousness comes in fits and bursts. Hunger and thirst follow close behind.

The sky shifts from stars, to sunlight, to clouds. Then eventide falls again.

At some point, I blink. Flames snap in my face, a boot kicks the cage, and a mortal accent grunts, "Still alive, monsters? Why waste your time? No one's coming. They abandoned you. Any others won't know where to look because they never saw where we put you."

The light vanishes. I plunge into nothingness once more.

Another rotation of lightness and darkness consumes the woods. My dry tongue gets drier, but the starvation gnawing on my gut finally lets up.

Visions sweep through. Figures chasing a doe who's my friend, my leg wedged into a set of jowls, my hoof leaking blood, and a small girl with green eyes.

Then a sound brushes against my ears. Muffled footfalls pat the grass, the steps light and quick. The noise stirs me awake, the world blurry except for a single figure kneeling by the cage, a hood draped over the stranger's head.

I squint as the compartment rattles like bones, hinges squeal as the door opens, and the visitor crawls inside on all fours. Alarm hits me like an axe to an oak. My fingers spider-crawl backward and slip under Cerulean's limp wings, searching for the knife.

Then a voice cracks through the space, crisp as a newly lit fire. *"Once in the dark forest, a Stag hunted a Doe."*

My hand stalls. A second later, my head snaps up. "I'm dreaming."

But the figure pushes back the hood, green hair spilling from its confines. Eyes of the same vibrant color glow through the darkness.

Juniper clasps the sides of my face and shakes her head, her cool breath rushing against my lips. "Then it's time to wake up," she rasps before sinking her mouth to mine.

21

Her lips slant, fitting with mine and pulling my mouth in deeply. The aroma of woodsmoke and the sweet tang of berry syrup drug my senses. Her nostrils flare, and she intensifies the kiss, as if consuming my own flavor and scent.

I'd rip myself away and make sure it's really her, check that I'm not hallucinating from the iron. But the second Juniper sighs, and I hear the voice that always sounds like kindling, I don't need to check.

I know every sound she makes. And Fables, I know every way she tastes.

I'm not going mad. She's here. This is real.

With a groan, I snatch her cheeks and grind my mouth into hers. My tongue lunges between the crease and strikes inside to lap up that voice, to swallow that taste.

Juniper's fingers sweep into my hair and grasp the roots, the sensation climbing up my antlers and capsizing the fucking world.

As our mouths clutch, a sob leaks from her throat. The noise shoves me from the delirium, the sound unlike my resilient huntress. And then I remember everything that happened before this moment.

I wrench my mouth from Juniper's but stay close. We pant for air as I hold her face and scan those pert features, then let my gaze drop down Juniper's frame. She's in one flesh-and-blood piece. She's breathing. I watch her stomach inflate and deflate, then launch my eyes back to those steady ones. They're as bright as they were before that hellish episode by the ancient oak.

"Puck," she chokes out, clasping my jaw and riveting her gaze on me.

"Juniper." I race my thumbs over her chin, then reality hits me, and I bark, "What the fuck are you thinking, coming after me? The kid—"

"Will be all right."

"You can't risk this."

"No, I can't. You've met me, haven't you? Do you honestly think I'd disregard precautions?"

"Then tell me what I need to hear," I growl.

"I'm okay," Juniper promises. "The Evermore Blossom worked. It took a day to penetrate, but it worked. Elixir extracted from it and heard the protective coating grow around the embryo, and I started feeling better." She clutches my face. "You're alive."

My panic deflates. "That's supposed to be my line, luv."

"What happened? Everyone else came back, but none of them would tell me anything other than my people took you and Cerulean."

"They just wanted to protect you."

"Then they should know it's worse to keep me in the dark." Her eyes tremble as she takes in the cuts and blood stains across my chest. "How badly did they hurt you?"

Because she hasn't seen my back yet, I shake my head. "We're not going there. It doesn't matter." I glance at the broken padlock hanging like a shocked mouth from the cage door. "How did you manage that nifty trick?"

Her lips tilt. "I have experience saving wild things."

My own mouth twists. "Smart woman."

"I thought I'd never hear you say that again."

"It's pretty hard to shut me up, much less for good."

"Truth be told, it wasn't just me." Juniper holds up an apparatus with a handle and two wands, one of them shaped into a curlicue, the whole thing constructed and polished from hardwood stems. "I have a certain sister who used to be a pickpocket and a thief. She can make keys out of anything."

Juniper looks like she wants to say more, but her lips clamp together. That systematic mind takes over, features rearranging themselves. "We have to move," she whispers. "I scouted the area, and the townsfolk are operating in shifts to monitor you. They still haven't decided whether to let you starve or take further advantage."

"Anger versus strategy."

She nods. "But instead of standing post near the cage, they're expecting another Fae ambush, so the trade poachers rigged snares around the area."

Huh. Nothing my woman can't get around. Lark must have gotten Juniper up to speed about the fuckwits from their recent past.

Juniper glances at Cerulean, concern warping her eyebrows. "How is he?"

"Ask me yourself," my brother suggests with his lids still closed. An instant later, two blue eyes find us through the darkness, then leap across the cage in confusion. "Where's Lark?"

Juniper winces. "Lark's hurt—but she'll be okay," she rushes out when Cerulean vaults upright, his face a frantic mask. "She tried to jump from Cypress's back while he was galloping through the forest. Lark didn't want to leave you, but Cypress was going too fast. The landing wasn't a smooth one. She broke her leg."

Cerulean hisses, both from the pain of moving and worry for his mate. Juniper gives him a swift rundown. Elixir brewed Lark a remedy to heal the leg, but it takes a couple of days to simmer, plus another day or so to take effect.

In the meantime, while our brother's toiling on that, Cypress is looking after Lark. Apparently, he blames himself for not keeping a hold on the spitfire, as if anyone can.

The news settles the weight on Cerulean's shoulders. He wouldn't have wanted Lark to endanger herself, but nothing else would have kept her away.

"Wait," I say, registering the crossbow hitched to Juniper's back. "You fucking came alone?"

She compresses her lips, as though I'm being fussy. "We don't have time to discuss logistics."

"Nonsense. You always have time for that."

"Not tonight."

She motions for Cerulean to get off his ass, then offers me her free arm. I grunt, wishing I didn't need the help, but my legs feel like they've disintegrated. Not to mention, the iron is making me woozy.

The Evermore Blossom must have equipped Juniper with added strength. She links her arm around my waist and helps lug my weight off the floor, but then we stop, crouching and glancing expectantly at my brother. Still, he hasn't budged.

His grim eyes click from Juniper to me. That look takes root, reminding me that although neither of us can lie, my brother is a master diverter. He can flip the truth inside out better than even I can.

And I know. I fucking know before his blue mouth pushes out the words. "I'll have to respectfully decline."

"What?" Juniper mutters under her breath. "Cerulean—"

"I'm too heavy."

"And I have two arms. I'll help you both."

"No, Juniper," he stresses. "I'm too heavy."

Stupefied, she glances from him to me. I bunch my mouth, then force myself to draw out the rest. "His wings were cut. He can't retract them."

Her eyes widen. She swings her head back to Cerulean, noticing the crevices where dozens of feathers used to be.

The iron has weakened him too much, to the point where he can't sheath his wings. The mass is impossible for him to carry on his own, and even with the Blossom's enhancement, Juniper can't take the brunt of two Faeries plus her weapon. As it is, it would require half a dozen centaurs to heft Cerulean's drooping wingspan.

Earlier, he'd implied he could technically fly, that his wings weren't torn beyond repair, that the only thing holding him back was the iron in his system.

But the prat never said he could get off the ground first.

Gliding and flapping while airborne are the easier parts for a mountain Fae. It's launching and landing that takes stamina.

Juniper's face tightens like it does whenever she's struggling to rationalize a way out. But for all her foresight and knowledge, she hadn't considered both Faeries lacking the vigor to hold themselves up. At least, not at the same time.

I'm shaking my head before Cerulean has a chance to piss me off further. "You immortal prick."

Cerulean sighs. "I'll survive."

"Bloody true because you're going. I'm staying."

"Puck," Juniper hazards.

I twist to her stricken features. "He's my brother. What would you do?"

She wavers, thinking of her sisters. She's about to answer when Cerulean's whisper reaches us. "Puck," he murmurs. "You're a father."

The words float across the cage and seep into my gut. My gaze fastens to Juniper, her irises flooded by so much green, so much life brimming there.

I drag my attention back to my brother and feel my face twitching. I hate this so much, hate that he's the one who's petrified of cages, hate that I'm leaving him to face a living nightmare.

"Fuck," I mutter, then reach out to grip his hand. "If you don't stay alive, I'll kill the shit out of you."

His lips flex into a half-smirk. He squeezes me back. "Go well and be swift."

Juniper fishes into her cloak pocket and presses a small flask and jar into Cerulean's palm. "Water," she says, her voice cracking. "And ointment I stole from Cypress's reserves when I left. It's supposed to alleviate pain and injuries quickly. And... *jvjalp mun joma.*"

Help is coming.

Cerulean's gaze swerves from the containers to Juniper. A grin slips across his face. "You're a fast learner."

Juniper swallows. "They're coming. I promise."

But what happens until then is the problem. While the ointment will nourish his wings, the iron will still be an issue. The longer he's here, the worse it'll get.

If that happens, my brother will deteriorate to the point where he'll permanently lose his ability to fly, healed feathers or not. Cerulean will relapse to his fledgling years, unable to remember how to use his wings or other powers, assuming he gets his magic back, all while trapped in the one place he fears most.

Neither Cerulean, nor I need to tell Juniper this. She knows, but each of us pretends that isn't a probability.

Juniper offers Cove's makeshift key to Cerulean, but he refuses. It'll do him no good if he can't haul himself to a standing position. Whoever comes to his aid will need the key more.

Instead, my brother tucks Scorpio's knife deeper into his wings, and we refasten the bolt. The humans will assume I found a way to pry open the padlock, then latched my brother inside and left him behind. With Cerulean still caged, hopefully they'll think he was abandoned, and they won't take their rage out on him.

But if the humans suspect I've gone for help, they might question him the hard way. In which case, Cerulean will need to exercise his devious silver tongue more than ever.

I cast him another glance. "Keep playing the game. Keep thinking of memories that'll rattle me. You'll need them when we see each other again. You'll need them to win. Understand?"

Cerulean puffs through his pain. "Tell her I love her."

I won't have to because he'll live to tell Lark himself. Nevertheless, I nod before Juniper hoists me out of the cage.

My arm hooks over her shoulder. With each lopsided step, my back and shoulder rage, and I sink my teeth into my lower lip, muffling the noises grating from my lungs.

We hobble down the vale until a gash appears in the briers, then slip through and scale the incline. Once we clear the slope and put enough distance between the cage and ourselves, Juniper starts multitasking. She balances my weight as best she can while trying to distract me from the wounds by listing a bunch of details.

Cypress and Foxglove are still infected by the iron. Although my best friend had been as stubborn as Juniper, wanting to return for me and Cerulean, he had been temporarily immobilized. Moreover, he'd known I would massacre him if he left Juniper before she got better.

Meanwhile, our band had been plotting a rescue once everyone recovered. Until then, they'd insisted Juniper stay put.

Because we'd talked about sending her father a letter, Juniper tamed her panic by writing one with her sisters and dispatching Lark's nightingale to deliver it.

As for Tímien, he still isn't back from wherever he'd gone. No one has seen or heard from the raptor, and at this point, that isn't like him. Even The Parliament are in an uproar searching every crevice of the mountain for him, which explains why the owl hasn't come to his son's rescue.

Anyway, the second she had regained her strength, my woman took off on her own. For the first leg of the journey, she'd hitched a ride with Sylvan, who fared better from the iron than everyone else. Once they got far enough, fast enough, Juniper sent the deer back to centaur territory, needing to make the final trek by herself.

Pure and simple, she had disagreed with the band's plot. As we'd already learned, a team of humans and Faeries are too loud, easier to ferret out.

By comparison, Juniper's light on her feet, can fit through crawlspaces, and knows the forest's shortcuts well enough now, in addition to how fluent she is in her homeland. She'd needed to move deftly, without being seen or heard, because that's what a huntress does.

But make no mistake, Elixir and the rest won't be far behind.

And when it comes to the mortals, their next move is anyone's guess.

Juniper theorizes. Sometime during these last months, the trade poachers had ridden back into town—once their balls grew back after the scare my brothers and I gave them when Lark first rode into Faerie, just before the sisters' games had started.

Back then, the poachers had followed Lark and stalled outside the border. Cerulean, Elixir, and I had enjoyed terrorizing those men, giving them a taste of trauma.

But who cares if they hadn't actually crossed The Triad? We should have done worse to them. Dammit, we should have let Elixir blind those fuckers like he'd originally wanted to.

They'd probably returned later, on a payback mission to find Lark, Juniper, and Cove. Instead, they must have heard rumors about the sisters' fate.

Clearly, the men had charmed the villagers. And feasibly, Juniper had been right about her earlier hunch. Maybe the neighbors had gotten riled up once they heard Lark had returned to Faerie, that she'd allegedly gone to be near her sisters, who were still being held captive.

That would explain the aerial signal the poachers had sent to the town once our battle had started. Both sets had unresolved grievances, the villagers especially.

Armed to the teeth, the poachers had decided to squat near Faerie and wait for an opportunity, a chance to trap our kin. If a grudge and an ego are a big enough combination, that'll make anyone stupid.

What matters is, they saw Lark. Now the village knows she's siding with Faeries. Easily, they've drawn the same conclusions about Juniper and Cove. It could be the final land mine needed to stir up shit, to get the humans to take action after nine years.

Our breaths puff into the night as we trundle down a backwoods path. Juniper moves confidently, without having to double-check the unmarked route. She creeps through as if she's done it a thousand times.

"You've been here before," I pant.

"It's a passage my sisters and I used to take when scouting for rescues," she replies while guiding me around a shrub. "We've done it so many times, it feels as though we've carved out a secret trail. See the indentations in the mulch?"

Small imprints and depressions have camouflaged themselves into the vegetation, the signs only visible to someone who knows how to hunt or track.

"Hidden in plain sight," I remark. "I approve."

"You would. Everything you do is hidden in plain sight."

"Oh, come now. I'm much more candid about certain things. You're not the only show-off in this relationship."

At my flirtatious tone, a chuckle trips out of Juniper's mouth. Partly, it sounds natural. But another part sounds forced.

She says this path will take longer to get to The Faerie Triad, but it'll keep us out of range from the market square. As a result, it's the slowest trip in the history of slow trips, worthy of its own epic Fable.

Eventually, we spill into the open plains, where a creek slithers through and flows toward a silhouette of jagged mountains. We follow the water. Based on its briny scent, it must be the creek from Elixir's past, back when Cove and my brother were young enemies during The Trapping. According to both, she had tried to drown him here, but Cerulean had swooped in and stopped it from happening.

That had been around the same time I'd been firing arrows at humans chasing me and Sylvan. That night, I had believed Juniper helped them track me down.

Despite the higher grass in this area, only sheer luck prevents us from getting spotted while staggering across the pastures and looping northeast. The Triad looms overhead like a gate. The instant we stumble past the hawthorn, oak, and ash trees, everything changes.

The stars shift position in the sky. The colors transform to white, teal, and gold, each one spraying the landscape with metallic sheens. The distant calls of fauna ring like bells or horns, the sounds endless and vast, as if we're in a hall of caves. And the air flooding my nostrils smells different from Juniper's world, as familiar as the soil.

Fireflies zip through the foliage, able to brand the skin of anyone they touch. We cross through the insects' colony and head to the cul-de-sac where three routes lead to three different regions.

A few steps later, two of those routes dissolve, and one remains. I swear, I've never been so fucking relieved to see candles twitching from the branches or the row of oaks arcing like a ribcage down The Solitary Forest's entrance.

Through the arcade and along a narrow lane, we reach a grove of evergreens—the place where Juniper and I first reunited after nine years. The Wicked Pines is our territory, so we tuck ourselves into the thicket. And finally, we stop to catch our breaths.

Juniper releases me against a tree trunk and dumps her crossbow on the ground. I roll my good shoulder, which does barbaric things to my back, but the waterskin Juniper fishes from beneath a patch of needles makes up for that. We guzzle the contents and devour cured meat and bread, also from the hidden stash.

I'd ask, but there's no bother. She must have planned for us to rest here, storing the provisions ahead of time.

Once we're sated, I slouch. "My, my, my," I heave, grinning through my exhaustion. "You are one determined woman."

Juniper wrinkles her nose, as if this should be common knowledge. "Well. It wasn't my sweet disposition that you fell for."

My thumb streaks across her cheekbone. "I fell for everything."

She gulps and steps back from my touch, about to reply when another voice gripes, "You know, when you told me to be patient, I didn't think you meant I'd have to be patient for eternity."

I whirl as a figure stomps from the fringes, his orange irises blazing. A bristling marten tail swishes from the Fae's ass. If his trim figure isn't a dead giveaway for his pubescent age, that sour puss scrunching his face like a dishrag does the rest.

Juniper packs away the rations. "You're immortal," she points out. "You have forever to live."

"Thanks for the reminder," the Fae grouses. "For a minute there, I forgot what the fuck *immortal* meant."

"My point is that patience should be the least of your chores."

"Fantastic. As if Cypress and Moth aren't already thorns in my side. Now I'm being lectured by a human."

"Ah, ah, ah," I interrupt. "That wasn't a lecture."

A quote hops off Juniper's tongue. "Choose diversions wisely, lest they lead to downfall."

I nod. "*That* was the lecture."

But my words snap the Fae out of his rant. The orange vine markings crinkling through his forehead smooth out when he sees me. "Puck."

"Tinder." Grinning, I plant my hand on his shoulder. "And here, I thought my woman had operated alone."

"Well," Juniper admits while coming to stand beside me. "I had a task that warranted help. Tinder came to my aid." Knowing he'll squirm at a verbal expression of gratitude, she offers an appreciative glance instead. "I knew I could rely on you."

Her compliment brings a rosy tint to the Fae's epicene features. He twists and plucks something off the grass, then nocks his proud chin and extends it to me. "We thought you'd miss these."

Another weight crumbles from my chest. I take the longbow and quiver, holding the weapons up to a shaft of starlight. Apart from a few scratches, the yew wood is intact.

The mortals either forgot to confiscate my weapons while carting me and Cerulean away, or they plainly hadn't seen the archery lying in the high grass.

Juniper suspected that might have happened, since our band couldn't remember us wielding our weapons at the point when they left. That much, she'd gotten out of them.

On the way to Reverie Hollow, Juniper had recruited Tinder for a mission to scout the area where I'd landed in the trap, in case anything had been left behind. Being slender enough to pass through unseen, Tinder had also reclaimed Cerulean's discarded javelin.

Lifting the archery for too long aggravates my shoulder, so I lower my arm and bow my head at Tinder. "A favor well done."

He beams. "It wasn't a favor—this time."

I laugh, the sound rumbling from my chest. But then a gasp cuts off the mirth.

Tinder and I glance at Juniper, whose eyes have dipped to something behind me. What she sees drains the peach complexion from her skin. That's when I realize how far I'd turned toward the Fae.

Juniper's haunted gaze crawls across my naked back, taking in what's sure to be a mess of pulped skin dried with blood.

My tongue is about to launch into a lame, sugar-coated explanation that she'll never believe. But instead, it's Tinder's turn to hiss.

"Fables eternal," he splutters, disgust etching his voice. "And they call us abominations."

A sigh blows from my mouth. Like my woman, I'd contest the point if I had the energy. My kin are just as guilty of brutality. Our cruelty isn't much different; it's just covered in a layer of pixie dust.

In our world, low-hanging fruit will suffocate as much as cure. Riddles are amusements as much as they're deceptions. The fauna are as sacred as they are feral.

There's beauty and viciousness here, just like there is in the mortal realm. The viciousness in Faerie merely looks prettier from a distance.

I could say all this. But instead, I mutter over my shoulder, "Tinder."

He nods and harnesses the javelin. "I'll...bring this to Lark."

"Not just that. Tell them we're alive, but they still have Cerulean."

I don't have the strength yet to call them through the roots. Tinder can do that, though manifesting means he won't need to.

Juniper hands her sister's makeshift key to the Fae and lists meticulous directions to Cerulean's cage, including every snare the poachers laid out. Because Tinder is skilled at remembering details, he doesn't need them written down. He dashes into the pines, his marten tail bouncing behind him, then fading as he evanesces.

After that, my woman and I are alone.

22

Everything goes silent but Juniper's haggard breathing. The constellations stubble her features in colorful specks. They shift erratically as her gaze jumps from the wasteland that's evidently become my back to my face as I turn fully in her direction.

I haven't peeked over my shoulder, but I don't need to. Her expression says it all.

Juniper's voice cracks like a twig. "What did they do to you?"

"It's just a few trivial scratches," I dismiss. "The mortals couldn't keep their hands off me. As usual, my animal magnetism was too much for them."

No surprise, the mirth falls flat. From about a mile away, the call of a bear cleaves through the forest.

I lick my lips and start again. "Juniper."

"Don't." Her ragged features work hard to prop themselves up, each piece clicking back into place despite her ashen complexion. She switches to efficiency mode and grabs my hand. "Come."

She drags me past a cluster of hollows, ushers me through a fence of pine saplings, and urges me into the ground pool where she'd once bathed during the start of her game. I remember ordering the forest nymphs to ready Juniper for me—for the hunt. What she doesn't know is how tempted I was to kick the nymphs out of the enclosure so I could spy on Juniper, observe her at my leisure while she ran soap down her naked body.

I hadn't given in to the temptation. But that hadn't stopped me from pacing, edgy with the strange desire to see her covered in nothing but suds. I hadn't known why yet, but she had strung me tightly from the start.

Without another word, Juniper presses me toward the depression until I dunk myself in. My naughty side wants to invite her to soak with me, so I can run my tongue up between her wet breasts, but the warm water is too overwhelming. I groan and wash myself while Juniper keeps checking the area, her eyes averted from me like a virgin instead of a woman who's had my cock inside her more times than either of us can tally.

This is the part where I'd put on a show and mosey out of the pool slowly, allowing rivulets to slide down my skin, all for her viewing pleasure. Sadly, she's having none of it. Juniper waits as I climb out, liquid splashing the grass as I step into my pants. They're covered in grime, but I can't have everything, and clothes can be remedied later.

She guides me from the hollow to our original location. A series of brisk, one-word instructions follow. Juniper tugs me to the grove's center—"Here"—and ushers me to the ground—"Sit"—then lowers herself behind me—"Turn"—and twists my shoulders away from her.

I listen to her cloak rustle as she fumbles either through her pockets or a pouch stashed under the mantle. Based on the slide of a drawstring, I'd say it's the latter.

Seconds later, a minty aroma fills the air. Cold cream slathers over the craters in my shoulder and down my spine. I cringe at the initial sting, then slump in relief as the chilled substance melts into my flesh. The lingering burns start to ebb.

My eyes shutter while Juniper's digits feather over the wounds, dabbing each one with the salve.

"Fuck," I exhale. "That feels good."

Juniper's tone sounds concentrated—or rather, distant. "It's the same ointment I gave Cerulean. It'll clean and relieve the wounds."

Although I can already guess why, I tease, "Any reason you brought two vials with you?"

"Of course."

"You going to tell me?"

"In case I lost the first one."

Planning for all inconveniences. That draws a light chuckle from my chest while the cream revives my mood. "Remember this place?"

"Yes," she replies, as if it's a trivia question. "This is where we reunited. I walked in on your bacchanal."

"Call it what it was: an orgy. Plus, you say that like it's a bad thing. Every memorable couple meets during a public sex binge."

"What books have you been reading?"

"What do you take me for? Naturally, the smutty ones."

She snorts, her palms coated in salve and gliding over my shoulders. "And that ostentatious throne of yours, woven out of stinging nettles."

"Ah," I reminisce with exaggerated wistfulness. "I forgot about the throne. I miss my throne."

"Do you miss the orgies?"

Now my grin broadens, hearing the censure in her voice. "Not lately. A certain mortal has provided me with an infinitely more satisfying alternative."

I expect her to stifle a grin, but her silence implies the opposite. She's still frowning, still remote. "Hey, luv?"

At my low murmur, her fingers stall. "What?"

"They'll heal."

Behind me, Juniper absorbs those words and then keeps going, sweeping down to the base of my spine. Lightly, she massages the salve into my muscles, the cold tingling and careful pressure making me hum in satisfaction.

Her touch is warm and intent. It's also detached like she's fixing a glitch instead of nursing a lover.

I try again. "You never finished the Fable."

"The Fable?" she repeats. "Which one?"

"From when you broke into the cage. Why'd you go with that one?"

"You know why."

"Maybe I want to hear you say it."

Her ministrations lag, thumbs rolling into skin and sinew. "Well. Some pairings have a song. I like to think we have a Fable."

My head twists halfway over my shoulder, so she can see my mouth slanting. "Indulge an injured Fae."

Her voice comes out faint, as if it might float away. *Once in the dark forest, a Stag hunted a Doe. So she hunted him back.*

She narrates the rest while brushing cream into my joints and the gashes made by the iron trap. Her voice and fingers leach away the pain, to the point where I feel tipsy from both.

At some point, Juniper guides me onto the grass and continues the Fable. The surrounding pines dissolve. All that's left is her voice reaching through the darkness.

What feels like seconds later, my eyes drift open. I'm lying on my side with a small form curled like a snail behind me, a pair of limbs tucked under mine and a set of booted feet tangled with my hooves. Juniper's heat radiates down my body as her fingers sketch my wounds, tracing the slashes. Based on the lines she draws, there are lots of them.

Despite that, the iron lashes don't burn anymore. And my skin's not raw to the touch, either. Also, my limbs feel lighter, stronger than they did hours ago. Although I'm not completely there yet, sparks of power filter through my veins.

But that's not what snaps me fully awake. It's the trembling set of fingers running across my back—and the subdued tears clogging Juniper's throat. Unlike before, she's touching me unsteadily, with less composure but more familiarity...like she's been studying the flog markings, memorizing their shapes.

As though she hasn't been sleeping at all. As though she's been awake all this time.

Juniper's voice shatters against my back. "I wasn't there," she utters, pressing her lips to one of the markings. "I wasn't there."

That fractured tone cuts me in half. I flip around and clasp her wet face in my hands. "No," I warn, my own voice gruff. "Don't fucking do that to yourself."

"I wasn't there to save you," she hiccups, her face leaking with tears. "I wasn't there to keep it from happening."

"Stop it," I rasp.

"I didn't know what happened to you. I could only imagine." Her voice collapses into sobs, everything she'd been holding back falling from her mouth. "I didn't know if you were alive. I didn't know if I'd ever see you again. And I just...what they did to you...I wasn't *there*."

"Shush." My lips swoop down and catch hers, planting an urgent kiss there and then dragging back to speak against them. "Shush, luv. It's over."

"I wasn't there, and I'm sorry. I'm so sorry, Puck."

I shake my head and take her lips again.

And again. And again.

With a whimper, Juniper kisses me back. Her mouth surges against mine, harsh and hard, and over, and over, and over.

I groan and fuse my arms around her waist, crushing her to my chest. We suck in air between each kiss, the pace hectic, the pressure furious, and the need primitive.

Until it's not enough.

My tongue spears through the crease of her mouth and pitches into that hot, deep place. A sweet noise coils from her throat as she flexes her own tongue with mine. My cock hardens, rising thick and high against the heat sweltering from the split of her legs.

My woman keens, feeling my dick flush with her thighs. Her nostrils flare, and her mouth shoves harder into mine. I growl and whip my tongue into Juniper, opening her wide and licking inside.

On a moan, Juniper tows herself back. "I don't want to hurt—"

"You won't," I grit out, sinking my mouth into hers again.

My woman knows what Fae ointments can achieve in a short time span. She'll only hurt me if she stops. That will wreck me to pieces.

Our mouths clutch and rock together. Feverish, we move at the same time. With my back no longer hurting like fuck, I hoist Juniper off the grass while she pushes me onto my back and scrambles on top.

Her compact legs spread around my waist, her limbs quivering. I'm about to rip into her, shred those leggings to ribbons when she grabs my shoulders and thumps me into the ground, fastening me beneath her like prey. More tears flare from her eyes, but they take on a predatory light, like a huntress of the wild.

A huntress who's caught herself a satyr.

"Stay down," Juniper orders. "And do not fucking move."

That seven-letter word slides from her prim mouth, scorching at the tip of her tongue. The command sends a bolt of lust up the stem of my cock. Now I don't give a shit that my back's newly mended, because this woman can have me under her until the world fades.

A thousand impish replies sit on my own tongue, but each one dies a quick death when she bends forward and snatches my mouth with hers. Her lips spread and tug on mine, that smart tongue diving in and plying against my own. I hum and meet her lips, stroke for stroke. My jaw works, putting enough pressure into the kiss that she moans again.

Inching back, Juniper sinks her teeth into my lower lip, pain mixing with pleasure. I hiss, liking it so damn much. She licks the spot, then kisses it before burying her face in my neck.

My head arches into the grass as she bites my chin, nips under my jaw, and grazes her incisors down my throat. In between, Juniper plants damp, open-mouthed kisses on my pulse point, which is pounding like a drum. Every contact of her teeth and lips floods my balls with lust.

It gets more agonizing as she descends. Air stutters from my chest while her forehead drags down my muscles, burning a torturous path over my flesh. Her tongue sweeps across my nipples before she seizes one in her mouth, mopping the tip until a hoarse sound rumbles out of me.

Juniper lets out a mewl of appreciation, then switches to the other nipple, drawing on the tight skin. She lets go and nibbles on my pecs, the rack of muscles across my abdomen, and the slopes of my hipbones. And when her fingers settle on the leather waistband of my pants, my blood hammers so furiously, it threatens to crack a few bones.

My cock aches, shoving up against the material to the point where it might break the seams. Her hands unbuckle the closures. Then Juniper cranes her neck and peers up at me, her expression ravenous—intentional. Those eyes trap me inside them, and that look brands itself into me, and those fingers bring every filthy word in existence to the forefront of my mind.

Without taking her eyes away, the huntress peels the leather from my waist, down my hips, and over my ass. My cock springs free. It stretches over my torso, the column broad and heavy, the head ruddy and a droplet leaking from the slit.

Juniper rivets on the sight, licks her lips, and gazes at me. Like that, she swipes the bead with the tip of her fingers, collecting the liquid with the lightest of brushes, then lifting it to her tongue. As she laps up the arousal, my own tongue slams into the roof of my mouth.

At the taste of me, her eyes sharpen. "I want more."

"Then take it," I urge. "Take more."

"It's mine. Tell me your cock is mine."

"It's yours. It's all yours to fuck."

Juniper nods, then does something that drains the oxygen from my lungs. She licks her palm and wraps her fingers around the base of my cock.

Fuck. Me. Hard.

Her hand swoops up and down, spreading the wetness from her mouth over my dick and mixing it with the liquid seeping from my crown. I grow firmer, longer, hotter in her fingers. Juniper watches my features while she works her hand from my balls to my slit, watches my eyes roll to the back of my head, watches my mouth fall open on a silent groan.

I grow so thick from her touch, Juniper can barely get a full grip. With a hungry sigh, she bends over. Her green hair falls like a curtain around me, dampness radiates against my shaft, and then a soft tongue rides up the column, licking from the bottom to the top.

"Shit," I grit out, my voice brittle.

"Mmm," she croons around my aching cock, the sound vibrating.

She licks again, and again, and again. The flat of her tongue laps on me, sketching up and over, then pats the crest until I'm swollen for her. Broken exhales push from my mouth as she skims her tongue across the fine line cutting through my crown.

She does this again, running the flat across the roof of my erection, sketching it over and over.

Finally, she takes pity. A pair of soft lips strap around the head of my cock, the tender pleat of her mouth splitting around me and drawing on the head. And then she sucks on it like a morsel. The restrained groan tears out of me, the noise shredded like paper.

My spine burrows into the grass. My hands drive through her locks and clutch her scalp, my hips desperate to move.

Stay down. And do not fucking move.

I obey while Juniper moans around my cock. Her mouth encases the crown, her tongue lashing the slit, licking back and forth across the seam. Eager, she cups my ass and lifts me to her, then plunges fully. Her lips splay around my cock and sucks my entire length inside her.

Oh, fuck. A disjointed moan launches hard and harsh from my lungs as she pulls rhythmically on my standing dick. With a steady tempo, Juniper's head rolls. She increases the pressure and siphons me into her mouth.

I cling to her head and stare down, gazing at her open mouth taking my cock, pivoting it into her. The vision is too sexy, too mesmerizing. My hips can't take it anymore, can't keep still. Every muscle begs to take action, to meet her thrusting mouth.

My groans turn plaintive, but somehow, I muster the willpower to let go, let her take me over completely. Juniper tightens her grip on my ass, as if sensing the frantic need. She keens and accelerates, plunging her mouth over my cock. Her tongue swirls around the head, her lips fucking me senseless.

My balls tighten. Ecstasy rushes from the sac to my tip as Juniper tows on me, driving up and down. Her mouth clings to my stiff flesh, sucking so fiercely that I'm shouting into the woods.

Too pent up to listen anymore, my hips let loose and charge ahead, pumping my cock into her waiting mouth. Primal noises fill the air. My woman takes it quickly, deeply, furiously.

When I tense, she seals onto me. I go still…and then come with howl. "Fuck, Juniper!"

My cock detonates, heat and liquid spurting from the crown. Juniper keens, swallowing my release whole, not letting go until I'm spent.

Spent as hell. But not done.

Faeries don't work that way. *Satyrs* don't work that way.

With a satisfied hum, Juniper releases my cock. I want to kiss her. I want to spread her wide and taste her back, rake my tongue between her pussy and feast on her clit. But with renewed determination, the huntress scurries across my lap and relishes my slack features, pride and desire stretching across her face.

A second later, we're clamoring again. She wiggles her hips, her pace urgent. I help her, stripping the leggings down her thighs in one deft move, and she shoves them over her boots, then chucks them aside. The cloak, long shirt, and shoes are still on, but we're too fed up to care.

The tight patch of hair covering her pussy glistens, her desire made clear.

I want in there. Right fucking now.

I grip Juniper's hips and jerk her toward me, positioning her over my cock. Its stiff length glides between the lips of her cunt, sliding across her slickness, prompting a whimper from her. I tease my cock through her folds, the head nudging the wet walls and probing her.

Our mouths fall open, guttural moans shearing into the air. How I'd like to vault upward and slam into her until she comes apart.

But again, Juniper stamps me down by flattening her palms over my shoulders. She seizes the hilt of my cock and sinks onto it, her wet clutch fastening around me.

I rasp her name, and she cries out. Astride my waist, she takes me high and hard, enclosing me from root to crown. Leaning over, Juniper drops a swift kiss to my lips before she sets her hands on either side of my head and whips her hips forward.

My groan hits an octave that must be heard within a three-miles radius. Juniper flings her waist, bucking onto my cock, taking every inch.

With a grunt, I grab her hips and yank her forward, whisking her inner walls against me. Her cries splinter as she hunches over, widens her knees, and uses that for leverage. She juts into me while her gaze clings to mine, our gazes locking.

Her cloak flares open, two pink nipples stud from under her shirt, and her naked waist gyrates. She grinds that sweet, soaked pussy onto me. Her back caves as she rows her hips, stroking my cock, chasing every fragmented sound that skids from my mouth.

Tingles scatter across my scalp. My teeth clench. I sprawl under Juniper, letting myself be ridden, letting myself be fucked by this woman, this huntress who captured me a long time ago, years before I captured her.

When another groan scrolls from my tongue, Juniper pants, "Yes. Do it. Come just like that, Puck."

I'll do more than that. I'll come and then fuck her back.

The onslaught mounts. I dig my fingers into her pounding hips and howl so loudly my throat burns, the orgasm smashing into me with a vengeance. My cock twitches inside her, a second bout of release shooting from my body.

Juniper whines, riding my climax. But before it's over, I vault upright off the ground, my earrings ringing with the movement.

Ah, she's given me plenty. But a Fae never loses steam that quickly.

"My turn," I growl, then pull out and lurch my cock up into her.

My huntress cries out. "Oh!"

I shackle her ass and snap my hips, pitching repeatedly into the hot clamp of her body. Juniper reaches behind me, under my arms, and loops her fingers over my shoulders, the better to take the brunt of my thrusts. She swats her hips, meeting the force of my waist, our hips slamming into one another.

The muscles of my abdomen clench as I piston in and out, my crown entering and withdrawing fully. We dip our heads, staring as her wetness coats my cock, which disappears continuously into her beautiful, slick, open cunt.

Juniper's forehead lands against mine. Our lips graze while our waists bump, the pace frenzied. Her legs fall apart when I drive harder, deeper, faster.

Her walls suck me in, hugging every inch, so long and fluid. I hit a spot that makes the huntress sob, a root buried so far into her it brings out the primal satyr in me. I wring my arms around her waist and blast my hips upward, striking that place endlessly.

The force is so great, my woman bounces, catching every punch of my cock. Not one to be outdone, she rocks her waist and beats it against mine, her folds colliding with my thrusts. We hurl ourselves at each other, our hips shooting together.

Her cloak and shirt flap over her naked thighs, and with her boots covering her feet, this vision is the sexiest thing I've ever seen, like whenever she wears those prim spectacles while I'm inside her. But right now, my tongue has a craving, and the rest of these tedious clothes are getting in the way.

I bat the cloak apart, revealing the slender curves of her tits as they jostle. From under the shirt, her nipples peek, the tips as firm as stones. I swoop in and snatch one between my teeth.

Juniper mewls. Her back arches, shoving that breast against my lips.

Through the material, I nip at the bud and toughen the skin more. Then I lick the fabric wet, sketching my tongue around the pink edges of her nipple before drawing the whole shell into my mouth.

Her fingers scuttle from my shoulders to my hair, where they yank on the roots. I feel that sensation to the bladed points of my antlers. Starved for more, I suck her nipple raw, then prowl my mouth across her chest to the other nipple.

"Puck," Juniper stresses. "Fables, please."

"Please, what?" I snarl. "What do you need? Do you need more of my cock?"

But she just crushes a fist into her mouth, muffling her grunts as if they're about to burst. The air crackles. The overhead candles flash with light. Juniper writhes on me, quelling her moans like she needs to contain them, like they'll carve this wild in half if she lets them out.

But I want her to let them out, to let everything out. I want the sound of her pleasure to fill this wild to the brink.

I grab her fist and pull it from her lips. "None of that. Let this forest hear you."

"So good," she pleads. "Too good."

"More?"

"Yes."

Marvelous. I jerk on the tassels cinching her cloak in place, and the mantle slumps to the grass, puddling around her bent legs. Grabbing the cloak, I toss the thing so far across the enclosure, it smacks into the pine trees.

Juniper crosses her arms, about to strip the shirt over her head. Except she halts, shakes her head, and kisses me before muttering, "Rip it off."

Hell, yes. My fingers capture the neckline and wrench it down the middle, the echo of sheared fabric scraping through my ears. Juniper's tits and curves pop through the sagging gap in her shirt, the muscles of her figure flexing with my thrusts.

I haul the shirt across the enclosure, then band my arms around her, and heft us off the ground. Rising on my hooves, I stand upright with Juniper's legs knitted around my waist and her cunt spreading for me.

And then I continue fucking her.

My cock lunges up into her wet folds while I fix her in place. She jolts, whines to the tempo of my hips. After a few pumps, she resumes her own attack by thrashing over me. The huntress knocks her waist into mine, her folds absorbing my cock with abandon.

I growl, clasp her ass, and lash my erection at a rampant pace. "Take my cock, luv. Take what's yours."

"Mine," she wheezes, clamping my jaw with both hands. "All mine."

"Always yours." I buck into her. "I fucking love you."

"I love you, too. So much."

"Then show me. Kiss the shit out of me."

Juniper half-moans, half-smiles. She burrows down and sheathes my lips, her tongue spearing into my mouth and tangling with my own. I flex my lips and tongue into her, and I drive my cock higher, deeper, rougher.

We've fucked, had sex, made love, and fucked some more in numerous ways, against countless surfaces. We've had each other fully dressed, half-dressed, and stripped bare. I've been above her, beneath her, behind her. She's taken me apart and put me back together.

But it's never been this powerful, this shrill, or this defiant.

I almost lost this. I almost lost her.

Sweat glistens under her tits and across her forehead. The same moisture surfaces down my spine. I groan and fuck into her, my cock plying her walls as they constrict.

My fingers trail down, shave through the coils of hair at her cunt, and find that kernel of skin. It projects from her body, swollen like a ripe cherry. I pinch her clit and brush my thumb over it.

My woman shudders, her pussy trembling like a spring ready to break. I feel that inflated stud throbbing like a heartbeat. Ravenous, I pulse my thumb against it, pressing and rubbing.

In response, Juniper drenches my cock. Her features tense, her mouth drops open, and her fingers curl sharply into my hair. Fables, she's gorgeous when she's about to come.

Her breathing speeds up, frayed and delirious. Tattered shouts build on my tongue, heat launching from my balls to my crown. While patting her clit, I stalk to the nearest tree and brace my palm on to the trunk behind her, careful not to ram Juniper into the bark. Keeping her flush against me, I put my ass into the effort, flexing it forward and whipping my cock through her soaked slit.

"Yes, Puck!" she hollers. "Right there."

"Almost, luv," I hum. "Almost there."

We charge into each other, my cock works us into a spiral, and her moans scatter across the woodland. Juniper flings herself back and shatters, her legs shaking around my waist. Her slick pussy convulses around my pumping cock, her orgasm squeezing the head—and I explode.

The roar tears from my mouth. A liquid rush of pleasure spills from my body into hers, so fierce and raw I nearly black out.

Juniper grinds on me, coming around me with such force that her cries span beyond the grove. I shout with her, my hips stalling with the release. We come for so long, my fingernails dig craters into the tree trunk, the climax quaking from my cock to the rest of me.

Slowly, our groans ebbs. Our hips roll languidly, riding out the last of it, then slump.

Juniper collapses into my shoulder. She brushes through my red waves and traces the peaks of my ears, making the earrings chime. My knuckles push a layer of green off her shoulder, and I drop a breathless kiss there.

All at once, Juniper's eyes lifts to mine. We gaze at each other and smile through the fatigue. The noises rush together, sated and amused.

I slip my cock from her sweet, soft walls and hunker to the ground with her, where we recline on the grass. The blades sink under our weight like a carpet. A breeze filters through, jostling the candles, which throw a sheen across Juniper's sweaty body.

She curls into my side, her cheek slumping onto my chest, and drapes one leg over my thighs. My bent arm rests beneath her head, and my digits rustle through her hair. Our stomachs labor for air, the respirations worn as we fight to catch our breaths.

My cock lulls on my abdomen, the length still as hard as a battering ram. Sometimes it takes a while for it to calm down. Not that I'm complaining, since I've got graphic plans before we leave The Wicked Pines, which involve a low hanging tree branch I'd like to bend her over, plus another trip to the bathing pool.

"Give me a few minutes," I tell her.

Juniper translates that, buries her face in my shoulder, and guffaws. "You are insatiable."

"I'm a satyr. And I'm in love. That's a double dose of kink. Plus, I don't hear you declining."

"You won't."

She looks up, flattens her hand on my pec, and perches her chin there. A peachy hue threads across her cheeks, her complexion bright and her irises even brighter from the life she's carrying.

Resting on her stomach, her legs bend, calves rising vertically and crossing at the ankles. It's a playful pose, so rare and candid that I revel in it. No one sees this side of her but me.

Matter of fact, I might have to dismantle any male who tries. Just because satyrs are legendary lovers doesn't mean they don't get jealous.

Anyway, her tears have dried. Besides that, my back has improved, based on the way she'd rescue-fucked me into the grass. I hadn't felt anything but the desire to sink my cock into her warmth and make her come.

When Juniper's close-mouth grin expands, I frown in amusement and skate my thumb across her jaw. "What's so funny?"

"I was just remembering this place," she quips. "The look on your face when I gave you a tongue lashing that first night."

"The first night or tonight? Because both were unforgettable."

She smacks my chest, which rumbles with laughter. "You know what I mean."

That, I do. "Ugh, that righteous quote you attacked me with. I wanted to sneer and take you down a peg, as much as I wanted to sample that outspoken mouth of yours." I sweep my lips across her nose. "You set me on edge from the beginning."

Juniper's mirth fades, her gaze trailing over my features. "No one will ever come close, Puck. No one ever has."

The words embed themselves in my heart. "The feeling is mutual," I whisper, cupping her face.

It's only ever been her. For all those years, she was the memory I'd never been able to extinguish. Every move I made had been wrapped up in this mortal.

Somehow, I've made her happy. Someway, she's given me the same fucking thing.

With a groan, my mouth sweeps down and claims hers. I haul her partway over me while our tongues fuse together. Her exquisite cunt radiates wet heat across my thighs, and now my cock is primed for a slower, more patient round of sex.

We'd fucked each other to the point of no return. In about five minutes, I'll make love to her until she's so lucid, she'll feel every inch of me for days.

But first, Juniper pulls away on a sigh, concern eclipsing her need. "What about Cerulean?"

Pain and fear clip my revelry in half. I frame the sides of her face and speak against her lips. "We didn't lose each other. We're not going to lose him, either."

"I love you," she whispers.

"Eternally, luv," I murmur, before taking her mouth again.

I roll on top of Juniper, my body aligning with hers. Her thighs flank my waist as I tease her entrance with my cock and kiss her breathless. My lips and tongue devour her, savoring these remaining hours.

My brother won't end in that cage. Not if I can't help it. Not if the rest of our band has anything to say about it. For sure, I know one brother who's prowling toward the mortal realm right now, hellbent on that task.

No one's coming. They abandoned you. Any others won't know where to look because they never saw where we put you.

I'd been half-conscious in the cage, but I remember that moment. At the time, the mortal's words had lathered salt into the wound. But not anymore, now that I'm feeling perkier and ready to give Juniper more bliss.

...they never saw where we put you.

Huh. The humans must have forgotten that us monsters are a three-some. And for all those Fables and cautionary horror stories, they should know a thing or two about Elixir. He doesn't need to fucking *see*.

PART 3

Elixir

23

Nothing survives without water. Not in my world.

It flows through this land like a vein, pumping life into the mountain, forest, and far beneath the earth. It is the beginning of many things—a storm, a seed, or a rushing river. Each begins with a single droplet.

Even in poisons and cures, water is a component. Even for immortal souls, it is vital. Even in me, it is an irreplaceable magic.

While submerged, my body shifts from one being to another, from a Fae with limbs to one with a tail. The river swirls as I flex my arms. Beneath the surface, my legs fuse into a single appendage.

This would not happen without water. It is my life force, as much as The Deep itself and the touch of my lady.

As I swim, the river parts like a gate, allowing me to pass. Liquid thrashes with each stretch of my arms, each whip of my serpent tail. My nostrils inhale the metallic scent of sharks, and my ears discern the si-phoning cadence of their gills.

The noise subsides quickly. I am moving too fast for the sounds to be more than an afterthought, for time is of the essence.

My brother needs me.

Tinder had arrived in The Heart of Willows with a message. Puck is safe, and Juniper is with him. But Cerulean remains caged by the humans, and I'm the only one who can free him.

Lark is healing, but the female's hobbling would have slowed me down. The remedy I had prepared several days ago will take another chunk of hours to fully cure the fracture in her leg. Although not much of an additional lapse, every second Cerulean is trapped is one second too many. I could not wait for Lark, nor had she wanted me to.

A small residue of iron still lingers in Cypress and Foxglove from having combated against so many weapons. Although not significant any longer, they would have also delayed me. By the time Lark is restored, the iron should be leached from the remainder of our band.

As for Coral, I had manifested to her side on the way from the forest and given instructions. She must lead our allies in The Deep while I'm absent. I trust no one more than her to do this—apart from my lady.

An image of gentle, kindly irises floods my mind. "Bring him back," Cove had whispered after pulling her lips from mine. "Bring him back to my sister. And come back to me."

My pulse stalls as her voice rolls like a wave through my head. A second later, the memory leaks away like a tear.

I whip my arms and tail faster through the depths. Whatever she requests of me, she will receive. Cerulean and Puck have served their roles, whereas I have stood by.

It is my turn now.

I hear the river swelling around a particular shape that's easy to identify. I spear upward, my body catapults over an underwater stalactite barnacled in moss, and I dive again.

The flux has a malleable shape, a powerful weight, and a glossy texture. But although I know each conduit and specimen that exists in this subterranean river, The Deep has been changing. It is no longer as predictable as it once was, no longer as effortless to navigate. More than ever, more than memory or routine, erratic sounds and current shifts in the water are my guides.

Be that as it may, the swiftest route to the mortal realm has not altered. My tail achieves a velocity that rivals manifesting, without expending precious energy.

A fever of stingrays flutters past me. They coast like blankets, their barbs carrying venom. I torpedo between them, and in a flash, all signs of the aquatic fleet are gone.

I shoot up an incline. The water's temperature decreases to a chilled degree. Its consistency thins, the river condenses to a stream, and the depth becomes shallow.

I set my teeth, leave the underground river behind, and launch into the mortal world.

My submerged body punches through the water like a fist and follows the direction Tinder had provided from Juniper. The moment my senses inhale the reek of iron and Cerulean's blood, I rage. For all the sharp edges that Cove has gentled in me, she has honed other edges—protective ones.

No one cages my kin. No one outlives those consequences.

How I want to blast into their realm, my arrival sending a tsunami gushing through that forsaken town. How I want to flood their haven, the same way their actions nine years ago resulted in flooding mine.

However, that would endanger their children and fauna. And it would get me into trouble with Cove.

I loop into a vertical climb and harpoon to the surface. Before emerging, I slacken my tail and arms. I slow my pace and slither toward the echo of fluid lapping at a bank. My head breaks through, oxygen replacing the liquid in my lungs.

I bob, materializing only enough for my eyes to float over the surface. Based on the stream's babbling resonance, it will taper into a brook from this point. On instinct, my orbs stray, as if able to pierce the void enfolding around me, to see through the wall of black and scan the perimeter. It's an impulse that has never left since I was a stripling.

Still, there are varied shades and shapes of darkness. Those disparities, my Fae eyes can at least distinguish.

This murk is blotchy, befitting a shrouded forest. Leaves shiver overhead, the environment vacant of humans. No footfalls. No faint breathing. That's good, for I would be forced to snap a neck or blind an unwelcome visitor.

Lack of vision is not a defect. But I do wield it as a weapon, for it takes the recipient by surprise, the sudden trauma shocking and confusing them, which incapacitates their ability to fight back.

I cruise toward the bank and rise to my full height. As my body smashes through the surface, my tail splits into a pair of limbs like the blades of a scissor. I hear my frame chopping the stream into pieces, beads of water arcing and pelting the bank.

My feet stalk from the depth. Rivulets coarse down my skin as I grope the baldric fixed across my torso, the strap woven from mer scales. A breeze rushes across my naked limbs. I hadn't given the slightest fuck about entering this land bare-assed, and Cove must have forgotten to insist I tether a spare pair of leggings to the harness. The thought of what she'd say at this moment lifts one corner of my mouth.

Recalling the strict instructions Tinder had passed on from Juniper, I prowl through the underbrush, picking around the snares the poachers had evidently installed. Several offshoots graze my shoulder as I pass. My soles crush a patch of mushrooms, imprinting them into the ground.

The scent of fungal toxicity reaches my nose. *Poisonous.*

But more potent are the stenches of crimson and iron, which ripen the closer I get. The latter odor seeps into my pores. My bones grow heavy, as if I'm swimming through saltwater.

A motley of images drowns my thoughts—a tank propped inside a well, iron bars above and below as I float within the tube like a specimen, my knuckles ramming into the glass but failing to shatter it, and the same heaviness draining my energy.

Fury, terror, and longing at the sight of a nearby lake, an escape route so near yet so far. Back then, my eyes had been able to see this world.

I purge myself of the memories. Yet shaking off the iron is less possible, for it slithers through my blood with each leaden step.

Before The Deep's great flood and during Cove's game, I had possessed a brew that enabled me to leach the noxious element from Juniper's crossbow bolts—a blend of river water, stingray venom, and an elfish metal from the Northern Frosts, all meant to "cure" the bolts by peeling the iron from their tips. Except the mixture had worked only in small quantities. It had been sufficient for the archery, but even if the flood hadn't washed away most of my supplies, a massive iron cage is another matter.

My pulse clatters. Sweat bridges across the scales encrusting my joints.

The sound of hinges resurrects my stamina. I trail the stream as it condenses to the brook I'd predicted.

On the way, my fingercaps sketch the air for shifts in its direction, any signs I can follow. This is never easy outside of The Deep, and so the effort is of little help.

I prowl through a snarl of bushes and suck in a gust of air. The putridness of iron and the tang of my brother's blood smothers me. His rhythmic breathing reaches my ears. Relief and fury expel from my chest as I cross the final distance and sink to a crouch.

With each unconscious outtake from my brother, the cage trembles subtly. Iron radiates from the grille like an airborne virus, so thick it slides along my tongue and down my throat.

"Cerulean," I rasp.

He jolts awake before I've finished uttering his name. My brother growls, lurches upright as if wrenched from a nightmare, and lunges my way.

At the last instant, the tip of a knife stalls against my jaw, the weapon halting in realization. "Elixir," he utters, the inflection scraped raw.

I listen to my brother slump. His wings drag him down, as though the plumes cannot hold themselves up. The scent of crimson seems to cover him from all angles.

A hiss vibrates off my tongue. "What have they done?"

Cerulean struggles for breath, as if each word bears the weight of a mountain. "Nothing we've never done to them."

Fuck his mercy. Fuck it to the bottom of the river.

Also, my exclamation hadn't required an actual response. Tinder had provided our group with the gory details of Puck's mutilation and the similar treatment Cerulean had likely received. Albeit Tinder told us privately, away from Lark and Juniper's ears, so we'd known Cerulean would need someone capable of bearing his frame.

Yet to witness firsthand what's happened to him…

To smell the evidence of his torture…

If I gnash my molars any harsher, they shall grind to dust. "Cerulean, I'm—"

But his body collapses like a pile of bricks. The cage tremors from the impact.

"*Minn ó brodir*," I snap. "Cerulean."

He doesn't answer.

"Fuck," I seethe.

I reach behind to unstrap one of the forked daggers from my back, then shove my free fingers into the baldric. Locating the makeshift key Cove had fabricated—which Tinder had returned from Juniper—I run my fingers quickly over the hardwood wands, one straight and one spiral. My lady had revealed a formidable ability to construct such objects, which cracks the most complex of mortal locks.

A convoy of centaurs would do better to balance my brother's wings. But what most Solitaries forget is that mermen shifters can balance the density of a river upon their shoulders. And as for water, it can sustain the weight of a continent. If we can do that, water and I can handle a set of Fae wings.

Or so I hope. Already, my knuckles ache from the iron. Haste is crucial, lest I'm unable to get him to the stream.

Without Cerulean conscious to guide me, I'll have to follow the sound of the padlock. I jab the cage with the prongs of my dagger, shaking the enclosure enough for the lock to swing. Trailing the noise, I locate the bolt, drop the dagger, and jam the apparatus into the keyhole.

Heat sizzles my fingers, and the stink of charred flesh permeates the air. I embed the tool deeper, yet the keyhole refuses to give.

My lady had imparted the mechanics of how to use this cursed tool. However, from her lips to my ears, some crucial step must have gotten lost in translation, an essential detail shuffled out of order.

Cerulean groans in his sleep, the sound frail. Anarchy surges up my arms. My wrist twists so hard the bones threaten to pop, but the bolt remains intact.

I grumble, "Fucking open, you motherfucker."

"Turn it the other way," a male voice instructs.

The blood in my veins spikes. With reptilian speed, I strike toward that voice and lash my free arm in the male's direction. My hand clamps like a manacle around his neck, ramming him into a neighboring tree trunk.

"Mortal," I hiss.

"Please," the man chokes while squirming like a pinned insect. "I'm h-here to h-help you."

"A mortal who lies."

"I can o-open that lock."

My lips curl. "I do not make bargains."

"Turn the lock the other w-way," he gags. "Then pump t-twice like a lever."

The instructions stay my hand. Cove's words rush in like the tide, her directions returning to me more distinctly.

Turn the lock to the left. Then pump twice like a lever.

My lady had assembled this key herself. No one outside of our band has seen it or knows how it functions. Or perhaps it's merely a replica of many, but something about the man's words uttered verbatim loosens my grip on his jugular.

His pulse taps against my palm, the beat stronger and steadier than I'd given him credit for. When mortals lie, their heartbeat changes pace, unlike with this one. Despite his aged baritone—likely a male in his fiftieth year—the human's intonation is robust, akin to a trained muscle.

It is the tone of a man equal parts nerve, endurance, and sympathy. The compilation reminds me of three other mortal figures I know.

My eyes slit. I make my choice.

With my other hand, I wrench the device from the keyhole, lift the object to his neck, and trace the wands down to his stomach. "Tell me how you know about this key."

The man wheezes, "Because I've used t-the s-same one before."

"If you are lying, I will gut you like a trout."

"If I'm t-telling the truth, you will ap-apologize for that."

The combination of bravado and civility reminds me of Cove. My mouth to twitches in hostile amusement. "Again. How do you know of this key?"

"Because…" In that single word, a newfangled emotion toughens his voice. The mortal's words grow thorns. "Because it belonged to my daughter."

24

My fingers snap open. They do so with a quick click of muscle and bone, the man's confession driving needles into my fingers and severing the choke hold. The mortal thuds to the grass, emits a guttural sound, and audibly clutches his throat while hacking.

I go still, listening to his fingers massage the area. The pressure of his words is immediate, water breaking through bedrock. I feel them yank my features into a different shape, from malevolent distrust to repentant disgrace.

Over the years, I have trained my eyes well. Only twice have I been so overcome that I've failed to suppress their blinding magic. The first incident had been with Cove in The Shiver of Sharks. The second episode had been with Juniper, when I heard the embryo inside her womb.

Thank Fables, this present moment won't be a third time. The shock doesn't outweigh my restraint. Otherwise, my eyes would have flung gold at him.

Nevertheless, I feel the orbs widen—a novelty, for they're more accustomed to narrowing.

Because it belonged to my daughter.

That solitary declaration haunts the space between us. This is Cove's father.

She had described him to me—darker skin than mine, more like Cypress; hair threaded with silver filaments; and a baritone like my own—yet not with any distinguishing particulars my senses would have registered. Especially not under these circumstances.

I cannot tell if it is guilt or humiliation that reels me backward. Perhaps it is neither but rather a hyperawareness of how he's looking at me. From the tension stringing in the air, I conclude the man is hurling me a rather volcanic expression.

"You had better tell me this isn't how you greeted Cove," he wheezes.

The threat embeds itself into my ribs like barbed wire. "You know who I am."

"Everyone in Reverie Hollow knows who you are."

"I meant—"

"I know what you meant." After consuming a thick draught of oxygen, I listen as he gestures to the key arrested in my grip and flaps his hand. "Give it to me."

My reflexes appear to have waned. It could be the iron. It could be intimidation. Neither of which I know what to do with.

The human swipes the makeshift device and grunts for me to move. I maneuver out of his way. Every motion is transparent in my mind's eye. He squats in front of the cage, clamps his fingers around the key's handle, and thrusts it into the hole.

My grimace is fully formed yet pointless as he touches the iron. No putridness of burning flesh. No sign of pain. It does not poison him as it does my kin, and the sounds of his movements are seamless.

One twist to the left. Two pumps.

Mechanisms clatter from within the padlock's shell. The bolt shudders and something loosens, splitting apart.

There's a pause. One that I'm familiar with, a prelude to discovery. It's the same dawning realization Cove had when she first beheld me after nine years.

"You can't see," the man says, his pitch low. When I nod, he stalls for a moment, then cautions, "Watch out for the door."

I could have assured him I would hear the hinges beforehand. However, the warning trips me into another bewildered state.

My eyebrows pinch together. "You know what we've done. Why would you help us?"

"I'll have my parental chat with you later," he mutters as the door screeches open. "For now, help me lug this raptor out of—"

But the man's tongue stalls, his voice fragmenting like something pushed through a grater. "Fables forgive them."

If his disclaimer about knowing how to use the tool hadn't already proven his identity, that exclamation does. I hear my lady's sympathetic voice reflected in his own.

A nodule burns like a miniature sun inside my throat. The man sees what his people have done to Cerulean. He sees, whereas I hear and smell the damage.

The man accelerates his movements and crawls into the cage. "Cerulean," he whispers.

My head ticks. "You know his name."

"Lark told me."

Of course. The iron must be diluting my comprehension. Cove's youngest sister had briefly returned to her father after winning her game in the mountain labyrinth.

My brother does not stir. A labored noise puffs from the human's chest. The cage floor shakes, a weight dragging across the foundation.

He won't manage. I reverse my baldric, rearranging it from my spine to my bare chest, and harness my discarded dagger alongside the second one. With my hands free, I hunker inside the cage. The floor is made of steel and the size considerable, enabling me to hunch between the bars without my weapons skewering me. Nonetheless, my proportions combined with Cerulean's wingspan and the robust physique of Cove's father make for a tight squeeze.

One of the rods sizzles, scorching my calf and another the side of my ear. I hiss, the blistering pain urging me to move faster.

I race my palms over the fringes of my brother's wings. Dried blood encrusts the plumes like scabs. And...a minefield of gaps burrows into the panels.

They have picked off his feathers.

The pockets behind my eyes singe. *For this, I will drown you.*

Vitriol rolls through my veins. I use that momentum to haul my brother from the cage's maw. Cove's father groans with the effort of helping, though I doubt he's able to do more than balance my brother's limbs.

We spill from the confines. Growling, I hunker my brother over my back. A mangled groan slips from his mouth, his head slumping on my shoulder.

I whisper to him the way Cove whispers to me, except I do so in Faeish. "*Éck jef fick. Éck á jef fick núna.*"

I have you. I have you now.

Cove's father insists, "Let me help."

"He is my brother," I grit out. "I must do this."

"For devil's sake. I see the surplus of muscles, but you're naked and armed as it is. Give me an occupation."

"You have done plenty. But sling any part of Cerulean across your shoulders, and your vertebrae will crack like a broken ladder."

His footfalls halt, then resume trailing me. "Well. If you say so."

Cerulean's wings pour on either side of me and scrub across the grass, their volume threatening to bring us down. It takes longer than it should, but I haul him through the underbrush and reach the boundary where the brook bloats into a stream. Then I sink, my jellied knees slamming into the earth.

"My goodness," the human exclaims. "He's heavier than a cliff. How in the world—"

"I am a water Fae."

"I wish that explained everything."

Muffled voices layer through the forest. Human accents and horse hooves shudder through the foliage.

I hear Cove's father whirl toward the commotion. "I wasn't followed. The poachers must be checking on the cage. They've been taking shifts guarding it."

Fuck. I adjust Cerulean more securely onto my back and position myself at the water's edge. Once I'm submerged, the journey will be easier.

My head swings in the man's direction. I would like to thank him. I would like to express more than gratitude. But Faeries do no such thing, and anyway, that window of opportunity is shrinking.

"She is well," I swear. "She is safe."

The air shifts as he whirls my way, desperation and anger clotting his reply. "Prove it."

I hesitate. "How?"

"Take me to her," the mortal demands. "Take me to *them*."

His tone is wrought of steel—firm, unbendable. His request is a debt owed, which I cannot ignore.

Yet if I do this, he will be deposited amid our war. Whereas if I leave him, he will find a way home without incident. I don't doubt the latter, for he has raised a bold and capable woman. She is like him.

In any event, it is not my decision. It is his.

Her family deserves this. They have earned this.

A battle is looming. If Cove doesn't see her father before then, she will despair. That notion is unthinkable.

And her father has made his choice. So I make mine.

The mortal voices splinter, amplifying through the night. They have discovered the empty cage. Boots thud into the grass, the commotion spreading across the woods.

"You must inhale as much oxygen as possible," I prompt the man.

"I'm not as skilled as my daughter," he concedes. "But she taught me how."

"And I shall be quick." I offer my hand. "Do not let go."

Without hesitation, his callused palm clamps onto mine. "I'll never do that."

His words are soaked in Lark, Juniper, and Cove. The foreign sensations of admiration and inadequacy squeeze their way through my bones. They percolate like a vortex, assaulting me to the core. If it weren't for me and my brothers, he would not have to say this.

I nod once, shackle Cerulean's wrists over my sternum, and lower myself into the water. The eddies splash. The chilled flux vibrates. Submerged, my skin drinks in the fluid, and my limbs weld together.

The man's stunned gasp resounds as my serpent tail whips beneath me. However, he recovers from the surprise long enough to fill his lungs.

Normally, I would have flipped headfirst into the stream. With a limp sibling plus a mortal attached to me, I dunk under the surface and melt into the water.

With a swat of my tail, we shoot into the depths. Gravity vanishes. The depth parts as we shave through. Water braces Cerulean's wings, as if they weigh little more than a single quill.

Holding my brother and my lady's father requires my tail to work harder. Though, not as much with the stream reinforcing me. Another lash of my appendage, and we launch across the current.

My scales draw liquid in and out like a pump. I detect a school of fish and pivot around them. The mortal's hand tightens at the sudden jolt.

The distance grows, the channel broadens, and the depth increases. Picturing Cove's face and thinking of Cerulean's empty lungs, I plunge lower. My tail burns, a foaming maelstrom of bubbles skates down my spine, and my mane flares behind as if windblown.

Moments later, the temperature rises as we smash through the boundary. The river's taste washes past my lips. Its balmy warmth rolls down my body.

At the crashing echo of a waterslide, I take a nosedive. To the mortal's credit, he doesn't scream and plug his lungs, nor does he panic as we crash into a pool littered with sharks. Still, he does use his limbs to punt the water, the motions harsh.

I hear the gills flapping, the fins swaying. I count twelve dwellers.

At our approach, the sharks scatter like missiles. It might be only me, but Cerulean's wingspan is likely another culprit, the panels startling the fauna.

I push deeper, propel through an underwater duct, and loop upward. We break the surface. Waves jet into the atmosphere and audibly smash into walls of polished rock.

The man heaves, "Hellfire and brimstone!"

That shall be the least of his problems here. We bob in a whirlpool that throws steam into the air, with a cascade splashing into its surface.

I swim to the ledge and beseech the water, which thickens around Cerulean. It acts as a brace, allowing me to prop him upright on an underwater bank meant for lounging. His head lolls against the ledge, but with the extra support, he shall not sink.

I divest my brother of his clothing. As my fingers pass over his back, fresh rancor spasms me in place. Scabs pulp across his skin, the lashes marking the areas where they'd beaten him, whipped him with something shaped like a rod. It seems, Tinder had prepared us only marginally.

A snarl curls in my throat. Carefully, I remove the rags that used to be Cerulean's clothing, then let the garments float like rafts, so the water may consume them as well. They're far too tattered to salvage.

I crawl out of the well on all fours. As my legs materialize, I slump to the ground, exhaustion sawing through me.

Cove's father splatters from the basin and drops onto the rim at my side. I decipher his limbs floating over the edge while he sucks in air and absorbs our surroundings. I imagine his first view of this place, embedded far beneath the earth. The cavernous ceiling and interconnected caves. Curtains of blue, green, and gold mist. Waterfalls glisten with unearthly hues, from aquamarine to emerald, illuminating the darkness.

"Where are we?" he marvels.

"The Deep," I answer.

"The domain where you rule?"

"Yes."

"But where specifically?"

Amusement nudges the corners of my lips. Now I know where Cove has inherited her inquisitiveness.

I heft myself sideways off the tiles, my palms flat on the ground to brace my upper body. "It is called The Mer Cascades."

The human's baritone remains calm. "As in merfolk?"

I nod once. Humans know of the three realms in the Solitary wild. Because the man does not interrogate further, I suspect he's scanning the enclave with its whirlpools and shower alcoves. His silence does not suggest he is frightened, nor impressed. Rather, it is the quiet of someone observing through a lens, someone searching for answers in every corner.

He is wondering if she's been here. He wants to know if she's nearby.

I must give him those answers, but not yet. My hand sweeps through the frothing pool from which we'd entered, sending a message through the river to our band.

We have him.

Belatedly, I register the *We*. I should have elaborated to them, but my perception is lagging to catch up. Between the journey and proximity to the iron, it shall take a few hours for the effects to wear off.

Condensation sails through the enclave. Humidity licks my flesh.

I smell the pool extracting blood and grime from Cerulean's flesh and wings. The vile evidence of his torture shall fade into the water like paint drops, leaving behind only clear fluid. The pool will infuse his pores with healing properties. Though, against this much destruction, it will take a while.

I cut my jaw toward the echoes of stirring fluid. "These waters will help my brother."

Concern wafts from the man. "Will he live, then?"

The question immobilizes me, tugs me in place like a noose. Suspicion sits on my tongue. "You could try to kill me now."

"How would I do that?"

"With the knife you took from my brother."

A beat of silence follows. My brother had been hiding a knife with familiar etchings on the hilt. It belongs to Scorpio, but that enigma is best left for a later discussion.

For now, I focus on the mortal who'd helped free my brother yet had done so while pocketing the weapon when he'd thought I was distracted. Had Cove taught him that trick? I wager yes.

I am naked, laced with iron, and I'm one-third of the Faeries who captured his children. What's more, I can barely raise my daggers at this point. This provides him with an opportunity.

Yet the man's respirations remain steady. "Do you expect everything that a person does to be out of vengeance?"

My throat contracts with shame. Something like pity has dragged his voice down an octave. I'm used to this sort of inflection, for it's another hallmark of my lady.

When I make no reply, he sighs. "Well, Fae. I'm not a murderer, however much I would like to castrate you."

With my cock hanging in plain sight, this certainly wouldn't be difficult.

"Cerulean is Lark's mate," I say. "He can lead you to them once he awakens. You have incentives to want him alive. Not me."

"My eldest hasn't told you? A nightingale delivered a letter from them. I know about you three."

I had forgotten. Lark, Juniper, and Cove had wanted to visit their father in secret, but too much had happened to make it possible. Cove had mentioned sending a letter instead, which she and her sisters had written from The Heart of Willows.

"What…did the missive say?" I dare to inquire.

"That you're not the enemy," he supplies. "That you're not monsters. That you matter to them."

My heart jolts inside the shell of my chest. The mortal does not sound placated, yet that hadn't stopped him from caring about Cerulean's well-being. It had not stopped him from exercising compassion.

The gesture has Cove all over it.

But like Lark and Juniper, he has questions, whereas I don't even have my fucking pants on.

I avert my gaze and gain my feet. "Wait here." Then I pause and think of Cove. "Erm, if you please."

Using the last of my physical reserves, I vanish before the man can open his mouth. I manifest to The Pit of Vipers, appearing beside the dome's central vat. I would have brought Cerulean and Cove's father here, amongst the restorative mixtures. However, with the flood devastation, it is still restricted. The Mer Cascades had been the next credible option.

Making haste, I stalk to the wall mantle housing the only elements and ingredients I have managed to restore thus far. My fingers flick among the bottles and vials, glasses clinking. Once I have collected the right vessel and stepped into a pair of leggings, I evanesce and materialize back in the enclave.

"Dammit!" the man grunts, startled when I reappear next to him. "Do you plan on doing that often?"

"No," I say while striding around the pool's rim toward my brother.

I feel Cove's father observing as I squat beside Cerulean with the vial. My thumb pops the cork from the lip, my free hand snatches his chin, and I angle his head while tipping the elixir down his throat. The brew emits a citrus scent and is a gilded effervescent fluid—I know how it looks from memory, back when both of my mothers taught me the fundamentals.

Cerulean's chest lurches, ingesting the remedy. He will need a few moments.

I flick the bottle into the water, which swallows it whole. At last, I drop beside my brother, dip my limbs into the whirlpool, and bow forward.

The scrutinizing gaze of Cove's father reaches me from across the whirlpool. I cannot muster the fortitude to lift my head. It might be exhaustion, but I do not think so.

Despite the crashing waterfalls, every move he makes is a tsunami in my ears. His clothes shift. He's reaching into his pocket, fishing for something. My ears pick up the man's fingers stroking a wooden object—the key.

"For years, Cove had one like this at home," the man reminiscences in a manner that suggests he is gazing at the apparatus. "She and her sisters would use it to free animals that had been poached for trade. Shortly before you took her, the original broke. Cove had been meaning to fix it."

His tone is cultured yet aggressive, like an heirloom weapon. "I consider myself a civilized man. Likewise, I trust my daughters' judgement. That said, it's taking every ounce of will not to curse the day you were born and reconsider what I said about not being a killer. It all depends on how you answer me."

Finally, I have the courage to draw my gaze toward his voice. "Ask me."

"For a start, tell me what I want to hear most."

"They are safe. They are near. They will be on their way."

Relief gusts from his lungs. "Good. That means I can put away the knife. Next, you never obliged my initial request when we met."

You had better tell me this isn't how you greeted Cove.

I wince. He had spoken those words after I'd had my fingers strapped around his gullet.

The reply pours from me like the river. "It was the same. Also, I nearly blinded her."

Water splatters the ground as the man rises like an alpha. "We were doing so well, lad," he speaks through his teeth. "But if you're hoping to make a good impression, you're failing spectacularly."

"Faeries cannot lie."

"The Fables say your kind manipulate the truth."

"I play mind games with my enemies, not my kin. That is not me."

"Cove is the sweetest soul on this earth," he feuds. "She trusts to a fault, tends to others before thinking of herself, and she's determined to see good in all creatures. Where others see bloodthirsty beasts, she sees lost souls. It would be tempting for any Fae to take advantage of that."

I blast to my feet, a growl snaking from my lips. "That is also not me."

"Then who are you?"

"I am the one who loves your daughter."

A slick voice carries through the enclave. "May I echo that sentiment?"

Like two waves colliding and then breaking apart, I feel our glowers smash into one another and then disintegrate. A brush of water alerts me to nearby activity—feathers twitching in the pool.

I spin toward that elegant tenor and fall to my knees. "Cerulean."

My brother's palm finds my jaw. "Elixir," he murmurs.

That is all I need. No other words.

His wings float limply atop the surface, yet I hear the water simmering around him, the flux illustrating his position. He's reclining, too weary to accomplish his usual sideways slouch. But his chin is perched high as his head swings toward the mortal across from us.

"You look like she'd said you would," Cerulean says.

A choppy breath cuts from the opposite end of the water. "So do you."

The three of us regard one another, the interim so sharp it could amputate a limb.

Predictably, the moment severs like bone as another male timbre bursts into the enclave. "Who the fuck is this?"

On reflex, my eyes launch heavenward. That cursed drawl can only belong to one brother. It is easy to envision the cataclysm of this scene, the unanimous manner in which we glance toward a very large prick clogging the Cascades' entrance. I picture the mortal's frown traveling from Puck's combustible red hair, to the leather ensemble with its surplus of buckles, to the cloven hooves that could snuff an inferno, to the antlers sprawling from his head like the skeletal branches of an oak tree.

Most notable of all, his lack of fucking filter.

I also know Puck well enough to conceptualize the troublemaker's cocksure squint and quirked brows as he takes the human's measure.

Now I had been worried about him. For the nightmare my brothers have been through, I would love nothing more than to turn our mortal enemies into carcasses. And for once, I am pacified to see Puck in one piece. Except the imp has inevitably ruined this impulse by opening his mouth to the only male human on earth with the power to eviscerate us.

Cerulean's sigh drifts from my right. I sense him palming his angular face in abject misery. "This is our other brother."

"I know who the fuck I am," Puck bleats like a disgruntled goat. "What about him?"

"Puck—"

"I mean, my days of orgies are through, but this is a new level of kink if you've decided to steal another mortal."

I cannot help it. My lips twitch as I foresee the bottomless hole Puck is digging for himself. Cerulean and I discern the fatal tone masked behind the droll remark. Our oversexed satyr of a brother is hardly serious.

But our guest does not know that.

He doesn't know that because he doesn't know Puck.

"Well," the rogue insists. "Anybody willing to let go of their dick long enough to answer me?"

The mortal's voice is hewn from stone. "I'm their father."

Dead. Silence.

At least from Puck.

Meanwhile, waterfalls smash into the whirlpools. Shower alcoves cough up steam. The muggy temperature rises, as though fermenting.

I fold my lips inward. This should not be funny.

It is very funny.

Puck's dangly earrings tinkle, the only sign that his jaw has unhinged. And it doesn't take a clairvoyant to know his eyes have leaped out of their sockets, nor that his throat has lost its ability to swallow.

A low, mumbling groan falls from his lips. "Ah, shit."

"Watch your damn mouth," the human snaps.

To that, none of us respond. A defenseless garble clots my brother's tongue. If Puck isn't careful, he might choke on it.

The prospect strangles my amusement. Cove says I love to hate Puck, as much as I hate to love him. Perhaps she's right. If this weren't so, I would not feel his mortification so acutely, just as I feel my own.

Few souls can wipe the smirk off my brother's face. Fewer can make him doubt himself, believe himself deficient. This is one such moment.

He's been fearing this meeting. Either he's making that physically obvious, or Cove's father possesses her skill for emotional perception.

The man's tone loses its whittled edge. "Juniper told me about you in the letter my daughters sent. You're the one she speaks about with such uncharacteristic intensity."

"I...," Puck babbles. "I..."

"She said you're quite the eloquent bloke."

My eyelashes flap. His testimonial gives me and my brothers new-fangled pause.

Puck draws out, "Juniper would never say that."

"Oh?" her father inquires. "What would she say?"

At last, I hear perception lift Puck's frown into a sideways grin, which reshapes his voice. "My, my, my. Like father, like scholar."

"I take that as a compliment."

"She would call me a cunning scoundrel."

The man's interest is piqued. I recognize the challenge as well. It is a quiz.

Puck audibly folds the tree stumps of his arms and waits for the rest.

The man deliberates. "What's her favorite word?"

"Book."

"Least favorite story?"

"Anything with smut, unfortunately."

"Cooking or baking?"

"Baking with a shitload of spice."

"How does she take her coffee?"

"She doesn't. Juniper drinks tea—sweetened with berry syrup, though she won't admit it."

"Quirks?"

"She glowers when she's wrong about something. She hates being interrupted. She talks in her sleep—"

"I'd rather not discover how you know that," the father grumbles.

"Sorry, luv. It's the satyr in me." A long, deep smirk fills Puck's tenor. "And her proudest memory is you teaching her to read."

That stumps the man, his reply teeming with the same emotions I feel for my lady. "Well," he mumbles gruffly. "Well."

"To the former, you must have meant Lark," Cerulean discloses. "I'm the eloquent bloke."

"And though you have not asked," I finish, "Cove would fondly say I'm the brooding viper."

The darkness alters. Black puddles shift from sooty to inky colors. I have described these signs to Cove. Along with my senses, different hues of black help me to perceive some of what's occurring around me.

The father is mobile. His head is straying from Puck, to Cerulean, to me. "Sit. Down."

I lower myself to the ground. Rustling linens shoot past my ears as Puck lobs a set of clothing to Cerulean, who catches the lot with a single hand.

"Figured you'd need these," Puck says, then seats himself. Instead of the usual cavalier sprawl, his exhalations tell me he's upright, one leg pitched and the other bent underneath.

Water sloshes. Cerulean vacates the basin, droplets sprinkling from his body and onto the tiles. A torrent rains from his wings as he shuffles into the pants but forgoes the shirt Puck must have brought. Unable to retract the plumes makes it impossible for Cerulean to sheathe his torso. The wings splat onto the floor and lag behind while he returns to a seated position.

From his end of the whirlpool, the mortal says, "My girls say they love you."

Warmth. Devotion. Pride. Remorse. Humility.

They converge like waterways and spill through me. Because my features struggle to remain fixed, approval floods his tone. "Those are exactly the reactions I wanted from you three." Then he pauses. "I want to see them."

In my message through the water, I had neglected to identify my unexpected companion. Lark's injury must be well on the mend by now, though it is likely consuming Juniper and Cove's attention in The Heart of Willows.

Nor can they manifest. They would need time to travel here, even with the aid of the fauna.

I do what I should have done at the onset. My fingers dice through the pool and send another missive to Coral. This time, I instruct my first-in-command to depart for the forest and convey the news.

"I have sent a dispatch," I answer. "But they must travel a considerable distance. It shall take a while."

The man huffs. "I wouldn't be their father if I weren't tempted to rip your heads off. But they're grown women, and I like to think I've raised them with a willingness to learn differently and practice forgiveness. In the meantime, I want to be wrong about you. I'll hear their stories soon enough, but for now, I want yours." Across the steaming pool, he says, "Start at the beginning."

Cerulean goes first, followed by Puck, then me. Our tales unravel like the river, fluid and dark. But there is lightness, as my lady has proven. We speak of The Trapping, of meeting his daughters as striplings, and of the games. We tell him of the wild and our kin. And we tell him of our days with Lark, Juniper, and Cove.

It is only one half of the saga. The other half is for our ladies to share.

The obvious, we omit. He doesn't want to hear that I've thrust my cock so deeply and frequently into Cove that she has branded me for eternity. And without his woman, Puck wisely does not mention the child he and Juniper have conceived.

We finish at the point where Cerulean and Puck were taken, including the rod whipping and Scorpio's flubbed intervention. I tack on the details of the rescue, up to when the father showed up.

The man sighs, carrying the weight of everything we've said. "So much destruction."

"So much to fight for," I counter.

I feel him nod. "I wasn't home when the whipping happened. I'd been making camp some miles off, intent on rescuing a poached fox. By the time I freed the animal and came home, the nightingale was waiting for me with my daughters' letter. The bird must have been there for a day, based on the message's date.

"Then this morning, I heard the reports in town, heard you two were caged, and saw the cobblestones painted in blood. I made a plan to get you once night fell."

"I'm indebted for the rescue," Cerulean says.

"It was mostly your brother."

"Yes, well." I feel Cerulean's blue eyes breeze toward me before returning to the father. "Then allow me to say something else instead: I apologize."

"Same." Puck's voice is humble, loaded with remorse. "For what it's worth, most days I want to flog my own ass. I'm sorry for what I did."

"As am I," I say.

The mortal is staring at us, wavering. "Did you tell *them* that?"

"We shall never stop telling them," I answer.

The cascades slip down tiers of rock. Mist floats through the enclave.

"In their letter, they said your names were Cerulean, Puck, and Elixir." There's a newfound tilt to the man's inflection—something smoother, easier. "Call me Thorne."

Warmth floods the space behind my eyes. Faeries do not take the offer of someone's name lightly. His manages to be piercing and trustworthy at the same time, protective rather than harmful.

It is the name of a guardian. It is strong, like his daughter.

Just then, my lady's tremulous voice slips through the enclave. "Papa?"

25

That sound, like a gentle flow of water passing over rocks. It washes through me and draws my gaze. When my eyes find her, the world takes shape, akin to waking up.

I see her, clear and luminous. My lady stands at the enclave's threshold, strands of teal trembling down her shoulders. Around her, the environment blurs like a puddle, offering mere glimpses of splashing water and mist.

Cove is the only vision my eyes are able to behold. It is the only one I need.

She's a prism of light, a vision glowing through the murk, defiant against the darkness. A door has swooped open, pouring color into a black hall. That is how it feels to look at her. This human is a siren, a temptress, and every crumb of goodness inside me.

She's barefooted and wearing the clothes I gave her on the night of Middle Moon. The porcelain white swimming suit clings to her like film, and the matching skirt of mer scales etched in silver wraps around her waist. The panels shimmer, and her thighs peek from the high slit.

My pupils brim as I soak up her presence. But she isn't gazing back. Her irises reflect the same brilliant shade as they cling to an image a dozen paces away.

Her father.

My pulse stutters at the sight of her slackened face. I have learned many of Cove's expressions—every contortion and lift of her features. I can interpret them, from vexed to aroused, from sad to peaceful. Several emotions combust across her features now. One of them tugs the edges of her mouth downward, another douses her complexion in pink, and the last glistens in her eyes.

Shock. Hope. Elation.

A second later, a smoky voice enters the scene. "Papa."

Unlike Cove's arrival, it is not a question but a statement. I cannot see Puck's woman, but I do catch a sliver of green tresses brushing my lady's arm. Juniper is standing immobile beside Cove.

I witness time suspend itself, not unlike diving into the depths and rising to the surface. The pause is thick, heavy. Neither party dares to move, as though doing so might break the spell.

At length, a stunted noise tears from Thorne's throat. "Juniper," he utters, as if the name is made of earth. And the next name is made of water, each necessary for his survival. "Cove."

My lady's hand shoots to her mouth. On a whimper, she breaks from her trance, races across the enclave, and flings herself into the man's arms.

I follow the trajectory. My gaze hooks onto the brief traces of this man who raised her, a flash of dark-skinned arms, slender yet robust and capable of holding Cove as she sags against him.

Then that glimpse melts out of view, leaving only Cove visible. She's clutching this man, wet rivulets streaking down her profile as she sobs openly.

My muscles tighten, alarmed until I realize…she's crying out of joy. She has done this with me as well.

Pleasure and pain clash like crossed blades spearing my chest. Her solace is all that matters. But she wouldn't be weeping if it were not for me.

I separated them.

My brothers and I did that. We tore this family apart.

The pair splits and glances toward an approaching figure. The diminutive shift of blackness tells me who it is. Thorne and Cove open a space for Juniper, who strays to them, her footfalls wooden. She's keeping herself upright, steady, but I hear the quiver of a fisted hand.

Thorne's intonation is riddled with love, his hand audibly reaching out to caress Juniper's cheek. "My tree of knowledge."

A dry sob racks the female's shoulders. I sense it, hear it, envision it.

Juniper's features collapse like a wave hitting the shore, and she snatches her father and Cove, gathering them to her.

They clasp each other, bonding themselves into one. Cove's head bows with theirs as they form an unbreachable cocoon. The sisters tuck themselves into Thorne's neck as the family cries.

"My girls," he chokes. "My beautiful girls."

Cove's nails dig into his shoulder. Her body lurches with every tear.

My retinas do something strange. They sting, as though doused with salt.

I avert my gaze and clamp my teeth together, fighting to swallow. I sense my brothers doing the same, glancing away in remorse and eager to give them privacy.

I love that Cove has this. I hate that I took it from her.

One final voice blows into the enclave. "Oh, my fucking Fables!"

Feet slap the floor as Lark bolts across the enclave like a windstorm. Except she isn't running toward her father, but her mate.

"Cerulean!" tolls from her mouth as she launches past me and Puck.

At the same time, our brother vaults to her. And he seems to have forgotten his injuries, the endless weight of his wings. Neither of them gives a solid fuck.

Halfway across the expanse, they fling themselves at each other. Their movements are succinct, Lark's body slamming into Cerulean's, and his arms snapping around her.

Their heads burrow into one another's necks, frames shaking, breaths uneven.

"Lark," he whispers harshly. "*Minn ó Lark.*"

"Cerulean," Lark shudders over and over, lurching back to ply his face with kisses. "I thought I'd lost you. I love you so mu—"

Her words are silenced by Cerulean's mouth, which captures her in a long-suffering kiss. Lips and tongues invade my hearing. These fated mates have never been subtle in their displays.

Now I have no clue where to direct my attention. The last resort is Puck, which I have opinions about. It does not take a genius to know he's admiring the scene with another of his pompous smirks.

I'm glad for these reunions. Nevertheless, a grunt drops from my mouth.

I peek at the huddle across from me. Cove is resting her head on her father's shoulder, but while the other two participants are clearly savoring Lark and Cerulean's reunion, my lady's gaze is on me.

I see relief that I'm unscathed. I see comfort that I've returned my brother to her sister. I see something unconditional.

Those glittering eyes drown my being as she mouths, *I love you.*

The rhythm of my heart shifts. I love her more.

But has she forgiven me? Can I ever forgive myself?

After a moment, Cerulean whispers something. Lark drags herself from him and rushes to her family. I listen to the hug expand, arms folding and squeezing.

Thorne heaves the final name—"Lark"—as though it's made of air. Sniffles and congested breaths overwhelm the enclave.

Finally, Lark inches back. There's a teary but snarky tilt to her voice. "Took you long enough, Papa."

Thorne chuckles and sucks up his tears. "The best things do."

I sense Puck tipping his head down, mirth crooking his lips. He likes that answer.

A slender body slithers up my calf. Its presence nudges a smile from my mouth, so that I squat and offer the water snake my bent arm. Lotus twines himself around me and rattles off a small, appreciative hiss. He senses Cove's mood and is pleased by it.

"And who's that?" Thorne muses with recognition.

Cove laughs at the prompt. "He followed me here. We found out his name is Lotus."

"Here, I'd thought the little rascal simply discovered a way out of the sanctuary after you left." Thorne clears his throat. "It seems he approves of your, erm, suitor."

My head jolts toward the word. "I am not her suitor. I am her lover."

Cove squeaks, a blush darting up her cheeks.

My frown deepens. What did I say wrong?

Puck tsks. "Might want to pace yourself, luv."

I grumble, "You did no better from the moment you darkened the threshold."

"Aww, come on. Everyone eventually loves me, including you." He blows me a wet kiss, which I do not reciprocate.

"Not lover in the sense that it's temporary," Cove rushes to explain to her father. "What he means is lover in the permanent sense. Or rather, not that I would choose someone temporarily, or that it's bad to do that. But well, this is something more."

She crosses to my side and cups my jaw. I want to burrow my face in that soft palm but restrain myself as she takes my hand, the temperature of her fingers seeping into my skin. "This is my Elixir."

My Elixir.

Hers. I'm hers.

I enjoy that expression and straighten for the man's inspection.

Juniper joins Puck, who slings his arm around her waist. "Papa," she begins. "This is Puck."

Lark hustles back to Cerulean's side and attaches herself to him. "And Cerulean."

Thorne's amusement fills the enclave. "We've met."

Much to the sisters' astonishment, we explain what has transpired since the moment everyone was separated. It takes considerable time. We sit around the steaming whirlpool, Cove curling against me while Lotus dunks himself into the basin and swims.

Lark's reaction is nothing short of mercenary and haunted when she finds out what happened to her mate. Cerulean murmurs to calm her down and promises to show her the damage when they're alone. He does not want to make a centerpiece of himself, nor of Puck.

Nevertheless, Lark vows to skin the trade poachers alive and "hang 'em upside down by their dicks."

It is not an empty threat. What's more, it is a fraction of what I would do.

The sisters confirm that Coral delivered my message and then escorted them to The Deep. It took a galloping herd of deer and an agitated boat trip to reach us.

And while Lark's leg has healed, and it was no chore to impart how she was injured, there is one factor the sisters do not share with their father. I listen to Juniper rubbing her stomach, indecision directing her movements. She is calculating when to speak.

Puck tucks her into him, letting her make the choice of what to say and when.

Once our chronologies have aligned, Cove reaches out and grasps her father's hand. "I'm glad you're here, Papa."

"I'd never want to be anywhere else," he says, then lets his voice travel as he inspects the enclave. "I'm not going to lie, though. It'll take some time getting used to what I'm seeing."

"Unfortunately, time is not on our side," Cerulean broaches. "We have enemies coming at us from two different fronts. We're on the cusp of battle, and we don't know who will strike first or how many days we have left to be ready."

Indeed. Scorpio and his enhanced-fauna threats. Our Fae enemies. The humans of Cove's town. There is much to prepare for and little to take for granted.

Waterfalls course through the enclave. Whirlpools stew in their own simmering heat.

This reserve has done Cerulean well. It is a good place for restoration, which is why the merfolk had chosen to dwell here—until they abandoned it after the flood, after opposing forces divided.

We all need time to rest before reconvening. That is the agreement.

"There's one thing I'm missing." Thorne's puzzled tone cuts through the discussion. "I'm still eager to hear from my daughters about their games, plus this second way to restore the land. But the Evermore Blossom you all spoke of? Puck said you needed it because Juniper got sick." He focuses on his daughter and the satyr, angling his body toward them. "What was wrong with you?"

It is a fatherly question. He would want to know the details, as both my mothers always did whenever a matter concerned me.

Everyone falls silent. Juniper's rigid posture is palpable.

Thorne's register lowers. "Juniper, are you unwell?" Concern slants his words. "You can tell me, my girl. If something—"

"I'm pregnant," she blurts out.

The words eject from her mouth like bubbles. I think she has stunned herself with the outburst. To say the least, the penchant suits Cove more than her.

Thorne draws in a rickety breath. "You're what?"

"May we be excused?" Cove hazards. "This is personal."

"No, you may not," Thorne says, his gaze still presumably frozen on his younger daughter.

Indecision compromises my lady's posture. She's no longer nestled against me but upright.

She knows Juniper wants privacy after detonating in front of everyone. She knows her sister had plotted this announcement, right down to the speech Juniper wrote and rehearsed in front of Puck and her sisters.

My empathetic lady knows her sister does not like when things don't go as planned. Cove also knows Juniper scorns being the center of attention, unlike the satyr beside her.

Cove wants to support her sister's wishes. But she also doesn't want to disobey her father.

Puck's scooting closer to Juniper, his body surrounding her like a fortress. He's guiding his arm around her middle and staring at Thorne over her shoulder, prepared to weather the man's judgement.

Juniper is tightening her fingers with his. "During the game, Puck and I...we made someone."

Affection slides off Puck's tongue. "To be more specific, we made a half-bookish-human, half-naughty-Fae."

I listen as Juniper swerves her head to gaze at him. "How do you know for certain what their traits will be?"

"I don't. But then again, I do."

Such a Fae answer. Doubtless, Cerulean's mouth is slanting with appreciation, whereas I grunt under my breath.

"Educated guess," Puck amends.

I think Juniper is trying to contain a beam. "Well. Half of each would be nice."

"Pregnant," Thorne repeats, drawing her back to him. "My Juniper is pregnant." The lack of reply means she's nodding.

And then her father sighs. "Oh, hon."

It is not weariness or worry. It is awe.

He is proud of her. He may not fully trust the Faeries who took his family, but this isn't about him. It is about his daughters. He is willing to understand more, and he yearns to see them happy.

Thorne is opening his arms for Juniper. She's crawling over to him and relaxing into his embrace. And while he's holding her, Thorne is exchanging nods with Puck, open and willing.

It is a good start.

My lips tip sideways. After planting a kiss to Cove's temple, I rise along with Cerulean and Puck. Together, we leave our ladies with their father.

As I stride from the enclave, the man speaks to them in a hushed tone, his voice drifting from between the cascades. "Tell me everything, my girls."

26

The Lily Pond surrounds me with noise. Water slices down rocky mantles into the pool. The surface agitates, solicited by the cascades. I stand at the ledge of the walkway leading from our hut to the pond.

This is where I first tasted Cove's skin, first filled her body with mine. This is where we have built a home.

From behind me, a draft nudges the front door. Its hinges reverberate like a snake's tail.

Usually, this is my haven. Tonight, every disturbance scrapes my flesh with tension. I cannot seem to escape it. Come tomorrow or the day after that, what we've newly erected might be dismantled to ruins.

I brace my fists on my hips. My head bows, long curtains of hair draping around my face. I'm scowling, seething. Once, it had been easy to find an outlet for rage, to target the nearest object and smash it to pieces.

Now I don't know where to throw this anger. And beneath that, foreboding crawls up my vertebrae like an insect.

The wood planks tremble under my bare feet. My ears click toward the sound, and my senses draw in the sweet scent of jasmine.

Her arms slip around my waist from behind, anchoring me to her. That warm body presses against me, her respirations steady.

I do not turn but align one arm with hers across my stomach. My eyes clench shut as I let myself be taken by those arms, which have never failed to haunt me, heal me, and hearten me.

The moment Cove tucks me against her, the noises from the pond soften. The cascade ebbs to a gentle spill. Instead of churning, the pool and its floating lily pads quiver.

With her, our home becomes sacred and safe once more. The fury I had felt seconds prior is forgotten, my wrath dissolving into the moist air.

Only the shape of her remains.

It has been a full day since my brothers and I left our ladies with their father. My brothers and I had agreed to take turns keeping watch outside The Cascades. I had gone first, stationing myself at the entrance before Puck claimed my place, followed by Cerulean.

The family had talked for hours before everyone retired to sleep and recover from all that's happened. Thorne went to the forest with Puck and Juniper, and Cove returned to our bed, where we slept like stones.

My joints relax into Cove as she rests her chin on my shoulder. Though I tower over her—over most Faeries apart from Cerulean—I like that my lady is tall enough to do this, to fit herself to me.

Her outtakes caress my neck. "What are you thinking?" she coaxes.

That I love you. That I am incomplete if you're not by my side. That without you, my demons would consume me. That I can see what others don't, yet I cannot predict what shall happen next. That I will shred the world in half if anything happens to you.

I will not hide this from her, nor must I expand beyond one answer. "I cannot lose you."

Cove's breath stalls, and her throat constricts against my shoulder. She burrows her face into me and muffles, "You're not alone there."

My heart winces. "You needn't worry for me."

"I worry about everyone."

"Yes, that is your penchant."

My lady's selflessness knows no bounds, her dedication no limits. It is humbling as much as it is confounding, aggravating, and terrifying.

I adore her for it.

"I was scared," Cove whispers. "When Tinder told us what happened to your brothers, I couldn't stay still once you went after Cerulean. Only Lotus calmed me down, whereas my sisters couldn't. I tried to distract myself by helping Lark with her leg, but…" a crack breaks apart her words. "I kept thinking of what my people would do if they caught you. And I…"

Tears clot her throat. I band my arms tightly over hers. "I am here now."

"But the iron got to you, too."

"It has passed."

The toxins have evaporated from my veins, their potency nowhere near what my brothers endured. I did not battle such weapons, nor was I beaten to a pulp.

At least Cerulean and Puck are on the mend. Time is the only guaranteed cure.

As for the rest, The Mer Cascades served its purpose where I could not. In this one way, it is fortunate the area has been vacant since the flood. Our enemies abandoned their recesses in favor of stalking the outer niches of The Deep, lurking where we can't find them.

To that end, our foes have us walled in, able to surprise us from any tunnel or cave. Even as we stand here, I feel The Deep shrinking.

The humans have learned of Lark's treachery and will conclude her sisters have fallen in league with the Folk as well. And just as I'd been fleeing with Cerulean and Thorne, the mortals had discovered the cage empty.

Moreover, I know the makings of anger, the skeleton that welds its pieces together. Torturing Cerulean and Puck has likely refueled their confidence, reminded them of their advantages more than their drawbacks. Scorpio had accurately predicted as much when he paid my brothers that visit to their cage.

They will not let this escape go. They will not tolerate the rift any longer.

They will use iron fire to breach Faerie. They will come here sooner rather than later.

Our Fae enemies are also mobilizing. Our meeting with Scorpio and his pathetic failure to recruit Puck after the whipping ensures that.

They say I can see what others don't. In this respect, my kin must be right. Visions of fire, steel, and blood inundate my head, along with crumbling mountain tops, fallen oaks, and roaring waves.

The only question that remains is which enemy lays siege first, if nature doesn't wipe us out in advance.

The bliss of Cove resting against me is temporary. Nevertheless, I hiss, "I shall never leave you. I would sunder an army to reach you."

"That's a lot of troops."

"I would mutilate them."

"And that's rather harsh."

"I would tear through the bars of my cage."

"Dramatics," she attempts to tease.

I grunt, "The truth."

The grim mirth drains from her voice. "Your brothers are just as powerful, and they could barely hold themselves up."

My mouth curls into a snarl. "What those mortals did to them..." My blood curdles from the memory. "I smelled Cerulean's wounds, felt the rod's shape across his back, the iron embedded into his flesh. Another three lashes, and they would have died. The humans—"

"Were no better," she admonishes. "They were mad with grief and terror, and they felt justified. They believed maiming Cerulean and Puck would avenge them and protect their future, but they were no better."

"No better," I repeat through my teeth. "We did not torment their fauna or children."

"Don't go in circles with me, Elixir. You know what I meant."

I have slowly peeled the flesh from a mortal's hide, all without a shred of remorse while they screamed. I have trapped human sacrifices in The Deep, dismissing their existence when a shiver of sharks got to them during their unbeatable game. I have forced them to choose between noxious brews, as penalty for losing their games. I have blinded them until their eyes hemorrhaged.

Yes, I know what she'd meant. Neither of our worlds are innocent.

Dew and mist coat the air. I draw Cove's floral scent into my lungs and surrender, my anger losing its fight once again as she rekindles the pond with her light.

Cove's arms ascend to hook over my shoulders. "Having my father with us means the world. Thank you."

"Never thank a Fae," I murmur, though my lips cannot resist tilting upward.

"I thought we'd gotten used to breaking rules," Cove quips.

"Then never feel the need to thank me. I would do anything for you."

"Including weathering my father's judgment?"

"That, and more." I grumble, "He does not like me."

A circumstance which I have thoroughly earned. The notion sits like a lump in my chest, the pressure calcifying.

Cove squeezes me tighter. "He doesn't know you, same as he doesn't know your brothers. But he will, eventually. Until then, Papa accepts you."

"That is more than I would afford," I concede. "If anyone touched you, I would disembowel—"

"Again, I know," she hushes me. "Papa is a good man. He may not be elated by my choices, but he's willing to try. We told him our stories after you left. It's still difficult for him to absorb, but he knows we wouldn't stay if we didn't want to. Though, he did threaten to stuff more iron down yours and your brothers' throats if you don't make good on your vows. Especially Puck."

I would expect nothing less. Nor do I have concerns. Everything I feel for Cove is beyond expression, limitless and bottomless.

But despite my pledge, I cannot control everything. I could lose all this tomorrow. It could end with Scorpio's trident in my gut, the mortals' iron searing through my bones, or the wild deteriorating to the point where I won't survive in my realm.

That could happen. But if I die, I shall accomplish two things first.

I will love my lady. And if the world shatters, I will make sure she's the last mortal left standing, so help me.

I growl, raise Cove's hand to my lips, and brush my mouth against her knuckles. "Make good on my vows," I echo. "That, I can promise."

"So can I," Cove says against my earlobe. "I'm not going anywhere."

Her whisper stirs my blood. Her siren's voice leaches the last vestiges of tension, replacing it with a sacred heat that flows to my cock.

Floral notes infuse the sweltering air. Her taut breasts rub against my back, separated by a thin swatch of cloth that would be effortless to shred.

I shudder, a deep rumble rising from my chest. The sound alters her own exhales, and her nails delve into my sternum, eliciting a mixture of pleasure and pain.

We siphon oxygen as one, her body rising, mine falling. The outtakes condense, thickening into shallow pants, rife with need.

Lily pads lick the bank. Water trickles from the rock wall bordering one end of the pond.

Our bed is a mere handful of leagues away.

Though, I could fuck her in any corner of this cavern. It would not be the first time.

I only hope it won't be the last.

I twist my head sideways. "You slay me with your touch."

"That's good," she murmurs. "Because I don't want to talk about the bright light of day anymore."

"What do you want instead?"

Like a temptress, she nips my earlobe with her teeth. "I want the darkness."

With a snarl, I whip around. My hands snatch her beautiful face, my head dives to her mouth, and I sink my lips into hers.

Cove whimpers, dices her fingers through my hair, and pulls on the roots. The sensation tracks down my vertebrae and smashes into my tail-bone like a violent current. She yields her mouth under mine, lips parting for my tongue as it sweeps between them. I lick into her, the flat of my tongue stroking against hers, the strength of my jaw kicking her head back.

Her moan ripples down my throat, sending a mixture of honey and the river across my palate. My eyebrows pinch, for the sound and taste are agonizing. Her pleasure is bliss and anguish, a miracle and a curse. It caresses and cuts me.

I want this. I should not deserve this.

I will never let this go. I cannot bear to forsake this.

My mouth clamps onto hers. Cove knots her fingers into my mane, crushing the long locks in her grip. Her tongue fights with my own, as if trying to draw my being into her, and the same impulse consumes me as I devour her mouth.

This is passion. This is love.

This is fear.

I know the wanton side of her. She wants it rough, desperate, because time is of the essence. But for once, I cannot give her that. No, I want this to last while it can.

With a groan, I peel my mouth from hers. Cove whines but hushes as I set a finger to the bridge of her lower lip. She materializes before me like a beacon, the vision swimming into lucid view. Her face contracts with need, an enticing deluge of pink spreads across her cheeks, her eyes remain squinted closed, and air rushes between her plush lips.

Cove clings to me, frame trembling and hair awry as it scatters over her shoulders. I commit the sight to memory. Her lithe shape is that of a swan, but that is not who she is.

My lady is a tidal wave. She is an empress of serpents.

My head tilts as I drag a thumb across that lower lip. The bronze claws encasing my digits flash at the tips. Lightly, I scrape them over her tremulous mouth, tracing their shape. Like a water ring broadening across the pond's surface, quivers expand across her figure.

The nectar dripping between her thighs drugs my senses, my nostrils drawing in musk and the sweet fragrance of her lust. My cock thickens, blood pounding from the seat to the crown. I have scented her arousal on countless occasions, even before the first time we tore into each other.

She has given me patience, and I have inspired ferocity in her. On this eventide, I'll make certain we give each other both. And I intend for it to last a very, very long time.

Even if that means controlling the brutal drumming in my cock. Even if it means resisting the divine throbbing in her cunt.

For those passions suffuse my being as well. She's already soaked for me, as I'm stretched to the brink for her. My erection is so hard it wrestles against the leggings and threatens to rip through the material.

Removing my fingers, I slide my lips across hers and hiss, "I'm going to fuck you softly, and you're going to make love to me hard."

A turbulent sigh rolls from her mouth. "Elixir."

That name uttered from her throat. I want to swallow the noise whole.

My capped digit skates down the column of her throat, skims over the erratic pulse point, and glides across her clavicles. I like when she shivers. Even more, I enjoy when it makes her suffer for my touch.

I feast on every detail of Cove as my caps graze back and forth along her collarbones. Her nipples poke through the supple bodice of her swimming suit. With a flick of my wrists, I could shear the material into ribbons. But tempting as that is, it might upset her later, if not while caught up in the moment. She cherishes this outfit, my gift to her.

Instead, I compensate with a gentle snap of my digits. My caps slice the dainty ties of her skirt. Yards of pearlescent mermaid scales radiate, glittering like a thousand shingles as the material splashes around her feet.

Cove gasps, her eyes about to fringe open. But I prowl closer, my shadow cloaking her in darkness. "Keep them closed," I order.

She does as bid, her obedience tilting one corner of my lips. It is rare for her to comply, to follow commands. It is one of the many reasons I could not stop thinking about her, wanting her from the moment she entered my domain.

Next, I hook my caps under the bodice straps and glide them down her arms. The malleable fabric peels like snakeskin, baring her flesh to my famished gaze. My breath tightens into a low rumble as her breasts spring from the material, the nipples as solid as shells, the points as rosy as her tongue.

The image parches my mouth, eager to lap on those delectable pellets. I strip the fabric over her stomach and across her hips. She steps out of the garment while I plunge it down her limbs.

Chucking the material aside, I rise.

As I do, I make a journey of it.

My honed caps encircle her ankles, ascend the backs of her knees, and skate a sharp trail up the backs of her thighs. Cove's panting fills my senses, surmounting the slosh of the pond's waterfall. I smile at her nervousness, how she awaits my actions, pulse ramming against her neck.

This is what the darkness does. It conceals, builds anticipation.

I prowl over every erotic curve and hollow, basking in my lady's quavering sighs, discovering her all over again. My hands trace the flare of her buttocks and the divots of her beautiful ass, prickles trailing in my wake. Then I skid my index fingers down the slopes of her hipbones, deeper still to the inner flanks of her thighs.

A roar builds in my lungs, not yet ready to break free. Rather, I keep my voice even. "Spread them."

Cove's legs broaden, giving me unbridled access to the swatch of hair tucked at the crux of her legs. The loveliest essence wafts from her cunt, sweet and savory. I lick my lips and gaze, observing as my fingercaps brush through the tight mound of hair.

My lady jolts but doesn't flee, because I won't hurt her. Never will I harm her.

Tormenting her is another matter.

My caps skim the delicate flesh of her slit, the walls swelling under my touch. So very lightly, I run the chiseled edges of my digits over Cove's skin, teasing her with the faintest of threats. The peaks are reminiscent of talons, deadly enough to use as weapons. But with her, they shall be a source of worship.

I rasp and gingerly etch the slot of her cunt, sliding my cap backward and forward, rowing over the seam. Cove whines, plaintive. Her hands grapple my hair, tangling it into disarray.

Liquid pours from her cunt, seeping through and wetting my finger. I growl and inch my digit into the pool of heat gathering at her nexus. Fables be damned, she's leaking onto the appendage.

I swirl my finger ever so carefully, etching the oval entrance. Cove's mouth falls open on a thin, swift cry. An endless stream of fluid pours from her.

My cock rises higher, the head strumming with heat. By sheer force of will, I keep my knees nailed to the wood planks.

Combing through the glistening hair, I find that tight kernel of skin projecting from her center. My finger pats it, feathers over it. Cove's spine tenses, and a sob drops from her mouth.

Not enough. I need her louder.

Gilded heat swarms behind my eyes, and I do my utmost to pull more noise from the well of her throat. With the slightest motions, I draw the back of my cap over her clitoris, orbiting the inflated nub. Her arousal gushes from her folds and drizzles down to my knuckles.

Fuck, my erection is going to rupture merely from this.

Nonetheless, if she wants a vicious Fae, that is what she'll get. I prolong our anguish and toy with her wet skin. Cove's frayed moans flood my ears, the climax hardening in her throat. I reap her pleasure, siphon it from her with my fingers coasting over the cinched bud of skin, then sinking across the rift in her thighs, then towing through the hair again before resuming its onslaught across her ridge of nerves.

Cove yanks on my scalp and tosses her skull back. Her moans fragment, ricocheting from that deep, dark place inside her. I croon, riveted by the flush of her cunt, the rush of wetness spilling from the recess.

"Now come," I demand. "Come on them."

With a last ruthless flick of my fingers, Cove unravels. Her body quakes, the orgasm ripping through her bones. She wails, the cataclysm of sound ravaging the cave.

Agony and euphoria cleave me in half. My muscles shudder from the impact. The second Cove's climax subsides, I lunge to my feet while stripping off the leggings. My cock jumps from the material, aching and as thick as a mast.

In one swift movement, I link my arms under Cove's thighs. She yelps as I haul her off the ground, crush my mouth to hers, and stalk naked across the walkway to the hut.

Keening, she clamps onto my nape and kisses me back. Our lips hurl at one another, rocking together, tongues swatting. Without breaking away, I lash my arm and shove the front door open, the facade ramming into the wall.

The ceiling is high, the curtains are sheer, and the walls are crafted of smooth stone. An assortment of black and white furnishings with wooden accents outfits the rooms. It is lightness and darkness, with splashes of greenery filling the empty corners.

Cove has described our home to me. But while I cannot see the interiors, I do not give a forsaken shit. All I need to know is how to maneuver past them.

I stride around the obstacles and strike toward the bedchamber while carrying her in my arms. Our lips pry apart. My forehead connects with hers, and gusts of air vacate our lungs.

She has not opened her eyes yet. Those luminous orbs remain hidden, clinging to the darkness, enabling her to feel me against her in an acute way.

Oh, fuck the bed.

I veer toward the wide divan fronting a bay window in the living room. We're panting and pent-up like fated mates in heat by the time my limbs hit the cushioned edge.

I drop Cove onto the surface, pillows tumbling off the sides. My mouth seizes hers again as I descend with my lady. Her hands swim through my hair. She uncoils across the divan, body sprawling beneath mine while I loom over her, my hips splitting her thighs like a gulf.

My eyes flare open to watch her kiss me, to see it happen. Her features pleat, as though afflicted, lost in the sensations, overwhelmed by the surge of our lips. My mouth burrows into hers, tongues swiping together, and the siren eats up my growl.

Perspiration beads in the trench between her tits, the humidity glossing her skin. The same outbreak drips down my abdomen. We're sweating and heaving—and slowing down.

At last, I pull back and sweep my mouth over hers. "Open them."

First her legs, which spread and hook over my waist. Then her eyes, the lashes fanning apart. Those orbs flutter, blasting me with light—blinding me.

Her gaze locks with mine. And I thrust my cock.

Cove gives a shout, her figure rocking upward. Rather than savage, my body pivots into her with a single measured stroke. The penetration is deft and full, the head of my cock pitching to the seat. She pulsates around me, her drenched cunt encapsulating my girth.

I seethe, a guttural noise slicing from my throat. Yet I wait, primed within Cove and watching her subside from the impact.

When the siren looks at me, understanding claims her features. The irises alight with ambition.

I have fucked her softly. Now it's her turn.

Make love to me hard.

Cove nods. As she does, my lady rolls her hips, taking me deeper. The delicate swat of her waist tugs on my cock. Her walls soak me in like a sponge, dragging a stunted growl from the pit of my chest.

Her hips beat a sinuous tempo with mine, the folds of her cunt sucking on my length. I broaden, the column getting larger. Blood floods my sac and surges to the apex. My muscles contort as she releases my mane and drapes her palms down my chest, fondles my scales, and rubs the nipples pitting from my pectorals.

Her fingers pinch the tips, inciting a jolt of pain. She stalks the noises I make, gyrating her core under me, wetness clutching my buried erection. Guided by her motions, I ply my cock in and out. The length withdraws fully, then swings into her compact little slit.

Cove directs the movements, dominates them. She grinds herself up into me, her folds grabbing each flex of my cock.

Her gaze cements to mine, her irises like two whirlpools drowning me. Her brows crinkle, pleasure blooming across her face. "Keep them on me."

I obey. We rock with concentrated urgency, my cock meeting her cunt, both striking slowly. She whimpers and pours her arousal over me, loosening another hiss from my throat.

Surely, I'll die from this someday. It isn't possible to feel this frenzy of sensations at once.

The pain. The fury. The fear. The desire. The love.

My lady skims the ridges bundled across my torso, tracing the stacked muscles. I sling my hips, the prow of my cock slipping through the lips of her core, probing the helm. Yet her knees steeple higher, lifting to change the angle of our fucking, tilting our lovemaking in a new direction.

This hauls me deeper. I release a prolonged groan and sling harder into the crook of her thighs.

Cove moans, mouth ajar and eyes steady on me. Her nipples skid over my chest. I give into temptation and bow my mouth to one, sealing my lips around the tip.

She whines. Her fingernails scour my back and claw the skin. I croon into her breast and lick the peak raw, then transfer my cravings to the other shell.

Our pelvises slide against one another, monstrously hard and sopping wet. Cove thrusts against me, sloping my cock into her, reeling her thighs on either side of me.

I grit out. My mouth releases her nipple, the disk of flesh gleaming and cinched. Wanting to savor the rest of my lady, I anchor my weight, hoisting myself over her. With my upper body buttressed, I apply all my reserves to the forward sling of my hips, my cock jutting into her.

We're a mess of noise, a steady drum of moans. Rough sounds drop from my mouth and cleave through the hut. My gaze returns to hers, drawn to that molten light.

Emboldened, Cove loops her legs over my shoulders. "Give it to me."

Fucking Fables eternal. She angles her cunt and my cock higher, then advances the pace by driving her ass down onto my groin. The merciless siren palms my buttocks, steering them into her.

With a grunt, I pursue that rhythm and piston my cock. If she wants the darkness, she shall have it.

I met her thrusts, pitch for pitch. Cove cries out in approval. At the sound, raging heat gushes into my pores, tingles rush to the tips of my ears, and my fingercaps puncture the divan. The whittled points stab the cushioned foundation, giving me leverage.

She rides my waist and oozes all over my erection. Her tits jostle, and her hair tangles around her face. Those broken sobs charge through my veins like a heady brew.

Her mouth hangs open, ass grinding into my pelvis. She engulfs me in her stare, daring me to try and avert my gaze. This siren knows I will fail.

"Love me," she pants. "Fuck me."

The command pares my flesh like a beautiful dagger, precious and penetrating. It's a delirious pleasure, a potent elixir of its own. I want to drain every drop of it, fill myself with every bit of her.

With a renewed growl, I straighten upright on my knees and heed my lady's request. Balanced vertically, I fling my cock into her. Her legs rest flush along my torso, heels braced on my shoulders.

I heft myself into her, striking deeply. My hands snatch her waist, and Cove grabs my ass, palming the indentations as they flex with each pump.

The siren chants, the noises beseeching for more, for all of it. I groan, and groan, and groan. My abdomen crimps, muscles working, putting every effort into her cries.

This is all I need. This is all I ask for.

We dash our hips together. My cock grinds into her slick cunt, the climax building at the juncture of our waists. A howl gets stuck in my throat.

I won't look away. Never shall I look away.

Cove's eyes squint, on the verge of tumbling into the void with me. I probe that impulse and attack with sharp, deft strikes until those eyes seal closed. She snatches my ass and shrieks with pleasure, her cunt spasming and coming around my cock, the magnitude plunging her into darkness.

The vision brands itself on my soul. The noise scores my heart.

I lash my cock, blood simmering from the stem to the roof. My joints tense, winding tightly—then snapping in half. The bellow shreds through my lungs, my release convulsing into her.

The frenzy races from where our bodies lock to the rest of me. The magnitude of it courses through my frame like a riptide.

My lower half sags, torso held aloft by a single bracketed arm at the side of Cove's head. I hunch over her, my waist flanked by her tremulous thighs, which I kiss before lowering them to the divan.

Though, I don't pull out of her body. For I could stay inside her until the wild fades and takes me with it.

My lady whimpers, satisfaction blooming across her face. Her lashes ripple apart, irises soft on me.

We suck in mouthfuls of air. Sweat trickles from my skin to hers.

I rush my fingercaps through her mussed hair, and she glides her palms up and down my tailbone, as if to stop me lest I attempt to withdraw my cock from her.

I shake my head. "Whoever said love is not more powerful than a weapon is a fucking idiot."

Cove bursts into laughter. "Meaning, your former self?"

Indeed. A grin consumes my face.

For a while, I content myself to stare at her. Outside, the pond licks against the dock leading from our door. The curtains whisper across the sill in a repetitive *shh, shh, shh*.

"And where is Lotus?" I wonder.

Sated, Cove nestles beneath me and runs her foot over the back of my calf. "Playing with the cobras in your den," she says fondly. "Because he's a mortal snake, I have a feeling they think he's a prophet or something."

A dry huff of amusement pushes from my lips. Cove's serpentine companion has attracted many of the river dwellers, including the reptiles in The Pit of Vipers.

"So we're alone," I conclude.

"Mmm-hmm," Cove hints while straying a finger down my chest and wiggling her hips.

I growl, that primal need rekindling swiftly. Explicit thoughts of what I could do to her in the next hour flood my mind. I'm grinning and lowering my mouth to hers when my senses attune to the lily pads floating outside, the cascade washing down the pond's overhang, and something else.

My descent stalls, mouth hovering over Cove's. A distinct stench poisons the air, tangy and charred. It's emanating from leagues away, yet it's intensifying, getting nearer.

I know that scent. I have never forgotten it.

Cove's forehead crimps. "What is it?"

My bones sizzle with recognition. Gold fizzes in her pupils as they throw my ferocious reflection back at me.

A snarl curdles from my tongue. "Iron fire."

27

I blast into The Pit of Vipers. My limbs cut through the terrarium, urgency biting its fangs into my bare heels.

To my left, a boa spirals through the crush of foliage, its body shaking the fronds. To my right, my ears cling to the reverberating tongue of a viper with saw-like scales riding up the cord of its body, the sound alone venomous to fauna prey. Several other quivering offshoots and rustling undergrowth alert me to the snakes gliding through their territory.

After the flood, I had leached this environment of the most pestilent toxins, though most of the reptiles are impervious to the pollutants.

Tragically, iron is the exception. The singular deficiency of Faeries. The one elemental chink in our armor, capable of diffusing our magic. The crawlspace leading to our weakness. Fatal to every living thing in this wild, a leviathan wouldn't outlast the effects.

Customarily, I would nod to the vipers. Tonight, I sweep by them.

Past the terrarium, I stride through the water curtain and into my den. The central vat boils, spitting noise into the dome. Dankness clots the air, the environment soggy with moisture and stinking of the residual poisons that cling stubbornly to the dome's walls.

Eons of brewing have infused my blood with the vigor to withstand these hazards. Like its dwellers, my serpentine origins have done the rest.

But that does not spare me from the pungent whiffs of iron. The odor peppers my senses, remote yet airborne and gaining traction.

The humans are getting closer. They have breached Faerie.

My teeth gnash. I do not bother threading my way across the expanse.

I smash through the mesh of lush foliage girdling the den, my shoulders cracking a few branches in half like a sickle.

Gone are the crescent tables and the containers dangling from ropes. Instead, I prowl to the rocky mantle protruding from the wall and shove my hand into the collection assembled there. Stoppered jars, glass bottles, and smaller vessels clatter like bones. The skeletal noise attests to how few ingredients I have managed to accumulate since the flood.

My thoughts cling to Cove's positive nature. Something is better than nothing.

Tendrils of flaming iron sneak under my nostrils. It percolates with the humidity and unsteadies my wrist, fingers shaking as I hunt through the cache. Anxiety and confusion crawl up my knuckles. I blink, unable to parse through the reserves, unable to find what I need—unable to remember.

For an instant, my lack of vision hinders me. Then my palm lands on a slender bottle ejecting warmth and a fizzing echo, these distinct features verifying my hopes. My fingers shackle around the vial and stuff it into the baldric under my robe.

Whipping around, my limbs carve across the den. In the atrium, the vipers' movements have grown restless. They rattle their tails. They agitate the foliage as they shift sizes, shuddering from cords to columns. Forked tongues unspool and vibrate because, however distant, mortal fumes are slowly dripping into the atmosphere.

My eyes burn, tossing gold through the area. Traces of the iron flames have gotten this far...this deep. That means there are many of them.

A pair of pythons large enough to swallow a carriage flank the atrium's exit. I stride their way, sensing their vertical pupils kindling on me.

I lower my voice. *"Deep beneath the water, a Snake bewitched a Viper..."*

With every sentence, a lull passes across the serpents. I narrate while stalking closer. As last, I finish in a murmur, *"For once magic has touched two beings, no other enchantments may prevail."*

Alleviated for the time being, the vipers shrink and go quiet. Too large, and they will be sighted. It is a great irony.

I set my finger to my lips. "Shh." My eyes stray across the atrium, hooking onto the essence of each dweller.

Leave. Hide. Now.

They take heed, filter into the den, and undulate toward the vat. It will lead to the river and its infinite crevices. Mortals may have iron fire. They may have that advantage against us, but not against the landscape itself.

And unlike Cove, they do not possess a fucking map. Burrow too far under, and they will be lost. The Deep will swallow them whole like a maw, even if our enemies take us first.

One of the serpents rustles over my toes on its way out. I make out its hood and count the large scales. It is a cobra.

I stalk from The Pit of Vipers and evanesce. My body dissolves, vaporizing like mist into the void. Gravity disappears under my soles. The seconds snare together. My pulse clocks like a beast shattering free of its confines.

The wind filters through my hair. Dry earth solidifies under my weight. Water gargles past my feet.

I sway briefly. Manifesting has zapped the precious amount of energy I've recouped since the rescue, but the adrenaline supplements that. Anyway, I'd needed to arrive quickly.

Peeling the hood from my head, I march between the trees. A gust lashes through the wild, and a nearby stream eddies. Tiny wings buzz around my head, glowing insects flitting through the environment.

The Colony of Fireflies cleaves a path to The Triad. I feel the trio of landscapes converge—the mountain, the forest, and the river.

"Sire," a voice squeaks from the bushes.

The words nail my feet to the soil. My eyebrows slam together, and I turn toward the source.

My attention jumps but fails to hit its mark until that same voice says, "Down here."

Because of the slender tone, I had anticipated a brownie or pixie. Instead, the clop of four hooves identifies the Fae. The centaur is young and female, her size and weight not yet vast enough to make the ground shiver.

Trenches dig into my forehead. Puck and Cove have a natural talent for interacting with striplings. This skill does not extend to me.

Once, I thrived on my title. I soaked its up its power like a stimulant.

Lord of the Water Fae. Ruler of the River.

But it does not feel right any longer. With my subjects divided, I cannot say I've earned the title on this eve. I certainly cannot argue I did my reign justice before then.

In any case, the wild and its fauna rule themselves. We are but servants and protectors.

"I am no longer *Sire*," I inform the wee one.

A tail flicks in irritation. "Don't you think denying your privilege is a disservice to us all?"

That is…true. Yet another privilege I cannot presently claim is time.

"Make haste," I grunt. "Go back to The Heart of Willows. You will be safe there."

"I don't want to be safe. I want to fight."

My brows straighten into planks. The clink of steel and strain of leather alert me to a band buckled around the filly's withers. Doubtless, it sheaths a weapon. Perhaps an axe or those shooting stars woodland Faeries are obsessed with.

Now I remember. This is the female Puck had anecdotally mentioned when taking my place to stand guard outside The Mer Cascades. She's the filly with a fondness for Juniper, a tenacious interest in humans, and a penchant for not doing what she's told.

The filly's defiance nudges the corner of my mouth. "Your courage won't be wasted. Returning to your kin is the best way to fight with us. Save your strength for the day you grow taller than me, and the wild will be grateful."

"You sound like Cypress."

"Is that supposed to be an insult?"

"And now you sound like Puck."

I don't need vision to know the spitfire's nose is crinkling. "The humans once took our youth," I remind her. "I was among them. Who will protect the young centaurs if you do not?"

Hesitation. Chagrin. Obstinacy. "I'm not falling for that, Sire."

Nor do we have precious minutes to waste. My baritone slithers from my lips. "Iron fire leaks into your pores with the potency of venom. It weakens you like prey crushed in the vise grip of a cobra. And once it's done sucking the magic from your blood, it feasts on your cartilage until you're nothing but a husk."

Silence. Her breathing splits like a twig.

Like I said. I have no special place in my soul for coddling. This filly has gotten the point.

I nick my chin toward the woodland. "You will do as you're told. Or I shall pin your hooves to the ground with the daggers concealed under my robe."

An audible gulp. "Yes, Sire."

There is no need to confirm her departure. My limbs snap into movement. I pivot and strike through The Colony of Fireflies.

At the path's end, the darkness shifts behind my eyes. It thickens into three distinct shades of black—a hawthorn, oak, and ash tree. The great sentinels rise from the earth, marking where the landscapes converge.

Here, the foulness of burning iron magnifies. All is quiet, despite the compression of bodies scattered along the border.

My eyes stumble across a halo of teal light. Cove stands on The Triad's threshold, her spear angled and ready. Starlight and shadows swirl around her. She glances my way, her gaze eviscerating the distance between us.

For a moment, we lock and hold.

Traces of white hair ripple from the margins, signifying Lark's presence beside Cove. And the click of a bolt being fed into a crossbow descends from the oak tree's branches. Because she cannot risk getting any closer, Juniper is stationed overhead and leveling a crossbow from one of the boughs. The leaves will shroud her, along with a scattered group of woodland archers, while offering them a clear prospect from which to fire.

"About time, luv." Puck's drawl resounds from several feet away, his voice accompanied by the strain of a nocked longbow. He's kneeling on the ground, under the oak's branches where Juniper squats, with his weapon poised. He has spoken without removing his attention from the borderline between Faerie and the mortal realm.

I huff. "I see you could not keep Juniper from the battle."

"Don't rub it in," the satyr gripes. "I might have threatened to haul the huntress over my shoulder and chain her in The Herd of Deer. One, she never does what I ask. Two, between her and her sisters, my woman knows how to bust through locks. So guess how long the argument lasted?"

Before or after they had pre-war sex? I would say not long.

In any case, the embryo is cocooned by the Evermore Blossom extract I'd given Juniper. Nothing can happen to their child.

And like her sisters, Juniper has a right to defend this crusade. Puck knows this, otherwise he would have made good on his threat to keep her out of the conflict.

The oak will shield Juniper, enabling her to fight from a distance. As an extra precaution, Lark's nightingale chirps overhead. Should any weapons fly in Juniper's direction, the bird can shift, pluck her from the branch within milliseconds, and catapult her to safety.

Unlike I had assumed, the mortals haven't breached Faerie yet. But they're about to try.

"Tell me," I say.

"One hundred leagues ahead," Puck briefs me. "Half on foot, the other on horseback. It's more than the village. Cerulean circled with the mountain Fae and counted a thousand strong, which means the humans asked for aid outside of their town."

"And they received it?" I balk.

"Come on. We're not dealing with the Unseelie Court. Mortals from different territories do help each other out, just like Solitaries."

That is true. Yet without bargains or guarantees, the notion strikes me. Either their neighboring provinces worried about being the Faeries' next victims or…the people simply cared to help, as Cove would.

On the other hand, I suspect it is both.

"Each one has a torch," Puck continues. "And I'd wager an iron-tipped weapon."

I seethe. "The humans could not have forged that many defenses so quickly."

Not since concluding Lark and her sisters have taken to our side. The intermission hasn't been long enough.

Puck's silence agrees with me. That amount of weaponry would have required an extensive period to amass. The mortals have been stewing on this moment for longer than we'd anticipated.

I trade looks with Cove. The dread strung across her face confirms as much. There must have been a select number of mortals plotting this revenge for a while, limiting the knowledge so that we wouldn't get wind of it through whispers and rumors.

Shifts in the thicket and the croaks of branches signal a legion of additional Fae nearby. Coral appears at my other side, her inflection catching as she grips her harpoon lance. "Sire."

"Describe it," I tell her.

She lists the allied Solitaries who currently wait in the vegetation. The winged and horned figures of the mountain, nymphs and dryads and leprechauns hunkering the bushes, and river Folk coiled near the stream, including merfolk bobbing over the surface and ready to leap from the depth.

According to Coral, Thorne has been armed with a pair of knives and is stationed among the shrubs with Foxglove, who's outfitted with a stockpile of daggers.

Cypress is further back and aiming his own longbow. Moth is squatting overhead on the hawthorn's bough, papery wings tense and fists balled. Tinder is waiting below her, with throwing stars bridled around his thigh.

Looming within The Triad's canopy, Cerulean is kneeling on his own branch. He's leaning into the void while gripping the hawthorn's trunk with one hand and his javelin with the other. Like a raptor, he's suspending himself and scanning the horizon beyond our world.

His father is nowhere to be seen. The Parliament of Owls is away, still looking for him. And Lotus and Sylvan have been left out of this, both tucked in their realms.

The whereabouts of our Fae enemies is anyone's guess, for Solitaries are masters at hiding themselves. Even so, they know the mortals are coming. They must smell it and taste the iron on their tongues.

Feasibly, they'll wait out the bloodshed. After that, they'll wade through the havoc and target the leftovers, the ones who haven't been butchered.

Speaking of which, my brothers' iron wounds are mending, but they're hardly suitable for combat. "How are you?" I ask Puck.

"Could have used another week or two," he answers. "But I'm not complaining."

Neither is Cerulean. Their bodies have weathered trauma, and now this before they've had a chance to fully recuperate. Yet they're alive for this event, Cerulean's once again capable of flying at least marginal distances, and Puck doesn't audibly wince as he wields the bow. Not only has The Mer Cascades done them well, but their resilience is a blessing.

Cerulean's wings twitch, the quills partially healed. A whispering growl ushers from his mouth. *"Feir eru jér."*

Despite the murmur, his warning travels. *They're here.*

Puck mutters, "Fuck."

He describes the rest in greater detail to me. Through the fringes and across the fields stretching from The Faerie Triad, torches rise like stalks. Balls of black flame writhe from the tips, the handles gripped by figures that multiply from dozens to hundreds.

Infinite footfalls coalesce with a percussion of hooves. As Puck had said, they've brought their equines, as humans do. Fables be damned.

Where mortals are usually shouting and chanting, this army of villagers is quiet. They have nothing left to scream. Indeed, they're done screaming for us.

My head thrashes toward Cove. I want to kiss her. I want to shove her behind me. I want to throw a tsunami at those who would touch her. But she just brands me with a brave smile that reaches her damp eyes.

Her whisper reaches out, not only to me but her sisters and each being standing with us. "The wind is a force, the tree rises high, and the water runs forever—just like us."

From within the oak, Juniper recites, "Whatever happens to one of us, happens to each of us."

Lark finishes, "Together. All or nothing."

And I am forever changed.

The words shake from the marrow of my bones, joining Puck's gruff voice and Cerulean's whisper. We speak separately and together.

"For the eternal wild."

As the humans reach the border, their collective shout finally hits the sky. And we charge to meet it.

28

The ground shudders under the weight of a thousand pairs of feet. A tumult whips through my hair. My limbs burn as they pump toward the clamor.

The atmosphere whirls, too many scents clashing—smoking iron, pouring sweat, ripe florals, and sharp brine.

One natural world against another. And somewhere between the two, a medium exists. It is the pause between one breath and another, between an exhalation and an inhalation. It's a sliver, a small chamber of space where their realm and ours converge—neither one, nor the other.

It is humanity and Faerie. Here, every sound, scent, texture, and taste merge.

Few recognize it. But I do.

We race toward that spot. The earth's quaking intensifies as we expunge the distance between us, a great percussion throbbing under my soles. The tangible beat of hooves and limbs. High grass oscillating like a tide.

I charge ahead while tearing off my robe, crossing my arms, and ripping the forked daggers from my baldric.

A wall of bodies spread on either side of me. Another wall of black expands ahead.

One second before it happens, sound floods my ears like a wave smashing into breakers. It's the sound of Cove when she first blocked my daggers with her spear. It's the jagged bedrock of The Deep before a flood tore through its foundation and sucked us into its depth. The convulsion of noise swallows me whole.

Howls slash the air. Whinnies slice through the quagmire. Steel rings, and arrows whiz.

And we collide.

At the rim between Faerie and the mortal world, bodies hurl themselves at one another. My canines grate together. A shift of wind pushes my way, coming from the right.

I duck as a mace spiked in iron swings overhead. I swerve and lurch upright while thrusting one dagger into a mortal's stomach. Fluid spritzes my jaw, and I imagine crimson spraying my skin like ink. With a thud, my kill hits the ground.

Puck's heavy panting blusters beside me. The crunch of bone signals he's just rammed his fist into someone's skull. After that, his longbow quivers, nocked and firing what sounds like a pair of arrows.

The projectiles dissect the air. Two more bodies go down.

Once, gratification and validation had consumed my waking hours as I contributed to human suffering. Now the divide claws through me. My fists and capped fingernails prickle with the urge to strike out and strike down. Yet my chest tightens with each fallen figure.

These are Cove's people. She came from them, as I came from my kin.

We were supposed to find a second way. I'd been expected to see what others cannot. This wasn't meant to happen.

It's them or us. It's them or my family. It's them or Cove.

It's fight now or die soon.

The stench of iron fire pulls on my joints, festering them like an infection, urging my reflexes to lag. The reek of it singes my throat with a single whiff.

A weight sprints in my brother's direction while he's driving an arrow into another figure's heart. Approaching flames emit the stench of more iron. The blaze will seize Puck like a match to oil.

The former half of me resurrects with a vengeance. I snatch Puck's attacker by the scruff before the man can turn my brother into a bonfire. The pockets behind my retinas burn, and heat pours from my pupils. I envision gold skewering the male's eyes, roasting the light from them.

The man screeches. His footfalls stagger in desperate confusion as I release him.

I don't bother finishing off the human. He won't last.

All the while, my eyes swerve. I hunt through the black abyss, ice-cold fear splashing through my gut until an oval of teal glows before me.

Cove thrusts her spear to block a person's sword. She rotates both weapons into a wide arc and uses the combined hilts to crush her opponent's kneecaps.

Pain, grief, and instinct glosses her eyes. She hates this, but she must do this.

A dark blot surges toward her. My dagger is flying and hacking through the predator's throat an instant later. The blot evaporates, the human having landed beside Cove, their frame pinned to the grass by my prongs.

She whirls my way, blood speckling her shoulder and collarbone. I race in her direction. On the way, I spin while stabbing my daggers into the belly of another mortal.

Faeries bellow in agony. Scalded flesh overwhelms my olfactory senses. Some of my kin are burning, others oozing from their wounds.

They should be faster, stronger. But the iron is heavy, dense in the atmosphere. It's giving the humans an equal chance.

Overhead, a hurricane of wind tosses a pack of mortals into the air. Their cries are airborne as they launch into the sky.

Cerulean is circling, his wings not as robust as they were but still capable of storming through. I hear those quills bristle and dive. Seconds later, a human yowls as they're plucked from a horse.

The lash of Lark's whip catches across someone's spine. The blast of Juniper's crossbow hails from the oak and impales an enemy. Their father intercepts a lunging pitchfork and stabs its wielder.

As I hew my way to Cove, my ears monitor the disorder around me.

Because Lark is fighting near her, I catch the wisp of white and attach it to a shift in the darkness. Then suddenly, my lady stalls. Cove's weapon braces as anger cramps her profile.

Whatever she sees, Lark must as well. The female's blot hovers beside Cove, then disintegrates in flash.

Lark must be charging toward someone. Cove breaks from her stupor and tracks after them. And from her perch, Juniper hollers something furious, though I cannot make out what.

The sisters are targeting a predatory voice that sneers, "Get the traitor bitches!"

Awareness slithers up my flesh. There's recognition in that mortal slur, plus an emotion I'm well acquainted with—spite.

Cerulean and Puck had mentioned the trade poachers of the sisters' past, the ones who chased Lark into Faerie, the ones who rallied the town when they caught my brothers. Venom stirs my nerve endings, as if brewed inside a cauldron. My limbs accelerate while I cleave through each form who gets in my way.

Thorne screams his daughters' names, but he's too far from them. The whizz and slickness of Lark's whip chops through the air. She's fighting the poachers—one in particular. Her movements are quick and fluid, as though she's been fantasizing about this encounter for centuries.

Her whip, Cove's spear, and Juniper's flying crossbow bolt resound as one. They're battling the men from recent history.

One of them heaves, blood congesting his throat. Another gags from the chokehold of Lark's whip.

Unlike my brothers and me, our ladies would have shown mercy in another life, in another setting. In this life and in this battle, they relinquish that luxury. The whip flicks audibly, blocking the poacher's attack, and the bones of someone's neck snap. I suspect she just brought down their leader.

Cove rams her spear downward. The blur of Juniper's bolt projects from the outskirts. And the final poacher goes quiet.

My lady's profile creases with exhaustion, protectiveness, and relief. Perhaps a tinge of remorse.

I twist my daggers in a succinct pattern and lance through an enemy. I pitch blinding gold at another weight hastening toward me.

Except the iron dilutes the effect. I feel the reduction behind my retinas, how the temperature has lessened.

Another nocked bow soars, the distinct quaver belonging to Cypress. At one point, the centaur bucks and rams his hooves against his opponent.

Moth's battle growl is impossible to miss, along with the mad flutter of her wings. Somewhere else, Foxglove is crossing daggers. Tinder is flinging his throwing stars toward a pair of mortals, the astral blades catching them mid-sprint. And Coral is wielding her harpoon lance, the clang of her weapon familiar to my senses.

But they're slowing, their outtakes dragging. My head fogs momentarily, the haze compromising my equilibrium.

Too late, a form materializes at my side. A knife snatches across my ribs. I hiss, fire licking my skin as the iron seeps into me.

Mindless, I whisk my arm but strike nothing. My second dagger strokes through open air, as ineffective as trying to cut water in half. In consequence, another scalding gash tears into the side of my neck.

Cove shouts my name. Countless roars eclipse her voice.

My veins boil. As iron residue leaks into my blood, visions douse my mind. I'm trapped in a cage plugged with water. Black bars lead to freedom but simmer with heat that singes me each time I touch them. I'm smaller, with fewer muscles, and a human girl is poking her bright eyes at me from the bushes.

Those irises draw me in like whirlpools. And how dare she gaze at me as if I'm something special.

I want to punish her for it. I want to retaliate against the mortals for the dying sounds of my kin and our fauna, and I'll start with her.

I will drown you.

It feels good to scare her, sending the girl scurrying back into the woods. I relish the sight. But then for some reason, I flatten my palms on the glass tank enclosing me and think, *Come back.*

Then I'm breaking free, raging toward the stream. A scrawny figure tackles me from behind, and we tumble into the depth. Hands wrestle me down, teal irises swirl with hatred, and salt stings into my pores.

Suddenly, my eyes cloud over. I sink into a void as terror gnaws on my ribs.

Then I'm waking up with a wet gasp, like gills sucking on liquid. I cannot see, only hear my mothers' voices and smell their combined fragrance wafting over me—lilies mixed with spring water, a comforting brew.

Then they're screaming, and mortals are firing, and my mothers are falling beside me. And they're not moving. I'm shouting their names, my eyes are lurching wildly, but I cannot find them. Blackness cloaks me in as I listen to them dying.

A mortal screech yanks me from the past like arms pulling me from the sea. A thud fills my ears, and I come to. The battle clamors around me. At some point, I'd collapsed on the grass. The metallic taste of blood drips across my palate, and its acidic scent permeates the field.

Teal engulfs the darkness. Cove's frantic gaze swims overhead, and she clasps my face. "Elixir!"

My lashes flap. Warm, cloying fluid dribbles from my side. A limp body is sprawled next to me, the scent of my blood clinging to the human's lifeless form. The mortal had managed two well-placed slashes before Cove got to them.

I would like to quip that she beat me to it, that I was on my way to her first.

"Elixir, no!"

But I do not mind her being quicker.

"Please, don't!

The vision of her face is a welcome one.

"No!"

Her eyes pool, but it's okay. I will be okay now that she's here. It's not the first time Cove has saved me, because she does it so well.

My knuckles glide across her trembling chin. "I see you."

A sob unhinges her jaw. Then Puck's voice appears next to her. "Motherfucker. Don't you dare, Elixir!"

I mutter words I cannot hear, then growl in protest as they search my frame. Sadly, they locate the vessel inside my baldric and fish the vial from its encasement. Before I can snarl for them to stop, fluid pours onto the wound, froths like foam, and drains into my skin. A soft wad of cloth is stuffed against my side.

My head clears. The mixture from my den fizzles inside me. It won't extract the iron, but it will staunch the bleeding and stitch the injury.

I'd had one precious dose. It was supposed to be for Cove.

Her eyes alight, features lifting in relief. Puck sighs, "Thank fuck."

Already, the wound is sealing. I sit upright, about to bark at them for sparing me instead of preserving the vial's contents. But their upturned heads stifle the urge.

A shadow passes through Cove's pupils. Horror bleaches her complexion.

Puck mumbles, *"Domisökurer almáttukar."*

Fables almighty.

Whatever they see, the rest of the battlefield is noticing as well. Hundreds of surviving bodies waver, both Faeries and humans. That's when more shouts mow through the field, this time from a distant ledge of the Solitary wild.

And I know the smell of him. Scorpio has a particular scent, like distilled algae.

And I know the sound of Faeries. Puck doesn't need to describe it, nor the troop of new Solitaries that flood the scene.

We had anticipated a battle with each of our enemies. We just hadn't expected it to happen at the same time.

My hunch had been right. Our Fae rivals must have heard the attack and held back for a dual purpose. They idled while we sliced through the humans. They waited for the mortal iron to penetrate and weaken us. They'd been standing fast until both fronts began to wilt, easy to ambush in one fell swoop.

It's devious. It's Fae.

This is their move in the game.

But it's not just Scorpio and his ilk. At the raging echoes of flapping wings, drumming hooves, and wild hissing, we know.

The merman kept his promise. He's brought the fauna.

Which…does not make sense. Against iron fire, against humans, they wouldn't be fighting a natural battle of survival in their habitat. It would invalidate the fauna's restoration and everything the Solitaries are striving for. That very point had been established during our meeting with Scorpio.

No, this does not make sense. Until…it does.

It does because there is a twist. Cove cries out, despair propelling her blood-stained hand to her mouth. Puck expels a tormented noise. From above, Cerulean's guttural shout of pain merges with the cacophony.

There are some truths that need to be seen. There are others that only need to be felt.

I know from their anguished reactions. I made the same sounds when my mothers died.

It is loss. It is denial.

It's the sound one makes when those who matter to them have been violated.

Scorpio hasn't enhanced the Solitary fauna in droves. He's chosen only three animals.

He has enhanced Tímien, Sylvan, and Lotus.

29

Cerulean had once called this a new game. A scrimmage of moves and countermoves. Full truths and half-truths. Lucid words and distorted words. Nature versus itself. In the end, someone loses, and someone else wins.

Yet that isn't so. This is a game where no one wins. The difference is how much we forsake, how much slips from our fingers like water.

Tímien spears into the fray. His wingspan shoves the wind out of his way, making it clear he has shifted sizes.

Sylvan gallops on hooves that stamp depressions into the earth. She rages toward the barrage, the weight of her approach testifying to her stature, which has tripled.

Lotus skates across the grass at an accelerated pace. The Evermore Blossom has worked on him despite his mortality, so while his slither is unmistakable, Lotus's violent hiss rings like a blade.

Their wild calls dominate the landscape. The furious caw of a Solitary raptor. The stomping limbs of a Fae stag. The rapid vibration of a mortal serpent.

This is why we have not seen or heard from Tímien. Scorpio must have gotten to him, trapped him when we weren't aware, along with our other companions while we were occupied.

And this is why Scorpio has not manipulated more animals from our wild. Such an action would have held water if the fight had been internal, had been in their habitat, and if any deaths had been natural.

Iron fire wielded by mortals has cancelled that option out. It has forced Scorpio to get creative.

The dwellers he's enhanced are sufficient. They're enough to make a vicious difference in battle, enough to jettison for the sake of our wild, enough without having to forfeit additional casualties of war—a few fauna martyrs in favor of the rest. Crucially, Scorpio has used the Evermore Blossom on three figures who would strike his opponents where it hurts the most.

He has made his choice. And he's made it well.

Cove's distraught eyes stray to mine. I grasp her face and beg her to tell me, to help me. Shakily and rapidly, she describes the anarchy in detail, and in this way, I see fragments of the chaos.

Puck is hunching beside her, his features ashen. In the sky, Cerulean's wings are swishing as he hovers, arrested in petrified shock.

He mouths the word, *Father*.

I hear Lotus shredding through the grass at an otherworldly pace he wouldn't be able to muster without the Evermore Blossom. The reptile is moving so fast, he might as well be immortal. He's baring his fangs, which are not venomous but capable of puncturing arteries to a fatal degree when suffused with the flower's essence.

When the snake camouflages into the high grass and disappears, Cove cries, "Lotus!"

I clutch her face tighter. "Show me."

Again, it takes her a moment to break from the spot where the snake had vanished. Her frightened gaze scans the area while narrating to me what she sees.

Cypress is mumbling a Fae incantation. From beside Cerulean, Moth is fluttering in a daze. And below her, Tinder is gawking.

Foxglove's wrist is trembling as she fights to keep hold of her dagger. And Coral's harpoon lance has seized mid-thrust.

A tempest of white hair is flapping around Lark's wide-eyed gaze. With Juniper stationed away from the battle's hub, Cove and I can only envision her stricken features. And as for their father, his split lip is hanging open.

The moment has suspended itself across the battlefield, humans and allied Faeries riveted and petrified.

At last, each world breaks into thunderstruck movement.

"Sylvan!" Puck roars, then lunges off the ground and races past me and Cove.

"Elixir," Cove whispers.

I snatch my lady's nape and fasten my forehead to hers. Her fingers curl into my hair and jolt me closer.

Then I release her. We lurch to our feet and sprint into the fray.

Three sides clash, punching into each other like a massive fist. The blow of bodies shatters my eardrums.

Cries splinter and screams blare like horns. Weapons clang and hit their mark. Bodies squirt fluid across my torso. Figures plummet to the ground or get snatched off the ground by winged Faeries.

A severed arm bounces off my shoulder. A dismembered head rolls.

Vomit splatters the grass. Blood bubbles from a person's gagging mouth.

I hear Cerulean swooping around the opposing mountain Fae. He's dodging their attack, trying to incapacitate them, to reach his father whose flight has blended into the quagmire. The owl's livid hoot scrapes across the sky as he attacks someone, giant talons surely carving into them.

The air shifts across my knuckles—Puck has swung himself atop an unseated horse and sent the animal bolting toward Sylvan's form. He launches a storm of arrows, shearing through anyone who tries to intercept.

Sylvan grunts in fury. Audibly, two fighters get caught in the deer's antlers, which hurl them into the sky like ragdolls.

Other Faeries either defend themselves against their rival kin or drive their blades, arrows, and axes into the mortals.

Sizzling wings resound overhead and collide with the lash of Lark's whip. She's combating a pair of firebird Faeries…the surviving ones who had targeted her in the labyrinth.

Seconds later, her opponents' skulls crack together. They split like eggshells as she yanks them into one another.

My limbs grow leaden. My joints struggle to bend.

Audible perception dwindles, leaking from me sensation by sensation. The darkness becomes less distinguishable, each shade of black reducing to a single void. Baffled, I swing my head from side to side. The erratic motions harken to the first moment I opened my eyes but saw nothing.

"Cove?" I bellow. "Cove!"

But she's gone. My lady has been swept into the vortex of clapping steel, burning iron, and screams of anger, fear, and pain. Likely, she's brawling a path to wherever Lotus might be.

Terror clamps like manacles around my throat. Rancor slithers down my arms. The agony lancing my bandaged side diminishes as I attune to the remaining vestiges of sensory awareness and hunt through the mob for a lone figure.

I know his gait and cadence. I know the vibrations of his breath.

I know he is coming for me.

As iron strips magic from my flesh like a layer of skin, two strengths keep me upright and propel me forward—love and hate. The memory of Cove's face clashes with the urge to punish, the familiar impulse to be brutish.

A lethal hiss ripples across my tongue. I stalk through the carnage, pace through the iron fumes, buoyed by new and old instincts. The iron may take my magic, but it shall not take my will. Nor that of my brothers.

Among the rampant bodies, his footfalls materialize. They stride my way, direct and with deliberate slowness. Mermen who can shift between water and land have a distinct tread. I have committed his to memory.

My blood's temperature reaches its boiling point. He has tried to kill my lady. He has tried to murder my brothers with the raven. Therefore, he has tried my extremely limited patience.

My ears blot out the surrounding cacophony. My mind envisions his cursed sneer, the ink markings glistening across his chest, the black drizzling from under his eyelids.

During Cove's game, I had plagued her with questions I knew she wouldn't want to answer. Deep, provoking questions that would do her damage. Yet she had bested me with similar ones, inquiries that peeled back my layers until there was nowhere left to hide, until my greatest weakness had been exposed. Where I had attacked with savagery, she had retaliated with empathy, because my lady knows how to bring vulnerability to the surface.

That's why her question in the aviary had made Scorpio shut up. Not long ago, she asked the Fae who broke him.

The answer is twofold. He broke someone first. And that someone had died before he could atone.

That someone had died trying to save me.

This is the part I haven't shared with anyone, including my lady. Scorpio had quarreled with his grandfather just before mortals thrashed into our realm. The merman had spewed words he hadn't meant.

After that, his grandfather raced to the human world, intent on saving me. My mothers had been weakened by iron fire and unable to so much as crawl to rescue me. They'd only begun to recover the night they died beside me.

Scorpio's grandfather had been their friend. He promised to help but got speared through by a human before he could succeed. And although Scorpio could have blamed me, he did not.

Not while I became a ruler, and he became my soldier. Not while I thrived, my ferocity eliciting his admiration.

Not until I changed.

Up until then, I had never raised a hand to Scorpio. He had respected me, relied on me to avenge our kin with him, to make sure his grandfather's death wasn't in vain.

That trust had ceased the moment Cove arrived. Each time Scorpio put her in danger, my punishment was severe, because she mattered more.

He'd felt betrayed. I had failed him.

I spin the forked daggers in my hands and prowl toward Scorpio. His trident vibrates as he tears it from the strap across his back.

The distance shrinks. We move faster, advancing across the field. I listen to his arm arching and shove my daggers upward.

Overhead, our weapons crash with a force that rocks the earth. Beneath the crossed blades, our foreheads thrust together.

Sweat and brine wafts from his skin. His voice shakes from iron-laced exertion. "I had no choice."

My own breath fuses with his. "But you did."

Not long ago, Cerulean had said as much. Faeries cannot lie to others, but they can lie to themselves.

We all make our choices.

His gasp is broken, unbridled. We shove ourselves backward at the same time, and we stalk around one another like vipers, like reptiles coasting around their prey.

Then in quick succession, our weapons blast forward. The noise floods my being, each blow another destructive wave.

We change angles at a breakneck pace. His trident bites into the points of my daggers. The prongs block his thrusts.

My arms glide, as if through water. They move in swift, serpentine motions.

I follow his labored exhalations and the weight of his attack. I tap into the past, from whenever he practiced against me while training with the water Fae.

His trident skims my back, its teeth peeling through my flesh. I grunt as liquid runs down my spine.

Both of us have a short fuse. The difference is, I fight with cutthroat precision, whereas he fights with nothing but undiluted anger. That is his error.

The more I thwart his attempts, the more Scorpio growls, the clumsier he combats. I strike back when frustration gets the best of him. With a howl, the merman spirals the trident and cannons toward me, angling the weapon for my heart.

In a move I have learned from the vipers in my den, I brace. Then I strike. Pivoting, I wheel under the trident and spiral behind it. One dagger catches the stem and uses the momentum to ram the trident into the earth.

My free arm shoots outward, the second dagger skewering Scorpio's lungs. He dangles at the end of my weapon, then hits the grass on his knees. A shocked gargle bubbles from his mouth.

I yank the prongs from his chest as he falls. A bereft sound sneaks from between his lips and penetrates me. Until Cove, I have never paid attention to such utterances.

This time, I slump on one knee before the merman and lean over him. He spasms, and something akin to grief bolts me in place.

If I had remembered my mothers' friendship with his grandfather, the elder Fae's attempt to save me, and what Scorpio and I both lost…

If I had listened to Cove during her game and been kinder, more compassionate to him...

If I had reacted differently...

He might have still tried to hurt her. He might have remained spiteful of her.

Or perhaps not. I will never know.

Scorpio's fingers trail across my own. I grab his hand and bunch it into a fist with mine, but I shall not speak. If I do, I cannot say whether Cove's compassion or my venom will come out.

For what he has lost, he has also taken. He might have done more and worse, yet I am sorry for him, and I am sorry it has ended this way.

I had no choice.

But you did.

Yes. And I have made it.

Scorpio hacks through the blood rushing from his mouth. He crushes our grips together, as if aware of my thoughts. "Save them."

Our kin. Our fauna. Our natural world.

When I nod, relief slides across his features, the scales glinting. Then the merman's digits loosen and go slack in my hand.

My eyes shut. I bow my head and then wrap the trident in his grasp, setting both atop his chest.

The battle's audible clamor resumes, sprawling across the fields.

A long sliding motion across the grass stalls me. My eyebrows stitch together, and I leap aside as another Solitary lashes my way. As I thrust myself from the figure, I veer behind them and skate my fingercaps along the scales and webbed hands.

It is a water Fae.

The male circles. I twist, evading his circuit.

His tongue vibrates. I wretch the other way, avoiding the lurch of his spiked net.

I drive my forked dagger into the Fae's weapon. The prongs pin the barbed mesh to the ground, driving my opponent to the grass. He squats, unleashes a sharp noise, and leaps forward like an amphibian—only to meet a pair of fangs.

In a short burst of motion, Lotus lunges upright in front of me and bores his teeth into the water Fae's throat. The snake is small and thin.

But with the Evermore Blossom, he is as fast as a viper.

My attacker howls and tries to bat the snake off, but Lotus holds fast and drills his fangs deeper. So deeply, I hear them rupture an artery. Blood spurts from the Fae's neck and sprays my skin.

Nearby, my lady shouts something to her sisters. Above the pandemonium, their voices unite.

Lark's whip vaults into the sky. As it does, Tímien squawks, and Cerulean hollers their names. I hear the cord strain with her weight. The woman has snagged the owl's leg, and she's fucking climbing her own whip to reach him.

Juniper's crossbow bolt clicks, soars from the oak, and stabs the earth. It succeeds in halting Sylvan, who rears in place. Then Puck's grunt signals he's jumped off the horse and reached the deer.

Cove's spear rams into the grass, the sound materializing beside me. She steals my hand and kneels, yanking us to the ground. I'm too stumped to resist.

As we hunker, she whispers, "Lotus."

Only then does the snake release his prey. The dead water Fae drops with a thud.

Cove's companion stops hissing, and his body undulates from the fallen body to us. Lotus slides up my thighs, my torso, and then links himself around my shoulders while Cove runs her palm over his scales. Her teary relief washes through me.

"Heavens," she utters. "Elixir, he's…"

Fables be damned. I know what she wants to say, what becomes clear.

And while I can hear some of it, I need to be certain. So once more, I beseech her to describe what's occurring. Close by, Lark is ascending Tímien's back, but he isn't throwing her off. In fact, her cooing voice is relaxing the owl's wings, biding Cerulean time to sail their way.

Sylvan is pausing to nudge her muzzle against the crossbow bolt lodged into the grass, while Puck is stroking her coat and heaving in amazement.

Yes. Of all beings, we Faeries should know by now. The fauna of our wild cannot always be predicted, and they belong to no one. But they do have their loyalties, which no amount of Evermore Blossom can dilute.

If only their natural instincts are enhanced, they will be fiercer. But that does not mean they will massacre the ones with whom they have bonds. Quite the opposite, they will defend their flocks, their herds, and their dens, including the Faeries and humans who matter to them.

Scorpio had not considered that.

Tímien, Sylvan, and Lotus hadn't been attacking merely to hurt anyone who got in their way. They'd been attacking to protect us.

The animals relent. With Lark on his back, Tímien is circling his son and fluttering his plumes against Cerulean's.

Sylvan is tucking herself close to Puck, a gentle puff shoving from her snout. And I feel Lotus glide from my shoulders to Cove's.

Gasps sweep through the field from our kin, who are witnessing us taming the enhanced fauna. Though, it fails to stifle the bloodshed.

Many of our Fae enemies are still battling against our side, as well as the mortals. But for this one snippet of time, Cove slants her gaze my way. I see hope brimming there—then I sense a new terror, just as her features pale.

"Dear Fables," she hazards, rushing to her feet with me.

Quickly, she tells me. There's a small face poking through the high grass. On the margins of the battle, a tiny form with raven hair has gone numb, their eyes widening.

Fuck. It's a child.

According to Cove, the little human can't be more than ten years old. He must have snuck here. The boy is stumbling nearer, awestruck by the devastation, his people, and the magical beings he's likely never beheld.

Then he's cocking his head in sudden amazement. His attention is fixating on something out of range.

One more step, and he'll place himself in a blade's path. Cove and I are about to catapult in his direction when I hear another small form galloping past us, veering in and out of the quagmire.

Recognition cinches my gut. The pattern and cadence of hooves tells me enough. It's a centaur, and a young one at that.

I know which stripling it must be, for I remember her stubborn plea to join the fight. Now I imagine the filly's hair flying her as she bounds toward the boy.

To that end, Cypress emits a distressed roar, which means he has spotted her.

From behind me, Puck hollers, "What the fuck?"

"Cease!" Cerulean shouts, his words charging from the sky like a hurricane.

But no one else is listening. No one else is paying attention.

I focus what remains of my senses, tapering my ears toward where the boy is standing. I hear combative footfalls getting near him and the whoosh of a swinging torch bursting with iron fire. He has placed himself in the line of the fighting.

The filly centaur crashes into the child, thrusting him out of the flame's path.

The nearby figure—who'd been wielding the torch against what sounds like a dryad—staggers to a halt. Both the figure and dryad freeze, registering what almost happened.

Quickly, more and more fighters notice. Their motions falter, slowing in place.

Cove tells me, and I envision it in my mind's eye.

The young centaur and boy fling their arms around each other. They huddle together, entwined like shields. Their heads cast about while trying to keep one another safe.

Two souls, neither of whom have ever met. One of Faerie, one of humanity. Yet there they stand, protecting each other.

One by one, the battle sounds ebb. All movement stops. Like a brushfire, the surrounding throng goes still.

Just like that, it ends.

30

Bowstrings relax as fighters lower their archery. The steely ring of blades subsides. Screams whittle to a collective hush.

Only three sounds remain. A belt of wind coasts through the field, treetops along the border shiver their leaves like cymbals, and the distant stream where I'd nearly drowned nine years ago eddies though the plain.

The echoes of nature harmonize like the strings of a harp. It is the melody of nature. For once, it is impossible to tell them apart from the resonances of my home.

The battle falls into a trance. Seconds filter through the quiet.

Slowly, another noise projects itself—the whimpering and wheezing of the striplings trapped amidst the crusade. I listen as the centaur and boy cling to another like caged creatures at the hub of this battleground. They sway, fenced in by three sides of a war.

My eyes stray. But at this point, and with this much iron contaminating my system, I can only sift through certain movements.

I lean into my lady. "Tell me."

"They're still holding each other," she whispers, spellbound. "They're peeking around, gawking at everyone, but they're not letting go." Cove's tone is slippery, like she might trip on her words. "They're protecting each other."

Now I recognize the emotion clotting her throat. It is the halfway point between empathy and memory.

Nine years ago, three sets of children crossed fated paths. The males came from a world of dark magic. The females hailed from a place of natural fortitude. Knowing so little about one another, these pairings found a connection, a crawlspace that existed between hate and love. Our feelings had varied, but the links nevertheless formed, steering us from one extreme to its opposite.

Cove and I share a hostile past. But there had been a sliver, an unbidden connection fusing us together. She does not know this, but I had wanted to retaliate against her as much as touch her face. And as much as she wanted to drown me in kind, her eyes had sparkled when she first beheld me.

I think Cove would have been tender, if I had allowed it then. At least, I did eventually.

If that can happen three times, why not once more? The centaur filly and mortal boy have no joined history. They do not know one another. Yet here they are, banding together like shields.

No malice. No magic.

No intolerance. No revenge.

In my recent past, I would have sneered at the display. I would have called the striplings mere fools—obstructions. I would have seized them by the scruffs and tossed them to the margins, then continued shoving my daggers into my prey.

Tonight, I disarm. As do the figures in our midst. Confusion and astonishment carry heavily in the air.

To bear arms takes strength and courage. But to defy three warring fronts takes a different sort of power—a true kind of sacrifice. It is both a reflex and a decision. I cannot say if there's a name for it, but I feel this enigma loosening the furious crick in my neck and cooling the vicious temperature behind my eyelids.

"Heroism," Cove utters into my ear, as though hearing my thoughts.

A great rustle of plumes cuts in as Cerulean appears beside me with Lark. Puck and Juniper funnel in next to us, along with Cypress's clomping hooves, Moth's flutter, Coral's solid footfalls, Foxglove's light steps, and Tinder's nimble gait.

The striplings emit petrified noises. Cove musters a step forward, intending to approach them. But her father gets there first.

My senses eke out the remnants of perception while Cove fills in the gaps. While Faeries and humans watch, Thorne weaves through the masses and kneels before the pair.

"What are your names?" he asks.

"L-Leif," the boy bleats.

"I'm Aster of the woodland," the filly declares.

"Leif and Aster of the woodland," Cove's father repeats. "Did you know in the ancient language of humans, Leif means 'descendent', and Aster means 'star'?" He pauses. "Of what came before and what might be."

The children remain quiet. I expect they're blinking, wondering how to respond.

"Well, now," Thorne says with a somber grin. "That was just about the bravest thing I've ever seen. But don't worry. It's over tonight, and no one will hurt you. Maybe you'd like to introduce yourselves?"

The pair swaps timid but curious glances. They peel themselves apart.

Cautiously, the boy extends his trembling palm. "Hi."

The filly hesitates, then takes his proffered hand. "Hello."

The moment shudders like a latch breaking open. The horde recovers from their unified daze, Faeries and humans ushering closer. Footfalls blur as everyone converges, mortals weakened by their wounds, immortals by the iron stifling their motions.

First, Cerulean glides through the tangle and joins the pair with Thorne. Lark is next, then Puck and Juniper. Cove loops her arm through mine as we take our places with them, followed by our friends and allies. We bridge the distance, spread into a ring around the children, and on Cerulean's lead, we lower our weapons. They settle on the grass by our feet, the scent of blood adhering to the armory.

As our band straightens, we wait. If need be, we shall arm ourselves again.

Make your choice.

Because we have made ours.

Uncertainty and distrust swoop through the field. The crowd wavers. I see what they see—beings of humanity and Faerie aligning.

Fauna from both worlds integrate themselves. Mortal horses calm down and swish their tails. Among them, Tímien paraglides alongside the nightingale who had been guarding Juniper in the oak. The birds land in their large forms while Sylvan stomps her hooves beside us, and Lotus entwines himself around Cove's arms.

It is a constellation of diverse warriors, of magic and nature melding into a single force. As one, we prove this kinship is possible.

But can we prove it shall last? Can we demonstrate eternal unity? Will anyone forgive what their enemies have done?

With time, perhaps. Lots of time. It worked for Cove and me, for her sisters and my brothers.

None of the bodies slumped and strewn across the field make a sound. The fallen have been killed, denied the chance to heal. Yet many lives remain.

It would be easy for someone to venture a word. But how swiftly a landscape can shift from upheaval to stillness, so much clamor reduced to a single breath. None of us have words left. At least, not on this eventide.

Speechlessness consumes the field. Death and loss have depleted us.

So instead, one human female grunts, "Oh, for shit's sake. Lay them down, you idiots."

"That's the blacksmith," Cove speaks into my ear.

That female had been responsible for creating the iron-tipped weapons. In my former life, I would have incinerated her for that crime against my kin. Now I understand this woman's skill had protected Cove in The Deep, and it's a means of defense that I would have taken advantage of as a mortal.

Cove resumes describing the pieces I cannot decipher on my own. Presumably, the blacksmith holds weight in the town. The mob folds, including the hunters who'd snared Puck as a stripling, and the glassblower who once kept Cerulean caged in a forge. Each of them relinquishes their defenses and snuffs out the iron torches.

That these humans make the ultimate second move stumps our Fae enemies. A portion of my subjects scowl in annoyance. They consider this gesture the equivalent of a favor or a deal, while the rest dare a fresh glimpse at me, Puck, and Cerulean.

Soon, we will convene with them. Hopefully, they will remember how they once trusted us. Perhaps they shall learn to do so again.

Until then, all Faeries shrug their weaponry to the ground. If not stunned, grieving, weakened, or shamed, our kin do welcome surprises. And they honor favors, even to mortals.

For a moment, we let the unspoken truce brim through the field. It shall keep for a while, enough time for us to heal and think.

Cerulean nods toward the blacksmith, then to our kin. Each head nods back, weary but willing.

It is an ending. It is also a beginning.

Sluggishly, we disperse to collect the dead. We set our fallen under The Faerie Triad, where they dissolve into the earth. The humans pile corpses and light a fire. The stench of burning flesh curls into the firmament, blending with the stars that arch through the sky.

Moments follow in slices. Tinder has lost a few fingers, which Cypress is bandaging. The centaur himself is enduring a knife wound to his haunches, and the tip of his ear had been sundered by the mortals. Moth has a cracked wing—extremely afflicting for an aerial Fae—and a host of grooves in her limbs. Bruises and burn marks swim through Foxglove and Coral's faces.

The Heart of Willows will be busy treating the maimed. I will join the effort and offer whatever brews I've restored. Other fighters with less trauma may recover in The Mer Cascades.

My brothers and their ladies suffer a range of injuries. I hear the tears fraying our clothes, smell blood coating the gashes in our flesh, and sense the actions of those closest to me.

Cerulean caresses Lark's bleeding cheek. Puck slams his scraped mouth against Juniper's. I trace Cove's wounds—several cuts and welts—to make sure none are severe, then balance my forehead against hers.

Stinging wet lines cover my torso, back, and scales, as though I've been dipped in saltwater. It shall pass. Though, that doesn't stop Cove from sketching every mark, as if to rid me of them.

Thorne groans from his cuts and a broken rib. At one point, his daughters tuck themselves into him, careful not to aggravate his fracture, and they stay that way for a long while.

The small portion of our band gather under The Triad. A gradient of warmth spills across my arms to signal dawn. When not taking me to watch the kelpies gallop through the rapids in The Deep, my mothers would bring me to this border. Lorelei and Marine had enjoyed watching the different mortal hues pile into the twilit sky, from ochre to violet.

Instead of asking Cove, I envision the colors my mothers had fancied. Right now, those pigments would be splashing across the horizon like the watercolors Lorelei and Marine also favored.

For a while, I sense our band resting their eyes there as well. The silence is worn and lacerated yet hypnotized. Everyone clings to the vista, looking above rather than below where blood must stain the grass like splatters of pigment. We have seen and shed enough crimson to outlast us.

From behind, the hawthorn, oak, and ash's shadows blend with the sunrise. The coolness of their silhouettes mingles with heat from the human realm's panorama. Both temperatures slide across my shoulders.

Each tree rustles its leaves. Berries from the hawthorn bump together, acorns rain from the oak, and the ash quavers.

Cove gasps and whispers, "They're coming back to each other."

She means the two striplings. It seems they intend to bid each other farewell. The filly called Aster and the boy called Leif stand in the high grass and thread their fingers.

As they do, awareness fill Juniper's voice. *"And the dragon said, 'I shall protect what I don't yet know, for therein lives my strongest magic.'"*

My mothers had read some of the Fables to me, but I'm not familiar with all of them. In particular, I do not recall this one.

My head swings toward Cove, who flashes me a grin. "Juniper wrote it."

She explains how the quote is from a story collection Juniper has been penning in her journal. Aster is a member of the Fae youths to whom Juniper has also been reading her work aloud. This story is one of them.

"Well done," Puck says with a grin in his voice. "Seems Aster took your story seriously."

"Is it supposed to be taken lightly?" Juniper contends.

The satyr chuckles. "No one would dare try that." After a moment, he adds, "Speaking of which, you can add this night to your journal."

The grass shifts as she turns to him and deliberates. "Well. It's certainly warranted."

"And when do we get to pore over this masterpiece?" Thorne wonders.

"And for which story would it be?" Cove asks.

"A new one, I'd think," Cerulean suggests.

"Preferably with a little spice," Lark pleads. "Can't be all action and tragedy. Who wants to read that after all the shit we've been through?"

Puck sniggers. "No wonder you and I get along."

"You wish, bloke."

Our mirth is tired and fleeting. Or so I gather. I'm the only one who does not react at all, their discussion fogging to the background while my mind strays.

"Wait," I mutter. "Wait a moment."

The group pivots toward me while my eyes jump through the darkness, and my thoughts cycle.

"A story that has not been written," I contemplate. "A new one."

"Elixir?" Cove inquires.

"What's he doing?" Lark asks.

The spaces behind my eyelids brim. It forces everyone but my lady to hop backward. And how offensive. Even if the iron hadn't already reduced that magic, I have enough willpower to stop myself from harming them.

I grunt, "I won't blind you."

Puck insists, "Then what—"

"Be quiet. I am thinking."

The suggestion of a new story written by Juniper blends in with the words from the Fable she had deconstructed. The one that had revealed the hidden message—the second way to save our world.

Fragments spin through my mind. The Fable's enigmatic contents. My Unseelie ancestor and her Seelie nemesis, both of whom played roles in the scribes' campaign to write the Book of Fables. Testimonial from the Horizon that Never Lies, who'd told us we have the capacity to discover this second way.

The second way is something far older than us. It is something that has existed since before our time, as has its source.

Sacrifice is the first option to restore our fauna and our realm. It is the one my kin have been enacting over the years through games.

From there, our band had made two loose conclusions. This means the second method is unity, which is older than sacrifice. And the source of this information is older than the Pegasi.

My ancestor was older, as was her nemesis. Both witches existed during the Pegasi's era, in addition to the era of the scribes.

My ancestor had installed a curse on a water well, and her nemesis placed a counter spell in one of the Fables. Both had linked Cove and me throughout her game.

But what else had the Unseelie and Seelie witches contributed to this chapter in history? If given the opportunity, would they not manipulate other bits of the Fables?

"Juniper." I lick my lips. "Tell me again. Recite the hidden message. Do it slowly."

Puzzled, she draws out the sentences. In my psyche, I picture the words, each one linking to the next like chains. The cadence is fluid, passing through me as water does. I recall how my mothers bequeathed to me some of the knowledge they'd inherited from my ancestor about brewing. Lorelei and Marine had memorized the instructions that were passed down to them.

The rhythms of those instructions match the Fable's text. The choice of words is familiar, explicitly so. The connection is concrete, I am certain of it.

I see those words like I see the darkness. I see what others cannot.

"The Seelie witch," I realize. "She created the second way."

Cove gasps. "The counter spell she'd forged to combat the curse your ancestor placed on the water well," she interprets. "Do you think it wasn't the only time the Seelie witch conjured such magic?"

Quiet floods the group until Juniper translates, "The second way is another of her counter spells."

I nod once. "Which means—"

"The Unseelie witch must have placed a spell on Faerie, in the first place," Cerulean theorizes. "Something she'd felt was necessary. Something her adversary was compelled to act against."

Indeed. We bridge the gaps, assemble the pieces. The ancient Unseelie witch had never trusted the scribes and their Book of Fables. She must have placed a spell on the Solitary wild to help her kin, a safety net in case the book did more harm than good: Should the Solitaries and their fauna perish from human hands, and the land is hence threatened, the way to save it is by human sacrifice.

Whereas the Seelie witch must have added a second way in the book. The hidden clue that Juniper discovered.

"Shit," Lark exclaims. "So we've got the source now. We just need the actual method of unity."

After a pause, Thorne's voice alights. "I think you've got it."

Puck hesitates, then his tone slackens as he whispers, "Holy fuck."

"A new story," I prompt Juniper.

A second later, her breath hitches. "The journal."

Yes. We have won this guessing game.

We know what must be done.

We have our second way.

31

We stand with this knowledge. No one dares mutter another word, lest the transcendent spell breaks.

Moth, Foxglove, and Coral stagger into our circle, having heard our conversation. Cypress clomps into the ring with a barely conscious Tinder slumped on his back, the lad's severed fingers consuming his consciousness. The rest of our allies funnel in behind them, along with batches of other Solitaries who'd combatted against us. Anxious footfalls and hooves merge with tentative ones.

Swiftly, our fellowship expands like a lung. While our dead fade and the mortals watch their fallen burn, the rest of us hover on a precipice.

I twist my head toward Cove. Her expression gleams with optimism.

To be sure, I address the crowd while keeping my eyes anchored to her. "Does anyone have the strength to manifest?"

After an exhausted moment in which no one replies, a small voice squeezes its way in. "I do."

The young centaur's response drifts from the outskirts of our huddle. Her tone is haunted yet determined. I picture her head raising despite some new trenches forming across her brow. She has aged a great deal today.

I remember that feeling after The Trapping. I remember so much hate. With this filly, I sense only faith. No sign of blame fills her inflection.

Cypress's baritone stretches toward the female. "You were ordered to stay away from the fighting."

"I was feeling rebellious," the stripling answers. "Maybe I was inspired.

It isn't the first time lately that a female has defied a Fae."

Beside me, Cove's profile flushes with mirth. She folds in her lips to keep from chuckling, whereas Lark snorts and Juniper huffs in amusement.

I feel my brothers withholding grins. A grumble sits in my throat, but the filly is right.

Cypress grunts, "For your transgressions, you will answer to me later." Then his tone lightens. "For now, you have a mission."

"Yes, sir," she says with elated pride.

"Bring us the Book of Fables," I tell her.

"And my journal," Juniper adds. "And a pencil."

"Um, why not a quill?" Moth wonders.

Thorne, Lark, Cove, and Puck reply in unison. "Editing."

Juniper defends, "It's practical. I don't want to run out of ink."

"Then have Aster fetch an inkwell," Tinder grits out sluggishly from his perch atop Cypress.

Puck approaches the lad and ruffles his hair. "You all right, luv?"

"I'll live, minus a few digits."

"Meh. Who needs that many anyway?"

"Indeed," Cypress says. "It is that thick skull of yours that could have used an adjustment."

"Fuck off, asshole."

"Glad to know you two still love each other," Puck slurs.

"Might we circle back?" Cerulean votes.

Foxglove sighs, "Yeah. I second that."

Coral's sultry voice drips in. "Third."

"Fine," Juniper admits. "The pencil is for revising. Are we honestly going to split hairs about this?"

"Grab her spectacles, while you're at it," Puck instructs the filly.

After he provides her with directions to their cabin, the centaur evanesces. Minutes pass until she returns. Winded breath whooshes from her mouth, and her hooves teeter before righting themselves.

Manifesting depletes our young most of all. Still, she possesses more reserves than any other Fae present. The iron hasn't afflicted her as much as it has the rest of us.

Cove opens the Book of Fables to the right page. Under the caps, the pads of my fingers coast over the words and trace the inky font.

Immortal wild. Immortal land. Dwellers of the mountain, forest, and river. You are born of eternal nature—of the wind, earth, and water. Yet that which is everlasting is not unbreakable. And should you wither by the hands of others, look not merely to sacrifice, for another path to restoration lies in wait. Therefore, follow your Fables, heed your neighbors, and look closer.

"Follow your Fables," I repeat loud enough for the congregation to hear.

"Heed your neighbors," Juniper continues, "…and look closer."

Yes. That.

It's a riddle. It's a cue.

It is rather fucking obvious.

Next, I seal my eyes shut and switch tomes, racing my digits over the pages of Juniper's journal. Nothing happens at first. Yet when I reach a fresh leaflet, the flesh under my fingercaps prickles. Unlike the previous ones, this page doesn't contain her handwriting. It is a blank slate waiting to be filled.

Heat crests behind my retinas. My eyelids flip open.

"I think we are right," I say.

Juniper accepts the spectacles and pencil from Aster, then takes the journal from me and stalls on that same unmarked page. "Wait," she realizes. "I can't be the only one."

Indeed. She cannot be.

This is also why her pregnancy hadn't been the answer.

The solution is not to create a new life. It is to write about one.

That is the route to unity. That is the way to express it.

And while the prompt may have been found in the Book of Fables, the response must be forged in a new volume. This is about the tales that haven't yet been documented, the ones we have lived and shall live, the multifaceted experiences of mortals and Faeries.

They are the stories where enemies become lovers. They are the stories of games, the players, and the fauna they cared for. They are the stories of before, of now, and of someday.

What has been written is not where things end. There will always be new Fables to tell, new stories to pen, and new ways to interpret them. It is eternal, like the wild itself.

But no, Juniper cannot be the only one writing. This collection can't be scripted by only one scribe. No one can bear the weight of the world from a single point of view.

Nor should they. The tales must have range, must be different, must be told from many perspectives.

The journal began as hers. It must continue as ours, as an anthology.

The huntress goes first. She pauses, thinks. Then the pencil scratches across the page.

The quick motions skim my ears. Short, sharp sentences.

Faeries are hardly renowned for their patience. Yet every soul—from the mountain, to the forest, to the river—waits as Juniper's pencil covers the page in text.

Suddenly, the noise stops. The instrument halts.

Juniper sighs. Puck's cloven hoofs stall behind her, presumably to read over her shoulder. "My, my, my," he admires. "Do the honors."

I imagine her nodding, adjusting the spectacles, shoring herself up. Then we all listen as she begins, *"Under the fated stars, a Human and a Fae played a game…"*

It is a short tale, but it is significant. It is about her and Puck when they first met, how they spent thirteen days learning about each other. She likens the memory to a game, implying there is always more to learn.

The moment she finishes, we hear it—a small crack in the foundation beneath the span of branches that make up The Triad. The sound reaches every figure in attendance.

In a flood of movement, the Faeries turn in stunned silence. Under the hawthorn, oak, and ash where the dead have faded, a tiny stem breaches the dirt. I hear the miniature stalk surface from the earth, a single leaf unfurling. Though the soil has been hardening throughout our land, now the parched ground softens under my bare soles, plush and releasing a fertile aroma.

One Fae lets out a dry sob. Another exclaims in Faeish. Someone else mutters, "Fables eternal."

From further afield, the mortals creep nearer as the same noises shudder across the border of Faerie. Alongside us, they bear witness, murmuring and gasping.

Reeds of grass shiver, wood crackles as the neck of a trunk repairs itself, and water gushes as the stream leading to The Deep overflows, where lately it had been running shallow.

Cove clutches my arm. Distant noises project from inside the wild. Our band's heads crank from the stream to the forest sprouting leaves that had long since wilted and fallen, then up to the mountain range, where crumbling summits vibrate into solid forms once more.

With a stunted breath, Juniper shoves her journal at me. "You're next."

I waver, "I do not—"

"I'll help you," Cove says.

When I nod, she takes my fingers and folds them around the pencil. I mumble the sentences in a low tone, a stream of consciousness that only she can hear.

In unison, we write.

As we do, more of the environment seals and flourishes as it once had. Fables are not long. I let the tale run like water, fluidly and without stopping. I strike out and contribute my story from a subterranean place within, letting it surface on the page like something long buried.

When I'm finished, Cove and I lift the pencil. And another cacophony reaches us. Caws, roars, and splashes resound, the noises crossing vast distances, as only the wild calls of Fae fauna can do.

Cerulean is next. His writing is swift and smooth, as though he doesn't need to deliberate what story to tell. The Fable is also short, likely a few paragraphs taking only moments to compose, as if it has lingered in his head for years.

Once he is done, additional reverberations spread from the cliff peaks, propel from the roots, and spill from the creeks and underground waterways.

It would be easy to assume we're hearing the fauna who have survived all this time. But it is even easier to believe it is not.

These calls are new yet familiar. I recognize the flutter of fins from the stream and the reptilian slide of vipers near the tunnel leading to my home. The sounds they make are fresh and magnified, as if they've been trapped for nine years, as if they've been dormant, suspended in a void. These creatures have not roamed our world since the night they fell.

While it is not yet the myriad of creatures we lost, it is a start. The more stories that come, the more nature will have the fortitude to replenish itself.

Cries spring from Fae mouths. Half of our kin sprint into Faerie.

The humans take careful steps to the borderline and go no further, not with their iron weaponry abandoned. Yet they watch as the environment shifts before them, revealing a portion of this conflict they hadn't known. None of the Solitaries threaten them not to enter. Our kin simply jet past the humans in a mad search to reunite with the restored fauna.

"Fables be damned," I say.

"Same," Puck utters with a grin.

Yet Cerulean's reaction surmounts ours. That's when the core of his story becomes evident.

Among the wild noises are those of a pack he's familiar with. The howl of a wolverine. The roar of a mountain lion. The call of a ram. My brother hasn't heard these sounds in what feels like an eternity, and as they descend from the zeniths, recognition constricts his voice.

"Father," Cerulean chokes out as Tímien shadows his son.

Moth's voice splinters, tears leaking through. "Well? What the hell are we waiting for?"

An excellent question. My brother kisses his mate, then shoots with his father into the firmament while Lark swings atop her nightingale companion, and Moth takes to the sky after them. Together, they launch toward the mountain.

As Tímien's hoot trumpets overhead, Cove describes the scene. Above us, flapping silhouettes merge with the flying group—another flock of raptors plus one dark figure. I can imagine The Parliament of Owls coasting through the welkin with the members of our band—and a raven flitting among them.

Cerulean once told me that ravens, like crows, remember acutely the deeds done to them. While this isn't uncommon in our fauna, the impression is everlasting with certain animals, including these corvids. Always, they remember who has wronged them and who has been kind.

Although Cerulean fought back that infamous night, he also stayed by the raven's side while I bathed its wounds. My brother's remorse had been palpable, perhaps as much as Scorpio's rage when he force-fed the raven the Evermore Blossom's essence.

The raptor has made his choice of what to commit to memory.

Puck and Juniper mount Sylvan and gallop into the forest. Thorne hitches himself onto Cypress's back, joining Tinder astride the centaur while Foxglove runs on foot.

Coral pats my arm, then marches toward the serpentine stream leading down into the river.

Lotus remains draped around my lady's bicep. She and I trade long looks that reach deeply, that anchor us to the earth. I clasp Cove's hand as we stride into Faerie and rush home, because there is so much to see.

More than it has been in almost a decade, the wild is alive. So very alive.

32

Many hours later, night pours over The Deep. Crickets wheeze, strokes of noise penetrating the tunnels. Mammals and fish join the merfolk spearing through the aquamarine river, liquid sloshing against the banks.

I feel the stalactites and subterranean foliage glowing in shafts of mellow light.

From the peaks, to the forests, to the depths, we have spent the daytime hours reacquainting ourselves with the wild. It has been a marvel. Many of the fallen fauna thrive once more, and the environment is repairing itself, filling in the gaps that have marred this world like gashes. It will take more time, more written stories, but the wounds are closing, leaving scars rather than eternal suffering.

From across the river, the canal colony stands quiet apart from the cascades racing down rock mantels. Strewn through the alleys, foot paths, and bridges, lanterns pulse with audible flames. Yet not a soul crosses through the underground city.

Allied and enemy Faeries alike have returned to their homes and hollows scattered throughout into the river's tunnels. Though this is the hour to rise, all Solitaries will sleep for a while, perhaps into the next eventide and longer still. The iron needs to drain from our systems.

Also, it was a long fucking battle.

Because of this, The Fauna Tides is vacant but for the aquatic dwellers. Plus, one other soul.

She sits like a beacon at the end of a pier balanced on stilts. Errant wisps flutter from the loose bun that slumps against the back of her neck.

For once, she wears a dark color, a swathe of black that glitters with a thousand mer scales. A single waterdrop glistens down her backless dress, the pendant shaped like a tear.

Her presence is a safe harbor, a marker in this darkness. Her light is strong enough to cut through the murk.

Bulrushes fence in the platform. Beside my lady, I hear a canal boat moored to the dock. The transport flutters over the water's surface, the prow's lantern jostling. It is the vessel I'd given Cove during her game.

She scissors her limbs in the water, her feet paddling through the aquamarine flux. Whatever creature she's engaging with, the exchange dabs her lips into a smile.

I stalk across the pier, searing a path toward that grin. A damp breeze stirs the hood of my robe and combs through my hair, which I have cinched against my nape tonight. I want the mane out of the way. Nothing is allowed to obstruct my view of her.

As my shadow pours across the siren's back, her voice swims in the air. "What took you so long?"

I squat behind Cove. My thighs encase her frame like a shell as I rest my chin on her shoulder. My words are low, a simmering broth of peaceful and feral. "What are you smiling at?"

"You, first."

"I wanted to make certain the den was secure." My arms snake around her middle and draw her spine into my torso. "It is safe now."

Cove's breath rushes from her lips. "Elixir, that's wonderful!"

It is. The restoration has seeped the toxins from my den, leaving behind only lush ferns, the whiff of freshwater, and the brews I've salvaged. And while this includes fewer cures than poisons, I'm not so redeemed that I've become an imbecile, nor wholly merciful. Poisons and venom serve purposes against those who would threaten my kin. Despite the restoration, I'm not about to yield that power.

I will never *not* be a vicious Fae. I just happen to be one who wields dark magic to protect what is mine—and to whom I belong.

Cove rests her arms over my own. She wants to turn, seal our mouths together, and then ask many questions.

I clutch my lady tighter, preventing her from doing so. "Not yet. Tell me."

"I was watching him." She swings an arm toward the river, which blurs before my vision can access it. Yet I hear the swish of a serpent. Lotus is rippling around Cove's calves and threading around her toes, the snake's play infectious and drawing chuckles from the siren.

My mouth presses into her shoulder, to keep from smirking. The flap of dorsal fins and stingers multiply from nearby. Nevertheless, this little viper is scarcely intimidated by the river dwellers surging through The Tides.

I remember this spectacle well from my youth. Jade river sharks, speckled stingrays with illuminated tails, and metallic dolphins are slicing across the depths. This flux, which abuts The Twisted Canals, is neutral amongst the fauna. Piranha are flitting through the underwater reeds and past rocks barnacled in vermillion moss. Schools of fish are sailing on the outskirts, their scales reflecting gradients of blues and greens.

Cove wiggles her submerged toes and laughs as Lotus cords around her feet. However, the passing fleet is too much of a temptation. Her mirth thins into a sigh when her companion weaves from the pier and slithers into the wild procession.

She squirms, preparing to get up and dive in after the snake. My mouth traces her rounded ear, stalling her. "We've been over this."

"Not lately," Cove objects.

"Then I shall recap. Trust me as you have before: Do not worry."

"How many times will it take before you realize—"

"That telling you what to do won't work? I learned that lesson ages ago."

"You have an entire pit of serpents taking up residence in your den," she frets. "Brood and grunt as much as you want, but you would protect any of them, same as I would. Worry comes with the territory, especially when your companion is a fish out of water.

"Well, not a fish per se. But a human reptile is kind of vulnerable around here." Cove gestures toward the river. "Any of these dwellers could hurt him."

"They will not. You know as much."

The fauna are territorial, and they have appetites, but they do not harm one another in The Tides. Even if they did, I would reach Lotus before a shark would.

But just in case, I sketch my fingers along the river's surface, which forms a wall of water around the snake. Although my reserves are limited until the iron drains, I have enough magic for this small act.

Cove sees what I've done and sags into me. "Thank you."

"No," I warn against her throat. "Never do that."

"Ah, I forgot for a second. Never thank a Fae."

"Never assume I expect gratitude. For you, I would do anything. It's not a favor, it's a…" My mind wrestles with itself, searching for the right word. "It is a certainty."

A destiny. An inevitability.

Whatever I do, she will never owe me for it. Not even with words.

To be frank, I should be thanking Lotus for leaving us alone. For I have other activities in mind, none of which involve rest until *after* I'm done with her. We had separated only for an hour, sufficient time for me to inspect the den and her to bathe in The Mer Cascades under Coral's guard. And more than enough time for my fingers to itch with need.

We've combatted here during her game. After the flood, we reconciled in this spot.

On this eve, I crave more. I yearn for a new consummation, a violent sort of desire. While at the center of this river, at the hub of this deep place, I want to release what has been, then grab ahold of what's to come.

"A certainty," Cove repeats, her outtake a wisp in this giant cavern. "Then how do you suggest I respond to your gallant offering? Maybe a hug?"

The invitation lures my mouth to her earlobe, where I rasp, "Try again."

Cove's skin pebbles. "A peck on the cheek?"

My teeth snatch the delicate flesh, pulling a stuttered gasp from her. "Again."

Her head flops onto my shoulder, giving my mouth unfettered access. "A compliment?"

"Again," I snarl, dragging my mouth down to her pulse point and sucking.

Another ragged sound melts from her as she clamps onto the back of my neck. "A handshake?"

Cursed siren. She's toying with me. My drumming heart and aching cock both know it.

I seize her tighter, run my lips across her jaw, and nudge my erection against her buttocks. My rigid cock thrusts into her tailbone. But once I scent the wetness leaking from between her thighs, my fermented blood reaches its boiling point.

"Again," I hiss.

Cove warms as she curls deeper into my body and grates her ass into me. Her words splinter into a moan, "A fuck?"

That same rush of blood launches from my sac to the roof of my cock. I snatch the side of her face and twist her gaze to mine. "That will do," I growl and take her mouth.

Cove's eager cry sets fire to my bones. My tongue spears through her lips, parting them with a rumble that collides with her moan. She digs her fingers into my hair, loosening the cinch at my nape. A strand breaks from the tether as she clings to my scalp and rocks her mouth under my own.

I lick into her, my tongue striking fast. My mouth angles and locks with hers, surging us together. Shivers wrack my lady's frame, and need scalds my flesh.

My groan dissolves against her whimper. My jaw thrusts, putting its weight into Cove's lips.

I kiss her harshly, and she takes the kiss, consuming it fully. Then her tongue flicks mine softly, and I fade into a million droplets.

But only for a moment. Damnation, only one moment.

Seething, I whip her around just as she scrambles to face me. With her legs straddling my groin, the tip of my cock twitches beneath the heat brimming from her cunt. Fables save me. I'm going to rip into her right here, right now.

Cove splits her thighs over my waist, grabs my face while kissing me, and swats her core against the column of my erection. Her tongue mimics the same tempo as those hot folds of flesh under her dress. I grab her ass and yank her repeatedly into me, my cock skidding along her clitoris.

Cove keens into my mouth. Where our hips row together, her walls throb and soak her undergarments, only to seep through my leggings.

Fuck. I will take her here, in view of every dweller, while the rest of our kin sleep within range.

Only the canal boat smacking the dock strips me of the impulse. I lash out my arm. My fingercaps slice through the rope mooring the vessel. Then I band my arms around Cove's middle and launch to my feet. Her thighs link around me, and while my tongue rides hers, I stride into the boat.

At my silent call, the water answers and lures the vessel across the river. We cruise over sharks and stingrays. I hunker onto the bench and drive my mouth against Cove's, and she continues to grind on my lap, killing me in the sweetest way.

Swiftly, the tide pulls us into a tunnel. The blackness intensifies, blotches of darkness shifting from sooty shades to ebony. We travel deeper, farther into the channel, where tails of foliage swing from overhead, one of them brushing my shoulder.

Faint globes dot the low ceiling, their radiance speckling Cove's features. But despite these fragments of illumination, we're lost in a chasm. I did not ignite the boat's hanging lantern for this reason.

The transport halts in a private artery beside a recess chiseled into the tunnel. On either side, slender cascades roll down chinks of rock.

Our heaving mouths echo into the throat of the cavern. My growl scrapes into the murk, and Cove's whine coils after it.

Her flushed face radiates through the tunnel like a blue torch. It's the only visible thing on earth, the only thing capable of shining this boldly while so far from the sun, so that even the globes cannot compare.

I pry myself away and slide my canines across her lower lip. "If I fuck you in this dark place, no one will know. No one will find you. No one will see or hear you except for me."

Cove trembles. "Then show me how loud I can get." She dips her head, licks up the column of my neck, and breathes me in, as if consuming my essence. "Show me how vicious you can be."

That, I shall. But not how she thinks.

I'm going to fuck her. But I'm going to do it gradually.

I'm going to make love to her. But I'm going to do it fiercely.

A primal noise squeezes between my clenched molars and rushes through the hollow. The boat tremors as I glide my palms under her skirt and grasp her thighs, spreading them wider around me. I haul Cove into my frame, then bow her backward.

My teeth skate along her shoulder and bite gently. She hisses, arms snapping tightly around me. I drag my mouth across her collarbone, sketching and nipping her skin while caressing the backs of her knees. My touch eases her thighs further, giving me an ample berth.

The vent between her legs pulses with heat. Desire sluices from her walls, the fragrance drugging my senses.

As I move down, I peel the elastic bodice down Cove's body. Her breasts push from the neckline, taut and swollen. I nibble the inflated swells and skim her ruched nipples. With delicate patience, my incisors circle the disks before my tongue pats the crest.

Cove moans, the reverberation breaking like glass and piercing through the tunnel. Yet it doesn't extend far enough. For my siren can be louder than that.

I continue this attack, teasing her nipple, grazing tenderly until it grows as firm as a pebble. The layers behind my pupils kindle with flames. My cock jumps as I imagine the tiny point of her breast flushing to a darker shade.

I sample my efforts and lap at the peak. The flat of my tongue races over her, towing across the compact skin, which toughens under my ministrations. Cove's body shoves into mine. Whimpers shoot from her own tongue, each one ratcheting down the jagged walls.

"Elixir," she pleads.

I know that entreaty. She wants more—and soon.

Instead, I taste her cruelly, prolonging her torment as I quest to the opposite breast and slant my incisors under the half-moon of skin. My teeth prick carefully, making her jolt as if hit by small shockwaves.

When I scale to the other nipple, she writhes on my lap. Her cunt abrades my cock, wetness pouring through the dainty fabric under her skirt.

My eyelids hood. A predatory groan ejects into the tunnel, which joins her sobs.

Still, the octave isn't high enough. We have done better.

We *shall* do much better.

I lick her nipple as I would her clit, with slow ferocity and an unquenchable thirst. I feather my tongue across the kernel, refusing to yield, denying my lady.

"Dammit, Elixir," she pleads. "You're...so...mean."

My chuckle rustles between the gulf of her tits. She has barely begun to learn how mean I can become. Though, I disregard pointing out that she'd asked for this. And let no one say I don't accept challenges half-heartedly.

What my lady requests, she will receive in spades. The more I anguish her, the louder she shall get. That is how it's done.

I hoist the siren forward, heft my face to hers, and seize her cheeks. "Grab the prow."

She nods and extends her arms behind me, strapping her fingers around the boat's raised curvature, bracing herself there. I strip the dress over Cove's hips and down her limbs. Yards of black scales fall limp in my hands. Never taking my eyes off her, I chuck the garment aside.

I slither down her front, plying her with quick snatches of my teeth and tongue along the way. Stretching out, I recline across the boat's cabin, positioning myself under the sprawl of her body.

My lady hovers over me, legs splayed on either side of my head. Those long thighs open themselves to my gaze, which trails over the sprigs of hair bunched at her cunt. The soft folds pinken, and the seam pools with arousal.

All hers. All mine.

She gazes down at me, eyes saturated with need while the vessel blurs around her like a fogged window. My parched mouth follows the line it had been drawing. I feast on her stomach, nip down her navel, and hook my arms around her thighs. Fastening my arms there, I shackle her in place.

I slide my teeth up one inner thigh, then venture along the other. Reaching the apex of her folds, my teeth brush her slit in the faintest, lightest contact.

Cove expires. "Oh, Fables!"

She grasps the prow and drops her head forward. Her eyebrows furrow, features strained and complexion feverish. A wet bead drips from her core, and my tongue leaps out to catch it.

The siren tastes of sugar and salt, of everything sweet and harsh. I palm her waist, pinning her as my teeth glide up her drenched crease, then track the motion with deft lashes of my tongue.

Cove cries out. She rotates her hips, swatting her soaked cunt over my waiting mouth.

Once she does, my canines abandon their onslaught. I alternate, draping my tongue up her slot and dabbing her clit with swift flicks. Her cunt swells, leaks with pleasure. I tighten my hold on her and dip my tongue between her slick folds, probing deeply, in and out.

Water sloshes against the boat. Condensation from the narrow cascades sprays Cove's breasts. At some point—I don't give a fuck when—her bun and the tether at my nape must have unraveled completely. Her hair splashes down her figure as she gyrates onto my lips.

I groan, pumping my tongue faster. She beats her waist astride the stem, her moans cresting like waves.

Still not loud enough. I withdraw my tongue and seal my lips around the sensitive bud jutting from her cunt. And I suck hard.

Cove gives a shout. Her thighs tense, knees pressing into the cabin.

That is more like it. Almost, my love.

I engulf her clitoris and suction it into my mouth with rhythmic tugs. My tongue circles the nub and then strikes the tip. I terrorize my lady in tempo to her priceless, endless weeping.

My hands descend to span her hips. Fixing her in place, I use the leverage to yank her back and forth. My tongue shifts from her clit and dives back into the damp clutch inside her.

All forces work in tandem. She rides my face, and I jerk her into me, and my mouth catches her cunt.

"Oh…my…fuck," Cove grunts.

Uttered from her mouth, that word sizzles through my blood.

My cock reacts. The length solidifies like a cursed mast and shoves against the bridge of my leggings. Shit, I may come merely from this. Were it not for my grip on her spread thighs, I would stroke myself to the brink.

Jasmine wafts from her skin. Tang and a honeyed flavor drizzle on my tongue, and I mop it up, flexing into her.

Her pleasure amplifies to new heights, exhalations fraying. The sounds taper and multiply down the conduit.

She is close. I plant my mouth on her cunt and kiss it fully. My lips fuse to her walls, my tongue lunges inside her, and I devour her clitoris.

Cove hunches over, forehead pressing into the prow. Her mouth falls open, wide and silent.

And then she hollers. And hollers. And fucking hollers.

Convulsions rolls down her form, wetness floods from her folds and slides over my tongue, which continues to pitch inside. I growl and kiss her lovely cunt as I have done to her mouth, consuming every droplet of her climax.

The noises gush down the artery, filling it to capacity. I want those sounds to last, to blend into the walls and resonate long after she comes.

Yet still, I can prove her louder. My tongue softens and pulls out, content to swab her gently as she rides out the tremors. Her thighs quaver, jellied and scarcely able to keep her aloft.

The instant my lady slumps, I vanish from beneath her. I vault upright, turn, and peel the leggings from my limbs, then align my torso with her spine. The swells of her ass cushion my throbbing erection. The water-drop pendant sparkles down her back.

My arm snakes around her midriff. I slope my head toward her profile and mash my lips to her cheek, our mussed hair spilling together. The palpitations drumming in her neck matches the one pounding in my wrists.

"Do not let go," I mutter, voice gravely to my ears.

"I never have," my lady swears.

That's all it takes. I bend Cove over, angling her toward the prow, which she clasps firmer. The lantern swings. I use my knees to kick hers aside, parting them as far as they'll go, and slant my cock toward her sopping entrance.

Our thighs fit together. My hands drop to her hips and bolt them against me.

I lean over her, kiss the pulse point thumping into her neck, and rotate my waist forward. The crown penetrates her wet lips. I ease out and sling my hips again, this time spreading her walls with half my length.

My mouth drops. My moan shatters against hers.

Fables, her beautiful cunt is so wet. It flutters around my tip and smears me in her climax.

My elbows shake, but I take care to keep my fingercaps poised from her skin. The rest of my hands weld against her, stilling my lady so that she feels each inch as I swipe my cock out…and in…and out…and in.

My waist swivels, jutting into her backside as I thrust my hardness steadily. My eyes sink to the knot of flesh where my bulging head sinks into her. I watch myself enter and retreat, the taut incline of my cock pivoting through Cove's cunt.

Sweat races down her spine. Perspiration washes down my abdomen.

She cries, desperate to move, eager to fill herself with me. But I will not allow it.

That is how vicious I can be.

The muscles in my abdomen contort. I whip my cock into her, out of her, into her. Each time her moan expands into the tunnel, I pump deeper.

Finally, my cock slips to the base. I strike into Cove from the apex to the hilt, urging her to make noises that crack the ceiling.

At last, she ascends that crescendo. I release her waist and cup her tits. With a joyous shout, Cove lets loose. She swivels her waist, whisking her ass into my erection.

Momentum increases. Our hips undulate, the collision pinning me deeper, deeper, deeper into her.

Her wet grip takes my thickening cock. Palpitations slam against my chest, and I veer my ass harder against her. Cove clutches the prow and takes advantage of this by striking back, her hips punting into mine.

The prow rocks. The boat jostles atop the water.

Light from the glowing orbs overhead swim across her skin like splotches of paint. She's radiant. She's everything. This is what I fought for; this is what I desire above all else.

I have never ruled The Deep as much as she rules me. Yet it's more. I am no longer alone, I have an equal, and within her, I have found my home.

I lean into Cove and drop kisses on her spine. I locate the pulse of her neck and suck, desperate to taste that lifeline.

Cove moans louder, her cunt spreading for my cock. I drown in her wetness, sink into her pleasure. My chin lands on her shoulder, the side of my face flush with hers. I thumb her nipples, then stretch my arms to grab the prow with her.

We hang on and charge against one another.

Her hips slam with mine. My cock vaults into her damp clutch, the muscles of her cunt pulsating. An effusion of cries packs the tunnel, the noises spreading far, wide, and endless.

"Yes," I tell her, pounding quicker. "Now show me how kind you can be. Take pity and come for me."

My waist lashes, her hips slap into mine, and we combust. Three... more...thrusts.

And Cove screams. And I roar.

Her folds ripple, coming around my cock. Heat shoots from my sac to the slit in my crown, then pours into her.

At last, her voice floods every crevice of this tunnel. I follow her into that void, growling through the rush.

We rock together, submerging ourselves in the frenzy. I haul Cove up against me, veer her mouth to mine, and kiss her while pumping to a slow halt.

We shudder and collapse against the prow. Our breaths smash together like river rapids.

My exhausted lips mold with hers. Our mouths cling, tongues swaying.

It is a long time before we split apart and dissolve into the cabin. As the hull bobs, I recline and tuck Cove into my side. One of her legs stretches across my waist, and her fingers draw over the grooves in my torso.

I comb through her hair and glimpse her staring up at me. I have witnessed this siren lost in pleasure, in laughter, in sorrow, in fear, and in wonder. But this expression is new, crinkling the corners of her eyes and raising the crooks of her mouth.

I could ask her, but I think I know. It is peace.

33

We sit at the top of the world. The mountain range stretches into the vista, a mural of summits capped in rowan trees and flaming torches. The pinnacles lance into a sky cluttered with stars, where raptors sail through the wind.

A small bonfire dances within the circle we make atop the promontory, where the cliffside of Cerulean's home extends over the void. This precipice is a boundary between life and death, the ending and beginning of things, of what is and what can be. It is a leap of faith into the wind.

Beneath, the forest rises. Trees of all species froth with green leaves that splay over the woodland. It is the center—the roots and the heartbeat of this land.

Further down, my home burrows into the darkness. Water flows through caves and tunnels like veins, fueling this world with life. It is the crust, the foundation of our realm.

I see all of this because I remember all of this. From my youth to now, some things are never forgotten.

Cove nestles into my side on a cushioned bench identical to the others surrounding the fire. I envision Puck lounging with his arm extended across the back of the seat, which he shares with Juniper. His wrist is hanging off the rim, fingers fondling the end of Juniper's ponytail, while his free hand thumbs over her womb. Juniper rests her spine into the shield of his chest, spectacles perched on her nose as she reads the journal.

Lark's position is clear. She's lying on her back, stretching across a bench with a pillow beneath her head and her calves propped on

Cerulean's lap. My brother reclines with the lazy fitness he has always embodied, his open shirt fluttering in the breeze, blue mouth tipping in a grin while he massages his mate's bare heels. He does this routinely, alternating between her feet and her scarred knees.

In the past three months, his wings have healed well. Though, he keeps the plumes tucked in tonight.

Thorne sits comfortably next to Tinder, whose missing fingers have also mended. The young Fae has been learning how to wield his throwing stars with the opposite hand.

Coral has elected to settle beside Foxglove, the females having developed a camaraderie.

Only Cypress and Moth take up residence on the lawn. The centaur is curling his limbs to his side, and the spitfire of a Fae is balancing at the edge of the promontory. I suspect one leg is dangling over the bluff, her posture indifferent to the thousand-foot drop. The current stirs her papery wings, and she's fiddling with Cypress's helmet, which she has confiscated.

Occasionally, I sense Foxglove's attention wandering across the fire to the centaur. The vibes are tangible, though my lady murmurs under her breath to confirm this hunch.

According to Cove, the centaur eventually notices. His eyes slide toward the nymph, and they share a tentative grin. He nods, and she returns the gesture.

Lark twirls a chalice of blackthorn wine and stares at the celestials while addressing Puck. "I still can't get over the thought of you in an apron."

"He's as skilled at cooking as I am at research," Juniper says.

"Admit it," the satyr croons. "You're being modest for once."

"*That's* modest?" Tinder balks.

"My charms in the kitchen go far beyond just cooking. Sadly for this group, I can't elaborate with my kid listening."

"The moppet is carrying a seed," Cypress reminds Puck with a wry grin. "It does not have ears yet. It will be a long time before you can refer to the wee one as if they're a sapling."

"In which case, let's circle back," Foxglove instigates, audibly twirling her manicured finger to illustrate. "What charms are you referring to?"

Moth huffs while propping what can only be Cypress's large horn helmet on her tiny head. "Leave it to a nymph to enable a satyr."

"For my part, I'd like to know as well," Coral adds, her aquatic tone so wickedly conspiratorial that I picture her crystalline eyes flashing. "Describe these charms."

"Sorry, luv," Puck answers with a smirk. "I wouldn't want to make my brothers jealous of my prowess."

I grumble but say nothing, whereas Cerulean chuckles. "Doubtful."

"Oh? How would you know, dear brother? You weren't in our cabin last night while I prepped a merry feast."

"I'm waiting for the impressive part," Moth says dryly.

Semi-distracted, Juniper thumbs through the journal. "He was naked."

Lark lurches from the bench, twists toward the fire, and spits out her wine. The chalice's contents spritz the flames, whiffs of blackthorns and grapes scattering into the air.

Her smarmy laughter soars to the firmament. "Hot damn. Between the lot of us, now I can't decide whose story will have spicier content."

"Oh, that will always be me and my woman," Puck advocates.

Thorne coughs. "Father, sitting right here," he reminds us. "As much as I'm willing to give my daughters my blessing, I don't need the details. You three—," he warns me and my brothers, "—are still on trial."

"Gladly," Cerulean responds on our behalf, which is better than me or Puck opening our mouths.

Beside me, Cove's skin heats in a manner that testifies to a rather expansive blush. I glance her way and find pink brushstrokes floating up her cheeks. "Um moreover, Fables don't have—" she flaps her fingers, "—explicit scenes."

"Well, my and Cerulean's story sure as shit does," Lark objects.

"Guilty," Puck adds, then clears his throat. "Apologies, Thorne. I promise, it's not all smut. There's also angst, redemption, and tears."

My eyebrows snap into a bridge. "Fables are less than three pages long."

"Yeah, and whichever imbecile made up that rule doesn't impress me."

Juniper sighs. "In one of my stories, I may have…added my own… romantic paragraphs, too."

"You?" everyone but Puck asks.

The female crinkles her nose. "Well. You don't have to make it sound like that."

"It's sexy," Puck upholds. "I read it before we got here."

"Tease," Lark accuses.

I'll bet that is not the only thing my brother and Juniper did before they arrived disheveled. According to Cove, their clothes had been in disarray. Puck's leathers and Juniper's blouse had been drenched in the scent of sex.

Matter of fact, so had Cerulean's and Lark's clothing. Not that either of them had been wearing much when Cove and I had knocked on The Fauna Tower's door hours ago. My brother's mate had sidetracked him to the point where they'd been fucking so intensely, they had forgotten the time of our gathering.

Aside from that, we'd heard them. It was hard not to.

I cannot blame either pair. For I have been keeping Cove busy in numerous places throughout The Deep and in a variety of positions. There has been much to celebrate. Aside from rebuilding the underground river, my greatest task of late has been to ply Cove with orgasms. That alone is a privilege.

As eventide soaks the land in darkness and lightness, a breeze carries native sounds from the wildlife park. The small boar who gave Puck grief with the Evermore Blossom has made its way here. But most vividly, a wolverine and a ram call out, then a falcon rasps. The surviving fauna drift among handfuls of the restored ones, including those who raised Cerulean, his wild family having taken a liking to this area.

Earlier, Sylvan and Lotus had retreated into the park to explore. Meanwhile, Tímien belts through the sky with the nightingale, the raven, and his kin. A dozen hoots from The Parliament of Owls project like metallic horns across the Solitary wild.

At last, Juniper shuts the journal with a satisfied breath. "It's done. For now, at least."

"And?" Lark insists.

"And you'll just have to read the whole thing for yourself."

"Really? No appraisal? That's a first."

"I've learned some things don't need to be perfect. Nobody's story is."

"There's my tree of knowledge," Thorne beams.

It is true. The journal has been passed from Juniper to her sisters, then from Fae to Fae. Each page has been claimed by a different contributor, everyone playing the role of scribe and telling their own story. It has turned into a Journal of Fables…and poems…and memoirs…and tales. It is a vignette of all who've lived here.

With the pages filled, the wild has repaired itself, the fauna restored, and our lifeline stitched back together.

Anyone who cares to read the collection may do so, be they Fae or human. Anyone who wishes to contribute to the anthology in the future will also have that right.

This is but the first volume. And life is long. But more than that, life is abundant, regardless of how much time one has.

Because it is crisp up here, I bundle Cove tighter in the blanket Cerulean has provided.

Cove huddles deeper into me. "I wonder what features the child will get from their parents. Aren't you rapt to know if you'll have a daughter or son?"

Juniper's vibrant eyes glint behind her spectacles, which she removes as she sinks further against Puck. "We'll wait and see."

I sense my brother ducking his head and grinning like an asshole with a secret. He knows. Somehow, he knows the answer, yet it doesn't matter.

They will be half-human, half-Fae. We suspect the child will have an extended life like their parents—like Cerulean and Lark, and Cove and myself. Because of the brew I'd made her, my lady can have an immortal existence with me. But instead, she has already chosen to last only as long as her sisters, and I have made the choice to fade with her.

But that will be a long time from now. A very long one.

"What happens next?" I muse.

All heads swivel toward me. Feeling the cumulative weight of their stares, I glower. I haven't said much thus far, but still. So dramatic of them.

Nor do I mean the obvious. A truce has been reached. In a fortnight, both sides of Faerie will meet at The Triad with representatives of Reverie Hollow to establish an equilibrium.

Until then, we have sworn neutrality, since an official pledge on paper may take longer than we expect. Yet to be worthy of verbal oaths and ink on parchment, this is hardly a shock. The humans have grievances, and Faeries are as stubborn as they are vindictive, for I should know.

But we are learning. Not only have the mortals seen what all forms of nature can do if not safeguarded, but the Solitaries have learned the consequences of viciousness.

Peace will take time. It will take practice. And at least we're willing.

There is hope.

If two striplings from opposing worlds can choose to rescue each other instead of destroying one another, the rest of us should be capable. Speaking of Leif and Aster, I've heard rumors about them meeting often at The Triad.

Cerulean lounges in his seat. "We'll continue to mend."

"We'll keep living," Puck says.

I think about that. "And we remember."

We remember what was and what can be. Everyone sits with this knowledge, a great calm sifting through the promontory while the flames pour warmth across the lawn.

Cypress whispers, "For the eternal wild."

The night has only begun. The centaur withdraws with Moth, Tinder, Foxglove, and Coral into the wildlife park. They slip past the gate, eager to meander with the fauna.

Thorne has spent these months dividing his visit. He has spent time with Cove and me in The Deep, then in the forest with Puck and Juniper, and since then in the mountain with Cerulean and Lark. While the man has enjoyed helping nurture the park's haven, he has a sanctuary of his own to manage.

Although Thorne had appointed mortal apprentices to the haven, he refuses to neglect it any longer. Also, he has pledged to speak on behalf of the wildlife in his world, intent on convincing the town to restrict trade poachers within their borders. After all that has occurred, he is optimistic about succeeding.

His daughters will live in Faerie with us, in the homes we've made with each other. But they shall visit their father often to help tend to the haven and advocate for mortal fauna, for there exists more than one place the sisters call their own.

Rising by the fire, Thorne gathers them close. "My girls."

I have never heard so much depth in so few words.

Tímien and Lark's nightingale fly us to the mortal realm, the raptors landing before the structure where the sisters grew up. Cerulean descends last, his wings flaring wide and tossing the wind against the treetops.

A horse whom the sisters have dubbed Whinny Badass neighs from an adjacent stable. Birds chirp and caw from the rear of the house. Creek water rushes through the property from nearby, and the scent of aged wood and cinnamon wafts from the structure.

Cove tucks her mouth against my ear and describes the scene. Timber walls, a front porch, and an overhand with an attic bedroom where she and her sisters used to sleep. She paints a picture of the Fable Dusk Sanctuary and the caravan where she, Juniper, and Lark would recite Fables to each other.

We pause in front of the house. I feel my brothers absorbing the sights with curiosity and intrigue.

My lady makes a comforted noise. I watch her profile slacken with memories and excitement, her eyes brightening as she turns to me. "This is where we grew up."

Juniper expels a breath. "Home."

Lark squeals. "About damn time."

Slats creak as Thorne strides up the steps, then pauses and turns half-way. A welcoming grin rumples his voice. "Well?"

Well, what?

I shuffle back and hear my brothers do the same. The words teeter on my tongue. Any one of us is about to wish our loves a festive reunion before we leave them to their evening.

The sisters step forward. When they notice we're not following them, they halt and swing toward us.

A grin shimmies through Lark's voice. "You three stragglers planning on standing guard? Or are you just stalling to watch our asses bounce up the stairs?"

Cerulean wavers. "We thought you'd want some time."

"In your house," Puck says.

"Alone," I finish.

The women object, speaking over each other when Thorne cuts in. "That's not how our family does it."

Family. Our family.

The term flows deeply through my chest.

My expression must match those of my brothers. And all three must stretch across our faces because Lark takes Cerulean's hand, Juniper loops her arm through Puck's, and Cove snakes her arm around my waist.

"Isn't that a picture." Their father's voice muses, and he rubs his hands together. "Now, then. Would you care to stay for dinner?"

The invitation produces an unrecognizable lump, which squats in my throat.

Puck smirks. "Fuck."

Thorne sighs, and I feel his eyes slide heavenward. "*Language,* son."

The latter word rinses the humor from Puck's tenor. It takes him a long moment to utter, "Sounds like a merry plan."

After a stunned pause, Cerulean's whisper stirs the grass. "We'd like that."

I swallow and incline my head.

The raptors shift to their normal size, launch into the air, and sail toward the sanctuary out back, content to wait for us from there.

As both pairs trail the man through the door, I lift Cove's hand and brush my mouth across her knuckles.

My lady smiles. "Welcome to my world."

And we follow them inside.

Epilogue

Glade

The Thirteenth Year

Under the vicious stars, a stripling is born. And well into her first year, she has already grown defiant.

The little girl waddles on shaky legs through the forest, determined to stay upright although she has just begun learning to walk. She gets that from her overachieving mama.

As for the reckless thrill she takes in risking a fall, all in the pursuit of mischief, that's from her papa.

She squeals and reaches up to catch the flecks of light dripping from the constellations, teal, gold, and white spangling the oaks. Her bare feet crunch acorns into the earth, and her leather dress flaps as she moves.

When a low-hanging branch snags on her wee antlers, she halts and purses her lips to contemplate this dilemma. However, she doesn't need long to free herself from this trap. The girl twists her fingers around the bough and loosens the knot, which springs free and releases her.

Then she's off again, unruffled by the episode. Layers of green hair flap behind her as she runs on unsteady feet. She's a confident little thing, with a boastful gleam in her brown eyes, the irises as rich as the soil. And because she's half-human, half-Fae, her acute senses perceive this world to a degree beyond her age, but they're not so exceptional that she dwells on it for long.

No, she's more interested in figuring out how her limbs work, what they can do for her.

Indeed, she's smart enough to realize the stars can't be caught, but other things in the wild can. A rustle in the bushes alerts her to a prowler. With brazen glee and steadfast determination, she staggers toward the sound and tracks the rhythm of cloven hooves.

It could be the deer she loves to play with, the one with shamrocks growing from its antlers.

Or it could be the snake her aunt and uncle always bring when they're here from the river. The serpent often tickles her whenever it twines around her leg.

Or it could be the owl she has flown on before, while tucked in between her second aunt and uncle, much to the dismay of her mama and the amusement of her papa.

Maybe it's the centaur who has engaged in this game with her before, or the filly and village boy who sometimes join in.

Maybe it's the moth, marten, nymph, or water Fae who let her play tricks on them.

Maybe it's her grandpapa coming for another visit.

But of course, the child knows better. Brows furrowing, she creeps toward the shrubs, stalks her prey—and shouts with laughter as she tackles the giant stag who leaps from the thicket.

"Ah, shit," her target snarls mirthfully. "Fables help me!"

He flops into the grass as she scrambles on top of his broad chest. She cannot speak yet, cannot say the word *shit*, but she shouts in triumph and milks this moment for all its worth. The little girl has inherited this habit from both parents.

She pins him down with her small palms and presses her head to his. Captured like this, their antlers hook together.

Her papa smirks. "You've trapped me, luv."

"She always does," a smoky voice declares from the sideline.

The girl and her father swing their gazes toward the woman leaning against an oak trunk. Her arms are crossed, with a bracelet of leaves vining around one arm. A green ponytail rests over her shoulder, and her perceptive expression is soft at the edges.

Only at the edges. Only for them.

Her mother has been watching the whole time, as she usually does. The little girl has never been allowed out of her parents' sights.

But someday, she will be allowed. Someday, she will become a sapling. After that, she will rise like a great oak and write her own story.

She might wield a bow of her own or some other powerful tool. Perhaps she'll hold a quill more than a weapon.

It will be her fate, as her winged uncle likes to say.

It will be her choice, as her serpentine uncle likes to add.

Until then, she's delighted to be here, between the mountain and the river, in the heart of the wild.

Her papa hefts himself off the grass, snatches the girl's waist, and launches her into the sky. She cheers as he spins her around, then scowls when he stops. For some reason, this prizes a chuckle from her parents.

Her father slings one arm around the child, able to bear her weight this way. He catches her mother staring at the pair of them, the woman's eyes glinting like a misted spruce tree.

But then her mama's attention travels down her papa's bare chest. Aside from a set of dangly earrings, he's wearing only leather breeches, which makes her mama's pulse race. The little girl hears it, though she doesn't know why this happens, why her mama's pupils swell or why the girl can detect the rapid beating of her mother's heart.

Even stranger, her father's heart makes the same racket. He mouths something to her mama, but the girl only makes out the word *soon*, which turns her mother's cheeks crimson.

They keep staring at each other. However, the wee one loses patience and grunts, which breaks the spell.

Her papa grins and swaggers up to her mama. He growls something sneaky, something like a secret promise, then he plants his lips on hers.

This happens a lot, so the girl sighs. Her parents split apart and huff with laughter.

They stroll through the woods to their cabin. Inside, flames crackle from the fireplace, and the scent of cloves makes the girl sleepy. She slumps on her papa's chest, limbs akimbo as he climbs upstairs with her mama in tow.

The girl's wooden crib is nestled in her parents' room on the second-floor loft, one level below the library. Their home is more like a tree-house than a cabin, and she likes that.

Her crib stands by the window overlooking The Herd of Deer, where the stags, bucks, and does graze. Sometimes she travels to the mortal realm with her Solitary family, to spend time in the sanctuary where her grandpapa lives. But tomorrow, he's coming to Faerie instead. They'll all be spending the day with her aunts and uncles, plus the rest of their kin, up in the wildlife park. She needs to slumber, so she'll have energy to race the fauna.

But she can't sleep yet. Their trio has a routine, and routines please the girl.

Despite her heavy eyelids, a word rolls across her tongue and teeters there. Finally, it bursts from her mouth. "Story."

It comes out like a wish, like a demand, and like a trick. Her parents halt on the threshold. Their gazes snap to one another, then to her.

"Did she say...," her mother breathes.

Her father shakes his awestruck head. "My, my, my. I'll be fucked."

Was her first word supposed to come later? But why wait?

Something bright strikes across their faces. The little girl must have impressed them. She enjoys the feeling and decides it won't be the last time.

Her mama and papa oblige the request. They pass the loft bedroom and mount the winding steps to the library, where bookshelves embed into the walls, each one packed with titles.

One special shelf displays a framed copy of something called The Wild Treaty, which humans and Faeries created before she was born. The girl doesn't understand what it is, only that it means both the townsfolk and Solitary Fae are friendly to each other. It also means they all take care of their natural worlds, from the land to its fauna. Each side does so equally.

Her parents settle with the girl on one of the wide reading chairs. The girl's mortal mama cushions their daughter on her lap, while the girl's Fae papa lounges on the seat's armrest.

Some of the books' pages make her parents grin, others make their faces sag. They're a happy family. Only sometimes, she'll catch her mother lost in a wounded daze. Or her father will awaken from dreams that make him breathe too fast, like something's got him trapped, like he's scared.

Does it have anything to do with the ink marked on her mama's back? Or the scars dotting her papa's calves and streaking across his spine?

The child doesn't know. But eventually, she will ask, and they'll tell her the tale.

Whenever her mama needs it, her parents hold each other close, and her papa murmurs a joke, and that makes her mother smile again.

Whenever her papa needs it, her mama combs through his red hair, and she whispers until he relaxes into the bed, and that makes him sink back into the pillows and close his eyes.

The girl has seen things like this happen with her aunts and uncles, too. Still, it isn't often. Most days, they have a merry time, their big family of humans and Faeries and fauna.

Although the child could do without the abundance of kissing and naughty comments between the couples—in addition to the strange noises her parents make from different rooms throughout their cabin, when they think their daughter is asleep—she doesn't mind. So long as she can run with the wild dwellers of this land and read stories about them, the girl is satisfied.

With that in mind, she picks out her favorite book from the library's bountiful collection. Her huntress mother slides on a pair of spectacles. Her satyr father stretches one bulky arm across the seat back and combs his fingers through his woman's hair.

With his free hand, he playfully taps his daughter's tapered ear. "Ready, luv?"

Glade is always ready for a Fable. So her mother opens the journal and turns to the first page. And she begins to read.

Thank you for sharing this wild journey with me. I will miss it eternally.

Ready for another spicy fantasy enemies-to-lovers series?

Meet my sinful jester in Trick
(Dark Seasons: Foolish Kingdoms #1)

Never Miss a Release!

Get new release alerts, exclusive content, and wicked details about my
books by subscribing to my newsletter at:
www.nataliajaster.com/newsletter

Author's Note

The tears are real, luvs. The end of a series is always bliss and heartache.

Vicious Faeries began with my love of *Labyrinth*, was amplified by my passion for nature, and came full circle with another subject that means a lot to me. By now, I've learned there's a distinct pattern to my world-building, something that comes up again and again: The power of writing.

Books, manuscripts, journals, fables, myths, decrees, and treaties always have a potent role in my series. I think it's because I'm so captivated by how deeply a text can inspire, how it can be its own force. In fiction, it rules kingdoms, unites allies and enemies, and reflects our weaknesses and strengths.

Yet writing malleable, constantly able to change. It can recreate and redefine itself. It's a formidable magic, with the ability to move worlds. In my series, it's often the trunk of the tree, the stem that bridges everything together.

We are all writers. We all have our own diverse stories to tell.

While we may share some universal experiences, they exist from different angles, from different perspectives, and in different voices. And I feel that's an essential—and beautiful—thing. It contributes to this wild kaleidoscope of a life, bringing lightness and darkness into the mix.

As for my characters, I've lived in The Dark Fables for over two years now and fallen in love with its vicious players.

Wicked and elegant Cerulean.

Bold and feisty Lark.

Sly and sinful Puck.

Smart and resilient Juniper.

Dark and brooding Elixir.

Kind and soulful Cove.

I adore every sexy, honest, flawed, strong, and empathetic thing about them. And while I LOVE writing spice (which I'm delighted to say is abundant in this series), what makes any romance memorable for me is its heart. The intensity and depth of the characters' emotions—the rawness of them.

If that's on the page, the story *has* me. The characters *own* me.

That is what sparks me to write. That's what keeps me going.

Of course, having special people in my life is vital along the journey.

Hugs to Michelle and Candace, for being there from book one and, more importantly, for your friendship.

To my family, for all the love.

To Roman, my eternal mate and muse.

And to my readers. To my ARC team, the Myths & Tricksters FB group, the Vicious Faeries spoiler group, and everyone who has given this series love.

Cerulean, Lark, Puck, Juniper, Elixir, and Cove have become my kin. And because you've made it this far with me, you've become part of that, too—my Fae family.

For the eternal wild,

~Natalia

P.S. Burning to talk about the series? Please leave a review and then come join the Vicious Faeries spoiler group or my Myths & Tricksters reader group on FB.

About Natalia

Natalia Jaster is a fantasy romance author who routinely swoons for the villain.

She lives in a dark forest, where she writes steamy New Adult tales about rakish jesters, immortal deities, and vicious fae. Wicked heroes are her weakness, and rebellious heroines are her best friends.

When she's not writing, you'll probably find her perched atop a castle tower, guzzling caramel apple tea, and counting the stars.

✺

Come say hi!

Bookbub: www.bookbub.com/authors/natalia-jaster
Facebook: www.facebook.com/NataliaJasterAuthor
Instagram: www.instagram.com/nataliajaster
TikTok: www.tiktok.com/@nataliajasterauthor
Website: https://www.nataliajaster.com

See the boards for Natalia's novels on
Pinterest: www.pinterest.com/andshewaits